I0692726

WHAT THE DEAD CONFESS

A MAYA FROST FBI THRILLER

DAVID ARCHER

MILA CROSS

RIGHTHOUSE

Copyright © 2026 by Right House

All rights reserved.

The characters and events portrayed in this ebook are fictitious. Any similarity to real persons, living or dead, is coincidental and not intended by the author.

No part of this book may be reproduced in any form or by any electronic or mechanical means, including information storage and retrieval systems, without written permission from the author, except for the use of brief quotations in a book review.

ISBN-13: 978-1-63696-461-4

ISBN-10: 1-63696-461-3

Printed in the United States of America

www.righthouse.com

www.instagram.com/righthousebooks

www.facebook.com/righthousebooks

twitter.com/righthousebooks

PROLOGUE

Teresa Morgan's problem was that she had too much faith in people, and that faith kept coming back to bite her in the ass.

Hardware had been Teresa's life since she was a teenager, and not the fancy computer hardware that most people thought she sold when she mentioned her job. No, Teresa was a connoisseur of the nuts-and-bolts type of hardware. Hammers, screws, things that kept the world safe and secure. *Man tools,* as her mother would have said. The building blocks of civilization.

The clock had just struck six p.m., and Teresa moved aisle to aisle to ensure all the stock was in its proper place. Not that there'd been much movement on the shelves because today had been a typical three-figure day. The total intake had barely surpassed $200 according to the register; the lowest intake this year, meaning it would be a miracle if the lights in this place still worked by next month. Outside the store, dusk began to settle in. No point staying open any longer. Teresa doubted she'd suddenly get an influx of construction workers desperate to replenish their supplies. Or any desperate builders looking for a new set of drill bits before a big job. Hell, even that weird guy with the Kromer cap hadn't stopped by this week.

No. Time to close up, go home, and wish for a miracle.

It hadn't always been like this. There had been a time when the local DIY store was a cornerstone of the community, especially here in backwater Florida. Families would visit when they needed to jazz up their new houses. Builders would stop by and stock up on the small things, even when they didn't need them. It was the community spirit: Help each other out not because business demanded it but because it was an effort in human connection.

But Morgan's Hardware was a victim of the megastores and the online hubs. Now DIYers could get everything they needed off Amazon for a fraction of the price, and it would appear on their doorstep the next morning. Teresa couldn't compete with that. She'd kept it old school for the sake of tradition, and she'd foolishly believed that such a decision would reward her with customer loyalty.

That hadn't happened. It was a brave new world out there, and Teresa had missed the boat. Now she was adrift in stormy waters with no shore in sight.

As she closed the window blinds, she considered retirement, embarrassing as the thought was. Who retired at fifty-eight? Well, normal people, but Teresa Morgan prided herself on being far from normal. She was from a long line of non-normal people, like her dad who'd only stopped working because his heart stopped beating, and her grandmother, who'd helped build this store with her own hands. If *they* knew she was considering throwing in the towel, they'd claw out of their graves just to call her a quitter. Hell, when she'd married, she hadn't even taken her husband's last name, because the Morgan name was hammered into the very foundations of Fernandina Beach, and she wanted to keep that alive.

Teresa went to the till, emptied it out, and bagged up the bills. Maybe she could transform this space into something else, she thought idly. A workshop where kids learned to use their hands instead of their thumbs? Teach them the difference between a Phillips head and a flathead before they forget how to hold anything that isn't a smartphone. The idea had merit, but the liability insurance alone would devour what little capital she had left.

Or pivot to the digital world? She could film "tutorials," whatever they were, like her niece kept insisting. But the idea of doing that—in the same aisles where her dad taught her to countersink a screw head so it sat perfectly flush with the wood, where he'd demonstrated the exact angle to hold a hacksaw so the blade wouldn't bind—felt like she was giving a giant middle finger to her forebears. Some things you had to learn through splinters, not tutorials.

As Teresa secured the register drawer, her phone vibrated against the oak counter. The screen lit up with Katie's name. Her niece had developed a habit of checking in at the best possible moment, presumably out of some misguided sense of duty since Teresa's husband had passed away last year.

She read the text:

Aunt T, got some ideas to help the store. Dinner at my place in an hour?

Teresa smiled the first real smile of the day. Not only was Katie the only real family she had left, but she was painfully optimistic in ways that only youth could be. Maybe there *was* hope, Teresa thought. Maybe the next generation of Morgans could step up and do what Teresa couldn't: fix this stupid place without having to resort to another loan.

She went to respond, but a sharp rattle at the window jolted her out of her mild fantasy.

Her pulse jumped up a notch.

Because there, through the blinds of the window closest to the counter, was a silhouette. And not just any silhouette. The flimsy blinds distorted it a little, but it was instantly recognizable.

It was the man who'd been appearing sporadically for weeks now. The man who wore the same clothes every time: plaid flannel jacket, Kromer cap, huge boots caked in mud. She'd never been able to discern any characteristics beyond the man's clothing, except for heavy stubble and the smell of cigarettes. Teresa had just taken to calling him the Anti-Freeze Man in her head because that was all he ever bought. Two gallons of it. Either the man had an anti-freeze fetish or he was a farmer stocking up for winter. Teresa had tried making small talk with him, but he never offered more than a nod or a mumbled thank you.

"Sorry, we're closed," she shouted.

There was no movement on the silhouette's part. Could he hear her? She was used to having conversations through glass—usually with kids outside causing trouble—and they never had a problem hearing her.

The figure, however, barely twitched. For a moment, she

wondered if those same kids had planted a mannequin outside and run off.

"Hello?" she called again.

Still it remained. A twinge of unease crept in. The guy admittedly gave her bad vibes whenever she saw him, but there were usually enough people around to offset any sense of danger. At this hour, there wouldn't be many people passing by. They'd be heading for the city along the main road. Nobody would stop by this little corner, at least not in large numbers.

Now the figure twitched. Definitely alive. Definitely looking straight at the window, maybe able to glimpse Teresa through a gap in the blinds if he angled himself right.

Something was off here. She could feel it. A part of her *knew* that he was watching *her*, not the store or the register or the reduced power tools in the window. God knew she'd had some eccentric customers over the years, and Teresa prided herself on being able to spot a pervert a mile off. Right now, a neon sign was going off in her head.

She grabbed her phone, considering calling the police. What would she say? One of her regular customers was standing outside her store? But then again, if she *did* call the police, once they busted him, she could probably say goodbye to that weekly anti-freeze sale.

No. Now wasn't the time to get what few customers she had left arrested, pervert or not.

But still—why was he here? And why wasn't he budging? Teresa wasn't sure of the politically correct term, but maybe Mr. Anti-Freeze was just a little slow on the uptake.

Better safe than sorry.

Teresa rushed over to the door to double-check she'd

locked it, then grabbed a hammer en route back to the till area. The good part about owning a hardware store was that you were never short of weapons, and while she'd never wielded such a weapon before, there was a first time for everything, even at her age.

But on her return, something had changed.

The silhouette had vanished.

On silent feet, she edged to the window and parted the blinds with two fingers.

No one there. The street was empty in every direction.

For a moment, she wondered if her imagination hadn't been playing tricks on her. They always said that losing a spouse did strange things to the brain, and maybe now that grief was finally catching up.

Or maybe a part of Teresa—the part of her that still dreamed of purpose—had wanted it. Craved the validation that she mattered enough for someone to seek her out, even if that someone was just a strange man with a silly cap and an inexplicable thirst for anti-freeze.

She put the hammer on the counter, breathed a sigh of relief, and then pressed her palms against her eyes until stars bloomed in the darkness. Behind the constellations lurked a truth she'd been dodging for months: this place was already a tomb. She was just the caretaker, dusting the headstones and polishing the plaques and keeping vigil over what had already died.

Dammit. This wasn't the time to feel sorry for herself. Sure, she'd lost a husband and a once-thriving business, but the Morgans didn't dwell on their misfortunes. They faced them head-on. Right there and then, Teresa decided it was time to move on to new pastures. She wasn't sure what that entailed, but she'd figure it out in time.

Time to close up. She closed the register, then grabbed her phone and began typing out a text to Katie as she walked back into the store room.

Then she froze in place.

A familiar scent assaulted her nostrils. It was a smell she knew, one that cooled engines and killed small animals.

Anti-freeze had a way of hanging in the air like that.

Click.

The deadbolt in the back door slid into place. Her dad's voice manifested in her head: *Always check the back door first, Teresa girl. The front's just for show.*

Teresa's breath caught in her throat. Her heart rate shot up, threatening to burst out of her chest.

Because standing in front of the back door was a familiar silhouette.

The jacket, the cap, the boots. The smell of cigarettes. The man from a previous era—he'd breached the back door.

And not only was Teresa sharing her store room with the stranger, but she was staring down the barrel of a rifle aimed squarely at her chest.

Her lungs seized. Her mind screamed commands her body couldn't follow: *Run. Fight. Scream.* But terror had short-circuited any rational thought, and the hammer in Teresa's hand felt embarrassingly inadequate against the opposition. She couldn't breathe, think, do anything but stand there while her heart hammered and her throat closed around a scream that wouldn't come.

"It's time, Bernice," the man said.

Bernice? Who the hell is Bernice?

"You've got the wrong person," she stammered.

"No. I've got exactly who I need."

Teresa saw the finger tighten. Heard the mechanism engage.

In the split-second before the rifle exploded, Teresa's last thought wasn't a highlight reel of her life, like they said it would be. It was the realization that her faith in people had finally killed her.

ONE

Maya Frost aligned her sight and emptied the magazine of her Glock 17 into the crude parody of a human being dangling fifty feet down the lane. Introspection had never been Maya's strong point, nor something she really sought to entertain, but here at the FBI firing range, the mind wandered to places it rarely trod during the cold light of day.

As a quantitative analyst who spent her days drowning in datasets, she had about as much practical need for marksmanship as a librarian. She wasn't required to maintain firearms proficiency beyond basic certification, but like her old man had always said, it didn't hurt to know how to shoot someone. Not to mention that she felt much more at home firing at this target dummy than she did behind a desk, plus it was the perfect way to end a twelve-hour day at the office.

The FBI headquarters in Washington, D.C. was a spectacle to behold at any hour, but once the worker bees cleared out at five, the place became a liminal space. Even the shooting range was unusually deserted tonight, probably because most people had better things to do at 7 p.m. on a Friday night.

Maya, however, did not. It could be Christmas Day and she'd still be blowing up cardboard targets because she needed this. For the past few weeks, she'd been assembling data about missing minors in the tri-state area of New York, and the patterns she'd uncovered had reminded her why law enforcement had the highest suicide rate of any profession. Abductions, trafficking, teenagers vanishing into extremist pipelines and emerging months later in grainy footage from Syrian training camps. It was enough to make even the most hardened bureaucrats want to give it all up, but here, letting out all of that frustration via 9MM bullets, it reminded her that the good guys had some tricks of their own too.

Maya pushed the retrieval button, and the target carrier brought her paper victim closer for inspection. Seven holes. Three in the chest, three in the forehead, one in the groin.

"Not bad, Frost," a voice said.

Maya spun and found Jack Kennedy standing outside her lane. Kennedy was FBI old guard—twenty years in special ops, and just like Maya, he was a fixture of these after-hours sessions, although she'd never asked exactly what demons he was shooting at.

"Thanks, Jack." She unclipped her ear defenders and hung them on the hook beside her lane. "Not bad yourself."

Kennedy gestured to the hole-ridden target. "Groin shot, huh?"

"Think it's too far?"

"We used to call that a white trash vasectomy. Can't say that anymore, though. The top dogs would have you over a barrel."

"Would they?"

"Yup, and speaking of the top dogs, your name came up in a meeting today."

Maya reapplied her black-rimmed glasses and loosened her ponytail, letting her raven hair fall to her shoulders. There was a thin sheen of gun oil on her fingertips. "My name? In one of your big-dick meetings?"

"Yeah. Surprised?"

She guessed there was some twist coming up, like she'd been nominated for something no one else wanted to do. "A little bit. Whatever rumors you've heard, I assure you only some of them are true. Can you divulge any details?"

"It was about that serial killer case over in Maine. The one you helped with."

Maya's eyebrows climbed her forehead. The Maine case. She'd expected Kennedy to mention her data work on the trafficking ring or maybe that algorithm she'd developed for catching financial fraud. Not the insights she'd quietly passed to the Behavioral team about the Bangor murders, a psychological profile she'd pieced together in her off-hours, nothing to do with Intelligence.

"Please tell them I appreciate the credit."

"I will. You caught something both forensics *and* Behavioral missed, so chances are you've made some new friends. And probably a few enemies."

Maya stifled a laugh. Even when it came to homicide, the political game never ceased. "Sorry for hurting their egos, but saving lives is important. I'm just glad it helped."

Kennedy checked his cell, then pocketed it. "You and me both. Anyway, must dash. Wife already thinks I'm having an affair."

"Are you?"

He chuckled. "Not yet. See you soon, Frost."

Maya saluted her goodbye, then turned and packed up her weapon with hands that had suddenly begun to tremble. Kennedy's comment had spiked her adrenaline because somewhere out there, the almost-mythical Behavioral team had not only become aware of her existence but that she'd actually contributed to their efforts—all because of something she'd put together in her spare time.

But that brief spark of optimism quickly fizzled out. What was she hoping for exactly? That it would lead to something bigger? No. There was a saying down in Intelligence that only the elite few graduated from the basement. You were either Desk or Field, and rarely did the two overlap. Just like in any office in the world, there was an invisible barrier between the white collar and blue collar, and it took a miracle to break that barrier down.

Maya packed everything away and made for the exit. Out of the shooting range, through the corridors. The basement corridors of the Hoover Building always reminded Maya of cerebral matter; gray, convoluted, and surprisingly quiet despite all the activity they contained. She was into the grand lobby when her cell phone pinged.

A text from Becky, her roommate.

Party at our place. Impromptu. ETA?

Goddammit. How old did you have to be before impromptu parties became unacceptable? Maya thought she'd left that stuff back at college, but Becky seemed insistent on keeping that part of their lives alive. Maya was about to hammer out a response—or maybe an excuse—when a voice snapped her back to the present.

"Miss Frost? It is Frost, isn't it?"

Maya glanced up and saw descending the stairs at a rapid pace a familiar face but not one she recognized by name. It was a man caught in that gray zone between middle age and elderly—late fifties, maybe early sixties. He was tree-trunk wide and kind of reminded Maya of a pro wrestler who'd stopped taking steroids. His salt-and-pepper hair was fighting a losing battle against his scalp, but he'd adapted his styling to minimize the retreat.

"Yes, sir. It's Frost."

"Hope I didn't startle you." He extended a hand. "Nice shooting, by the way. I was watching from the first floor."

"Thank you, sir." Maya accepted the shake as her analytical brain kicked in. His blue suit was perfectly pressed except for a slight rumple near the left cuff, which meant he was right-handed, wrote a lot, and leaned on that arm during long meetings. The red tie screamed old guard FBI. They all wore them, like it was a secret signal. Her eyes caught a few telltale signs on his left hand too – particularly a white band of skin on his ring finger. A phantom wedding ring, the skin there several shades paler than the rest of his hand. But what truly interested her was the thinner gold band he now wore above the white strip, as if trying to obscure the evidence of a recent divorce. Then there were the dry patches of skin under his eyes. Tobacco user but not cigarettes. Pipe smoker. The pattern of irritation matched the way pipe smoke would curl around the face.

"Sorry, I should introduce myself. My name's Vernon. You've probably heard me under some other name, maybe one with four letters."

Then it clicked. Maya did know this man. She'd seen his

face on billboards around HQ enough times but had never equated it with the name. "Mr. Raymond Vernon. Head of Behavioral, is that right?"

"Got it in one. I just wanted to extend my thanks to your crew in Intelligence. Your help with the tri-state missing persons has made our jobs in Behavioral much easier. I don't get out of the meeting room very often, so I just wanted to show my face to the people who make a difference."

Maya was suddenly stuck for words. Here was the director of the Behavioral Research and Instruction Unit, a man who mingled with the Washington, D.C. elite, raining praise on her. His team was the FBI's dark priesthood. They were the agents who mixed field work with psychological magic to hunt down America's worst of the worst. The Behavioral Unit mostly dealt with serial cases and ultra-violent crimes, but they'd usually be consulted on any case that involved a dead body and a lack of forensic evidence.

And Maya would have given anything to be one of them.

She wanted to return the gesture of gratitude but wasn't sure how to articulate it. "Thank you, sir. I appreciate the kind words."

Vernon waved a dismissive hand. "Kind words don't catch killers. Results do. And word of your Maine profile made its way to us, too. Within a week, we found the Bangor Ripper working the desk in a guitar shop."

"I heard, sir. I'm really glad we got him before victim six."

"*We* didn't get anything. *You* did. You made us in Behavioral look like fools, and I love that."

A ringtone interrupted their conversation, and Vernon fished his cell out of his pocket. He held up a finger, took the call, then took ten steps toward the stairs. Maya watched him go, a big man with a bigger shadow. *You made us look like fools, and I love that.* It was a strange mix of praise and a verbal razor to the throat, but Maya welcomed it. Vernon began to pace, and then his expression dropped. The transformation reminded her of time-lapse footage she'd once seen of a flower closing its petals.

Should she leave him be? Head home to her roommate and her friends pretending they weren't all too old for house parties?

No. She might never get another chance to speak to this man in the flesh, so she waited. Twenty seconds passed. Thirty. Vernon's words turned monosyllabic, and then he hung up. He reassembled himself and returned.

"Apologies. I should let you go. You probably have a husband waiting at home."

"No husband, sir. Not really my area."

"Very well. Someone like you could be useful to the Behavioral team, so if my name pops up in your inbox, don't be alarmed. Take care."

Maya opened her mouth to speak but couldn't find the right words. She finally managed a muted "Absolutely. Bye, sir."

Vernon rushed back upstairs to his ivory tower, and Maya was left alone. She had to replay the past few minutes in her mind to make sure she hadn't hallucinated them because she was sure she'd dreamed this exact scenario more than a few times over the past twelve years.

Someone like you could be useful to the Behavioral team.

TWO

MAYA WAS HALFWAY HOME WHEN SHE DECIDED TO detour through Shelby Avenue, the street where the Cuckoo Oak Bar just happened to be. She couldn't face a night with Becky and her loud nail salon friends, not when Maya had spent the past twelve hours tracking down missing children. The juxtaposition was too great, like laughing at a funeral. So instead, Maya parked her Honda Civic around the back of the bar and found a quiet booth inside.

Most bars in Falls Church would be heaving on a Friday night, but the Cuckoo Oak was a law enforcement bar for law enforcement people. Maya didn't exactly fit the bill, being a desk jockey and all, but she needed neutral territory to process whatever the hell had just happened with Vernon. There were about twenty other patrons inside, most propping up the bar, some hiding away in the corners. What Maya loved most about this place was how sound died as soon as it was born. Soft furnishings, fabric curtains, and carpeted floors. Modern bars were designed with metal furniture to amplify sound and give the illusion of high energy, but thankfully the Cuckoo Oak predated that philosophy.

At her booth, she fired off a text to Becky saying she was stuck at work. Then she pulled out her laptop and browsed those pesky unfinished documents on her desktop. Her device connected to the Wi-Fi automatically.

"What'll it be?" a voice asked. Maya glanced over and saw a waitress lost in the act of wiping down a table.

"Coffee please. No sugar."

"Irish?"

"No thanks. The opposite of Irish."

"Coming right up." The waitress finished her duties, then locked eyes with Maya. "Hey, it's you. The mind reader woman. Got a deck of cards?"

A sudden memory resurfaced. A few months ago, Maya had been here with her Intelligence crew. What had begun as a low-stakes poker game ended up as Maya doing a spontaneous magic show.

"Damn, sorry, I haven't got a deck on me."

"Just wait there. I was telling Marge about you. Two seconds." The waitress disappeared behind the counter, shouted something into the back area, then emerged with another waitress by her side. They came over, and the new arrival threw an ancient deck of cards on the table. Maya had been doing magic tricks since she was ten and had never seen a brown deck in her life.

"Do that thing you did. I've been wracking my brain over it ever since." The waitress nudged her colleague. "Watch this, Marge."

Maya slid the deck out of their box and found that the

cards were probably older than she was. That sudden adrenaline spike of impromptu performance hit her because the brain always jumped to that single burning question: *What if I screw this up?* There was probably no bigger embarrassment in the world because magic tricks were all about the big reveal at the end. If you got that wrong, that's all the spectator would remember.

She pushed the thought aside and gave the cards a riffle shuffle. It wasn't smooth, but she got there. Then she fanned the cards out and held them toward this woman apparently named Marge.

"Pick one. Don't let me see it."

Marge plucked one from the middle, glanced at it, and held it to her chest. "Got one."

"Say it in your head. Over and over. Imagine you're saying it aloud."

The woman nodded along. Marge seemed to humor her, and she didn't seem the type to try and catch Maya out. Maya clasped her hands together and dissected—or at least appeared to—Marge's micro-expressions.

"The sides of your mouth keep flinching, which suggests it's either a two or a... ten?"

Marge grinned at the mention of ten. One out of three.

"I'm going to guess it's a red card because people are more open with their body language when they pick reds. So it's either a heart or a diamond, and when people say one of them over and over in their head"—Maya gestured for Marge to keep mentally repeating her card—"you can sense twitches in the lower jaw that resemble the first letter. And your mouth is slightly widening every few seconds, so I'm going to say it's the ten of... hearts."

"What!" Marge screeched. She flung her card on the table, and Maya was as relieved as anyone to see the ten of hearts staring back at her. "How'd you know that? Did you cheat? Was Linda here in on it?"

"Nothing like that," Maya laughed. "Believe me, if you knew the secret, you'd be very disappointed."

"Well, I love it," Marge said. "You should do a gig here one night. Magic or mind-reading or whatever it is. God knows we need something to liven this place up."

Maya boxed the cards and passed them back to the waitress. "It would be a short show. I'm no Copperfield."

Linda, the first waitress, nudged Marge. "See? Told ya. It's freaky. Is it some fed training thing?"

"Misspent youth. I always had cards as a kid. Dad was a gambling addict, Mom was sort of a magician."

"No kidding?"

"Yeah. She disappeared when I was six."

The waitresses laughed in tandem, then Linda said, "Love it. I'll get that coffee for you."

"Appreciated," Maya said. Her joke had landed, and she didn't correct their assumption that it was part of the act. Some truths were easier to deliver as comedy. When the waitresses disappeared, Maya got back to her laptop.

She loaded up a saved document and stared at seventeen faces in thumbnail photos, all teenagers who'd vanished throughout New York, New Jersey, and Connecticut. Seventeen kids whose parents kept their bedrooms exactly as they'd left them, just in case they ever came back. Maya had a theory about hope: It was the cruelest emotion on the spectrum because it prevented proper grieving. The families of these missing kids were stuck in purgatory because they couldn't mourn what might still be alive.

With the tri-state cases, she still needed a deep dive into the latest cell tower pings. Then the financial fraud algorithm was throwing up anomalies she needed to dissect. Lots to do, not enough time to do it all before Monday.

Then Maya's laptop pinged. A new email popped up in the corner of her screen.

Great, she thought. Another Friday night worker but one who wanted to make sure *everyone else* knew they were working. Maya was ready to dismiss it, but then she saw the name of the sender: *raymond.vernon@fbi.gov.*

Goosebumps suddenly prickled her flesh. The man—the director of Behavioral—who she'd been speaking to not one hour ago. Maya clicked the message with her heart in her throat.

Subject: call me.

Hi Miss Frost, apologies for the late message. I found your email address in the directory. Could you call me? Number is below. Vernon.

Maya's vision went blurry, the way it did when she'd glugged too much caffeine on an empty stomach. The bar around her became background noise, and her hands suddenly went cold. It was that peculiar feeling that preceded vomiting or fainting.

The possibilities came in waves. Had she screwed up somewhere, and now Vernon wanted to ask questions? But he'd praised her work, hadn't he? Or maybe this was about the serial case in Maine she'd helped solve.

Too much thinking, Maya told herself. Her cell phone sat in her bag. All she had to do was call the number in his signature block and find out what the hell was important enough to interrupt his Friday evening.

She grabbed her cell and rushed to the back door, trusting that her laptop was safe among the Cuckoo Oak clientele. She burst out into the smoking area, thankfully deserted, and dialed the number.

One ring.

Two.

Three.

Then a voice picked up. "Vernon speaking."

"Hi, Director Vernon? It's Maya Frost."

"Ah, you got my email then," he said. "I wasn't sure if you'd be online."

"Always. Is everything OK?"

"Yes. Well, no. Far from it. Do you have a moment to talk? This could take a while."

Maya adjusted the phone with a trembling hand. What the hell was Vernon talking about? "Of course. Are you at HQ? I'm just at the Cuckoo Oak, but I can—"

"No, that's perfect," Vernon interrupted. "Wait there. I'll be there in twenty minutes."

"Here? Really? Wouldn't HQ be better?"

"No. I need to talk off the record."

THREE

MAYA RETURNED TO HER BOOTH AND POURED THE entire creamer into her coffee so she could consume every drop of caffeine before Vernon arrived. Twenty minutes. A director of the FBI wanted to meet her off the record, and Maya had no clue what the hell he wanted to discuss.

She thought of her early beginnings, and now here she was, about to sit face to face with the director of the most prestigious unit in the FBI. The trajectory seemed impossible when she traced it back to its origins.

Nine years ago, Maya had been a criminal science graduate who, by some stroke of fortune, managed to land a job with Massachusetts State Police. It had been an entry-level position that involved admin work and not much else, and she'd actually believed that maybe some patrol officer would call in sick and she'd get to ride along, solve a case, become the day's unlikely hero. The embarrassment of that wishful thinking still made her wince. To subsidize the hero complex, she'd volunteered at a battered women's shelter on the side too.

The fantasy, of course, remained just that. Two years of paperwork drudgery morphed into a data analysis role. More responsibility but the fieldwork opportunities remained firmly zero. She was stuck behind a screen, drowning in statistics while the real action happened somewhere else, to someone else.

She'd been good at the analysis work, better than good. Patterns emerged when she stared at spreadsheets long enough. Numbers told stories that witnesses couldn't or wouldn't tell. But every breakthrough felt bittersweet because she was always three steps removed from the action.

Her break had come at twenty-four, when an old colleague from Mass State mentioned her name to the intelligence director at the FBI. One medieval interrogation disguised as an interview later, Maya Frost was the Intelligence Department's fresh meat. She had her toe in the door of the dream, but now, at the ripe age of thirty, she was still in the same position as she had been six years ago.

It wasn't the worst thing in the world because while most people saw work as something they *had* to do, Maya saw it as something she *got* to do. Every day was an exercise in saving lives, putting monsters behind bars, and bringing a little light to the dark, but it never felt like enough. Maya had made no secret of her ambitions, but positions in the Behavioral Unit were never advertised. They were filled in-house, usually via word of mouth.

Sometimes she'd start chatting with special agents and behavioral profilers at FBI events, and the stories they told made her hungry to experience the field firsthand. Sometimes she'd catch glimpses of the real work when Behavioral requested intelligence support. Details that never made the evening news. A victim with an occult symbol carved in their skin. A handwritten note left behind at the murder scene. These tiny shards of darkness would alight her imagination, theories would spark, but any insights would hit a brick wall because intelligence analysts weren't invited to theorize about murder. That was left up to the real players.

Except for her theory about the Maine serial killer. That had somehow obliterated the invisible barrier between the Behavioral Unit and every other department in the Bureau, and that was certainly the trigger that had set this discreet meeting in motion.

The door chime announced a new arrival to the bar. Maya glanced up and saw Raymond Vernon's bulk filling the doorway. The man was dressed in a black woolen coat and had a scarf covering the bottom half of his face despite it being a mild autumn night. He made a beeline for Maya's table and took a seat opposite her without waiting for the invitation.

"Miss Frost. Sorry for the cloak-and-dagger routine. It's not common, I promise."

"I expected nothing less. Do you want a drink?"

Vernon removed his scarf, then scanned the room like he was about to reveal the secrets of the universe and didn't want anyone eavesdropping. "I'm good. Haven't touched the stuff in years. Can I cut to the chase?"

"Please do."

"So we're in a mess at the moment."

Maya arched a brow. "A mess?"

"Yeah. The Bureau. Every department. Mine especially.

We've got thirteen thousand special agents in-house, three hundred within Behavioral specialty, but it's still not enough."

Maya had heard the statistics time and time again. Thirteen thousand agents sounded like a lot until you considered that hundreds would be deployed to any given state at once. Terrorism task forces in New York, organized crime units in Chicago, cybercrimes in California. Then there were the cold cases that could keep entire teams busy for months or years. Missing persons investigations that required agents to canvass entire counties. International operations that pulled specialists away for half a decade at a stretch. Not to mention that a lot of agents were stuck behind desks or testifying in courtrooms rather than doing any actual legwork. Considering that most rookies didn't qualify for field work until their late twenties, and then throw in the mandatory retirement age of fifty-eight, you could get thirty years at most out of a good agent.

"I've read the numbers, sir," Maya said.

"Good. We're losing agents faster than we can replace them. Retirement, burnout, and just plain old suicide. The next batch of rookies aren't expected for another six months, and we can't just sit around with our thumbs up our asses until they arrive."

Maya swallowed a lump in her throat. She'd never had a meeting where the term suicide—or thumbs up asses—was mentioned within the first minute, even at the FBI. "So how can I help with this? I assume that's why you wanted to meet?"

"Got it in one. The truth is, I want to try something new.

An initiative not yet cleared by the higher-ups. But I think it could work. With the right people."

Every nerve ending began to tingle. Maya's nervous system couldn't decide whether to celebrate or sound the alarm, so it did both. "What would this initiative involve?"

"Think of it as a crash course in field work. We'd take people who showed promise in other areas"—Vernon gave her a subtle nod—"and team them up with a veteran agent. A mentor and apprentice deal. How would you feel about that?"

Maya's throat closed up. Words suddenly abandoned her. Field work. Without the academy. Without the six months of tactical training. Without waiting for an opening that might never come.

Her body betrayed every poker face lesson she'd ever learned. Blood drained from her face and pooled somewhere in her feet because Vernon was offering her a shortcut to her dream job.

"Are you serious?" she asked. A part of her wondered if she hadn't accidentally shot herself back at that firing range and this was all some comatose hallucination.

"Dead serious."

A thousand questions fought for dominance, but one in particular won out. "But... why me? Why not someone who does a physical job? How do you know I'd be good at it?"

"Call it intuition. Call it me seeing you at that firing range every week. You obviously know your way around a firearm, not to mention your work on the Maine case. You saw patterns Behavioral veterans didn't, and that alone is enough for consideration. Would you be interested? There'd be no formal training period or anything like that. It's a completely new—and risky—initiative, but like I said, the Bureau's methods need an overhaul, and risks are par for the course."

"But what about my job?"

"I've already spoken to Weston. He doesn't want to see you leave the department, but he knows you don't want to be there for the rest of your life. Intelligence will survive without you."

Maya felt like she was being offered a winning lottery ticket. Sure, it was an unconventional lottery ticket, but it offered things money couldn't buy: a chance to be the hero Maya had always dreamed of being, a chance to put monsters behind bars with her own two hands.

"I... would love to," Maya said. "But I need to ask a few things. Is that all right?"

"Of course. I understand this is unconventional."

"This is embarrassingly simple, but how does the Behavioral Unit... actually work? I mean, day to day. I know the theory, the profiles, but the logistics..."

"You don't know because Intelligence keeps you in a box." Vernon said it like it was a universal fact. "Here's the reality. Local law enforcement hits a wall, usually for one of three reasons. Either the bodies start piling up, there's no physical evidence to go on, or the crime is ultra-violent in nature."

Maya got it. Despite what most people thought, most local PD offices weren't equipped to deal with anything more than gangland shootings or domestic crimes of passion. But the FBI had resources local police departments didn't, like face-analysis software, ballistics experts, cellular forensics, access to the VICAP database. "Understood."

"We dispatch agents to the locations to draw up psychological profiles of the unsub, and we stay there as long as it takes."

"How long is typical?" Maya asked, but she regretted the question as soon as it left her lips.

Vernon leaned forward. "There's no *typical* in this game. Back when I was on the ground, shortest case I worked was three days. Longest was twenty-two years. In this gig, you'll miss your kids' birthdays. You'll forget what your husband looks like. Your mailbox will be fit to burst every time you actually get to see your own house. Are you OK with that?"

Maya absorbed this information. Months away from home. Away from her tiny apartment and Becky's impromptu parties and her Friday night routine at this very bar. The prospect should have triggered some anxiety about leaving her comfortable patterns behind.

Instead, it sounded like paradise.

"No kids or husband. And my mail is all junk anyway."

"So you're in?"

"I'm in," Maya said without hesitation.

"Perfect. There's just... one other thing."

"I'm listening."

"We need someone now. Tonight."

"Tonight." She heard herself repeat the word like it might change meaning the second time around.

"Yeah. We've got an ultra-violent crime in Fernandina Beach, Florida. It's nothing like what the local PD are used to. Are you ready?"

"Ready? But I haven't—" Maya stopped. Hadn't what? Hadn't prepared? Hadn't told her roommate she was apparently leaving for Florida for God knew how long? Hadn't finished that report on money laundering patterns in Baltimore? None of it mattered if she said no. And she wasn't going to say no.

"Problem?"

"No problem, sir. Just adjusting to this sudden timeline. What's the case? Can you tell me more?" Maya was already mentally running through everything she'd need. Laptop, firearm. How many pairs of underwear did you need for a murder investigation? Vernon's expression suggested he was watching her work through the panic in real time.

"No. I don't know much about the case myself, but I'll tell you what—head back to your place and pack your things. I'll get a cab to pick you up and take you to the airport. A handler will fast-track you through the boarding gate, then Devon will explain the rest when you're on the plane."

Maya blinked hard. Had she heard Vernon right? "Devon? As in... Devon Lynch?"

Vernon had already risen to his feet. His scarf was hanging loosely around his neck. "Yes. Devon Lynch. Are you familiar with her?"

Maya knew Devon Lynch, all right. Everyone in the Bureau knew Devon Lynch.

FOUR

MAYA FLOORED THE GAS ON HER WAY BACK TO HER apartment, but her mind wasn't on the road. Not only was she still wondering whether or not the past hour had been a fever dream, but now her brain was tunnelling backward through seven years of Bureau gossip to excavate everything she knew about Devon Lynch.

Devon Lynch was *the* psychological profiler in the FBI. From what Maya could remember, Lynch was a career agent, now in her mid-fifties, most likely. She'd been trained by Ressler and Douglas, the godfathers of behavioral profiling themselves, and had since added her own contributions to the profiling knowledgebase. She'd written a book called *Hands Don't Lie: Reading Truth Through Subconscious Movements*. The premise was seductive: that our hands were constantly writing confessions our mouths would never speak. Lynch claimed she could spot a killer by the way they held a coffee cup or a sex offender by how their fingers moved during questioning. It was either brilliant or complete horseshit, and Maya had never decided which.

She'd seen the woman in the flesh precisely once, at an award ceremony honoring Lynch's capture of the Chicago Ripper. Rumor had it that Lynch had crafted a psychological profile so accurate that she predicted the Ripper would be disguised as a cop with a bulletproof vest beneath his uniform when they caught him, and that was exactly what had happened.

Maya ditched her car in the parking lot, then rushed into her complex, up the stairs, and stopped at her front door. Voices were bleeding through. Maya's phone pinged.

A text from Vernon.

Car will be there in 20. Pack for warm climate – RV.

Twenty minutes to pack for what might be the most important assignment of her life. Maya's throat constricted. She wasn't ready. Nobody would be ready. But the chance might never come again.

So she pushed inside and aimed for the living room. She poked her head around the door and found five bodies occupying the floor. The wine glasses being so precariously balanced near the rug would usually spike her anxiety, but tonight she felt no such concern.

"Hey, everyone. Hope you're all having fun."

"Maya." Becky emerged from the couch in a satin robe. "Where the hell have you been? We saved you wine."

"Drink it. I can't stay. Listen, my room will be free tonight if anyone wants to crash."

One of the girls, a peroxide blonde that Maya knew only by hair color, gave her a thumbs up. Maya escaped on the advent of delivering good news and made for the bedroom.

As she began pulling clothes out of her closet, Becky appeared in the doorway with a wine glass in hand.

"This is concerning," she said.

"Yes, it is."

"Where are you going?"

"Fernandina Beach."

"What? A beach? There are no beaches in DC."

"True." Maya stuffed three casual tops and two pairs of jeans into her bag. They took up more space than she suspected. Was this a suitcase situation? No. That would mean going through baggage claim, and Maya guessed that Devon Lynch would scoff at such procedures.

"You're being weird. Weirder than usual. You want to tell me what's going on?"

Maya located underwear, then decided five pairs was either too optimistic or too pessimistic. She grabbed seven, then looked up at Becky with her golden locks and robe that revealed a little too much. "I'm going to Florida with work. They want me on a case."

Becky's eyebrows shot up. "A *case*? You? Why?"

"I've been asking myself that."

"Wait a minute. You're going to Florida? For how long?"

"No idea." Maya searched for her necessary electronics. "I've been offered field work. Don't worry. I'll be fine."

Becky gulped the remains of her drink and then held it out like an invisible hand might refill it. "Maya, what am I going to do about the bills? Or those forms that come in the mail? What about the lottery numbers? I'm supposed to do it all myself? None of this makes sense."

Maya found a copy of Devon Lynch's book underneath her bedside table. Should she take it, or was that sucking up?

She decided to leave it behind because she was losing the battle of bag space anyway.

"None of that will change. It all happens automatically, Beck."

"Do you know how many people die from alligator attacks out there?"

"Hardly any."

"Fine, but I'm just saying. You don't fit. You're the least Florida person I know."

Maya stopped her frantic packing and studied Becky's face. Beyond the wine flush, a note of concern lurked in her roommate's expression. Being alone was Becky's worst nightmare. For reasons Maya would never understand, being alone made Becky invite strangers from wherever the hell just to fill the apartment with noise. Maya ditched her bag by the door and put her hands on Becky's shoulders.

"Woman, I'm not going to Iraq. I'm going to Florida. It's the same as DC, but it has pelicans."

"And crackheads with guns."

"We have those here too."

"That's not the point."

"Hey." Maya gently squeezed Becky's shoulders and gave a mock massage. "I'll miss you too, but I'm going to call you every day, OK? It'll be like we're long-distance lovers."

"We're not lovers because I think I could do better than you, honestly. And you don't need to call every day. I don't like you that much."

Maya smiled. "Deal. You've got a room full of people out there who think you're the life and soul, too. You won't even notice I'm gone."

"Fine. Don't forget your toothbrush."

"Good call." Maya moved to the bathroom and found her necessities. Becky followed her in. Her bag was fit to burst, but that was the thing about packing. You didn't know what you were missing until you needed it. "I'll call you when I can."

"FBI people always say that in movies. Right before they get shot."

"True. Why don't you ask one of your girlfriends to stay in my room? I'll probably be gone a few days at least."

Becky glanced back at the living room, then leaned in and whispered, "They're kind of annoying me, to be honest. I'm not ready for that commitment."

"Fair enough."

"Speaking of commitment, have you got protection?"

"Protection?"

"Yeah. *Protection.*"

"From what?"

"Herpes. Babies. Deadbeat dads."

Maya shot her a look. "It's not that kind of trip."

"You say that now, but Florida's full of Florida men. It's where they keep them." Becky propped herself against the bathroom doorframe. "If you do meet someone, which you need to, wrap it up. And don't be coming back here with a face tattoo or anything like that either."

"No herpes. No face tattoos. I promise."

"And don't trust anyone named Kyle. Or Alfie, or any guy who has an X in their name."

Maya threw her bag over one shoulder and hugged her roommate. "You got it, partner."

"You're really doing this. The fieldwork thing."

"I think so."

"What if you're good at it?"

"That would be a great thing."

"No it wouldn't. We had this chat the other day."

Maya remembered. Tuesday night. They'd watched a documentary about a celebrity chef who'd burned out so spectacularly he'd ended up living in a van, making grilled cheese for tourists.

"The passion-to-profession paradox," Maya murmured.

"Exactly." Becky jabbed a finger toward Maya's chest. "You turn what you love into work, and soon you hate both."

The theory wasn't without merit. And the question gnawed at her; what if she *was* good at this? What if Devon Lynch saw something in her that went beyond basement-dwelling number crunching? Becky studied her with the alarming focus of the moderately drunk.

"I don't know, but there's only one way to find out. I'll text you when I get there."

"Be good."

"You too."

Maya said her goodbyes and made her way downstairs and outside into the evening. Any minute, a cab would arrive to take her to a new life. She'd miss Becky while she was gone, but suddenly, parties and data analysis felt a million miles away.

FIVE

Maya's handler met her at the entrance to Reagan International Airport and shuttled her through security and the boarding gate in record time. Now as she walked through the tunnel toward the waiting jet, she realized she'd been deceived.

A part of her had expected the full cinematic treatment. Black SUVs with tinted windows. A private hangar. Maybe a sunglassed pilot who called her "Agent Frost." What she hadn't expected was the sterility of Terminal A, with its wine bars and Wolfgang Puck Express. She always assumed special agents flew in private jets, but that image, she now saw, was as fictional as the hero cop who never filled out paperwork.

Maya ascended the steps to the airplane's doors and felt her pulse rate spike. An hour ago, this whole thing had been mere words and fantasies, and now it was as real as the jet fuel invading her nostrils. She gave her boarding pass to the stewardess, who guided her left through the heavy blue curtain that separated economy from the luxury option.

"There." The woman pointed. "You're in E3."

Maya blinked hard. "Really? First class?"

The stewardess checked the ticket again. "Business, but yes."

Maya wasn't sure of the difference between business and first, but she wasn't about to complain. She'd expected to be knee to knee with Devon Lynch for two hours in economy, which might not have been an ideal environment to sell herself.

She moved down the aisle. Business class had a different configuration than she'd expected—pairs of seats facing each other across fixed tables, like a train compartment. Privacy without isolation. Row E appeared, and Maya stopped dead.

Devon Lynch sat in the opposite seat.

The woman wasn't like Maya remembered, nor did she resemble the headshots that were pinned up around HQ. This Devon Lynch had light red hair—which Maya guessed was her natural color—tied back in a bun. She was one rung above skinny, and even sitting down, Maya could tell she was a tall woman, no thanks to those heeled boots that matched her black dress. She was rifling through a stack of papers.

"Miss Lynch?" Maya asked.

Devon glanced up. The woman had razor-sharp cheekbones and porcelain skin that could have come right out of Ireland. She had hazel-green eyes, and Maya's brain supplied the useless fact that red hair and green eyes occurred in less than one percent of the population. Rarer than both left-handedness and perfect pitch. Devon Lynch had apparently been assembled from the universe's limited edition resources.

"That's me. You're the rookie, right?"

Maya had never been called a rookie before, and the title felt strange. Instinct screamed at her to say something intelligent, something that would prove Vernon hadn't made a mistake in choosing her, but instead she stood frozen in the aisle. "Yes, ma'am."

"Sit." Devon gestured to the chair opposite her. Maya shuffled into the seat and stuffed her bag beneath it. This was it. She'd arrived. Now came the hard part.

"Miss Lynch, I'm not going to tell you I'm your biggest fan or anything like that, but I've read your book. And seen some of your articles. And attended a ceremony of yours a few years ago."

Devon placed her stack of papers down on the table, sat back, and folded her arms. "Please call me Devon. And what should I call you?"

"Maya. Or just... Frost. Either is fine."

"Frost it is. So, Miss Frost, why are you here?"

"Mr. Vernon sent me."

"Yes he did. But why are you here? What made you say yes to a strange request from a man you barely know, to a partner you've never met, to fly to a murder scene a thousand miles away?"

Maya's mind went blank. What kind of question was that? The real answer—because Vernon thought she had potential—sounded too broad. The safe answer—to assist in the investigation—was the kind of nothing answer that would get her sent back to the basement before the plane had even taken off.

"I'm here because..." Maya stopped and caught the way Devon's eyes tracked the movement of her hands as she reached for words that didn't exist. "I know how the human brain works."

"You know how the human brain works," Devon repeated, and somehow made it sound like Maya had claimed she could juggle planets. "Is that right?"

"Yes."

"And does that qualify you for this job?"

"No."

"Do you know what this job entails?"

The captain's announcement came over the speaker. Maya must have been the last person to board. "Yes I do. Vernon gave me the rundown."

Devon Lynch regarded her for a minute, then pulled a pen from her jacket pocket and began clicking it to the level that other people might find it annoying. Maya recognized the technique from her own analysis work. Create a pattern, then watch how the subject responds to it. See if they mirror the rhythm, fight against it, or pretend not to notice. Maya did the latter.

"I'm going to be honest with you—I don't want a partner. I've been working alone for fifteen years, and I like it that way. But Vernon says I need to help train the next generation, and that I'm willing to do."

What was Maya supposed to do? Thank her? Maya hadn't expected this level of confrontation. "I'm sure you've got a lot of advice to give."

"Tell me about you," Devon said, clearly ignoring the compliment. "You're from Intelligence, is that right?"

"Correct." Maya waited for further invitation to speak,

but none came, so she launched into the spiel she'd been practicing on the way here. It felt safer than Devon's psychological archeology. "Six years in Intelligence, twelve in law enforcement. I've helped identify three terrorist cells operating in the mid-Atlantic region. Found financial patterns that led to the dismantling of an abduction ring in Baltimore. My algorithm for tracking cryptocurrency transactions resulted in forty-seven arrests related to human trafficking."

Devon turned her pen over in her fingers, examining it like she'd never seen one before. Her incessant clicking continued. Maya pushed on.

"I've processed over two thousand missing persons cases, identified statistical anomalies in organized crime financial networks, and my work on the tri-state trafficking analysis led to—"

Maya stopped just as the cabin lights went out and the plane surged into motion. It hit her then, the way understanding sometimes did. Not gradually but all at once, like stepping off a curb you didn't see. Vernon hadn't sent her here to quote her résumé. The FBI had cabinets full of people who could boast similar success rates.

"And I helped find the Bangor Ripper."

Devon's clicking stopped. She leaned forward slightly, her first sign of genuine interest. "Go on."

"Five victims in six months. Three women, two men. All stabbed in their own homes with their index fingers cut off."

"I know the case. I looked into it myself at the time. How did you uncover the unsub?"

"Profiling but from a different angle," Maya said with a surge of confidence. "Serial killers usually stick to a specific type of victim, but the Bangor Ripper's victimology was massively inconsistent. Young men, young women, old women. It's unheard of in the realm of serial murder, especially from someone everyone thought was a lust killer."

The plane rumbled and began its ascent into the sky. Maya's stomach churned, and she had to avoid looking out of the window because this part always made her feel sick. She'd always been a bad flier.

"Correct," Devon said.

"But the Bangor Ripper wasn't a lust killer. Usually, when a perp uses a knife, we think it's a substitute for penetration, right? That's what historical cases tell us. But that wasn't the case here. The people he was killing weren't surrogates for someone else. He wasn't symbolically killing his mom or his ex-wife over and over again. He was killing very specific victims."

Devon Lynch's body language underwent an abrupt realignment that Maya felt across the table. Her languid disinterest evaporated. "How'd you reach that conclusion?"

"He wasn't a thrill killer because of the lengths he went to to invade the homes. He wasn't a lust killer because there weren't any sexual components present. He wasn't a sadist because he didn't mutilate the bodies. These victims meant something to him. So I dug into their lives."

"The investigators already determined the victims didn't run in the same circles."

"No they didn't, but I found that they all had one thing in common. The first was that they'd all lost something. A baby, a wife, a house, a limb. One had been diagnosed with cancer. All of the victims had posted about their losses on social media. So the question became: why would a killer target these people?"

"You tell me," Devon said.

"Because he related to them. He saw himself as a savior, not a killer. Someone to take the pain away, the way he wished someone could take *his* pain away. So with this theory in mind, I searched within five miles of the first crime scene for anyone who'd also suffered similar losses. Sure enough, there was a guy who'd lost his whole family—and his index finger—in a car crash. Then six months ago, he'd been diagnosed with cancer. I figured that was the stressor that finally made him snap. He took their index fingers to symbolically replace what he'd lost. I gave your team the details and... here I am."

Silence descended, and Devon regarded Maya for a moment that was just the wrong side of uncomfortable. Maya searched for some sign that she'd passed this impromptu examination, but all she found was the unsettling realization that Devon Lynch was easier to admire from afar.

"OK." Devon gestured toward the galley area where Maya could see a station set up for business class passengers. "Get us a drink from over there. Neat whiskey and whatever you want. It's on me."

"Sure."

Before Maya could rise, Devon reached into her bag and threw a brown folder onto the table. "And this is for you."

She eyeballed the front cover. Stenciled in the corner was CASE: *137495, FERNANDINA BEACH, FL.*

"We're going to put that brain of yours to use," Devon continued, "because we've got a woman who's been strung up like a deer."

SIX

MAYA SET THE WHISKEY DOWN IN FRONT OF DEVON AND
gripped her Diet Coke like it might somehow help her credibility. Was Coke lame? Should she have gotten something
stronger in Devon's company? She had stood at the drink
station for a full ten seconds before choosing it over the
miniature bottles of vodka and gin. Now the choice felt like
she was revealing something. *The rookie who couldn't loosen
up, even at thirty thousand feet.*

Maybe she wasn't thinking straight because Devon had
told her they were dealing with a victim who'd been strung
up like a deer, whatever that might look like. Maya was
itching to get close to it.

"Thanks," said Devon. She took a sip, then gestured to
the brown folder on the table between them. "You seen a
case file before?"

"Not in such proximity."

"Now's the time."

Maya grabbed the file and unearthed the stack of papers

within. The first page was a police report, and among the stack Maya recognized a wad of eight-by-ten crime scene photos. They were the unglossed versions, the premature ones before they went through official processing. She swallowed against her suddenly dry throat. This was it. Not a report filtered through three departments nor statistics on a screen. This was real crime scene documentation, only an hour removed from the printer.

FERNANDINA BEACH POLICE DEPARTMENT.
INCIDENT REPORT #2024-10847.
TYPE: HOMICIDE.
VICTIM: Morgan, Teresa Lynn
DOB: 03/14/1967 (age 58)
ADDRESS: 1247 Palmetto Street, Fernandina Beach, FL
SUMMARY: Victim discovered deceased in storage room of her place of business. COD undetermined. Body positioned post-mortem in unusual display.

"Unusual display?" Maya asked.

"Check the photos. Pictures say more than police reports ever could."

Maya obliged. She skipped to the first photograph in the pile and felt her heart plunge to the pit of her stomach. Consuming awful imagery was the backbone of any job in the FBI, but something about the scene in front of Maya bypassed that shield of detachment. The photo showed a naked woman hanging upside down, legs spread, with a giant laceration running down the middle of her body. Her arms hung downward, while her fingertips caressed the lake of blood that had pooled on the floor. Long wet brown hair concealed her face.

This woman—named Teresa Morgan, according to the

report—had been strung up and nearly cut in half. A bisection, as it was officially known.

"Jesus Christ," Maya blurted out.

"Not pretty, is it?"

Maya rifled through the rest of the shots. The next one showed a close-up of the giant gash running through the victim's torso. It began between the legs and ran down to her ribs. Maya was no expert on corpse mutilation, but she guessed that there wasn't a hacksaw in the world that could do this. Another photo showed a close-up of the restraints that kept the woman's legs in place. The killer had wrapped heavy-duty ratchet straps around each thigh and attached them to eye bolts in the wooden rafters. Maya knew those things. She'd helped her father load lumber countless times back in her farm days. "What the hell is going on here?"

Devon regarded her, probably to check that she hadn't gone pale. "Tell me what you see."

"I see..." Maya had always prided herself on being able to see the fifth dimension behind crime scene photos—the human element behind the blood and severed limbs. She scanned each picture in turn, suddenly desperate to unleash the unique insights she was convinced dwelled in her brain.

But she had nothing.

All she saw was a dead woman hanging from a ceiling.

"I'm not sure. What else do we know?"

"Come on, rookie. We read crimes scenes. That's what Behavioral does. If you can't do that..."

Maya pinched the bridge of her nose and chided herself. As much as she wanted to say, "Well, why don't you help me, since you're the expert?" she maintained her calm. She'd been devouring anything true crime related since she was old enough to read, she reminded herself. Didn't matter if it was an infamous case or some obscure murder in buttfuck nowhere. She knew this game. This was what she did in her off-hours, lying awake at three a.m., replaying details in her head and constructing psychological profiles for fun. Any spare hour she had, she dissected something homicidal. She only needed to catch a news segment about two unsolved homicides in the same city and the theories would start blooming.

So why, when it actually mattered, was her mind so goddamn blank?

The answer came before she'd finished asking the question, and it was simple: Because this was real. This poor woman, Teresa Morgan, had woken up this morning and gone about her day under the foolish assumption that she'd still be alive tomorrow. This wasn't some murder puzzle to be solved vicariously. There was a human being running free out there that had done this.

That revelation cleared some mental fog, and the thoughts came in waves.

"Given the profile of the victim, this isn't a sexually-motivated crime. Lust killers overwhelmingly target young women, but Teresa Morgan is pushing sixty. The killer has an intimate knowledge of the location, so this wasn't his first time in there. He came prepared, and he's got a stomach made of iron because he must have spent at least an hour with the body. Something like this takes time."

Something akin to a smile twitched at the corners of Devon's lips. She controlled it admirably, Maya thought. "What about the killer themselves? Who could do this?"

Maya inspected a wide-shot of the body. "Probability

says it's a man, because I doubt the average woman has the physical strength to pull this off. Teresa looks about what, one-forty? And our unsub hauled her up to the ceiling? This guy is built, sturdy."

Despite what people thought, few people were capable of lugging around a dead body. Maya had heard it described as like trying to carry four bags of compost that had been tied together.

"Agreed. And the staging?"

"It's pure overkill, but..."

Devon cocked a brow. "But?"

"But I'm not going to say that it implies a connection between killer and victim. That myth has been debunked. But something this precise means that the killer has a specific fantasy he's trying to address. He's been planning this for a long time."

"How do you know that?"

Maya gulped her drink. She felt it all spewing out now, things she hadn't even realized until her tongue began moving.

"Nobody wakes up one day and decides to saw a woman in half. This is the culmination of his darkest fantasy, one he couldn't keep contained anymore. And if someone just wanted Teresa dead and not humiliated in death, he wouldn't have gone to these extremes. He'd have just shot her and left. He probably doesn't know her personally either because killers get theatrical when they're confident there's no paper trail leading back to them."

"Not bad," Devon said.

Maya barely heard it because there was something else

about the scene. Was she imagining things? Jumping to conclusions?

Maybe. She decided to put this sudden new theory on hold for a second. "Thank you. Did I miss anything?"

Devon flipped through her own copy of the case file. There was a beat of silence before she said, "A few things. The angle of the entry wound suggests our unsub is about six-one. You said there might not be a connection between killer and victim, but the killer obviously knew the layout of this place. This is Teresa Morgan's place of business, so he could be a disgruntled employee or customer. Yes, killers usually only go to these lengths, but there are always exceptions. Given how he's strung her up and nearly bisected her, it suggests he's comfortable with corpses, be they animal or human. We could be looking at a butcher, surgeon, undertaker. When we land, we need to get eyes on the scene to make sure PD didn't miss anything."

Maya glugged down her drink but found it did little to quench the dryness in her throat. With how she felt right now, she doubted there was enough liquid in the world to do that.

She concluded that she'd done adequately in whatever test this had been. Devon Lynch had shifted from testing to teaching, which meant something. Maya couldn't quite get a read on her yet. She couldn't decide if Devon genuinely saw potential or was simply making the best of being saddled with a rookie on a new case. She guessed time would tell which version of Devon Lynch she'd be working with, and if Maya would last long enough to find out.

But then she found herself drawn back to the crime scene photos, to Teresa Morgan's inverted form.

Something about it didn't make sense. Or made too much sense.

It felt like a misremembered song lyric. The kind that made you stop mid-hum because the words that came out weren't what your brain remembered.

No. It couldn't be, could it?

SEVEN

DEVON LYNCH HAD KNOWN THIS DAY WOULD COME EVER since Vernon started his recruitment crusade three months ago and wouldn't accept no for an answer. Devon had done her part to make this whole operation as painless as possible, and now she was sitting in the back of a cab beside the fruits of her labor.

But while the rookie pool was often shallow and full of rocks, Maya Frost didn't seem so bad. The academy produced plenty of smart agents and plenty of brave ones, but rarely both in the same package. Devon just hoped Maya had enough common sense to survive what textbooks couldn't teach her. They were headed to the crime scene, and Maya had reeled off the address to the driver like she'd rehearsed the words on the way here. Their destination was a tucked-away street on the eastern edge of Fernandina Beach. Devon had been to Florida more times than she could remember, but this was her first time on Amelia Island, and as far as memory served her, she'd never seen a partially-bisected woman in the flesh either.

"Miss Lynch, what do—"

"Please call me Devon."

"Sorry. Devon, what do I do about, you know—protection? Firearms?"

"Say it like it is. You need a gun."

"I need a gun."

"Got your firearms license?" Devon asked.

"Updated last month. Federal qualification current through next April."

"Good. What about your carry permit?"

Maya fidgeted in her seat. "I have my concealed carry for D.C., but I don't know about other states. Vernon didn't explain."

"Vernon doesn't explain much, but it's simple. You're FBI, temporarily assigned to a federal investigation. Local PD will issue you a duty weapon tomorrow morning, probably the standard Glock 17 or 22. I'll handle the paperwork to make sure everything's above board."

"Thank you. What about tonight?"

Devon checked her watch. "Well, it's nearly midnight, so we probably won't get much shooting done before dawn. If you spot anyone suspicious, you tell me. Don't do anything crazy because you're not properly credentialed yet. That means no interviewing suspects, no arrests. Clear?"

"Crystal. I'm here to learn."

The girl was saying all of the right things, Devon had to give her that. By this point, newbies had usually reached the question-asking stage, but Maya had only asked the basics, all of which fell into the selfless category. She hadn't once asked if she'd be getting a raise. "You seen a dead body in the flesh before?"

"One."

"Been to an active crime scene?"

"No. Never."

"Three things to keep in mind. Wear gloves, but only touch what you have to. If you need to throw up, do it outside. And keep any theories to yourself because cops have mouths, and word travels fast, especially in small towns like this."

"Understood. Do we work alongside the police, or do they leave us to our own devices?"

"Ha. I wish. Local PD only call us when they're desperate, and nobody likes admitting they're desperate. The sheriffs and chiefs usually hover around, but the uniforms stay back. And when they see two women taking over, we'll be about as welcome as a Tabasco enema."

Maya almost smiled. It was the first one Devon had seen since this eager young thing had stepped onto the plane. "That's quite the image. Feel free to keep the advice coming."

"You respond well to analogies?"

"Exclusively. They're the best way of condensing the complexities of life down to short sentences."

"Good, because I've got loads." Devon watched the streets blur past outside the window. It had been nothing but coastal highway and the odd salt marsh since they'd gotten in the car, but now life was beginning to emerge. Shops and gas stations and an endless array of seafood restaurants. Beside her, the rookie had taken to looking at the crime scene photos again. Every agent went through this phase, like it was a compulsive itch they had to scratch. They always thought that there'd be some hidden detail in the pictures that solved the case before it had even begun, but Devon wasn't ready to hit Maya with the cold reality that investigations never worked like that. The truth was dirty—and always hidden.

"Something about that scene bothering you, Frost?"

"Sort of. Isn't it bothering you?"

"It's a dead woman strung up by her legs. Of course it bothers me."

"How so?"

"Because there's some asshole out there who thinks he can do this and get away with it." Devon tapped the photo in Maya's lap. "This scene tells me that the killer thinks he's an artist, and artists piss me off."

Maya regarded her for a moment. "You hate artists?"

"I don't mean like Da Vinci. I mean killers like this. They think they're making some grand statement by butchering women, but really they're just perverts who can't get it up. Don't make the mistake of thinking guys like this are tortured geniuses because they're not. People romanticize these scumbags too much these days, and if you want to get results in this job, you have to see these people for what they are."

"What's that?"

"Man children. Murder is an adult temper tantrum. Most adults can control their impulses, but guys like this can't."

"Couldn't agree more," Maya said before returning to the pictures. "But this scene. It's... I don't know."

"Spit it out, Frost."

Maya mentally chewed something over, then said, "Seriously, ignore me. The altitude is messing with my head."

"We're about a hundred feet lower elevation than D.C."

"Maybe that's it. I'm not used to being this low."

Devon eyeballed the GPS on the driver's screen. "Well, get used to it, because we're about to get lower. Crime scene is two miles away. The body is still there according to the brief I got back at HQ, so try not to throw up on your shoes."

"I'm ready."

Yeah, Devon thought. *That's what they all say.*

EIGHT

Maya could see Morgan's Hardware Store from the other end of the street where the cab dropped her and Devon off. Not because it was bigger or prettier than the neighboring buildings but because the place was gift-wrapped in yellow tape.

Here she was. Into the belly of the beast. The nerves had stirred up a tsunami in her stomach, and she was struggling to keep her hands from shaking. Across the road, Maya spotted a lone cruiser, although its presence wasn't doing much to deter the few strangers who stopped to stare.

"What do we do about the gawpers? Ignore them?"

"Exactly that. They might be journalists, so don't say a word to them." Devon adjusted the collar on her jacket and surveyed the street. "Not the most isolated place in the world. Our unsub took a risk here."

There was a row of shops leading to Morgan's Hardware, all of which were different in size and scale. Their destination was lodged at the end of the row, which then overlooked a stretch of salt marsh.

"If he was smart, he'd have climbed up the other side. There are six shops here, and what I guess is a bar just over there." Maya pointed to an old brick building with a swinging sign out front saying *Black Horse Tavern*. "Some of these places must have cameras outside."

"Let's hope so. Come on."

Devon led the way. They passed a few shops that were uniquely small town, all of them long closed given the hour. A barber shop, a pawn shop, a small grocery store. Orange street lamps illuminated the row, and then the brass signage of Morgan's Hardware came into full view. The place was a perfect square of green cinderblock and two lines of windows on either side of the door. Three cops in uniform were standing out front, and one of them ambled over as Maya and Devon approached.

"Feds?" he asked.

"That's us. Are you in charge?"

"Yes, ma'am. Harrison Riggs," he said as he extended his hand. "I'm the sheriff and the unlucky son of a bitch that has to deal with this mess."

"Special Agent Devon Lynch, and this is agent-in-training Maya Frost."

They exchanged greetings. Maya was quietly grateful for the dignity of *agent-in-training*. But if she was being honest, they could call her *Field Test Subject #1* and she'd still have taken the job.

"Training, huh?" Sheriff Riggs said. He was in his fifties at a guess, and he boasted the weathered skin of a man who'd suffered through many a Florida summer. Up in D.C., his tan would have taken out eyeballs.

"Training indeed, but I'm ready to dive right in."

"Well, I'm glad someone is. You'd think this case was radioactive with how my guys have backed away from it. We don't get a lot of homicides in Fernandina, especially of this... level. So we're in uncharted territory, honestly."

Maya said, "A place like this, I imagine it's mostly crimes of passion, burglaries gone wrong, arson."

Riggs regarded her with his index finger. "Bingo, lady. You check the stats before coming here or something?"

"Coastal city, slow way of life. Lots of traditional couples and bored kids."

"You're not wrong, but I don't think a bored kid could do what they did in the back of that store."

"Did you know the vic?" asked Devon.

"Yeah. My wife is always doing some DIY project around the house, and she inevitably ropes me in once she gets bored. When I couldn't get something done, Teresa was my go-to. She'd give me what I needed and tell me how to fix my wife's screw-ups. Teresa saved my ass a hundred times."

"Does everyone around here know her?"

"Yup. Most of my guys do. The veterans knew her old man too. This store's been in Fernandina for generations."

"And your guys are still reluctant to help?"

Riggs sighed through his nose. "Yeah, because they don't want to let the community down. The longer we *don't* find Teresa's killer, the more we're the bad guys."

"Sounds familiar. Who called it in?"

"The vic's niece. Said she was trying to get ahold of Teresa all night. When her cell kept going to voicemail, she came down here to check on her. Found her about seven p.m."

"Was the door unlocked?"

"The back door, yes. Front door was locked."

"This niece of hers—have you checked her out?"

"Yup. She's no killer."

"How do you know?"

Riggs huffed. "Because she's barely five foot and weighs a hundred pounds."

Maya made a mental note of everything. Pillar of the community. Locked front door. Found by the niece, who was apparently too petite to be a killer. Across the street, a few stragglers had edged closer to the crime scene. The officers guarding the door rushed over to keep them at bay.

"The body's still in situ?" asked Devon.

"The scene is exactly as the killer left it. Forensics team should be here within the hour. We don't have a dedicated forensics team around here, so they've had to come in from Jacksonville."

"Great." Devon nudged Maya. "Ready, rookie?"

Maya took in two lungfuls of air. A fine tremor ran through her fingers as she flexed them. Ready as she'd ever be. "Let's go."

NINE

THERE WERE DEFINING MOMENTS IN A PERSON'S LIFE, Maya thought. The moment you were born, the moment you reproduced, and the moment you first saw a mutilated corpse dangling from the rafters in the back of a hardware store. Maya was yet to reproduce, so she'd had two out of three.

"Jesus wept," Devon breathed. "What the hell are we looking at?"

"I was hoping you'd tell me," Riggs said from the door. The sheriff had his forearm over his nose. "Gloves up, ladies. Lots of places for sticky prints in here."

Maya's entire nervous system was on fire, maybe because her conscious mind was still playing catch-up with the carnage in front of her. Even ten years in law enforcement hadn't quite prepared her for the sensory assault that had suddenly ambushed her. This poor woman was dangling gracelessly in a *V* shape above a pool of blood, and if not for those stubborn muscles in her neck, she'd be in two separate halves. Bones and ropes of intestines jutted from within, and a mask of blood-matted hair concealed her face. Tears welled up behind Maya's eyes out of sympathy for Teresa Morgan, so she paid a moment of silent tribute to her because the dead deserved at least that much.

Devon knocked her with her elbow. "You all right there, rookie?"

"Yeah... I mean...."

"You want a mask?"

"Please."

The sheriff's hand appeared clutching a surgical mask. Maya took it. He offered Devon one, but she declined. "We checked the front of house. The place is pristine. No sign of anything out of the ordinary. No blood."

"Any CCTV in there?" Devon asked.

"Yeah. There's a camera that covers the whole place, but it's outsourced to some security company. It's not a feed that goes into a hard drive here."

"Get that footage, if it exists. The camera might just be for show."

"One of my guys is working on it right now."

"Good. Frost, what do you think?"

Maya had been lost in the onslaught that apparently came with proximity to death. She didn't know where to start. Inspect the body? Recreate the killer's possible pathway in and out of the store? Canvas the street for people who might have seen something? Was there a procedure here, or did you just do everything non-linearly until you'd done everything you could? Maya said, "I think whoever did this is acting out a very specific fantasy."

"Why?"

Maya reached forward and pointed to the mutilated

fleshy tissue, careful not to step in the pool of blood. "He used a power tool for this. Look at how swollen the flesh is. A hacksaw would give you clean lines, but a power tool would completely blow it out."

"How's that relate to a specific fantasy?"

"Have you ever seen a killer bring his own power tools to a crime scene?"

Devon scratched her cheek. "Tools, yes. Power tools, no."

"This guy lugged a chainsaw or an angle grinder here. You don't decide to do that on a whim. This idea has been brewing in his head for a while, until it reached the point he couldn't control it anymore."

"Frost, we're in a hardware store. Of all the places in the world to find a tool to cut someone in half with, this is probably number one."

Maya looked out onto the shop floor and conceded that Devon had a point. "But if this guy is smart, or if he knew the layout here, he wouldn't have ventured out front. The sheriff said there's no blood out there, plus there are cameras. If you ask me, he brought his own tools, came in through the back door, and ambushed Teresa here."

"There's no way of knowing that for sure. The vic could have invited him in. He could have walked in the front door and locked it before he left. Never make assumptions because they're just poison in a well. Any theory you pull from that water will be tainted from the start."

Devon really did like her analogies, Maya thought. "OK. So what *can* we know for sure?"

"That our killer's not squeamish, and someone in this town is running around with Teresa's blood on them because there's no way of doing this without making a mess." Devon pointed to a step-ladder resting against the far wall. "And he's resourceful. He couldn't reach that ceiling without help, not unless he's eight feet tall, so I'm betting he used that ladder. Sheriff, make sure forensics sweeps every tool in this room."

"Count on it."

"You're right that this is the culmination of a long-standing violent fantasy. Impossible to determine the killing method, unless there are bullet holes somewhere in this mess. We could be dealing with a lust killer, but it's impossible to tell if there's any sexual component here. Even an autopsy won't confirm that."

Maya shuddered at the implication, then knelt down and inspected the clumps of hair masking Teresa's face. Death had transformed this poor woman into something that no longer appeared human on the surface, and Maya needed to look beyond and see the victim beneath. That's how she'd always done it in Intelligence. If you saw the humanity, you might just glimpse the story. And in that story might just be the reason they died.

But as she peered closer, she spotted something in the gaps between the tangles of bloodied hair.

"Sheriff, have you or your guys touched the body at all?"

"No, ma'am. Her niece made the identification, and we've stayed back ever since. Didn't want to contaminate the scene before forensics got here."

Maya's heart slammed against her ribs because there was something here that the crime scene photos hadn't picked up. Nor would they, because this thing had been invisible until the intrusion of bodies and draft from the opening-and-shutting door had brought it to light.

"Um, Devon? Have you seen her face?"

"No. It's covered in hair."

Maya reached out over the pool of blood with two gloved hands and parted the curtains of matted hair. There, staring back at her, was a skinless canvas of fleshy tissue, muscle, cartilage, bone, and vacant eyes missing their lids.

What the hell?

Nausea burned her stomach. Maya struggled to look away. Somewhere behind her, Sheriff Riggs began choking.

The killer had skinned Teresa Morgan's face.

"You gotta be kidding me," Riggs breathed.

"No kidding here." Devon kneeled down beside Maya for a closer look. "Our guy took a scalpel to her. He must have done this first. Before he cut her in two."

This didn't make sense. A surge of frustration hit Maya because this all but destroyed the theory she'd been mentally working on since she first saw the crime scene photos. A skinned face had no place here, yet here it was, staring back at her with eyes that would never close.

Strung up by her feet, cut nearly in half, stripped of her most human feature, and left to bleed dry in the back of her own store. Ten years of looking at crime scenes through a computer screen hadn't prepared her for death in the flesh, and she had to question if she hadn't been foolish giving up her cushy desk job to stare horror in the face. Or lack thereof.

A part of her said that yes, she had.

TEN

Maya felt like a diver coming up for air when she stumbled out of Morgan's Hardware and back onto the street. The forensic technicians had arrived to sweep the place from top to bottom, and she had to pray they'd find something useful because all Maya could see back in there was a gutted woman with a distinct lack of face.

Part of it was familiar in the way that old memories felt familiar but when so long had passed that you weren't sure if they actually happened or you'd just invented them. Maya had plenty of them to go around, and now this was another one for the pile.

"Feel free to take my car," Riggs said. "It's a long walk to the nearest motel."

"Are you sure?" asked Devon.

"Yup. I can get a lift back with one of the guys when they swap shifts, plus I need to stay here and keep an eye on the CSI guys anyway. We can reconvene at the precinct tomorrow. You know where it is?"

"No, but we'll find it."

"Sure. Just hit the home button on the GPS in the car." Riggs passed his keys to Devon. "I'll clear a space for you when I get back there."

"Appreciated."

Riggs turned to Maya. "Miss Frost, you good? You're as white as old dog shit."

"Yeah. Just kind of nauseous after seeing that."

"Go and sleep it off. If we get anything here, I'll buzz you both."

"Thank you, Sheriff," Devon said, then Riggs saluted and left the agents alone. Maya guessed that this was the point where the real work started. She was desperate to get some solitude so she could compartmentalize this mess, because if she could somehow rearrange the puzzle pieces here, there might just be an answer hiding in plain sight.

And while Maya didn't think it was appropriate to say it aloud, Teresa Morgan's killer had a psychopathology that she'd give anything to analyze. In the law enforcement game, you were always told to see things in black and white. You were the hero, and you put the villain in the ground and then moved on to the next villain with little in the way of analysis or self-reflection. Was it the same in Behavioral? Or could she voice this fascination? Yes, she wanted this unsub in chains, but she also wanted five minutes to talk with him to see what madness lived in his head.

"Frost, you ready to go? No point hanging around here. With any luck, we should have forensic results and the coroner's report by the morning."

Maya looked at the Black Horse Tavern across the street. It was after one a.m., so only the most stubborn drinkers remained. "Shouldn't we interview some of those guys in the bar? What if our unsub is one of them? You know how killers like to keep an eye on their crime scenes."

"No, only serial killers do that. We're not dealing with a serial killer. This is an isolated case, and if our guy has the patience and determination to gut a woman and saw her face off, chances are he's smart enough to get a million miles from the scene after he's finished."

Maya nodded, but she didn't quite agree. Murders of this level of brutality were rarely one-offs and were rarely the first in a sequence. If this killer hadn't killed before, he was certainly going to kill again. Maya was sure of it.

"Understood. Then I guess we better find our home for the night."

"And the rest. We could be in this town a while."

"I can deal with that."

Devon dangled the keys. "I promise you, things will look a lot different in the morning."

"You think?"

"I know, and by the way, you did pretty good in there. You didn't freak out, or if you did, I didn't notice."

"Thank you. All the vomit was internal."

"Best place for it. Ruminate on things for the night, then we'll see what tomorrow brings. Let's go."

MAYA QUICKLY DECIDED that Devon drove like she was actively trying to die. However, they made it to the Golden Hibiki Inn, a small motel with a needlessly Japanese name, still with all of their limbs attached. The place wasn't much to look at, but it had beds, and after this surreal day that she was still convinced was some kind of fever dream, Maya would have slept on a cactus if it meant getting horizontal.

"Home sweet home," Devon said as she reached her room. She was ten doors down from Maya according to their keycard numbers, which struck Maya as strange given that there were only three other cars in the parking lot out front.

"What's the process for the morning?"

"What time did you start work at HQ?"

"Nine."

"Then be ready for eight."

"Roger that."

"Get some sleep, Frost, because you'll need it. See you in a few hours."

Maya waited until she heard Devon's door click shut before leaving because if nothing else, it felt rude not to. Then she found her room, dropped her bag next to the nightstand, and surveyed her home for the foreseeable future. There was a desk, TV on the wall, and a mattress topper on a bed that might have been white once upon a time. She familiarized herself with the layout and the adjacent bathroom and then collapsed on the bed. Some water stains on the ceiling reminded her of the Rorschach tests that the Bureau shrinks used to determine whether a worker was fit for duty or not. Maya had never seen a damn thing in those tests, even in the ones that were purposely shaped like genitals.

Sleep should have come easily, but after forty-five minutes of lying on top of thin sheets in complete darkness, Maya was still wide awake. It probably had something to do with the image of a gutted, faceless woman burned into her eyeballs, and she doubted that image was going away. Her dad always said that if you weren't asleep within twenty-five minutes of hitting the mattress, you weren't sleeping any time soon. So Maya figured she might as well get up and put her insomnia to use.

She switched on the bedside lamp, rummaged through her bag for her notebook, and began writing. Theories were crawling out of her brain like insects from old wood, and she needed to get them down before they scattered.

Killer profile - preliminary:

Male, white, 25-50, well-built, lives locally, is familiar with the layout of Morgan's Hardware. Competent with power tools. Knowledge of human anatomy. Medical training? Butcher? Hunter? Surgeon? Facial mutilation suggests personal connection to victim or symbolic significance. Removal of identity? Trophy taking? Deep-seated issues with identity, recognition, or maternal figures. Mother complex? History of childhood abuse/neglect? Possible dissociative episodes during commission of crime.

Psychological indicators: Extreme compartmentalization. Ability to function normally in social settings while harboring violent fantasies. Most likely lives alone but a significant distance from the crime scene. If unsub had his own private space, he would have carried out mutilation at his own residence to negate possibility of capture.

Post-offense behavior: Likely experiencing emotional high followed by crash. May seek validation through media coverage or insertion into investigation. Could revisit crime scene or attend victim's funeral.

Trigger event: Recent stressor precipitated this level of violence. Job loss? Relationship ending? Death of family member? Killer reached breaking point where fantasy became insufficient.

Maya read it all back. There was one other thing she needed to add, but as she put pen to paper, she almost felt stupid writing it.

But she did anyway.

Copycat?

ELEVEN

THE TWELVE PIGS SNIFFED THE AIR WHEN HE ENTERED the platform above their pen because even these domesticated swine could smell blood from fifty feet away. It wasn't his blood they could smell, of course. It was the blood of a woman who'd been foolish enough to be the perfect target, and it had since dried itself into his clothes and hair and skin —and that made him feel alive.

Down below, one of the pigs began squealing. He fed them twice a day, but never at three in the morning, so the poor things probably thought it was Christmas. But it wasn't Christmas. Nor had he come here to feed the pigs. He'd come here because the pigs had always been his invisible line to the strange world of death, ever since that fateful day a few years ago when the pigs had feasted on the heartiest meal in their short little lives and his world had changed for the better.

He'd never known much outside of this farm. He'd been

born here, pushed out into the world in the old barn next to the chicken coop, and his old man's favorite joke was that he'd put him to work in the pig sty as soon as the boy had stopped crying. It might have been true for all he knew because his earliest memories all involved these animals in one way or another.

From that point, the boy's mere existence was apparently enough to infuriate his old man and his mother by extension. When the tractor seized up one winter, they both blamed him for not staying on top of the oil levels. When the chickens died of coccidiosis one year, his mother blamed him for not keeping them warm enough, as though ten-year-olds could control the weather. All of these mistakes ended with lashings from his old man's paddle, and he still felt that phantom sting even thirty years later when something went wrong. He could barely remember his mother and father being in the same room together, even though the photographs in the hallway told him that yes, once upon his time, his mom and dad had been a loving, affectionate couple. After he'd been born, it seemed that his parents could only agree on one thing: Life had been better before he arrived.

The old man hadn't lasted long, thankfully. The poor bastard smoked himself into an early grave, and that left him alone with his mother from twelve onward. But the old man's death knocked something loose in her, like a screw that been holding back her full capacity for cruelty. Before, she'd been content to ignore him most days and save her venom for when the chores weren't done. But after the old man's funeral, she'd lock him in the cellar for breathing too loudly and make him clean floors that weren't even dirty. Sometimes she'd drink herself into oblivion and occasionally disappear for days on end and leave a boy barely in his teens at home to fend for himself. The beatings got worse whenever she was sober enough to dish them out, and even when he grew to match her size, his body seemed incapable of fighting back, like a dog that had been kicked so many times it had no teeth left to bite.

Then one day, at the ripe young age of fifteen, his mother took things one step too far. All of the piglets fell sick with classical swine fever, and it was his responsibility to put them out of their misery. Even at such a young age, he was used to slaughtering all manner of creatures, but his mother wasn't content with giving the pigs a captive bolt to the head this time. Instead, she forced her fifteen-year-old son to trap them in heavy duty sacks and hammer them until they stopped screeching.

He didn't remember the hammering part. There was a black hole in his memory where that hour-long slaughtering session should have been, but he was sure that he cried and did whatever he could to drown out their futile squeals. The part that he *did* remember, the part that was burned into his retinas like a flashbulb afterimage, was opening those bags and emptying the remains into the incinerator. He saw what was left of those pigs, the only friends he'd had.

His mother had watched the carnage of the mass slaughter, but she hadn't seen the part that came afterward. While she was back in the farmhouse, drinking herself into a stupor, he suddenly realized what had truly happened here. When he poured out those hammered remains, he'd also poured out a part of himself. He should have refused, fought back, denied that stupid old bitch for the first time in his life. He was the same size as her at that point but heavier, stockier. He was the pure farm boy his father had always wanted for a son, and working day and night in the fields instead of going to school had given him a warrior's physique. If he could just summon the willpower to do so, he could have laid his bitch mother out without breaking a sweat.

Years later, the police ruled it an accident. The stupid old drunkard had stumbled into the pig pen after one too many gins, fallen over, and passed out from a combination of shock and an unstable blood alcohol level.

"And those pigs, they'll eat anything," he'd told the investigator.

To his fortune, the pigs had devoured nearly every inch of his mother. If not for the teeth coming out of their backsides, there wouldn't have been any trace of her left at all, which meant that no autopsy in the world would discover that both of her ankles had been broken at the time of her death, and her larynx had probably ruptured from screaming.

Teresa Morgan hadn't reminded him of his mother. The only thing they had in common was that they'd met each other once upon a time. But while Teresa and his mother were at opposite ends of the motherly spectrum, it was the moment that Teresa shouted, "Sorry, we're closed" that he lost himself to the fantasy. It was the world closing the door in his face. An older woman giving him orders. He'd thought, for years, that the day he watched the pigs excrete his mother's remains was the end of the story. He thought the pigs had finally fixed what his parents had broken.

Sadly not. It just showed him the tool, and tonight he'd

picked that tool up again and found that it felt like an old friend coming home.

And tomorrow night, he'd pick it up again.

TWELVE

THE RABBITS ON THE WALLPAPER HAD BUTTON EYES, and that was the only part of the story she could remember with any clarity.

Maya was five years old again, and she was weighted down by a pink comforter in the top bunk. It was her first ever night in the top bunk, because the younger sister was usually forced to the bottom bunk as per the sibling code. Only when one of the sisters reached the age that bunk positioning became uncool would she get the top bunk with any regularity, but given that Maya was five and Abigail was seven, that stage was still many years away.

But Maya had earned the top bunk on that night because she'd won the teacher's award at school that week for blowing her classmates away with an impromptu magic performance. The trick had been a simple card illusion, and the handling had been clunky. Still, it had fooled the whole class and apparently Mrs. Owen too, and that was cause for celebration in the eyes of Maya's parents.

Sleep had come easily for Abby, judging by her lack of movement, but Maya's adrenaline rush kept her awake past standard bedtime. She'd eventually dropped off around half past ten, but despite the cosiness that came with the heavy comforter and the success of claiming the top bunk, she woke up again while it was still dark outside.

Maya rarely woke up before the sun rose. She could see through the gap in the curtains where her mom always forgot to pull them all the way closed. No light coming through. Still deep night. The only light came from Abigail's night light, a plastic star that spun slowly on the dresser and threw moving shapes across the walls and ceiling.

Something had woken her up. Maya was sure of it. She hadn't just stirred awake the way kids sometimes did. Something specific had pulled her out of sleep, some sound or movement that never occurred this deep in the night.

Then she heard it.

Footsteps on the landing.

Right outside the door.

Mom? Dad? Maya had never once heard them go to the bathroom or sneak in to check on them in the middle of the night. Maybe they did it all the time and Maya was just too lost in the blissful ignorance of sleep to notice.

She held her breath and listened, and then the creak of the bedroom door made her tiny heart pound.

A strange smell filled the room. She knew the smell from her walks along the Nashua River with her dad—the scent of earth, rain. The outdoors. Whoever this person was, they'd just come from outside.

Maya couldn't think or move or cry out. She lay paralyzed beneath her comforter while the stranger crept closer to their bunk, and it was at this point that the memory—in whatever form it surfaced—broke into a million pieces, like an explosion of glass she could never reassemble. She remembered a pale hand, a black jacket, a man's voice, none of which she could say for certain were actually present or whether they were figments of a confused child's imagination.

Knock knock knock.

The rabbits on the wallpaper vanished, and Maya found herself staring at a nightlamp in front of a yellow wall. She was no longer in yesteryear, Massachusetts and was actually in today, Florida, in a crap motel that her clogged mind concluded was in desperate need of re-painting. She grabbed her phone and checked the time. 7:03 a.m.

Knock knock knock. Louder this time.

Maya pulled herself back to reality and jumped out of bed. Who the hell was knocking at this time? She still had an hour before she had to get going.

At the door, she peered through the spy hole.

Devon.

Maya cracked the door open and found her partner leaning against the frame. "Devon? You're early."

"One hour ahead of schedule. Right on schedule."

"Should I meet you downstairs in... a few minutes?"

Devon swiveled her head. "You going to talk to me through the crack? What are you hiding in there?"

"No." Maya swung the door open a little wider. Thankfully she'd slept in a T-shirt, so she wasn't embarrassingly unclothed. "Is everything all right?"

"I got a text from the sheriff an hour ago. The tech guy at

the precinct has the CCTV footage from Teresa's store. He's waiting for us before he plays it."

Sweat beaded on Maya's forehead. She was still in recovery mode from the dream. It always took a few minutes for the body to catch up with the emotional hit. "Why's he waiting?"

"Protocol. FBI needs to witness the initial viewing to ensure that the evidence stays admissible in court. If he watches it alone first, defense attorneys could argue tampering or editing or any of that tech crap. We need to go see Teresa's niece, too."

"Right. I'll be ready in five."

"Please do. Meet you downstairs."

Devon left, and Maya rushed to get everything done in record time. Shower, teeth, deodorant, clothes. The dream had left her drained, as it always did, and she knew that the burden of shame would be lodged in her chest for the rest of the day. She was only a minute overdue when she grabbed her bag and headed out into the corridor.

A new feeling pushed through the old familiar sensation of post-dream guilt. Excitement. If fortune was in their favor, she might just get a real look at Teresa Morgan's killer, caught on camera doing whatever he'd done to get inside that hardware store.

THIRTEEN

AFTER WORKING IN THE FBI OFFICES FOR SEVEN YEARS, Maya's makeshift office at the Fernandina Beach PD felt tiny in comparison, but there was something refreshing about working out of a room that didn't pretend to be anything more than a big cube. Riggs had kept his word about clearing them a space, and that space had nothing but the basics: two desks that faced opposing walls, a giant whiteboard, and a few outlets. It was as salt of the earth as offices came, and Maya felt at home the moment she walked in.

"Hope you weren't expecting windows," Devon said as she plugged in her laptop. "Police stations are pretty over-crowded these days, so outsiders get stuffed in the closet."

"I can live without windows."

"Same, but I can't live without coffee. Are you a coffee person?"

"Cut me and I bleed coffee," Maya said. She hooked up her laptop and laid her notes down on the desk. Setup didn't take anywhere near as long as she expected. "I'll take anything, though. Tea, coffee, that green stuff they have in Japan."

"Well, I need to call Vernon and update him on what we found last night. There must be a kitchen in here somewhere."

Maya fixed Devon with a stare. Was that what this was? Was she really asking her to do a coffee run? "You want me to get it?"

Devon grabbed her cell and began scrolling. "Is that a problem?"

She liked to think that Vernon had sent her here to be a little more than the coffee bitch, but could she protest? Was that a sense of entitlement she hadn't earned yet? They always said you had to start at the bottom, but last night she'd stared a dead woman in what was left of her face, and surely that gave her a pass from junior duties.

No. She could argue and get labeled as a prima donna, or she could swallow her pride and fetch coffee.

"All right. How do you take it?"

"No sugar. Black as a raven's asshole."

"Back in five."

Maya's geographical instincts took her down the corridor to the right. She passed a few empty rooms with glass partitions and then stumbled across an empty kitchen that was barely wide enough to fit two human beings. The cupboards and sink were as old as hell, but a gleaming coffee maker was sitting on the counter with a note attached to it:

OUT OF ODER. ALFIE's WORKING ON IT.

Whoever Alfie was, he'd spelled *order* wrong, but more concerning was a lack of a caffeine provider. Maya rifled through the cupboard, found some instant coffee that had gone hard, and decided it would have to do. She found two mugs and a spoon in the drawer. Next came the question of hot water.

"Having trouble?" a voice asked.

Maya nearly jumped out of her skin. She hadn't heard anyone approaching. She spun around to find a tall, casually-dressed man holding a screwdriver. He had black glasses, messy hair, cheekbones that could cut glass, and the posture of a man whose spine had been reshaped by a desk chair. His eyes were red raw.

"Something like that. I'm just looking for... coffee."

"Don't worry." The man tapped his screwdriver on his hand then began tinkering with the coffee machine. "I've got a tool. It's not big, but it gets the job done."

Maya backed up to the sink and felt herself blush. She wasn't sure why. "That's what they all say."

The guy laughed. "You must be one of those pesky federal people we were warned about."

His accent was unremarkable. There was no Southern drawl there, nor was there a hint of that Miami English she'd heard so much about. "That's us. Are you Alfie, by any chance?"

He stopped tinkering and shook Maya's hand. Up close, she could smell a hint of vanilla on him, and he had soft palms that, if not for the screwdriver in his hand, would suggest that he had never held a DIY implement in his life.

"Alfred Kustka, but no one calls me Alfred. Or Kustka. So I'm stuck with Alfie."

"Kustka? Is that Swedish?"

"Close. My dad was from Finland, and my mom was from... Jacksonville."

"Exotic. I'm Maya."

"Oh yeah. You're in charge of this murder investigation, right?"

"My partner's the one in charge. She's in our closet-turned-office. I'm just the newbie around here."

Alfie pocketed his screwdriver, then gave the coffee machine a hard whack. It suddenly gurgled to life. "Would you look at that? Sometimes all it takes is a good slap. You don't look like a newbie, by the way. I don't mean that you look old; I mean you look the age you are. I don't know what that age is, but you look like you've seen some stuff. I'd never expect you to be new to this. Am I rambling?"

"A little."

"Sorry." Alfie flushed red, then began tapping his foot. "Here, just put your cup underneath the nozzle, then grab a pod out of the drawer and push the button. Actually, you probably know how to use a coffee machine. Ignore me."

Maya wanted to chuckle, but it felt inappropriate. She put her mug under the nozzle and then took a moment to inspect what she called the trinity—the three parts of the body that always told the story a person wasn't rehearsing in their head. First were the hands because hands gestured, pleaded, created barriers, and hid in pockets. Alfie's hands were baby-soft and pale as cottage cheese, but the cuticles were damaged, and the fingertips had hardened. Office worker, gamer, didn't like the sun.

Next was the mouth. The first thing they taught you in acting school was how to control the points of your mouth because a tiny up or downturn could completely alter an expression, and few people could control this consciously. Alfie's mouth kept twitching up and down, like he wanted to smile but had forgotten exactly how that particular expression went. The skin on his lips was dry, too, like he'd been biting them recently.

Most people thought the eyes were the final giveaway, but that was an outdated belief. People had learned to control their eyes, thanks to tired myths like "liars can't maintain eye contact." When confronted with a lie, today half the population stared you down like they were trying to laser through your skull. The real tell was something most people didn't even know existed—the hollow at the base of the throat or the delicate space between the clavicles. This was the panic button. The place liars touched when they felt vulnerable, because it was where the body's most primitive alarm system lived.

Maya concluded that Alfie Kustka was what her roommate Becky would have called a standard nerd. Slightly awkward and mostly harmless.

And then something else hit her.

The bitten lips, red-raw eyes, the concave posture, the screwdriver.

"You're the tech guy," she said.

"Ha. What gave it away?"

"You must have been working through the night to get us that security footage, and I know what a man who's been up all night looks like."

Alfie blushed this time, then said, "Lucky them."

"If only. We pull all-nighters at HQ all the time, and I'm the only woman on our team." Maya finished preparing Devon's coffee and ensured it was as black as black could be.

Shockingly, her pride didn't seem to have taken a hit being the coffee bitch, and maybe Alfie had played a part in that.

"Tell me about it. Law enforcement's a sausage fest. I'd love to do something else but... I'm stuck here. Anyway, if you want to see that footage, my office is next door. The crypt is open."

FOURTEEN

MAYA, DEVON, AND SHERIFF RIGGS CRAMMED themselves into Alfie's office, and Maya could see why Alfie called this place the crypt. It was another windowless room, larger than her own but made smaller by the tower of hard drives in one corner and a giant fan in the other. Alfie had spiced up the room with a shelf of action figures, an empty goldfish bowl, and a poster for the movie *Blade Runner*. It was the weirdest office she'd ever seen.

"Quick rundown," Alfie said. "Teresa Morgan's shop wasn't running a closed-circuit system. She was using a budget cloud system called Securi-Live. They terminated the feed about two a.m."

"Less of the geek speak, Alf," Riggs said.

"The security footage was stored off-site, probably because it was cheaper than the electricity costs of cameras all day," Maya said. She didn't think Riggs' geek comment was necessary.

Alfie snapped his fingers. "What she said. Securi-Live

sent me footage going back a week because that's all they have stored. Anything before that is deleted. Where do you want me to play from?"

"From Teresa closing up her store yesterday. Not sure what time that would be."

"Six p.m., according to the sign in the shop's window," said Maya.

"Six p.m. it is." Alfie loaded up the grainy, grayscale footage that was 168 hours long, according to the timecode in the bottom right corner. The video showed a static shot of Morgan's Hardware's shop floor. Every aisle was visible, along with the checkout counter and the front door. The corner of the feed showed the date and time.

Alfie zipped through the footage in one-hour intervals. It became a time-lapse of a shop in motion. Customers darted around the aisles while Teresa herself did cashier duties, and then there were long stretches through the night hours where nothing moved except the timestamp. The footage grew lighter as dawn broke each day, then darker as evening fell. Maya noticed that the store didn't exactly pull crowds. Most hours showed Teresa alone, restocking shelves or reading something behind the counter. When customers did appear, it was usually one or two at a time.

"She ran that place solo," Maya observed.

"Help wasn't Teresa's style," said Riggs. "And even in places like this, the family businesses aren't exactly thriving. The only thing that's still going around here are the bars. That and the undertakers."

"Death and booze are here to stay," Devon said. "Alfie, is this the highest quality you can get? I can barely make out the faces."

"Afraid so, miss."

"My cell has better quality than this."

"These feeds run all day, every day, so we're talking terabytes of data. It costs a lot to store it all, so people go for the cheapest option."

"We got audio?"

Alfie maxed out the volume and let a scene play out. Voices were audible, barely. "Sort of."

"It'll do."

The days blurred together until Alfie hit the 160-hour mark. The footage slowed to normal speed as he hit four p.m. yesterday afternoon. He jumped through in one-minute intervals. One customer appeared at half past four and then left without buying anything. The store then remained empty until the clock showed six p.m. with only Teresa left.

"There she is," Riggs said.

Teresa appeared on screen, moving through what looked like her closing routine. The grainy footage made details impossible, but Maya could see her walking between the aisles, closing up the blinds and then disappearing behind the counter area. She checked her cell phone, then dropped it and looked toward the front window.

Her body language changed. She stepped back from the window, then moved closer again.

"What's she doing?"

"Someone's outside. She's talking to them through the glass."

Teresa moved away from the window. She seemed agitated, checking something—maybe the lock on the front door.

"There." Devon pointed. "She just grabbed something off the counter. Looked heavy."

"Weapon?" Maya suggested.

Teresa stood by the window for another moment, then the footage showed her walking toward the back of the store and disappearing from view.

Maya was mentally fitting the pieces together. A stranger outside the shop. Teresa with a weapon in her hand. Alfie let the footage run, and it stayed on an empty, static image of the shop.

Then something crashed.

Mumbled voices came next. The camera was fifteen, twenty feet away from the counter and subsequently the store room, but Maya was definitely picking up something through the hiss of the max-volume speakers.

"You were right, Frost. He came in through the back."

Maya was lost in the scene. She edged closer to the speaker, as much as the hissing pierced her ears.

BANG.

The sound was a shockingly loud percussive blast that made all four of them flinch. The speakers crackled with distortion, and then a silence fell over the room again.

"He shot her," Maya said.

"That's strange," Devon added. "Most killers capable of this level of mutilation stab or strangle. Shooting her means he needed to get the upper hand immediately."

Maya noted it down. This meant he wasn't comfortable with his own skills. He couldn't subdue Teresa physically—but then how did he hoist her up to the rafters? There was a contradiction here, and it was driving Maya crazy.

Devon said, "Skip through it in short bursts, Alfie. Every ten seconds or so."

Alfie complied. He began zipping through the footage but stopped around ten minutes later when a violent whirring sound began. It lasted only a few seconds on each jump, but it was enough.

"Jesus. Sounds like a chainsaw," Riggs said.

Maya's throat closed. She'd seen what that saw had done, and now she was hearing it, feeling it. The vibration of the saw, the spray of gore, the absolute desecration. This was how Teresa Morgan had been cut in half. Alfie continued skipping. Ten minutes, twenty, thirty.

Devon said, "It's useless. The camera can't see the one thing we need. He's not going to come out front covered in blood."

The sounds kept coming. Thuds, whirring. Maya wanted to be anywhere but listening to Teresa Morgan being torn apart, but she stayed glued to the screen.

"Keep going 'til the end," Devon said. "There's a microscopic chance he'll screw up and appear on screen, even if it's just an arm or a hand. It's better than nothing."

Alfie kept skipping. The sounds eventually stopped. Just empty store, empty aisles, dead air. The total time elapsed had been over two hours, which was more than enough time for this unsub to get in, carry out his dirty work, and leave.

"Yeah, he's gone," Riggs said. "Damn it to hell."

"Yup. Cut it there, Alfie. We need to get this whole tape analyzed. Every face that appears going back all week. We need to put names to them all."

"Wait," Maya said. "Riggs, did you find Teresa's cell phone?"

"No. That wasn't on the manifest."

"Well, she laid it on the counter before she went in the back, so if it's not still there, someone took it."

All eyes in the room moved back to the footage. "Fair catch. Alfie, keep skipping through, but slowly," Devon said.

He sped through in one-second bursts. More of the same followed. Just an empty store and no sign of any further mutilation taking place just beyond the reach of the camera. Maya fixed her stare on the hole that led to the back room, willing something to appear. *Come on, come on. Please still be there. Just one mistake. That's all we need.*

Another hour of on-screen time passed in a blur of fast-forwarded minutes. Riggs cleared his throat like he was ready to call it a day, but Maya leaned closer to the screen as though she might telepathically conjure up something useful.

And then she saw it.

Riggs began, "Well, I think—"

"Wait. Look. Right there."

Everyone leaned in.

A shadow appeared in the doorway. It swayed, grew darker, and then from that shadow, a human figure manifested. Arms, legs, torso, a cap covering his face. Blood rushed behind Maya's eyes because everyone in that room was staring at Teresa Morgan's killer.

"Holy sh..." said Riggs.

"We got him," Devon added. "The son of a bitch was crazy enough to show himself."

Maya's gaze didn't falter. She took in everything she could about him: about 5'11, 180 pounds, wide shoulders, flannel jacket, weird cap, black gloves. There were dark stains on his clothes, which Maya guessed was blood in grayscale.

The figure kept his head down, as though he knew there was a camera on him. He slowly picked up Teresa's cell phone off the counter and pocketed it, and then he just stood there.

"What the hell is he doing?" Riggs asked.

As though he'd heard Riggs through the screen, the figure positioned himself below the camera and removed one black glove.

And waved.

Not a regular wave. He wriggled his fingers up and down, like a kid saying goodbye to their mom on the first day of kindergarten.

Like he was saying hello.

FIFTEEN

"Devon, have you seen this?"

Maya had gotten Alfie to put the security footage on her laptop, and she'd spent the past hour scrutinizing it to high heaven.

Devon leaned in. "What am I looking at?"

Intelligence work had taught her that there was always a story in the details if you looked hard enough, and sometimes those details could be as minor as a black smudge. "Look at the killer's hand."

"He's waving, Frost. You know what waving looks like?"

"I don't mean that, I mean—"

"Surprised he didn't flip us off. His patronizing little wave means the same thing."

Maya rolled the footage back and paused it at the exact moment the killer's hand turned, palm open, toward the camera. She jabbed the screen. A dark, misshapen smudge was visible against the pale gray of his hand. "Can you see that? There's a mark on his palm."

Devon squinted like she was trying to read fine print. She looked unconvinced. "He just power-sawed a woman in half. Of course he's going to be covered in marks."

"It doesn't look like blood," Maya insisted. The theory screamed at her and begged for validation. "Blood would be a smear or a splatter. This is... a shape. It's solid. Black. Circular at the bottom with a V in the middle."

"It doesn't look like anything, which is why you shouldn't be focusing on it. Don't try and get blood out of a stone. Let's focus on what we *do* know."

One more sarcastic comment from Devon and Maya might have blurted out her working theory right there and then just to shut her up. Maya was convinced there were connections here, connections that went back in time to a previous era. But as the words assembled in her head, she felt crazy even entertaining them, and the last thing she wanted was for Devon—as annoying as she was being—to think she was fantasizing.

"And what *do* we know?"

"That our killer knows the layout of Teresa's store, which means he's been there before, which means someone's seen him, and he *might* be on the camera footage. Let's go and speak to Teresa's niece while the tech guy works his magic, because she might know something about Teresa's regular customers."

"Got it. I'll be ready in a minute. I just need to check something with Alfie."

Devon somehow grinned without showing her teeth. It was an odd expression and seemed to be the closest thing Devon had to a human emotion that wasn't annoyance. "You like him."

The comment tripped her up. "What?"

"The tech guy. You're into him."

A hot flash of indignation shot through her. Part of it was the mortifying feeling of being so transparent, and the other was pure irritation at Devon reducing their brief interaction in his office to a high school assessment of who-likes-who.

"No I'm not. I don't even know him."

"Please. I saw how you leaned into him back in his office. Plain as day." Devon's not-quite-smile widened a fraction. "Just do your business, and don't let a pretty face get in the way of the work, all right?"

Maya left without another word. First she was the coffee bitch, now she was some lovesick rookie who apparently couldn't keep it in her pants around the first nerd who smiled at her. She stalked down the hallway and idly wondered what a woman actually had to do to be taken seriously around here besides bleed to death in a back room.

"Alfie, could you help me with something?" She found him hunched over his computer with the CCTV footage running on all three of his monitors. His posture explained the curve she'd noticed in his spine. She almost launched into a lecture about proper desk posture, then thought better of it.

"I've got 160 hours' worth of faces to get through. I might be here a while."

"I get it. Can you enhance images?"

"Images? Yes."

"At the end of the video when the perp shows his palm. There's something black on there. Would you be able to isolate that part and make it clearer? I know it's a long shot, but..."

"Long shots score the best goals."

"Bingo. And what are the chances of you enhancing the audio too?"

"It's on my list. You get out there and do the dirty work. Leave me your number, and I'll text you if I get anything."

"I owe you one," Maya said as she gave Alfie her business card, then headed out of the office with his vanilla aftershave still lingering under her nose. Back to Devon, who, despite how she was acting today, maybe hadn't been so wrong about the leaning-in thing.

SIXTEEN

Maya sat on the edge of Katie Morgan's leather chair because sitting back would have been comfortable, and comfort felt at odds with the topic of conversation.

"I just... don't get it. I keep thinking she's going to call, like this is all some sick joke, and she's going to phone me and say that someone robbed her store or something."

When Katie Morgan had opened the door to her apartment, Maya understood why Sheriff Riggs had immediately dismissed her as a suspect. She was a tiny young blond woman swallowed by a thick terrycloth robe. Her taut face, which Maya guessed was usually pretty and bright, was now a puffy, tear-stained mess. Now she was crumpled in the corner of her sofa, and she'd been chain-smoking since the moment they arrived.

"That's what we're here to find out," said Devon, who had opted to stand. "Can you walk us through how you found her?"

"I already told the cops."

"It's the little details."

"There are no little details," Katie breathed. "I was calling Teresa for a few hours, and she didn't answer, so I drove down to check on her. The front door was locked, but Aunt T's car was still around the back. I went through the back door and... yeah."

"Did you see anyone nearby? Maybe a car hanging around? Anything like that?"

"No. The only people I saw were in the bar across the street."

Devon nodded. "Can we ask what Teresa was like? She seems to be something of a hero around here."

Katie lit another cigarette with the embers of her current one. She grabbed a tissue and wiped away a new slate of tears. "Yes, a hero. Everyone loved her, but she didn't love them back."

Maya committed every detail to memory. She wasn't sure whether to interrupt Devon with her own questions or let the woman take the lead, but when Devon went quiet for a moment, Maya took her chance.

"She didn't love them back? How come?"

"Business was crap. Teresa was stressed about money and keeping the place open. She thought about selling it but thought her dad would have laughed at her."

"Would he have?"

Katie shrugged. "Who cares? He's been dead for years."

Maya knew it wasn't that simple. The primal need to win the admiration of a parent—dead or alive—was a poison that the modern world could do without. A person could destroy themselves all for the approval of a corpse that had long rotted in its grave. She should know.

"What did Teresa do in her spare time?" she asked.

"Not much. Her husband died a few years ago, and ever since then she's just kept things simple. If she had any crazy hobbies, I didn't know about them."

"Any enemies?" Devon asked.

Katie looked at Devon like she'd just asked her to explain quantum physics. "Enemies? No."

"Ex-employees? Rival business owners? Tricky customers?"

"None. Aunt T has run that shop alone since my uncle died. The only business rival is the online stores. She hasn't mentioned any tricky customers."

Maya noted the use of present tense, as if Teresa was still alive. The subconscious took longer to process death than the rational mind, and in Maya's admittedly limited experience in this area, guilty people didn't mix their tenses.

"No one at all?"

"No. Teresa knew everyone."

"Which is exactly why somebody with malicious intent wouldn't stand out," said Devon. "But even so, Teresa might have mentioned something in passing because—"

"I don't know!" snapped Katie. She dumped her cigarette in the ashtray and then buried her head in her hands. "You don't think, you know? Maybe she did mention someone, but you don't always take it in."

Devon audibly sighed, and Maya had to wonder how the hell this kind of sledgehammer approach had aided her in the past. Maya was no interrogation expert by any means, but human instinct told her that you didn't get answers by bulldozing someone who was already in pieces.

So she took the reins. Maya got up and sat next to Katie on her couch. She put a hand on the poor woman's wrist.

"We're not trying to push you. There's every chance that some random stranger did this to your aunt, but we believe her attacker knew the layout of her store intimately. Therefore, we have to work with the theory that your aunt knew this person on some level. Sometimes it's the tiny little details that make all the difference. Could have been a name Teresa only mentioned once, could have been weeks ago, months ago."

Katie withdrew her head from her hands. She looked at Maya with a fresh batch of tears in her eyes, and Maya could see cogs were turning behind them.

An idea formed.

"Where did you talk to Teresa the most? Here? At her place?"

"At her shop."

"Then do me a favor. Close your eyes and picture yourself there. The smell. Sawdust, paint thinner. Hear that sound of the bell over the door. Look at Teresa behind the counter, doing whatever she did there. Imagine her face when you walk through the door. Hear her voice. You got all that in your head?"

Katie's eyes were closed shut. She nodded. "Yeah, but it's—"

"Don't worry if it's not perfect. Don't try to find a specific memory. Just be in the room with her. What's she doing? What's she talking about? Complaining about?"

Katie was silent for a long moment, then the tells came. Her brow furrowed and her nose twitched. She was there, in the hardware store of her memory.

"Everything. No sales."

"That's good." Maya let go of Katie's wrist, then she caught Devon on the other side of the room, regarding the scene like it was some kind of abstract painting. "Picture everything you can. Is it dark outside? Is it daytime? Can you hear anything? Smell anything?"

"It's bright but cold. I can hear the till beeping. And it smells like..."

Katie froze, but Maya continued to push. Smell was the sense closest linked to memory. It was the reason the scent of wet pavement could throw you right back to your childhood driveway, or a stranger's perfume could remind you of your first-grade teacher who you hadn't thought of in decades.

"What's it smell like?"

"Anti-freeze."

For a second, Maya thought she hadn't heard Katie right. "Say that again."

Katie's eyes snapped open. She looked confused, like she'd surprised herself. "Anti-freeze. A few weeks ago, Aunt T mentioned someone. A guy who came in and only ever bought anti-freeze. Same thing every time. She said it was weird because who needs that much anti-freeze? And he never talked, just pointed at what he wanted and paid cash."

Maya turned to Devon, who regarded Katie with a solemn glare. Maya's pulse beat to the point that her hands began to shake because this was a jigsaw piece she'd never expected to appear, let alone slot into the puzzle seamlessly.

"You're sure?" she asked.

"Yeah. She said he smelled like the stuff constantly."

"Got a description of this guy?" asked Devon.

Katie blinked away a few tears. "No, sorry. She just said

he acted kind of odd. Thought maybe he had a disability or something."

Maya's phone buzzed in her pocket. She stole a quick glance and found a message from an unknown number.

Get back to precinct ASAP. Found something super weird on the footage - Alfie.

"Katie, you've been a great help," she said as she put a hand on her shoulder. "You did amazing. Thank you."

The grieving young girl scrubbed a hand over her face, which only amplified the inflammation around her eyes and nose. "Catch him?"

"Come again?"

"Promise you'll catch him?"

Maya looked over at Devon, whose eyes had narrowed even more than usual. Devon said, "We can't make promises, but—"

"We'll catch him," Maya said. "Trust us."

"Thank you." Katie leaned in for a hug, and Maya returned the gesture. On the other side of the room, Devon was staring at her with the kind of look you'd give someone for stepping in dog crap and tracking it through the house, and Maya knew why. She'd just broken the cardinal rule of victim relations: never make a promise you can't keep.

But Maya had no intention of letting this girl down.

SEVENTEEN

"You shouldn't have done that," Devon said without taking her eyes off the road. Maya was making notes in the passenger seat, and the theory she was cooking up had begun to take on a new and terrible shape.

"I'm sorry."

"No you're not. We can't touch civilians, even if it's to offer comfort. And we definitely can't promise we'll catch whoever killed their family members because that's not a promise we can make good on, understand?"

"Isn't it better to give them a smidgeon of hope?"

"No, because false hope is worse than no hope at all. It stops people from grieving properly. You should know better, with all the stuff you see in Intelligence."

Maya had to admit Devon had a point, even if she hated it. She'd seen enough families clinging to impossible hope to know what it did to people. The way they refused to accept death certificates. The way they mortgaged their houses chasing false leads.

"You're right," Maya said quietly. "I just wanted to give her something."

"Give her the truth instead. It's kinder in the long run. What are you writing on that notepad of yours?"

"Notes."

Devon merged into the traffic that led back to the precinct. "Notes about what? If you've got any theories about this anti-freeze weirdness, now's the time to speak up."

She did indeed have a working theory, but even though they were dealing with a butchered woman who'd been killed by an eccentric who apparently stockpiled anti-freeze, the words seemed to clog up as they reached the tip of her tongue. "Not quite. It's all a bit... crazy. What do you think?"

"I don't know what to think because this anti-freeze guy might just have been a run-of-the-mill screwball and not a killer, but we still need to track him down."

"Well, Alfie said he's got something weird, so maybe that'll give us a launching pad. We can check till receipts from the store too."

"Yeah. I've got software running at the precinct to track down Teresa's cell as well, but the cell is turned off."

"Of course."

The outside world thought the Bureau could just find any phone, anywhere, like some all-seeing eye in the sky. The reality was depressingly low-tech. A turned-off phone basically ceased to exist until someone powered it back on. The best they could do was run historical data and check which towers it had connected to in the hours before the murder. But if this guy was smart enough to turn it off, he'd probably dumped it in a river by now.

"Let's see what Alfie's found, and let's hope it's something useful."

"Let's hope."

Devon focused on the road for a minute, then turned to Maya and lowered her voice. "By the way, that hypnosis thing you did? That was quite good."

"I DID WHAT YOU ASKED, Maya, and I found two really odd things we didn't catch the first time around."

Maya thought Alfie looked as if he hadn't slept in days, and given that he'd been in this precinct since at least last night, it may not have been too far from the truth. "Hit us."

Alfie pulled up some printouts from beside his keyboard. He handed one to Maya and one to Devon. "I enhanced that section of the footage, and look what I found."

Every detail of the photograph had been sharpened for clarity. The killer's face was still a blur beneath his cap, but his raised hand was now much more visible. Maya could see the individual lines on his palm, the creases around his knuckles. And there, dead center in the middle of his palm, was a perfect black circle. It wasn't a smudge or a bloodstain. It was a solid, black mark, sitting unnaturally in the center of his hand.

Maya squinted at the image. "Is that a... tattoo?"

"I don't see what else it could be. He's not holding anything solid because I'd be able to tell from the depth. I don't think it's blood, because while I'm no expert, I don't think blood could be shaped so perfectly."

Devon said, "I'll be damned. This is a good find, Alfie."

Maya looked at her so-called partner and blinked. She'd been the one to notice this, to get Alfie to enhance it, and he was the one who got the praise? She breathed, then decided to let it go. "Great work. What's the second thing?"

Alfie spun back to his computer and opened up a folder packed with files that ended in the extension .wav, so Maya guessed they were all audio clips. "Well, this is where it gets really weird. I did what I could to enhance the brief conversation between the victim and killer in the back room, and..."

"And what?"

He hovered his mouse over one of the files. "Are you sure this victim's name is Teresa?"

Maya and Devon exchanged a look. "That's the one thing we *are* sure of," Devon said.

"Because... well, take a listen to this."

Alfie clicked the file, and static whistled through the speakers. A male voice broke the hiss.

"It's time, Bernice."

A quieter female voice came next. *"You've got the wrong person."*

"No. I've got exactly who I need."

The world stopped. Every single hair on Maya's arms and neck snapped to attention like she'd been electrocuted. "Play that again."

Alfie did. He put it on a loop, and Maya could confirm without any doubt that the killer referred to Teresa as Bernice.

The theory that had been scratching at the corners of her mind since yesterday suddenly became a very real possibility, and if Maya was a betting girl, she'd have put her life savings on this being right. There were too many coinci-

DAVID ARCHER & MILA CROSS

dences for it not to be. It was the truth, and it was staring back at her beneath a cap on some grainy CCTV footage.

"Alfie, thank you." She turned to her partner. "Devon, could I see you outside?"

Devon nodded and led the way out into the corridor. Maya shut the door to Alfie's office behind her.

"What is it?"

This was it. This was the connection that had been eating at her since she'd first walked into that hardware store and seen Teresa Morgan hanging like a slaughtered deer.

"Devon, I think we've got this all wrong. I don't think our killer is some local psycho with a vendetta against Teresa Morgan."

"No? Enlighten me. Who is it?"

This time, Maya didn't feel so stupid. "I think our killer is Ed Gein."

EIGHTEEN

HE LOOKED DOWN INTO THE BLACK, UNBLINKING CIRCLE of water in the well, the one that his dad had told him went all the way down to hell. Most days, he just saw his own reflection in there, but sometimes his mother's pale face would float up from the bottom and remind him from beyond the grave how much he'd failed at the game of life.

He'd let this farm go to ruin. He'd never met a woman, never procreated. His bloodline would end with him, and short of a miracle, it was too late to do anything about that. His mother's voice was emerging from that well more and more recently, and he could even hear it from the other side of the field. Even at night, when he bolted himself in at the farmhouse and shunned the rest of the world, his old lady's phantom criticism still bled through the walls.

But since last night, he hadn't heard his mom's shrill cries or seen her ghostly presence once.

He had not banished her. No, he knew she was still there, rattling her chains somewhere in the dark cellar of his mind. It was just that the ghosts that had haunted this farm and his head for thirty years had finally met something they were afraid of. Last night, he'd brought home a real demon, and there wasn't enough room in this place for the three of them.

There was still work to do before tonight's big event, so he busied himself. The shovel scraped concrete under the muck. He worked in a mindless rhythm the way he'd learned to, scooping the slurry of shit and piss-soaked hay and flinging it into the wheelbarrow. The stink was honest. It was the smell of the world he knew.

As he worked, he got to thinking about heroes.

Idols. Inspirations.

His heroes were supposed to be his father. A man who taught him nothing except how to cough yourself to death. His mother hadn't been much different, and he'd had no teachers to speak of. After he'd been left alone as a teenager, his Uncle Wade had moved into the farm because he was too young to inherit this place himself. The house had filled with a new stink then, mostly sweat. Wade was a big man with a wet cough and hands that were always looking for something to grab, something to squeeze.

The beatings from Wade were different. They weren't the hot anger of his mother's paddle but perverse declarations of love that hurt him more than any slap ever could.

For three years, he just took it, because he had no one else to confide in. Just added it to the pile. A boy just trying to get from one sunrise to the next without leaving too much blood on his clothes.

Then he found the book.

It was in the county library, tucked away in the back. Just

a cheap second-hand paperback with bent pages and a tombstone on the cover. A book about ghouls. Real ones. He'd read about the old fellow from Plainfield, Wisconsin. A quiet man on a dead farm, just like him. A man who'd danced with the dead by night, and a man with a troublesome relative to boot: a brother who was always in the way.

And the book explained, in simple, clear prose, how the old ghoul had solved that problem.

Fire. It looked like an accident. A brush fire that got out of hand. Nobody ever suspected a thing.

A good idea was a good idea forever.

Funny how that happened. One day, Wade was there. The next, he was a pile of ashes in the barn. It had started in the chicken coop right next door, just like the sheriff figured. A faulty heat lamp, maybe. Bad wiring. Nothing more than a freak accident. The fire had taken all the chickens with it, and that night he'd repeated the phrase: *If you want to make an omelet, you have to break a few eggs.* Even now, that line was the funniest thing he'd ever said.

That was the day he finally understood. Heroes weren't real. His father, his teachers, the men in the town who tipped their hats but never saw the bruises—they weren't here for him. The only people who had ever offered him a workable solution to a problem was one of the world's villains.

He came back to the well again and peered inside one more time. It wasn't his own face staring back at him, nor was it his mother's. Now he was looking at a creature of the night, one that had died years ago but would return to life tonight.

It was the face that made people check their locks.

The final visitor that no one ever saw coming.

NINETEEN

"Frost, have you gone crazy?"

"No, listen to me. It all makes sense."

Maya was scrambling around her office, assembling the evidence in a linear pattern so she could present it to Devon without coming across like a nutball who saw the face of Jesus in clouds. Or the face of long-dead serial killers in hardware stores in backwater Florida.

"No it doesn't. Ed Gein's been dead for forty years."

Ed Gein was a notorious serial killer from Wisconsin who operated in the 1950s. He began as a grave robber, unearthing corpses from a local cemetery by night. He'd haul the bodies back to his farmhouse and skin them, dissect them, and fashion them into all manner of bizarre curiosities. Lampshades made from skin, bowls made from human skulls. Gein intended to create a skin suit so he could role-play as his deceased mother who, in life, had been an overbearing religious fanatic.

But eventually, grave robbing wasn't enough for the lonely farm boy, and so he turned to real women.

"I don't mean the real Gein." Maya found a crime scene of Teresa Morgan's bisected corpse and slapped it onto the whiteboard with a magnet. "Gein started by robbing graves, right?"

"I'm familiar with Ed Gein, Frost."

"So you'll know that he murdered two real women. One of them was named Mary, and the other was Bernice."

Devon crossed her arms. "Yeah, Bernice Worden. What about it?"

"Because he didn't *just* murder Bernice Worden. He took her back to his house and did exactly this to her. He cut her in half and strung her up like an animal carcass. Upside down, gutted, blood leaking out. Not only that, but Bernice Worden ran a store. A hardware store. Sound familiar?"

Devon plucked the photo off the whiteboard and studied it. Maya could see her mental gears turning.

"There's more," she continued. "What did Ed Gein buy from Bernice Worden's hardware store the morning he killed her? What was the last item on her sales ledger?"

"I don't know."

"Anti-freeze."

"Was it?"

"Yes. It's well documented." Maya let that sink in for a second, then continued as the connections came hard and fast. "And the skinned face. Gein skinned the faces of some of the women he dug up so he could make a skin mask."

"Did Gein skin Bernice Worden's face?"

"No, he didn't."

"So there's at least one inconsistency."

"Yes but..." Maya stuck a printout of the CCTV footage on the whiteboard. "Look at our guy. He's even dressed like Gein. Flannel shirt, work cap, heavy boots. Right down to the smallest detail."

Devon threw her photograph down on the desk and rubbed her temples. "So what? You think our guy is pretending to be Ed Gein?"

"No. Well, yes. I think he's roleplaying as Ed Gein, and he's just taken this roleplay to the absolute extreme. He's dressed like him, targeted a woman that looked like an original Gein victim, and butchered her the same way too."

"Frost, I've seen a hundred copycats in my years, but I've never seen someone pretending to *be* another killer. There isn't even a name for what you're talking about."

"No, but the evidence doesn't lie. Don't tell me you don't see the similarities."

"I do, but..."

Maya watched her partner wrestle with the theory, and if Maya didn't know any better, she'd think that Devon was finding any excuse to disagree with her. "But?"

"What about this little mark on his hand? If he purposely showed that to the camera, then it must fit the theory somehow, shouldn't it?"

Maya's confidence suddenly wavered. She'd been hoping Devon wouldn't circle back to that detail because the truth was that she didn't know how that fit in. "I'm still working on it, but you have to agree there's something to this."

"Maybe." Devon walked over to the whiteboard and stared at the CCTV photo hanging there. "Look, I'm not saying you're completely off base here, and if you'd have asked me thirty years ago, I'd have jumped at this connection. But a lifetime in this job teaches you that coincidences happen, and they're not as rare as you think. The brain makes connections it wants to see, and following what you *want* to see instead of what you *do* see is a straight road to frustration. Not to mention that we're in farm country. Half the men in this county dress like that every day of the week. Flannel shirts and caps aren't exactly rare in rural Florida."

"But combined with everything else—"

Devon spun around. "And is it possible our killer is just so mentally scrambled that he got the victim's name wrong? Maybe he's having some kind of psychotic break, and Teresa reminded him of someone else entirely."

Maya felt her theory deflating slightly. "It's possible, but the details are too specific. Who buys anti-freeze in September?"

"People getting ready for October. I'm not saying this anti-freeze guy isn't our man, but your theory sounds like a conspiracy you'd hear on one of those trashy documentaries. You don't think aliens built the pyramids as well, do you?"

"No."

"Good. Even if this was true, what are you suggesting we do? Put out an APB for the ghost of Ed Gein?"

"Obviously not, but if we can confirm this weird Gein obsession, we might be able to predict his next move. What if he targets someone who reminds him of Gein's other victim? What if we check local cemeteries for disturbances?"

The office door creaked open, and Sheriff Riggs' face appeared in the gap. "Agents, sorry to interrupt you. The pathologist is ready to see you. She's with the body at the Baptist ME's office. It's only a ten-minute drive away."

Devon straightened up and grabbed her jacket from the back of her chair. "Copy that. We'll be right there."

Riggs disappeared back down the hallway. Devon was already at the door, but Maya was still standing next to the whiteboard. Devon's verbal jab had landed right between the eyes, and it had hurt more than she'd expected. Humiliation crept up her neck, not just because Devon was poking holes in her theory but because she'd done it with the condescension of a parent explaining to a child that monsters weren't real.

Devon was the veteran. Maya was the newbie who'd been handed the job less than forty-eight hours ago, the coffee bitch with a single good call to her name. To argue further would be to cement her status as the hysterical rookie, so she opted to keep her mouth shut.

And Maya wasn't above admitting that maybe she was trying so hard to prove herself worthy of this partnership that she'd invented an elaborate theory out of thin air. Maya grabbed her things and met Devon again out in the corridor.

"Look, Frost. Your theory isn't completely insane. But in this job, you learn to follow the evidence where it leads, not where you want it to go. Now come on. Let's go and visit a morgue."

TWENTY

THE NASSAU COUNTY MEDICAL EXAMINER'S OFFICE was an annex attached to the local hospital. Maya had only been in a morgue once before, years ago, for a duty that had nothing to do with police work and everything to do with saying a final goodbye. She'd hated the places ever since and had never been able to reconcile the smell of bleach with anything but the sight of a face that would never smile again.

"You not a fan of morgues, Frost?"

Maya looked over at her partner, who was sitting two chairs apart from her in the waiting room. A bored receptionist sat behind a Plexiglas counter on the other side of the room, and a cabinet of urns sat in the corner. Maya thought that some plants would liven this place up, but she figured that putting something living in here would be a cruel irony.

"No. What gave it away?"

"You're shaking like a dog shitting razor blades."

"I'm just cold. Don't you think it's cold?"

"It's freezing, but that's the point. You ever smelled a warm corpse?"

The comment caught her off guard, but Maya couldn't keep her response at bay. "Once."

"You want to tell me about that?"

"Maybe another time."

Devon spun her feet around. "Frost, you're keeping something locked up in that head of yours. I can see it a mile off. I knew you had some grand theory about this case, but I didn't push. But now I think it's time I *did* push because if we're going to be partners, we need to know each other inside out."

Maya stared at Devon. A hot flush burned her cheeks because the hypocrisy of Devon's comments almost choked her. Devon had struck her as the type who kept her own counsel and expected others to do the same. Now she was demanding Maya's life story in a morgue waiting room like it was perfectly normal.

"Does this work both ways?"

"Yes."

"Then why don't you tell me about *you?* I don't mean all the achievements you've made at the Bureau or anything like that. Give me something real. Maybe something about why you're giving me such a hard time. Quid pro quo."

Devon almost smiled. "First thing to know is that I hate Latin."

"Omnino non miror."

"And that means?"

"Who knows?" Maya said.

Devon looked microseconds away from delivering a smart-ass comment, but the receptionist interrupted.

"Excuse me, Agents. Dr. Liang is ready for you in room B2. Up the corridor, second door on the right."

"Saved by the bell," Devon said, "but this isn't over."

Maya led the way this time. Two days ago, she had thought Devon was a legendary FBI profiler with a sharp brain and sharper wit. Now the rumors about her being thrice-divorced came back to her, and Maya finally got it. She knocked on the door to autopsy room 2B, and a faint voice came back.

"It's open."

Maya entered first, and the olfactory assault sapped the breath from her. The autopsy suite was a chemical overload and distantly reminded Maya of swimming pools. There were stainless steel lockers against every wall and one concrete slab at the center of the room with a bumpy figure draped in a white sheet. A masked, dark-haired woman stood behind a desktop computer at the other end.

"Agents Lynch and Frost? There are masks and gloves next to you," the woman shouted. Maya complied, but Devon opted for gloves only.

"Thank you for seeing us, Doctor," said Devon.

The mortician sauntered over and dropped her mask. She was a young Chinese woman with glossy skin that might as well have been airbrushed by angels. Maya, who rarely thought twice about her own appearance, felt an absurd pang of envy. She had a sudden, insane thought that the formaldehyde they used down here must be the world's best-kept anti-aging secret.

"No problem. I'm Dr. Liang, and I just finished the preliminary on Mrs. Morgan an hour ago. Where would you like to start?"

"I'd like to go linearly through the process," Devon said. Maya didn't quite know what that meant, but she nodded along.

"Very well. Brace yourselves; this isn't pretty."

"It's fine. We saw the body last night, Doc."

Dr. Liang slowly peeled away the white sheet and unveiled the desecrated remains of Teresa Morgan inch by inch. Maya had seen it once already, but the green tint of this autopsy room somehow made the sight even more appalling. She winced as the mutilations revealed themselves one more time, and now what remained of Teresa Morgan had shrunk in on itself. Maya struggled to look at her raw skull, but she forced herself to out of respect. Teresa deserved at least one person who wouldn't look away.

"There's good news, and that's that all of these mutilations took place postmortem. Mrs. Morgan likely didn't suffer because the bullet to her heart killed her instantly."

"Bullet?" Maya asked. "We didn't know about any bullet."

"You wouldn't." Dr. Liang pulled out a metal pointer and aimed it at Teresa's split ribcage. "There's a wound here consistent with a bullet hole, and the heart is punctured too. It's around two-point-five in diameter, which by my math would be from a rifle or a shotgun."

Rifle, thought Maya. Exactly what Ed Gein used to kill Bernice Worden.

Devon said, "So our unsub shot Teresa to subdue her. What about these cuts? Were they surgical or amateur? What's this guy's skill level?"

"Difficult to say. He's certainly no surgeon, because a surgeon wouldn't have made the errors he did."

"No?"

"Certainly not." Dr Liang moved the pointer to where Teresa's face used to be. "He used a scalpel to remove the face, and I hate to be so graphic, but doing so isn't exactly hard."

Maya breathed heavily through her nose. Bile had begun to rise in her throat. "It's not hard?"

"No. The skin around the face is thin and malleable. He wouldn't have needed to dig deep for this part, nor would he have needed to hack, but even so, he didn't maintain a steady hand. The score lines are noticeably jagged, which means his hands were trembling throughout."

"What about the bisection?"

"Again, a surgeon wouldn't use a power saw to sever a corpse. Your perp *might* be familiar with animal butchery, but that's the extent of it. This was definitely his first time severing human bone."

Devon said, "Got it. Did you find anything else?"

"Sheriff Riggs said you already know the time of death, which is good, because any pathologist who claims to give you an accurate time of death is lying. There were no defensive wounds, no ligature marks, and as strange as this might sound, no sign of internal penetration. At least as best as I can tell."

Maya ran through her profile of the unsub and quickly concluded that the autopsy hadn't revealed much more about him. All they could tell was that he wasn't a surgeon but might be a butcher. She tried not to sigh.

"As far as the mutilations go, that's all I can really tell you." Dr. Liang put her pointer away. "However, I did find something that didn't quite make sense, at least not to my brain. Maybe you two could shed some light on it for me."

Maya's pulse quickened. "What did you find?"

Dr. Liang hurried over to a steel table and picked up a small plastic bag. She held it up to show the agents.

Maya squinted. Inside was what looked like a thin piece of charcoal, but Maya guessed it was anything but.

"Is that skin?" asked Devon.

"Yes it is, but it's not Miss Morgan's skin."

"How can you tell?"

"Different people have different epidermal thickness, melanin distribution patterns, and the way collagen fibers are arranged. Under a microscope, skin is as individual as a fingerprint." Dr. Liang held the bag closer to the light. "This sample has a completely different cellular density than Mrs. Morgan's tissue. Plus, the DNA markers don't match. See the dermal ridge patterns? They're intact enough to show this came from someone at least ten years younger than our victim. Skin loses elasticity with age."

Devon moved closer. "How old would you say that person is?"

"Twenty-five to forty."

Maya regarded her partner. Her throat had gone dry. "We've got the unsub's DNA."

"Yes you do, but the bad news is that the lab has already processed this, and it doesn't match any DNA in the database. Both medical and law enforcement."

"Dammit," Maya breathed. "How is that possible?"

"A person's DNA is only in a database if it has a reason to be. That means our guy has never been in trouble with the law and hasn't had any major surgery."

Liang said, "Exactly, but there's more. I can't say why this skin is this color because this isn't a skin tone I've ever seen. It's also scabbed, so it might have been infected. The lab results came back inconclusive on that. Aside from this, that's all I can really tell you about the vic."

Maya stared at the evidence bag. Black skin. Scabbed edges.

Suddenly, she knew exactly what to do.

"Devon," she whispered. "Can I talk to you outside?"

Her partner nodded. "Thank you, Dr. Liang. Please call us if you find anything else."

"I will. I'll be running some more tests over the next few days."

Maya barely heard because she'd already shed her mask and gloves and made for the door. She rushed outside, breathed in the sterile air, and then turned to Devon, who was sauntering behind her. For the first time since they'd been partnered, Maya felt like she was leading instead of scrambling to catch up.

"What is it, Frost?"

"I think I know how we can find this guy."

TWENTY-ONE

MAYA WAS CONVINCED THAT THE BLACK MARK ON THE killer's hand was a tattoo.

And tattoos only scabbed over when they were fresh.

Devon unlocked the car door and talked to Maya across the hood. "So what, we canvass every single tattoo place on Amelia Island?"

"Yup."

"What if he didn't get tattooed here? What if he went to the mainland?"

There Devon went again with her pessimism. "Then we canvass every tattoo shop there too."

"And ask them if anyone's gotten a hand tattoo recently? I imagine they do hand tattoos every day. Every guy I see these days has tattoos in weird places. How those guys get jobs I have no idea."

She'd had a thought there too, but she was keeping it from Devon because no doubt the old veteran would find a problem with it. "Let's just get back to the precinct. I've got an idea."

Loath as she was to admit it, Maya's job in Intelligence had been good to her. Spending ten hours a day with data-obsessed brainiacs had taught her a thing or two, and now it was time to make good on the seven years she'd spent in the FBI's basement.

MAYA LOCKED herself in the office because she needed solitude for this. She drowned out the precinct noise with earplugs, found a marker pen, and approached the whiteboard. She wiped it clean, and then pinned the CCTV printout of the killer and his hand tattoo to the metal frame. Somewhere outside the office, Devon was calling tattoo parlors in the area to see if any had tattooed palms recently.

Leave her to it. For Maya, it was time to see beyond the grain.

She knew the base of the tattoo was circular, and there was something akin to a *V* shape in the center.

And from that—with a little luck—she could work out the rest.

In the Intelligence world, you didn't see people. You saw data, and data was only useful if you could read it. A radio signal pinging off a tower meant nothing if you couldn't interpret it, and the same went for black smudges on a killer's palms.

Maya drew a circle on the whiteboard. Then she stared at the printout again, this time ignoring what it looked like and focusing on what it was: pixels captured during motion, thousands of individual data points captured by a digital sensor. Each pixel was a coordinate on a grid, a number representing light and shadow at a specific location.

When the killer waved, his hand moved. The tattoo moved with it. Sharp edges would blur into curves. Points would smear into arcs. But some parts would leave heavier traces than others.

The killer had been moving when the camera captured this frame. His hand was in motion, completing that mocking wave. And motion created blur.

But motion blur wasn't random. It followed rules. If you knew how an object was moving, you could predict how that movement would distort its image. Sharp edges became curves. Points became streaks. But the distortion wasn't always uniform. Some parts of the moving object would leave heavier traces than others.

She thought about the wave. The killer's hand lightly swaying as his fingertips moved up and down. Any sharp points or edges on the original tattoo would have been smeared into arcs by that lateral movement.

But what if the original shape wasn't a circle at all?

Maya picked up the printout and held it inches from her face, squinting at the individual pixels that made up the dark mark. Her eyes watered from the strain, but she forced herself to focus on the details that everyone else would dismiss as photographic noise.

There. At the edge of the supposed circle. A slightly denser cluster of black pixels. And there, about seventy degrees clockwise. Another cluster. Maya counted them, mapping their positions in her mind.

Five clusters. Evenly spaced around the perimeter.

Maya's heart began to pound. She grabbed the marker again and made five small dots around the circumference of her drawn circle. The spots where motion blur would be thickest if the original shape had had corners.

Five corners. Five points.

Her hand trembled as she connected the first two dots with a straight line. Then the second to the third. Third to the fourth.

The shape that emerged made her blood freeze in her veins.

Just then, Maya distantly heard her office door burst open. A voice spoke to her, but it was drowned out by both the earplugs and the revelation staring her in the face.

It had never been a circle.

"Frost. You listening?"

Maya slowly unplugged her ears. Devon was saying something.

"These tattoo places," Devon continued, "they need more info than just a palm tattoo. They need to know exactly what design, or we'll be here for—"

"A pentagram," Maya said, staring blankly at her drawing on the board. She spun around to face her partner. "Tell them we're looking for a pentagram."

And with that, her theory got a lot more complicated.

TWENTY-TWO

Blood Moon Tattoo was the next stop on their journey. As it turned out, tattoo parlors didn't seem to be the most helpful establishments, especially over the phone. Devon had figured that they might be more cooperative in person, so she and Maya had hit the road.

They were looking for someone who'd had a pentagram tattooed on their palm, and it would have been inked in the past month.

"You're sure it's a pentagram?" Devon asked as they exited the car. Fernandina Beach had more parking spaces than people to fill them, which was a welcome change from fighting for every inch of space as Maya had to in DC. Devon had pulled right up to the front door of Blood Moon, between a rusty Silverado and nothing else.

"Unless you know another five-pointed star that fits in a circle."

"I do not. How does this tie in to Ed Gein? I'm not as

clued-up as you on the guy, but I'm guessing Gein wasn't a Satanist."

"It doesn't tie in with Gein, but a pentagram doesn't always mean Satanism," Maya said, though she wasn't sure why she was defending occult symbolism to her partner. "They're used in paganism."

"He cut a woman in half and skinned her face. Chances are he's into Satan."

Maya couldn't argue with the logic. They entered Blood Moon Tattoo, and Maya was beginning to think that all tattoo places had been designed by the same, somewhat-depressed interior designer. Flash art on the walls, skulls and dragons at every turn, and it was all punctuated by that annoying stop-start buzzing of tattoo guns. At the far end of the studio, Maya could see a young guy tattooing what looked like a detached prosthetic limb.

"Don't do it," said the girl behind the counter. She was about twenty-two, with bright green hair and a face full of metal.

"Don't do what?" Maya asked.

"Ruin that skin of yours. Virgin skin is the new black."

"It's a bit late for that. I've got a flower on my leg."

"A flower?" The girl twizzled her green locks. "That's a symbol of virginity. You know that?"

"No. I don't know anything about tattoos, which is why we need help. We're working with local police on an ongoing investigation, and we're looking for someone who we believe has a tattoo on their palm."

Devon flashed her badge, then slid the CCTV photo across the small counter. The woman eyeballed it like it might bite her. "An ongoing investigation? I've never heard that term in real life."

"First time for everything."

"Sure is, flower girl. But sorry, but we don't do palm work here. Some places will, but we've got morals." She pointed to a sign on the wall that said NO HANDS, NO FACES. WE STICK TO OUR GUNS.

"Never?"

"Never. Hand tattoos come with a stigma."

"Which is?"

"That the person is a criminal."

"Fitting," said Devon. "Has anyone *asked* for a palm tattoo in the past few months? Perhaps a pentagram or similar design?"

The woman idly checked her computer. She typed in something, then began scrolling. "Sorry, I don't remember anybody asking for that, and there are no search results for *pentagram* in our messages. I can have a more thorough look, but it might take a while."

"All of your correspondence is done on there?"

"Pretty much."

Maya sighed. This was their fifth tattoo shop in the past two hours, and the story had been similar every time. In the back of the store, the noise of the tattoo gun died out, and the man who'd been inking a fake leg stood up and came over to the counter. Maya read his body language. Legs together, shoulders hunched, lips one inch apart. He had something on his mind.

"You guys looking for a palm tat?"

"Not for ourselves. Do you know anyone with one? Or

anyone who requested one?" Maya pointed to the CCTV photo on the counter. "This design?"

The tattooist scrutinized the photo. "From what I can tell, yeah."

Maya and Devon swapped a look. This could be exactly what they needed. "Tell us everything."

"First of all, it's hard to tell because the photo quality sucks, but this tat doesn't look professional to me. An amateur did this. Or he did it himself."

Devon said, "Who was the person who asked for this tat? Do you have a name, address, picture?"

"Bear with me. He messaged me personally, not the shop." The artist fished out his cell phone and scrolled through, then he passed it across to Maya. "Here, look. This guy contacted me a couple of weeks back."

The screen showed a messages tab on a social media page. The sender was named Lucien K, and his profile picture was too small to see in any detail. Maya speed-read the exchange.

Lucien K: Hi, I am looking for a particular design for my palm. Reference picture is attached. Please quote prices and availability.

Damien: Hey, sorry but I don't do hands at all. I'm sure there are other places in the area that will though!

Lucien K: I can pay more?

"Reference picture," Maya said. "Can I open it?"

"Sure."

Maya clicked the attachment.

And there it was.

A perfect black pentagram. Maya compared it to what she could see on the CCTV picture, and it was a perfect fit.

Devon leaned closer. "That's it. We got the son of a bitch. Who is he? Can you see his profile?"

"Yeah," the tattooist said hesitantly. "I'm not violating privacy laws or anything, am I?"

Devon's icy stare said more than words ever could. The tattooist raised his hands in surrender.

"OK, OK. Here." He clicked the sender's name, pulling up the social media page of one Lucien K. He scrolled through all of the available information, but the only forthcoming details were a name and a profile picture, both of which could be fake. There were no posts, no interests, no date of birth or education.

"Not a whole lot about him."

"Can you enlarge the picture?"

The tattooist clicked, and a grainy shot of Lucien K.—possibly the man who'd murdered Teresa—filled the screen. It was a distant photo of a figure in a field; ninety percent scenery, ten percent man.

But there were enough details in there for Maya to maybe get an idea of the man behind the monster.

Mid-thirties. Buzzed hair. About one-sixty, just over six feet tall, on the lean side of stocky.

Devon began, "Sir, we're going to send an officer out here. We might need to confiscate your cell phone for a day or two, but we'll —"

"Wait," Maya interrupted. She was still burning the image of the man into her brain, and there was something both she and Devon had missed staring right at them. "Devon, look. The guy's T-shirt."

"What about it?"

"Looks like... words," the tattooist said.

Maya ignored the commentary. Letters began to separate themselves from the digital sludge. It was curved white strokes across black cotton, spelling out something that was no brand logo. This wasn't Nike, wasn't Adidas, wasn't a beer label. It was local.

Her mouth went dry as the name came into focus.

Fernandina Hunting Club.

"You guys might have just helped us catch a monster," Maya said, although she was unable to truly articulate the extent of her gratitude. She scribbled down her cell number, gave her thanks, and rushed for the door.

The killer was a butcher.

A hunter.

And if he wanted to fight a real predator, Maya was going to make that happen.

TWENTY-THREE

Their destination was the lodge owned by the Fernandina Hunting Club, and Maya had a good feeling about this. How many people could there be on a single island that hunted *and* wanted a pentagram tattoo on their palm? The road leading to the lodge was more of a dirt track than a public right of way, and Maya could sense Devon's annoyance as she continually had to drop below ten miles an hour.

"Don't think of me as dumb," Maya said, "but what's a hunting club do?"

Devon side-eyed her. "Hunt."

"I got that much, but their website says their lodge is open every day, and they meet there for hunts. Surely these people don't hunt every day?"

"You ever wonder why everything is going extinct? Because of guys like this."

"Wow."

"They probably don't hunt every day. It's probably a social club for men who love guns. Do you like guns, Frost?"

"Yes and no. You don't grow up in the Massachusetts wilds without a passive knowledge of guns. What about you?"

"I only know what I have to."

A weather-beaten road sign pointed Devon left. She eased the car onto a dusty track, and moments later, the Fernandina Hunting Club spread out ahead. A rutted gravel lane funneled them toward a low cedar-board lodge fronted by broad windows and a wrap-around porch. Trucks, SUVs, and some old beaters populated the lot. Off to one side of the lodge, a covered patio held picnic tables where half a dozen men sat with coffee mugs and, by Maya's estimation, weapons. Their rifles leaned against the railing like walking sticks. She caught snatches of conversation and laughter carrying across the lot. Out front, an American flag and club banner hung from a metal pole, the logo of which showed a buck's head over crossed rifles.

"There's life within," Devon said. She parked the car just out of sight. "Ready?"

Maya wasn't ready. Never in her life had she approached a huge crowd of men, one of whom might be a homicidal psychopath. "I don't mean to state the obvious, Devon."

"But you're going to."

"Yeah. We're about to infiltrate a hunting group, and they all have guns."

Devon checked the ammunition levels on her Glock. "Do you know the first rule of gun control?"

"No?"

"If there's a gun, control it."

"Meaning what? Shoot first?"

"Yeah," said Devon.

"But I don't have a gun."

"Then just focus on finding this Lucien person. If anything kicks off, I'll do damage control."

A hundred thoughts fought for dominance. What if Lucien's profile had been fake? What if he wasn't a member of this club at all? What if this all went sideways and Maya became the subject of a cheap funeral with a template eulogy from a priest she'd never met?

She banished her concerns, stepped out of the car, and shook herself back to the present. A wise man had once told her that fear was the passenger, not the co-pilot, and if you didn't keep it in the back seat, it would drive you off the road. "Let's go."

The men's chatter got louder as Maya and Devon approached the front lawn, and as they came into view, their conversations died out. Both she and Devon were dressed casually, but the lack of plaid shirts and hunting boots made it obvious they weren't here to join the club.

"You ladies lost?" one of the men asked. All eyes turned to them—six pairs of eyeballs by Maya's count. She felt that sudden rush, the same one that came before someone asked her to do a magic trick.

Devon spoke first. "We're with the FBI. Are any of you gentlemen in charge here?"

"That'd be me. My name's Jeff. What do the FBI want with us?" The one who'd spoken scratched his gray beard that had clearly never been trimmed in its existence. He was a burly man in a brown jacket, and by Maya's estimation, he had a Winchester Model 70 at his feet.

"We're looking for someone we believe is a member here. Lucien. That name ring any bells?"

The men regarded each other with blank stares. "Sorry, we don't know any Lucien."

"We? You speaking for everyone?"

"It's a figure of speech, miss."

Maya noticed a couple of the men tense up. Two of them clutched their beer glasses tightly, and then this Jeff character followed suit. Maya had always believed that honest drinking only took place after dark, and anyone who self-medicated during the day was not to be trusted.

"Well, Lucien is a person of interest in an ongoing investigation. We found a photograph of him wearing a shirt with the logo of this club on it. We need to know if he's been here recently."

Jeff finished his drink, then pulled out a tobacco tin. "A lot of people come and go, miss. Some people buy our shirts even if they're not members."

Maya's turn. "Really? I checked your website on the way here, and it said the exact opposite. Merchandise is for members only. Is that not accurate?"

Jeff pulled his jacket around himself as the wind picked up. He glanced around at his associates, who offered little in the way of support. They were all suddenly staring over at the building entrance as though they'd never seen a hunting lodge before.

"I don't know what to tell you. Lucien isn't here."

"So you do know a Lucien," said Devon.

"I don't know what to tell you. This is a private club, and

I know the law. Get a warrant, or you might be hearing from my lawyer."

Maya had met a lot of people who claimed to *know the law,* but anyone who said that usually didn't. One of her life rules was that if someone used the term *my lawyer,* they didn't have a lawyer.

Devon asked, "Is that so?"

"Yeah. Or learn to hunt."

That got a cackle from Jeff's buddies—and everything about it slid under Maya's skin.

Go away, little girl. That's what these men were saying, and she'd heard variations of that theme weekly ever since she first stepped into a police precinct ten years ago, from sergeants to training instructors to higher-ups in the Bureau. From every Neanderthal who thought a woman's place was anywhere but here.

This wasn't those people. This was a potential witness, maybe even a suspect, in the murder of an innocent woman. And here was Jeff, sitting on his plump ass with his afternoon beer and stupid beard, making jokes about hunting to the two FBI agents trying to do good in the world.

"Did you just say *learn to hunt?*"

Silence fell. Jeff glanced at his cronies, then up at Maya. "Yeah. City folk don't tend to know much about these things."

"These things?"

"Hunting. Guns."

Maya lost it.

"Pal, I was sifting through pig shit at stupid o'clock in the morning since I was seven years old. I know the weight of a rifle in my hand. I know what cordite smells like when it's still hot in the chamber. I know what it feels like to put food on the table with a clean shot, not sit around drinking beer and playing weekend warrior."

"Hold up a minute—" Jeff began, but Maya stepped closer so he had to crane his neck to see her.

"Nice Winchester 70 you've got there. The rifleman's rifle. That scope is probably good for five hundred yards if you've actually zeroed it, which I'm betting you haven't. It's a bit too clean too. Your boyfriend polish that for you?"

Jeff went red. He went to raise his hand, but Maya slapped it away and turned to the next hunter. "You there. Flannel boy. What's that, a Remington 700? See that wear pattern on the fore-end? You're gripping it too tight when you shoot. Probably pulling it right every time." Next hunter in line, a man in a Jacksonville Jaguars cap. "You, is that a Colt in your pants or are you just pleased to see me?"

"It's a Colt," he muttered.

"Of course it is." Maya grabbed Jeff's tobacco tin, took out a pinch of the brown stuff, and shoved it in her cheek like she'd been doing it since kindergarten. "You boys sit up here with your expensive scopes, hunting things from a hundred feet away that can't fight back. Me and my partner here aren't looking for Bambi. Do you understand?"

Jeff shrugged. The other men had gone noticeably quiet. "Good speech."

"Look, I get the whole boys' club thing, but we're working here." Maya spat a globule of tobacco between Jeff's boots. "So I'll ask you one more time. Lucien. Who is he? And if I get a feeling you're holding back important info, well, maybe there's a shooting range in Jackson Correctional you can use."

"Lucien," spat Jeff. "He goes by Luke. He's out in the back. Target practice."

Maya looked at Devon, who was already aiming herself toward the lodge. "Thank you."

"Don't hurt him. He's just a little... odd."

"We'll be the judge of that."

TWENTY-FOUR

THE LOBBY AREA WAS VAST, AND THERE SEEMED TO BE A distinct lack of any character in here, unless Maya counted the giant boar's head that looked like it had died pissed off mounted on the wall.

"There." Devon pointed to a door that said *Members' Area.*

Gunshots echoed somewhere deeper in the building. Maya picked up speed, yanked open the door, and found herself in a corridor leading past a collection of locked rooms. She followed the sound of gunfire with Devon a few steps behind, trying not to think about what might lie ahead. She had a good feeling about this, but one wrong move could mean a bullet in a vital organ. Anyone capable of severing a human being in two was capable of anything, especially in the face of capture.

At the end of the corridor, Maya skidded to a halt at a large glass partition with double doors in the middle. Beyond it was a backyard. Maya counted twelve men, all of them pointing rifles at targets nailed to trees. She turned to Devon. "You see him?"

"I see a lot of things, but I can't see any hand tattoos."

Everyone in the firing range had gloves on, and even if they didn't, any identifiable marks were too far away to see with any clarity. "Lots of civilians here. That's not good."

"No it isn't, and we need to play this smart, because if Lucien gets a whiff of us, then he'll bolt into the woods over there. There's eleven innocent men here too, so this isn't a place for bullets."

"Ironic."

"Yeah."

Maya and Devon both instinctively shadowed themselves against the wall as one of the shooters came in their direction. He opened the door, stepped inside, and then Devon ambushed him.

"Sir, we're looking for Lucien. Is he out there?"

The man regarded Devon like he'd never seen a woman before. Confusion and suspicion warred on his face. "Lucien? Yes. Why?"

Devon flashed her badge. "Because we need to talk to him. Which one is he?"

With a shaky hand, the man pointed to the figure on the far left of the range. "That's him. Is he in trouble?"

"Maybe. Do yourself a favor and make yourself scarce. This could get ugly."

He nodded, then disappeared down the corridor. Maya caught him idling at the door, probably waiting for the show to begin so he could watch from afar. She squinted to make out the figure that was apparently Lucien. He was taller than he'd seemed on his profile picture, a clump of blond hair atop his head, a hunting jacket with the club logo embroidered on the rear.

"What's the play?" Maya asked. Her heart was beating at cardiac arrest levels, because she'd never been this close to a murderer of this magnitude before. All those years of dreaming, and now she was living it—except it was nothing like what she'd imagined. She didn't have the security of her imagination here, where she could model the fantasy until it had a neat resolution. Fantasies didn't account for variables like Devon's gun jamming or the killer having a rifle of his own.

"I'll approach him. You round up the civilians and get them the hell out of here, got it?"

Maya breathed heavily. A part of her was disappointed she wouldn't get any close-up action, but she reminded herself of the goal: Get Teresa Morgan's killer in chains. Nothing else mattered. "Got it."

"Stay alert."

Devon stepped outside, and a few pairs of eyeballs turned in their direction. Devon moved across the lawn to Lucien's area while Maya grabbed the other shooters by the peripherals with her manic hand gestures. *Get out. Clear the area.* Two of the older men near the front got the message immediately. They exchanged a confused look, reluctantly lowered their rifles, and started shuffling back toward the safety of the clubhouse.

But the others, cocooned in their earmuffs and locked in the zen of their targets, didn't even notice her. Either that or they chose to ignore her completely. She moved closer, with one eye on Devon and the man who might just have gutted

Teresa Morgan last night. She saw Devon flash her badge, but the conversation was lost to the wind.

As more men gathered at the entrance to the lodge, other shooters followed suit. The arrival of these two strange women must have told them that this wasn't business as usual, and men like this didn't respond well to change. Now only two men lingered at the edge of the lawn, and they seemed too drawn by the magnetic pull of potential violence to move any time soon. Maya rushed in their direction, but movement between Devon and Lucien caught her attention.

Lucien nodded, said something to Maya, and then—to Maya's shock—laid his rifle down on the floor.

She breathed for a moment.

Was that it? A clean surrender?

Maya scrutinized Lucien's body language. His shoulders twitched, and then he shifted his weight to the balls of his feet. He began to rock as Devon closed in on him, and Maya caught her casually placing one hand on her firearm.

Not a good sign. It didn't take an expert to recognize that deer-in-the-headlights look.

And then Lucien exploded into motion.

He became a blur. His feet ate up ten feet of the lawn in seconds.

"Shit!" Maya forgot about the two remaining civilians. Forgot about her lack of a weapon. Forgot about everything except the lanky figure in the hunting jacket now tearing across the grass toward the lodge. Maya saw Devon raise her gun and scream for him to freeze, but Lucien paid no attention. Devon hesitated, and Maya knew that there was no way she'd risk a bullet with the other hunters around.

Only one option remained.

Maya burst into pursuit.

She put boots to grass and trailed the moving blur toward the civilians, toward the lodge. Teresa Morgan's killer was escaping, and Maya wasn't going to let that happen.

"Stop him!" she screamed, but the other hunters abruptly parted as Lucien barreled toward them. He yanked the lodge door and disappeared inside, and Maya was at the same spot a second later. She pulled the door nearly clean off its hinges just in time to see Lucien turning at the end of the corridor.

Pain shot up her ankles, but she'd logged thousands of miles on Massachusetts back roads, and now it was time for those miles to pay dividends. She shot forward, channeled her inner bloodhound, and reminded herself of basic criminal psychology. Fleeing suspects looked for space. The smart ones didn't zig-zag, and only the really foolish ones tried to hide in enclosed spaces. If not the woods at the back, then Lucien would head for the entrance.

When Maya turned the corridor, she spotted the now-familiar blur corkscrewing through the lodge and crashing into furniture, heading toward the patio area out front. Maya was dimly aware of bodies behind her, but as the frontrunner, she had to lead the charge. Devon might have been among them, but Maya couldn't wait for her—nor the security of her loaded Glock.

Maya followed in the same direction. She shaved a few seconds by vaulting over a small table, and Lucien must have either slowed or caught on something because he was suddenly within grabbing distance. Maya reached out and grazed the fabric of his jacket, but Lucien surged forward. Maya stumbled, almost toppled, shouldered off a cabinet, and jolted herself back upright. Adrenaline propelled her forward, and up ahead, the lodge's front door exploded outward. Maya was only a few heartbeats behind, and the transition from dim interior to Florida sunshine momentarily veered her off course, but the sight of Lucien's fast-moving figure corrected her. The transition must have affected him too, because he was closer than Maya had realized, close enough to smell, to hear his violent breaths.

The patio materialized piece by piece. Beer cans, rifles, tobacco tins, and the six men who Maya had scolded only a few minutes before. With the oncoming bodies, their earlier bravado disappeared, and they scattered to the wind. The commotion made Lucien scramble for direction. He ceased, recalibrated, and in that microsecond of confusion, Maya made her bid for capture.

Her hand shot forward.

Contact.

The rough weave of Lucien's jacket filled her palm.

For one crystal clear moment, she had him in her hands. This bizarre shadow creature who'd haunted the CCTV footage of Teresa Morgan's store was suddenly, impossibly tangible.

Lucien's body jerked sideways as her grip found purchase. Maya's arms windmilled and searched for equilibrium that was already lost. Electricity shot through her veins, and she inhaled the sweet smell of victory because she was certain that Lucien was now her defenseless prey. With the momentum carrying them both, they fell forward together in a graceless roll of violence. Maya felt her feet leave the ground, and then they both fell to the mercy of gravity. In that brief, airborne moment, Maya was reminded why she'd left her desk, why she'd endured Devon's condescension. This moment was proof that her theories could bleed and breathe and be brought to the ground.

They hit the ground together. Maya's shoulder bounced off the bench, and her knee scraped concrete. Beer cans fell on them both, and then Maya found herself rolling to the point that she couldn't tell where Lucien ended and she began. Time reasserted itself as they skidded to a stop. Until the world stopped spinning and she realized she was staring up into pale eyes that held no surprise at all, as if their violent collision had been choreographed from the beginning. And Maya found herself lying on her back.

With Lucien's writhing form on top of her.

But it wasn't his weaselly face she was staring at.

It was the barrel of a rifle.

A Remington 700. One that had been waiting here at the bench. She realized Lucien must have snatched it as they were entangled.

Goddammit.

"Don't move," Lucien breathed.

Maya showed her palms. "Put the gun down, Lucien. It's over."

Voices shouted, but they were distant. One of the hunters said something about calling the police.

"Move and I shoot you."

Maya stared up at the rifle's dark mouth and felt her mind split into competing voices. The analyst in her processed the finer points of the Remington 700. The field agent she was supposed to be searched for tactical options but found nothing but gravel digging into her spine.

But it was the woman underneath both identities who whispered the question that mattered: *Is this how it ends?*

Seven years of dreaming about moments like this, and she'd never imagined the mundane details, like the way beer foam still dripped from an overturned can beside her head or how one of her cuticles was sore from picking at it earlier.

Negotiate. The word surfaced from her FBI training from years ago. *Keep him talking. Establish rapport. Find common ground. Buy time.*

"Why'd you do it?"

"Do what?"

"You know what."

Lucien pressed the barrel to Maya's forehead. "I needed to! I had no—"

"Freeze! Get off of her!" Devon's voice cut him off. "Put the gun down, Lucien."

Maya's position awarded her nothing but a direct glimpse to a sky that was quickly becoming overcast. She couldn't see her partner.

"I'm not going back," Lucien cried. "I won't do it."

"You'll do exactly what I tell you to. Now get off."

Lucien turned his head toward Devon for the first time, and Maya *felt* it. The barrel had shifted a crucial few inches away from her skull as his attention divided.

This was her opportunity. The first rule of gun control. If there's a gun—control it.

She grabbed the rifle's stock, pushed it farther off-target while her right hand found the bolt handle. She twisted the bolt upward with force, and the Remington's action opened with a metallic snap, ejecting the chambered round in a bright brass arc. The cartridge hit the gravel beside her ear with a small ping.

Lucien snapped back to her. "What the... You bitch!"

Maya clenched her fist, put every ounce of might into her knuckles, and smashed them into Lucien's nose. A spray of blood covered them both, and the sound of cracking cartilage was so satisfying that Maya almost felt bad about it. The gun clattered away from them as Lucien instinctively grabbed his face, and then Maya followed up with another right hand to the temple.

He toppled. Devon rushed in and trained her gun on his limp torso. She dug her boot into his spine. "Move and I shoot, got it?"

Lucien didn't respond. His body deflated with the reality of capture, and Maya climbed to her feet. Devon stole a glance at her. "You OK, rookie?"

"I am now. You?"

"I'll be better when we see his hands." Devon gestured with her head. "Do the honors, will you?"

Maya stepped over Lucien's torso, unhooked the Velcro strap, and tore the glove off his left hand. She twisted his wrist to see his palm.

And her heart stopped.

No. It can't be.

She did the same with the other hand.

Maya looked up at her partner, then back down at the hands that should have held all the answers but instead offered only more questions.

If Lucien was Teresa Morgan's killer, then why wasn't there a pentagram on his palm?

TWENTY-FIVE

Maya looked at Lucien through the one-way glass into a locked office that doubled as an interrogation room. Dusk had turned to nightfall, and the suspect hadn't said a single word since Maya and Devon had hauled him in in the back of their car six hours ago. Devon hadn't given Maya an earful about her takedown of Lucien, so she assumed that she'd finally done something right. The adrenaline of the capture had subsided, and so now Maya was left with a mute suspect with an absence of a pentagram on his palm.

Sheriff Riggs approached the agents with two coffees. "I come bearing gifts."

"Thanks. What did you find out about him?" Devon asked.

"Here's what we do know. The guy's name is Luke Kavanagh, but he calls himself Lucien."

"Of course he does."

"He's thirty-two, and he's got two priors, both from a year

ago. One for indecent exposure, one for spiking a woman's drink. Unemployed, but he doesn't need a job because his parents are well-to-do. According to his bank account, they transfer him five grand a month. That's how he survives."

"What a life."

Riggs said, "Yup. And his lawyer is coming as fast as he can, but if he's not here within the hour, we can do the preliminary interview. I'm not sure how long we can hold him."

"For an investigation this serious, we can hold him as long as we have to. The circumstantial evidence will hold up," said Devon.

"Good. Has he moved a muscle since you stuffed him in there?"

"Only to ask for the bathroom."

Riggs regarded Lucien—or Luke—through the glass. He put his hands on his hips. "Well, he looks pretty good to me, but you say there's no tattoo on his hand?"

"No."

"Weird." Riggs nudged Maya. Until now, she'd been lost in her own world. "You're quiet, rookie. I heard you took this guy down pretty good."

"Something like that."

"Any wounds?"

"Just a scraped knee and a bruised shoulder. I'd say I got off light."

"Yes you did. What do you think of this guy? Is he our man?"

Maya tried to reconcile the man in front of her with the monster on the CCTV footage. They had similarities, and if she asked a hundred detectives what they thought, half of them would say charge him immediately. The hunting background and the tattoo request went a long way, but there were a few things that didn't add up.

"I don't know."

"Why not?" Riggs asked.

"Lucien doesn't look strong enough to haul a dead body up a ladder, and if he's got priors, then surely he'd have been on the database somewhere. The mortician said that Teresa's killer's DNA wasn't on any database. And the skin that had peeled off his hand was inked black. There's no blank ink on his palms at all. I inspected the hell out of them."

"Laser removal?" asked Riggs.

"In a day?"

"What if he drew it with a marker?"

"Then why had it scabbed over?"

"Beats me." Riggs shrugged. "Sit tight for an hour, and if his lawyer doesn't show, you can get in there and question him. If you need to open him up, I've got a few spare screws that fit perfectly between the knuckles."

"Thanks, Sheriff," Devon said, "but I'm pretty sure we can get him to talk."

"Let's hope so. I've just got to check on something with Dispatch, but I'll be back for the interview." Riggs disappeared down the hallway and left the agents alone. Maya turned to Devon, and there was a new glint in Devon's eye that hadn't been there prior to Maya risking her life to take down this potential killer. A grudging respect, perhaps. A concession that the rookie, for all her theoretical posturing, could actually perform in the wild. Apparently risking your life and nearly getting a rifle shoved down your throat was all it took to gain a field agent's approval. It felt both earned and infuriatingly trivial.

"You didn't do bad out there, Frost. Thanks for chasing that asshole down."

"Thanks for pointing a gun at his face."

"That was the easy part. You did the leg work."

Maya was oddly grateful for the compliment, and she wasn't sure how to process it properly. "Do you think he's our killer?"

"Yeah. I can say without a shadow of a doubt that Luke Kavanagh is our perp. What about you?"

Maya caught a smirk on Devon's face, like a professor who had just asked a question she already knew the answer to, waiting to see if the student would give the response she wanted to hear or the one that seemed obvious.

It felt like a test.

"I think Luke Kavanagh is a two-bit pervert. You don't go from flashing and spiking drinks to bisection and face skinning in the span of a year."

"Sure about that?"

Maya nodded. "Pretty sure."

"What about running from the cops?"

"Running from the cops doesn't mean you're a murderer. It just means you're an idiot."

Devon tapped her shoulder. "Fair enough."

"Why'd you ask if I thought he was our man?"

"Because I needed to know if you'd stick to the evidence or get caught up in the excitement of making an arrest. Field work can mess with your judgment. Adrenaline makes you want to close cases even when they're not really closed."

Maya tried to hide her disappointment and failed. "So you don't think he's our killer either, and that was a test."

"Yup. And you passed. Let's let this son of a bitch stew for a while. We'll come back in an hour."

TWENTY-SIX

ELAINE HUTCHINS ALLOWED HERSELF A SIMPLE pleasure tonight, and that was to stay up late and watch brainless television. Seventy-three years of life had taught her that what time didn't steal from under your nose, circumstance did, and so the small indulgences like staying up past bedtime mattered more than ever in these twilight years.

Cecil, bless his heart, had been too tired from fishing to share this rare moment of rebellion with her and had retired to bed half an hour ago. Elaine had different ideas, and tonight she was going to watch an old Western that reminded her of her youth, or maybe she'd try out one of those true crime documentaries her daughter kept raving about. Elaine didn't have a streaming subscription, whatever that was, so she had to channel hop. That suited her, because she didn't know another way of watching TV.

There were more channels than she knew what to do with, and none of the programs seemed to ignite her interest. Only when she came to *Where Eagles Dare* did she stop, and memories of theater trips back in the sixties surged back. She remembered seeing this alongside Cecil back when she was fifteen, sixteen? Everyone in that cinema was engrossed in the spectacle on the screen, and that felt like a phenomena that couldn't be replicated today. People these days seemed to live in their own bubbles, their own niches, and that was something Elaine couldn't get on board with.

Upstairs, Cecil rolled in bed and made the springs creak. That man had been her one and only since junior year of high school. First love, last love, every love in between. Fifty-seven years of marriage, three kids, four grandkids, and enough ups and downs to fill a library. She'd never so much as looked at another man, but she had to admit that if Clint Eastwood showed up at her door with that crooked grin, she might have to give Cecil the bad news.

On screen, Clint was dispatching Nazis with his characteristic cool. Lord, that man could wear a parka. He must be pushing a hundred himself now, but Elaine had no doubt that he could make her feel sixteen again. The action on the film brought her back to sitting in the dark theater with Cecil's sweaty hand creeping toward hers across the armrest. He'd been so nervous that date, the poor thing. Kept wiping his palms on his good pants every few minutes before making another attempt. It had taken him half the movie to finally make contact, and when he did, Elaine had grabbed his hand firmly, putting them both out of their misery.

The memory made her smile. Those were the days when holding hands felt like the most dangerous thing two kids could do. Now she and Cecil barely touched except in passing. Not because the love had died but because familiarity had made them complacent. Even at her age, she missed that electricity, and Elaine firmly believed that a working libido had no age limit.

A thud from upstairs brought her back to reality.

What was that?

Cecil never got up once he fell asleep. The man had a camel's bladder, a fact that filled her with great envy.

Another thud.

Then what sounded like footsteps ascending the stairs.

"Cecil? Is that you?"

Nothing. The sounds ceased, and so Elaine went back to Clint Eastwood and his rugged good looks. She turned up the volume, but then another thud sounded upstairs, followed by the unmistakable creaking of the bedroom door.

Dread traced its way down Elaine's spine. This wasn't right. Cecil might be getting on in years, but his sleep patterns were as predictable as sunrise. He went to bed, read three pages of a novel, and then passed out with it on his chest until morning. There'd been the sleepwalking phase a few years ago, back when Elaine would find him wandering in the garden at three a.m. or when she'd find him dressed for work despite having been retired for ten years.

Maybe it was just the moisture in the floorboards. Winter wasn't far off, and the change in humidity played havoc with old houses like this. Or that bat in the attic had finally bitten its way through the hatch.

And what? Become life-sized? Given up on flying and started walking instead? A giant bat was the most preferable of her paranoid imaginings, because at least she could call animal control or hit it with a broom. She couldn't hit Cecil with a broom, for many reasons.

The footsteps came again, and this time there was no

mistaking them for anything else. Concern gnawed at her, perhaps amplified by the rash idea she'd had ten minutes ago of watching a true crime show. She'd inadvertently gotten herself into a state of paranoia, and now she had to reassure herself or she wouldn't be able to focus on Clint.

Elaine rose out of her chair and briefly considered calling the police. But what would she say? That she'd heard a noise upstairs? She could play the helpless older woman card, but she liked to think she had more pride than that.

THUD.

Louder than the others. Something was going on up there—and Elaine needed to see. Her heart began to race as she looked for a weapon because what if this was an intruder? She was seventy-three and not exactly in peak physical condition, but this was her house, goddammit, and she'd defend it until her last breath.

Elaine hefted the brass lamp beside her chair like it was Excalibur itself. She moved toward the stairs and edged up. They'd never felt this long before. "Cecil, are you OK?"

No response.

She took three more steps, and now the landing area came into view. The thuds had stopped, but Elaine could see that the bedroom door was ajar. Cecil never left it open. He liked his bedroom darker than the inside of a cow, as he'd often say.

"If you're messing with me, I'm going to kill you," Elaine said. She wasn't sure why that particular comment spilled out because Cecil had never played practical jokes on her before. He was serious to a fault. Elaine found herself gripping the banister, and she thought herself pathetic for doing so. Clint Eastwood wouldn't grip the banister. He'd shoot whatever had disrupted him and go back to his whiskey.

Elaine pressed herself against the hallway wall like she was trying to become part of the wallpaper, then edged closer to the bedroom door. Any second now, she'd see Cecil sound asleep and would probably have to apologize for waking him up. Any second now, she told herself. She couldn't breathe, could barely think straight.

The door creaked as she nudged it with her elbow. She crept in with her lamp-turned-weapon held high.

Her vision adjusted to the darkness, and there she made out the familiar outline of her husband of fifty years.

But the picture was different.

Cecil always slept curled up like a shrimp, with his knees pulled to his chest and one arm tucked under his pillow.

This wasn't that.

This Cecil was spread out like a starfish. Arms stretched wide toward the headboard, legs splayed. Her eyes found the glint of metal at his wrists first and then the silver stripe across his mouth that caught what little light filtered through the curtains. There was movement in his limbs and mumbles trying to escape his throat, and then he looked Elaine and violently shook his head.

"Ce...Cecil? What the...?"

Panic burned Elaine's lungs. Someone was in her house. Someone had done this to her husband.

Then she felt warm breath against the back of her neck.

She didn't even have time to scream before the steel bit into her throat, and then the lamp fell from her hands, taking the last of the light with it.

TWENTY-SEVEN

AN HOUR HAD PASSED WITH NO SIGN OF LUKE Kavanagh's lawyer, which meant Maya and Devon had a legal right to interview the suspect without any legal aid present.

Devon said, "Ready to interrogate this asshole?"

Maya had spent the past hour dwelling on the details—alone—because Devon had disappeared outside, and neither Alfie nor Riggs were anywhere to be found. Now they'd assembled outside the interview room. "No. I've never interviewed a suspect before. What's the process?"

"Give a guilty man enough rope and he'll hang himself."

"Meaning?"

"If he slips up, press him. It's funny, but catching a killer in a lie sometimes means more than a confession."

Maya cocked a brow. "How do you figure that?"

"Because criminals give false confessions all the time, but none of them ever give false lies."

"Huh?"

"The smartest thing you can do is let stupid people think they're smarter than you. Killers always think they're the smartest person in the room, even when they're handcuffed to a table."

The wisdom—if it could be termed as such—made Maya's head hurt. She'd quickly come to realize that Devon Lynch ran on her own bizarre logic, and perhaps that was the real secret to her success in the field. Maya guessed that if it worked, it worked, however unconventional.

"No. You've lost me."

"Just follow my lead. Ready?"

"Ready as I'll ever be."

Devon pushed into the interrogation room that Maya now realized was as cold as a refrigerator. Luke Kavanagh—or Lucien—was sitting at the table in the center of the room with cuffed wrists. The bruise where Maya had punched him had bloomed into a purple stain that wrapped around his eye, and the satisfaction it brought made her question her moral compass. She hadn't agreed to this job so she could punch criminals, but she guessed it was one of the perks.

"Mr. Luke Kavanagh?" said Devon. She took a seat opposite him, and Maya sat beside her. Devon laid down her folder, reached over, and switched on the tape recorder.

The suspect shrugged.

"Is that your name? Yes or no."

Another shrug.

"Fine." Devon gave the date and time for the recording, then sat back and folded her arms. "If you don't say anything, we're going to slap every charge we can on you. So if you don't want to spend Christmas in prison, we suggest you say something."

Luke pursed his lips together. Maya could read the body language a mile off. The man had no shortage of stubbornness, so she was already convinced Devon's approach wasn't going to work.

"How'd you get the name Lucien?" Maya asked.

The suspect eyeballed her, then shrugged again.

"Come on. How'd you get Lucien from Luke? What is it, French? Italian?"

"No," Lucien said. The first word he'd spoken since she'd punched him.

"Then how'd you get it?"

"I gave it to myself."

Maya laughed. "That's not how nicknames work."

"Why not?"

"You can't just name yourself. Other people have to give you nicknames, which is why I'm going to call you Luke the Murderer. How does that sound?"

Luke tried to pull his hands apart, then realized they were bound with steel rings. "I'm no murderer. Lucien is Latin. I studied it."

"Did you study Ed Gein too?"

"Who? Ed Gein?"

"Not familiar with him?" Maya asked.

"I know him, but..."

"Fine, let's change course. When we caught you, you said the words *I needed to*. Want to explain what that meant?"

The floodgates were open, and now Maya just had to keep the water running. She was no interrogation expert, but she was very aware that psychopaths couldn't help but correct any misinformation about themselves. If Luke thought Maya could control the perception of him, he'd be quick to put her right, and then once he opened his mouth, he'd fall victim to a psychological phenomenon known as the commitment escalation trap. The psychological need for narrative consistency meant that once a suspect began constructing their story, they would feel compelled to keep building it.

"I... needed to run."

Maya went quiet. She nudged Devon to take over. "Explain," Devon said.

"Because I knew."

"Knew what? You're not making sense."

"It's just... I couldn't..." Luke trailed off, but Maya could see a mile off that he was fighting for the right words, weighing up which ones he should spit out and which ones he should hold back.

"All right, let's start from beginning," said Devon. "We're here investigating a homicide, and our investigation has—"

"Wait. What? Homicide?"

"It means murder."

"I know," Luke said, "but I haven't murdered anyone. Who's been murdered?"

Luke's expression was one of genuine surprise, but psychopaths were naturally good actors, because acting was just lying. Devon reached into her folder and laid out a crime scene photo on the table. It showed a wide-shot of the hardware store back room, with Teresa's halved body swaying front and center.

"Recognize this?"

Luke's face purged itself of color until a ghostly white remained, then he jerked back so violently that his handcuffs rattled. "Jesus Christ! What happened to... Is that a person?"

"Yes. A murdered person."

"Who?" Luke breathed.

Maya watched his pupils dilate, watched the way his breathing ebbed and flowed. This reaction couldn't be faked because it happened in the nervous system before the brain had time to lie about it. Therefore, Maya was quick to conclude one thing: Lucien's body was screaming the truth. He'd never seen this before in his life.

"A local woman. Her name was Anne Smith," Devon said. Maya watched Luke's expression again, and there was no hint of irritation at Devon getting the name wrong. A murderer would want to correct her on the mistake, but Luke bought the lie.

"You don't think that... I did this? Do you?"

"We have our suspicions."

"Me? A murderer? Are you kidding me?" Luke's voice had risen an octave. "How the hell did you link this to *me*?"

"Because we believe our perpetrator has a pentagram tattoo on his hand."

Luke inspected his palms like he wasn't sure whether he had a tattoo there himself. "Umm, and what's that got to do with me? I don't have any tattoos, anywhere."

"But you inquired about one, didn't you?"

"Did I?"

"According to Damien Walker at Blood Moon Tattoo, yes."

Luke slapped his forehead with one hand, bringing the other with it by virtue of the handcuffs. "Of course. Now I remember."

Maya had already made up her mind regarding Luke's innocence, but she had trouble believing that anyone could forget they'd recently requested a tattoo on their hands. "You... forgot?"

"Yeah. Well, no. I never actually wanted one."

"What?"

The suspect began laughing, which Maya thought was brazenly inappropriate given the circumstances. "I was just trolling them. I do it all the time."

Devon leaned forward. "Trolling?"

"Yeah, you know?"

"No, I don't know."

Maya elbowed her partner. "It means he was just messing with them. Just to get a rise out of them."

"Why? Don't you have better things to do?"

"It was for our online group. We're called the Chaos Collective. We call up businesses, ask for the craziest shit and then post it online. Last month it was pet groomers. Brazilian waxes for cats. This month it was tattoo shops. It's just a joke."

Devon sat back and stared a hole through Luke to the point it became uncomfortable. Luke began to shrink like a slug who'd been salted. "What the hell is wrong with you? So you and a bunch of other virgins just harass businesses?"

Luke could only nod. Maya didn't blame him because she felt that if Luke said another word, Devon might reach over and strangle him just for daring to talk. "Why'd you run from us, then?"

"Honestly?"

"No, we want you to lie," Devon yelled. "Of course honestly."

"Right. Sorry." Luke took a breath. "I ran because I tried it on with this woman last week. She wasn't into me, and maybe I pushed a little harder than I should have. I figured she reported me, and my dad... He said he'd cut off my allowance if I did anything dumb again. I panicked. I'm sorry. You believe me, right?"

Maya pressed her fingers to her temples. She peered over at Devon, who looked like she'd just learned that not only was Santa Claus real but he was also a sex offender. Maya had been hopelessly optimistic that her assessment had been wrong and that Luke Kavanagh *was* capable of mutilating a woman beyond recognition, but now that optimism had been all but destroyed. Luke Kavanagh was many things, but a murderer wasn't one of them, and now Maya had to live with the fact that they'd spent nearly all day dealing with this idiot instead of chasing an actual killer.

But before she or Devon could voice their thoughts, the door to the interrogation room burst open.

Sheriff Riggs filled the doorway. "Agents, I need to see you outside. Now."

Maya led the way. Devon shut the door behind them when they got into the corridor. "What is it?"

"The call came in two minutes ago."

"What call?"

Goosebumps prickled Maya's flesh. She'd never been in this position before, but she could instinctively sense what Riggs was about to say.

"He's killed again."

TWENTY-EIGHT

ONE BEDROOM, TWO BODIES.

The house was in the middle of the closest thing Fernandina Beach had to suburbia, and Maya and Devon were staring at the desecrated bodies of what Maya guessed had been, in life, a married couple. An elderly gentleman was cuffed to all four corners of the bed, and the woman was curled up next to his torso on what little space remained. Both of their throats had been slit, and they'd been stabbed multiple times in the torso. Rumpled bedsheets covered the woman's legs, but Cecil's naked figure lay completely in view.

Maya's stomach twisted into knots at the sight of it all, not because of the brutality or the excessive blood but because the man and woman's hands were still interlocked, despite the contortion necessary to make it so. Even in death, they'd stayed together.

"Frost," Devon said. "What do you think?"

Two super-bright bulbs cast the bodies in high-definition

orange. Maya stepped a little closer and looked over the wounds, beginning with the man. These poor souls had been killed in the place they should have felt most safe.

"I think... we need to ask a difficult question first."

Sheriff Riggs entered the room, removed his mask, and asked, "What difficult question?" He had wrinkles on his forehead that Maya was sure hadn't been there yesterday.

"The question of whether this is the same perp or not."

"Why wouldn't it be?"

Devon turned to Riggs. "Because the M.O. is completely different, as is the victimology. Our perp shot Teresa Morgan and then mutilated her entirely post-mortem. If this is the same guy, then he's altered his approach significantly, and budding serial killers don't do that. They stick with what they know. He's also carried out what we call a double event, which is extremely rare in the annals of serial killing."

"I don't know what to tell you," Riggs said. "We never see murders like this, and we suddenly get two in two days? Unless someone's poisoned the water supply around here, I can't see that happening."

"You're probably right, but we're going to need something solid that connects these two cases. What do we know about the vics?"

"Cecil and Elaine Hutchins, both seventy-three. Lovely couple, according to some of my guys."

"You knew them?"

"Me? No. But two of my uniforms, Gary and Stu, did. Said they were quiet as mice, kept to themselves. No trouble. No run-ins with the law."

Maya took it all in. "So inoffensive targets, like just Teresa."

"Yup."

Devon moved over to the bodies and ran a gloved finger over the deep laceration in Elaine's neck. The woman's eyes were frozen up in a crude parody of life. "Who called it in?"

"Neighbor. Said he heard a man screaming about ten p.m."

"Didn't mention a woman screaming?"

"No."

"Did he come by to check on them?"

"Yeah, a few minutes later, then he called us when no one answered."

Maya was mentally fitting the scene together. "So if he didn't hear Elaine screaming, that means he killed her before she had a chance to scream."

"Right, and the blood is contained in this room, so he killed them both in here. But how? Even if he's physically capable, subduing two people at once is a risk."

Maya shut her eyes and tried to reconcile this scene with her Ed Gein theory. She mentally ran through Gein's life story but nowhere did it feature two elderly folk butchered in their beds. In fact, it was almost the polar opposite of Gein's crimes. So as much as it pained her, maybe it was time to discard that theory.

But in that moment of historical reflection, another thought jumped into her brain, and her subconscious filled in the blanks.

"Wait a minute. How did our guy get in?"

"We don't know yet," Riggs said. "The front door was locked until we broke it down. Back door is still locked."

"Windows?"

"One in the study is open, but it's not very big. The study is downstairs."

Devon said, "Climbing in through the window is a bold choice, especially around here. The houses around here are packed in tight, so there're tons of potential witnesses. It's not like he was secluded."

"Which means he specifically targeted this house," Maya said.

Riggs said, "But why? Why'd he need an old couple?"

"Because it's crucial to his fantasy. We just don't know what that fantasy is."

"I've got an idea. Getting his rocks off to killing poor folks in my town, that's what." Riggs wiped the sweat off his brow despite it being freezing in here, then waved a dismissive hand. "I've gotta deal with the neighbors outside. They're hysterical. Shout if you need me."

The sheriff left, and now it was just Maya, Devon, and two corpses. Maya ran a gloved hand over the wounds on Cecil's chest. "He used a knife to kill them both."

"Something bigger than a knife, Frost. Look at the length of those gashes. Even a butcher's knife would struggle to make something that big."

"So what, a sword?"

"Could be. Or a machete."

The word *machete* gave her pause. That meant something to her. Why? "Have you ever known a killer to use a machete before?"

"Not to my recollection, but I try not to think about the past too much. Did you see the TV was on downstairs?"

"Yeah. So if we're thinking linearly, then Elaine was watching TV downstairs; meanwhile, the killer snuck in through the kitchen window and made his way upstairs. You can't see the kitchen from the living room, so he'd have been invisible as long as he kept quiet."

Devon circled around to the other side of the bed. "Yeah, and if he was smart, he'd have taken out Cecil first since he was the primary threat. Cecil must have already been asleep, so the perp used that to his advantage. Then Elaine would have heard the commotion and came upstairs. That's when he struck."

Maya glanced around the room and didn't see much out of place except for a discarded lamp on the floor. She pointed at it. "That lamp seems out of place. Think Elaine tried to use it as a weapon?"

"Could be. Futile effort, because a machete beats a lamp any day of the week."

Again, the word *machete* sparked something in the back of her head, and this time, Maya fully acknowledged it. She faced the terrible stillness in Elaine Hutchins' eyes, took everything she knew about this case so far, and threw it into one big mental blender.

Hardware store, mutilation, butchery, skinned face, Ed Gein, pentagram, double-event, double-homicide, home invasion, machete.

Devon was saying something across the room, mostly to herself, it seemed. "Well, if we can ascertain it's the same offender, this officially makes him a serial killer. Three victims to his name puts him in that special list, so when the press hears about this, it's going to be a shitstorm. I haven't seen a double-event in, Jesus, ten years?"

Maya didn't know how it happened. There was no doubt

an explanation for the psychological process that followed, but she was ignorant to the exact mechanism.

It all connected—and it all made sense.

"Devon, we need to search this place. Every inch of it. We're missing something."

"What are you talking about?"

Maya was already on the hunt, as difficult as it was searching a scene where touch was frowned upon. "Our killer isn't done talking to us. There'll be a message here. A clue. Something."

"What makes you think that?"

She couldn't handle anything with any vigor because doing so could contaminate a fresh crime scene. Instead, Maya picked and plucked gently through every object she could: drawers, cupboard doors, ornaments, jewelry boxes. She worked herself in a circle around the body while Devon stayed stubbornly rooted to her spot.

"Because this isn't what I thought. This isn't about Ed Gein. It's about something bigger. Something much—" Maya's throat closed up when she came to the bedframe, then she glanced up and saw the bedsheets covering Elaine's bottom half. Nobody had disturbed the victims' positioning yet because that was a job for the forensics team.

This had to be it.

"Frost, if there was a message, we'd see it. It's not exactly a maze in here."

"We're not seeing it because it's hiding right in front of us," Maya said. The more she spoke it aloud, the more sense it made. It had to be right there, where her subconscious was telling her it was. "Can I move the bedsheet?"

"What? No. There could be prints on it. Don't disturb—"

"Devon, please. Trust me. I just need one peek."

Her partner sighed, then moved to the door and checked there was no one nearby. "All right, but be quick."

Maya's hands shook as she gripped the thin sheet with two fingers. It whispered as she peeled it back.

And there it was.

"Holy shit," Devon breathed. "You were right."

Written across the pale terrain of Elaine's thigh in bright green letters were three words.

CALL ME FRED.

Now she knew, with absolute clarity, what this killer's fantasy was.

He wasn't a serial killer. He was just playing the part of one. Or two.

"Devon, our killer is a copycat."

TWENTY-NINE

THE PROJECT HAD TAKEN HIM TO SOME STRANGE PLACES, made him do some strange things, but he trusted that the master's advice would guide him right. The adrenaline of tonight's double-event was still going strong, but now, standing above the pigs, paranoia had diluted the high somewhat.

He'd expected this. The serial killer, like any creature, went through predictable stages of metamorphosis. First came the euphoria and the feeling of invincibility. Then came the suspicion and hypervigilance, when you were certain that you'd made a mistake and you'd wake up the next morning with the police surrounding your house. This was normal, the master explained, but by the time you reached the paranoia stage, you were already trapped. The addiction had taken root during those glorious highs, and so the serial killer was forced to spend the rest of their lives chasing that rush, even as the paranoia grew stronger with every kill.

The master had explained the psychological progression in painful detail, but he'd also provided the most important piece of advice of all: Being aware of this metamorphosis was what separated the lifers in prison from the killers who were still walking free.

Tonight could have been messy, he had to admit. There'd been so many places it could have gone wrong, but he thought he'd weathered the risks with the skill of someone who'd been doing this for decades. Breaking in, sneaking up the stairs, keeping the man quiet, luring the woman upstairs, slaughtering them both, and then leaving the message. He'd expected more screams and more moments of improvisation, but all things considered, it had gone as smoothly as it could.

The pigs circled below him, as they did when they expected a feed, but once again he was here for personal reflection and nothing more. He wondered if it was cruel to mislead the poor sows this way, but he couldn't reconcile the notion of cruelty with something as trivial as starving pigs. Last night had numbed his awareness of cruelty in general, and tonight had rendered him barely able to acknowledge it at all.

At least toward others. He remained acutely aware of slights against himself, and one slight was cutting him deep right now.

The master hadn't contacted him at all.

Of course, they'd agreed to part ways before the project began, but he expected a word of encouragement, perhaps acknowledgment of a job well done once news of Teresa Morgan's death had hit the news.

However, there'd been no such thing. It was just him, the pigs, and a dead farm. To make the moment comically sadder still, he still had the tube of green lipstick in his hand. The same one he'd used to scrawl the message on the woman's legs. He threw it on the floor, stamped on it, and then kicked the shards into the pig pen.

It must have been getting late by now, and he needed to rest because his head was spinning a carousel of disparate imagery, and he couldn't focus on one or thing or the other. Only when the idea of rest popped into his head did he remember that the night wasn't over yet. There was still one more thing on the agenda.

He went into the shed and found the blowtorch. He took a seat on his dad's old chair and looked down at his palm.

The tattoo had been a stupid idea. He'd known that when he carved it in there himself, but he was convinced it would help with his mindset, calm his nerves, remind him that he'd been chosen for something greater than the mundane shit that had been the past forty years of life.

But he couldn't go around with this on his hand forever. He couldn't wear gloves forever, either. Sacrifice was the price of transformation. The master had taught him that nothing worthwhile ever came without cost. He'd sacrificed his old life, his old moral constraints, even his sense of self to become what he was now. What was a little more pain compared to that?

He fired up the blowtorch. Blue fire hissed out.

Yes, this was going to hurt.

Do it, the voice said. *Burn it off. It's not you.*

No, don't burn it off, another voice jumped in. *You can't erase the transformation because you're scared. We did this together.*

Two voices occupying his skull, both of whom believed they knew the path to survival.

You're weak. Just like you've always been. Burn it off before it burns you.

Look at what you've accomplished. The pentagram is part of that.

"No. Be quiet. Both of you."

He lowered the flame to his palm, winced at the sudden heat, and pulled away. The two voices hurled more arguments at each other, and then a third voice joined the fray. This one was more eloquent.

It won't hurt. You need to destroy the evidence. Escaping from jail isn't easy. Believe me.

And a fourth.

BURN IT. BURN EVERYTHING. THE HAND. THE FARM. THE EVIDENCE. START OVER.

The cacophony built, voices layering over each other until he couldn't distinguish one from another. His head felt like it might split open, spill all these fractured selves onto the shed floor where they could fight it out properly.

"Shut up! All of you! I'm going to go crazy!"

Like you're not crazy already.

Listen to yourself. Pathetic.

That's right. Keep the pentagram.

They didn't stop. If anything, his outburst had given them strength. The noise in his skull was unbearable, worse than screaming pigs at slaughter, worse than the Hutchins man's final wheeze. He couldn't listen to this, couldn't do this. He needed distance.

The truck keys were in his pocket. Yes. A drive. Get away from the farm, away from the pigs, away from the scene where all these selves were trying to tear each other apart. Maybe moving would quiet them, the way it quieted crying babies. Maybe the night air would blow some of them out the window.

He hurried out of the pig pen, still in the clothes he'd worn to slaughter two people, but he had no intention of changing. The air quieted the voices, and then he found his truck, slammed the door, and shut out the world.

But it couldn't shut out what was already inside with him.

HE HADN'T MEANT to drive toward the Hutchins house, but his hands had steered the wheel in that direction anyway. This must have been the compulsion the master talked about. Serial killers couldn't help but insert themselves into investigations, and he'd always thought any killer who did so was a fool. Now he was in the street he'd been in just a few hours ago, but it was awash with red and blue lights and a horde of gawkers outside the residence in question.

With the truck parked out of sight, he walked toward the commotion. Just another curious neighbor drawn by the circus. The voices in his head had quieted now, perhaps satiated by this pilgrimage to the scene of their triumph. The neighbors were wearing pajamas and robes, as if they didn't have the self-respect to dress themselves before indulging their morbid curiosity.

Not that he could get on his high horse, because his cargo pants and T-shirt were still wearing the blood of the victims, although he'd covered himself up with a long jacket he'd found in the truck. He was also reminded of the time he attended his mother's funeral in jeans and a T-shirt, but because he was a living victim, no one had the nerve to say anything.

How ironic it was that the police officer guarding the yellow tape was within spitting distance of the author of this chaos. The thrill sang in his veins, but he kept himself from showing anything other than feigned grief on his face. He wedged himself in between two clusters of neighbors and listened to their idle chatter, but it had devolved into hollow nothingness. He was late to the party, because it seemed they'd given up trading theories by now.

Shame. Perhaps this had been a bad idea. Now he needed to disappear without anyone noticing, which shouldn't be too difficult given the lack of streetlights around here.

He was already calculating his retreat to the back of the crowd when the front door of the house opened and two figures emerged.

Not police officers. Or at least, they weren't dressed as such.

They came down the pathway, close enough that he could make out their features in the strobing lights.

Two women. One middle-aged. One young, thirties maybe. Dark hair. Long. A bit too long for his liking. She was the kind of woman he never saw around here, the kind of woman who wouldn't look twice at him even when his clothes were caked in blood.

As they passed within arm's reach of where he stood, he

heard the older woman speak: "Come on, Frost. Let's go back to the precinct."

Frost.

His lips formed the word, but he didn't dare speak it aloud. The master's voice whispered caution. Be invisible.

The women got into a car, and a moment later, a van began reversing up the street. The officer cleared out the gawpers, telling them to get back to their homes because officers would need to come and interview all of them.

And that's when he made his escape, swept away by the exodus of neighbors.

Frost.

There was another piece of wisdom the master had gifted him with.

There was a great comfort in knowing your enemy's name.

THIRTY

It was after midnight, and Maya had spent the past hour staring at the theory she'd stamped on the whiteboard in her office.

She'd laid it all out for Devon in black and white.

Their unsub was not roleplaying as Ed Gein.

He was roleplaying as multiple serial killers.

Everything about the Teresa Morgan scene had been an homage to infamous murderer Ed Gein. The victim, the location, the method of murder, the postmortem mutilations, even the way he'd dressed. Maya had stuck a grainy printout of the original Gein victim's butchered torso next to the glossy photos of Teresa Morgan.

It was a perfect match, except for one thing.

Except for the pentagram on his hand.

That pentagram had absolutely nothing to do with Ed Gein, and that was the point.

Because the pentagram was the bridge that led to the next victim.

When the perp had killed Elaine and Cecil Hutchins, he'd been channeling a different serial killer. He'd been channeling Richard Ramirez.

Richard Ramirez, also known as the Night Stalker, had operated in California in 1985. Ramirez had been a violent, opportunistic killer who'd invaded homes and raped and killed whoever was unfortunate enough to be inside. He had no preferred victimology; men, women, and children were all fair game in Ramirez's book. He'd amassed a grand total of thirteen kills, and two of those thirteen had been an elderly couple who Ramirez had killed in their beds.

He'd killed them with a machete.

And once the deed was done, he'd left a message at the scene in lipstick.

A pentagram. Which he'd drawn on both the walls *and* the female victim's thigh.

Devon chose that moment to re-enter the office. She was mid-conversation with someone on the other end of her cell, and then she hung up and threw the phone on her desk. "Shit news. Riggs checked with all of the Hutchins' neighbors, and none of them saw anyone suspicious hanging around the street."

"Dammit."

"Three doorbell cams nearby, but they're all past the Hutchins house. The unsub wouldn't have stepped in front of them."

"Any strange cars?"

"No sightings. Have you figured out what the message means yet?"

Maya examined the veteran for any sign of mockery. What was the subtext behind Devon's sudden cooperation?

It felt weird that this woman was actually engaging with her theory instead of just shooting it down like a clay pigeon at a gun range, as she had done up until earlier today.

She couldn't hold the question back. "Wait. Do you actually believe any of this? My theory about the copycat killings?"

Devon's mouth twitched. "I believe in my own two eyes, and what my eyes saw was a message that said *Call me Fred*, so let's focus on that."

It irked Maya that Devon wouldn't admit it, but she was right. There was a time and place for everything, including ego feeding, and this wasn't it. "Fred. Do you really think our killer is stupid enough to give us his real name?"

"No. So we need to figure out what this message means."

"Maybe it *is* his real name but he goes by Freddy or Frederick or something. There are theories that the Zodiac left shortened versions of his real name in his ciphers."

"Don't remind me of the Zodiac. I spent one of my first years at the Bureau going through old evidence on that. It led nowhere because none of his ciphers made sense, and if it's the same here, then we might be looking in the wrong place entirely."

"Our killer wrote it in green lipstick too. Richard Ramirez wrote it in red."

Devon collapsed into a chair and stared at Maya's whiteboard ramblings. "Maybe green was all he could find in their house."

"Devon, come on. A guy as meticulous as this? Nothing is an accident. Besides, I checked Elaine's makeup drawer before we left, and there was no green lipstick in there."

"First of all, you shouldn't be touching things at an active crime scene. Second of all, it just means he took the lipstick with him when he left. He took Teresa Morgan's cell, so we know he has no problem taking evidence."

"Maybe."

"So what's it mean?"

"Well, the pentagram at the first scene was the hint that led to the second scene."

"So he's leaving breadcrumbs. He's telling us where he's going to strike next."

"It seems so, but why would he do that?" asked Maya.

"Because it's a game he's playing. Serial killers get a thrill from fooling the cops. Ego is the second most common driving force after sex, and we know our guy isn't a lust killer. He's doing this out of insecurity because he thinks that outsmarting the police will give him the sense of power he can't get anywhere else."

Maya wrestled with the profile. She tried to pull everything that she knew about this unsub and throw it into a single pile. She grabbed the marker pen and attacked the whiteboard once more.

"So our guy studies serial killers and is maybe even obsessed with them. He's at least ten years younger than Teresa Morgan, according to the mortician, so he could be anything from 20 to 48. He's probably white, doesn't seem to have a rap sheet, and he's able to pivot between M.O.s on a whim."

"Yeah, and that takes some commitment. Changing your M.O. so drastically on the second murder is practically unheard of."

"He's patient, organized, capable of subduing alive victims. The pentagram tattoo suggests dedication, because you don't carve symbols into your own flesh on a whim. It shows he's willing to leave evidence too, which means either arrogance or stupidity. Given the precision, it's probably arrogance."

"He took the cell phone and lipstick as a forensic countermeasure, but they might have been trophies too."

"Gein and Ramirez are polar opposites in terms of psychopathology too. Gein was a sheltered mommy's boy. Ramirez was driven by rage. Their crimes addressed different psychological needs. What kind of person needs to embody multiple murderers?"

Devon said, "Someone who can't settle on a single identity because his own personality is too broken to sustain."

Maya's head pounded like someone was using her skull as a drum kit. She needed sleep, needed food that wasn't vending machine garbage, needed this bastard to make a mistake before he killed again.

"Frost, I have a question," Devon continued. She'd stripped her voice of the professional tone she'd kept up until now.

"Go ahead."

Devon's lips clamped shut, and if Maya didn't know better, she'd have thought that Devon looked nervous. "No. It doesn't matter."

"No, please. Ask anything."

"All right. I guess my question is... how do you know all of this?"

The question tripped her up. "Know what?"

"Criminal psychology. Human psychology. You worked in Intelligence, and you studied criminal science, right?"

"Yes. Data analytics."

"So... neither of those involve behavioral profiling. Where'd you learn all of this shit? Where did you even find time?"

It was an odd question, Maya thought, but a necessary one. She didn't know that Devon cared so much, but she appreciated the curiosity in her background.

"I could show you, but I need something before I can do that."

Devon stood up. "Is it a drink? Because I'm dying for a whiskey. What's say we hit that bar opposite Teresa's store?"

Maya checked the time. Ten past midnight. "Isn't it a bit late?"

"No." Devon grabbed her bag. "It's never too late. So what do you need?"

"Are you sure you want me to tell you? It's kind of... weird."

"Try me."

"OK." Maya hesitated, but if she and Devon were going to be partners, she had to lay it all out. "I need a deck of cards."

THIRTY-ONE

Maya didn't have a deck of cards on her, and neither did the precinct, but the Black Horse Tavern might, and it was right across from Teresa Morgan's hardware store, which meant they could kill two birds with one stone: get Devon her whiskey and maybe find Maya the tools she needed to explain her unusual education.

Even at half past midnight on a Saturday, the place was pretty dead. Only one table showed signs of life, and there Maya saw three men hunched around half-empty beer glasses. They looked up when Maya and Devon walked in, whispered something between themselves, then went back to their own business. One of them lit up a cigarette indoors, something that could get a person arrested in D.C.

Devon headed straight for the bar while Maya hung back, taking in the sight of Teresa Morgan's darkened storefront through the grimy window. Crime scene tape still crisscrossed the entrance, and knowing what had happened in there just yesterday churned her stomach.

"Frost, what are you having?"

Maya headed over to the bar. The bartender was a sour-faced old woman who looked like she'd rather be anywhere else. "Coke, please."

"And a whiskey and Coke."

"No whiskey," Maya said, but Devon put a hand on her shoulder.

"It's Saturday night. You're having something stronger than Coke."

Was this unprofessional? Maya guessed not, because if Devon was doing it, it must be fine. "All right, but I'm no drinker."

"You will be."

The bartender said, "Take a seat. I'll bring them over."

"Thanks. You don't have a deck of cards back there, do you?" Devon asked.

"Cards? No. But Billy Big Mouth over there probably does." The bartender nodded at the three men, and Maya instinctively knew which one was Billy Big Mouth. Wide, shaved head, and what Maya would have called noncommittal facial hair. He'd trimmed parts of it and was left with some kind of handlebar-soul patch hybrid. He had two heavy gold earrings in both ears.

Devon nudged her. "Go on. You've got me invested. We're not leaving here until you've explained what the hell you're talking about."

Maya approached their table, feeling like she was walking up to a pack of wild dogs that would probably start growling any minute. They all eyeballed her for a beat too long, as if they were trying to figure out if she was trouble or entertainment. "Sorry to bother you, guys. The bartender said you might have a deck of cards on you."

The man who Maya assumed was Billy necked the last of his drink, then sized her up. "You're not from around here."

"I never said I was."

Devon appeared by her side, and it was pretty easy to conclude that they weren't welcome here.

"Cops? Come to find out who killed Teresa. Is that right?"

"FBI, but close enough."

"FBI, huh? A real woman, Teresa. Salt of the earth. We've got some sicko running around our town, killing our best people, so what are you doing about it?"

"Everything we can, sir."

Billy laughed. "Like drinking and playing cards? Yeah, seems like it."

Devon stepped in. "It's not like that. We assure you we're doing everything in our power to bring this perp to justice. We came here just for a moment, then we'll be straight back on the case."

"I'll believe it when I see it." Billy pulled out an old, worn deck of cards from his pocket and slapped it on the table. "Why do the cops need the feds here anyway? They not man enough to find this freak themselves?"

"We approach the investigation from a different angle," Devon said. "We're just here to assist them."

Billy took the cards out of the box and started dealing them on the table into three piles, one for him and two for his pals. "Angle? What angle's that then? Some of your mystic mumbo jumbo, like off those TV shows? How you can tell what toothpaste a guy uses from just looking at him?"

Maya said, "Yeah. I can see a mile off that you don't use any toothpaste."

Billy's pals laughed, and Billy himself had the decency to grin, but it faded fast. "Yeah, so I got bad teeth. You're gonna have to do better than that. If you ask me, cops are just pretending to do something by calling in the feds. Makes everyone feel better, but there's still a wacko out there."

His buddies nodded along, emboldened by their leader's hostility. A thinner one with glasses leaned forward. "My cousin's a cop in Jacksonville. Says half the time you FBI types come in, talk a bunch of fancy crap, then leave without solving nothing."

"Exactly, Ken. Mumbo jumbo."

Maya recognized Billy's type. He was a local who felt ownership over any tragedy that befell his community, and he needed someone to blame for such a violation. He fanned out his five cards sloppily and stared at the hand he'd dealt himself. He wiggled his empty beer glass at the bartender. Devon touched her wrist, as if to say *let's go,* but Maya wasn't ready. This was her moment, and she had something to say.

"You. Billy. That's your name, right?"

"Yeah. Is that the best you got?"

"You're right to be angry, because your father left when you were a kid. Your dad was a military man, Navy I assume. You've seen him a few times since, but you're not military yourself, even though you wanted to be. Those earrings are solid gold. An old sailor's tradition, so if you died at sea your pals could sell the earrings to pay for your funeral. That's your subconscious link to your dad."

Billy's eyes widened. He glanced at his pals, then back to Maya. "Oh yeah?"

"You've been angry at authority figures ever since, but you still respect them enough to want their approval. That's why you're testing us. You want us to prove we're worth respecting. Your handlebar moustache is new, maybe a few weeks. You grew it after your girlfriend left. Trying to reinvent yourself, show everyone you don't need her. But you keep touching it when you're nervous, which means you're not sure it suits you."

Mr. Big Mouth gave nothing away, and Maya had to hand it to him for remaining so stoic. "You've got paint under your fingernails. House painter, self-employed. Good work when you can get it but seasonal. You've got a gambling problem, and you're angry about Teresa's death because you knew her personally. She extended credit when the hardware chains wouldn't. Oh, and the cards in your hand are the king of hearts, the queen of clubs, the three of spades, the four of hearts, and the nine of diamonds. Oh, and your little friend Ken over there has the two aces. And if I'm not mistaken, two jacks and the ten of clubs."

Billy gawked at the cards in his hand, and the other two men threw their cards back on the deck. Maya reached across the table, picked one up, and displayed it. "Ace of spades. See how there's a crimp in the bottom right? That's called a breather crimp. Billy puts them there so he can tell which cards are the aces from the back. Classic gambler trick, right, Billy?"

The man stared at her like she'd just pulled a rabbit out of his ass. He had the expression of a man who'd been caught red-handed but wasn't about to admit it in front of his buddies. He checked his cards again, then threw them on the pile. "Well, God damn. You even got the order right."

"How'd you do that?" asked Ken. "Some mind reading business?"

Maya displayed the ace again, then took it into her other hand. When she opened her hand, the card had vanished. Then she reached behind the silent man's ear and flicked it back into full view.

"No such as thing as mind reading, and anyone who tells you otherwise is talking out of their ass."

———

"MAGIC?" Devon asked.

They'd found a table on the other side of the room, away from Billy Big Mouth and his crew. Maya had left the cards with them because she hoped she'd proven her proficiency already. "Yeah, magic."

"How'd you read that guy like that? I caught the paint under the fingernails and the nervous tics, but not much else." Devon drank her whiskey faster than Maya had ever seen anyone drink anything. If she didn't know better, she'd think Devon was a functioning alcoholic.

"Easy. The earrings were pure Navy, but someone who'd been in the Navy wouldn't treat feds like that. I read online that this place was a hub for military folks in the eighties, about which time Billy would have been about ten. Probability did the rest. The moustache was another statistical likelihood. What kind of man in his fifties with a beer gut changes his appearance? One who's trying to impress someone or prove he's better off without someone. If he *was* with someone, he probably wouldn't be drinking and gambling with two other middle-aged guys in a dead bar on Saturday night."

Devon nodded. "I should have seen this. What about the gambling problem?"

"Only two types of people carry decks of cards with them. Magicians and gamblers. If he was a magician, he'd have better dexterity. Ergo, he's a gambler."

"And the house painting?"

Maya drank her whiskey and Coke, which was akin to drinking battery acid in her book. They must have put some strong liquor in there. She leaned in and said, "I saw his work van parked outside. It said *Billy Woodsworth, painter and decorator*. Sometimes the solution is so obvious you just look right past it."

"Brilliant," Devon laughed. "Here I was thinking you were some kind of savant. What about the cards?"

Maya looked back across the room, then to her partner. She whispered, "I can't tell you that secret."

"Oh, come on. Why not?"

"Because it's..." Maya trailed off. What was it? A violation of the magician's code? Such a stupid trick that revealing it might undo some of this mystique she was building? Yes, it was both of those, but the method was also so ridiculous that keeping it secret felt equally as pathetic too. "OK, but don't tell anyone."

"Scout's honor."

Maya picked up Devon's empty glass. She held it to the light. "Look closely. What do you see?"

Her partner squinted. "I see myself."

Maya shrugged. "There you go."

It took Devon a second, but then the magic clicked into place. She snapped her head back up and laughed. "Dammit. The reflection from his beer glass."

She felt her cheeks flush red. Whether it was from embarrassment or alcohol, she didn't know. "Yup. I got lucky with the angles and just ran with it."

"How'd this start? I need to know. I've always had a love-hate relationship with magic."

"Have you?"

"Yeah. David Copperfield. Me and him... had a thing."

Maya nearly choked on her drink. "What? Seriously?"

"Seriously. It was twenty-five years ago, though. He was doing some corporate show in D.C., but there was a terrorist threat on the building the same day. I was part of the team that got dispatched there. I met Copperfield and, well..."

"What about the terrorist threat?"

"The threat was a hoax, but there were definitely a few explosions."

Maya tried to reconcile this information with everything she knew about Devon, as little as that might be. The no-nonsense profiler who'd made her fetch coffee and the world's greatest illusionist. If someone had have asked Maya to list a million people Devon might have slept with, Copper-field wouldn't have made the cut.

"You're messing with me," she said.

"God's honest truth. Then the next morning—poof. Vanished. Left a rose behind and everything."

The whiskey was definitely hitting her now, because she

was sure this was all some kind of surreal dream. Perhaps everything, from Vernon cornering her outside the shooting range to Devon's magical confession, was all a dream. "This is going to take me a few days to process."

"Sure, so in the meantime, tell me how it started for you."

Maya lifted her glass and downed the rest of her whiskey and Coke in one burning gulp. The alcohol scorched its way down her throat, and she welcomed the pain. It was easier than the ache that came with this particular memory.

"I was about five, and I found a deck of cards in my mom's drawer. Mom taught me this simple trick where you make a card rise up without touching it. That was it."

"Gotta start somewhere," Devon said. "That's it?"

"Well, sort of. I had a sister. Abigail. Two years older than me. One night we were in bed, and I had the top bunk that night because I'd won some award at school. We were asleep, but I woke up in the middle of the night, which I never did."

Devon stayed quiet.

"I heard someone outside the room. I thought maybe it was Mom or Dad, but you know how you can tell? You can feel the difference in their size, how they move?"

"Definitely."

"Well, a figure snuck into our room, and I just lay there terrified underneath my blanket. I couldn't see much through the slats on the bed, but I remember seeing a black jacket and a pale hand. I think I heard a man's voice, but I can't be sure. And I just lay there, paralyzed, too terrified to do anything. I didn't scream or run or anything. I just... let it happen."

Devon's expression had lost all of its earlier humor. "Let what happen?"

"I don't know. The next thing I remember is standing outside the bedroom in the middle of the night. Mom and Dad were in hysterics, and Abigail was... gone. They were screaming at two police officers, *People don't just disappear.* But now I know that they do. People do just disappear."

They both fell silent, and Maya wondered if she hadn't crossed a line blurting all of this out. She'd never spoken it to anyone before, at least outside of a police station. By this point, she should have had tears in her eyes, but she'd spent twenty-five years crying over this in solitude, so that well had dried up long ago.

"Jesus, Frost. I'm sorry. I didn't mean to pry. If I'd have known..."

"No one's seen or heard from Abby since. Two months after that, my mom's body washed up on the shore of the Nashua River. She'd thrown herself into freezing waters. Couldn't handle the heartache."

Devon rubbed her temples. "Shit. I'm sorry."

"And the worst part was that it was all because of magic. If I hadn't done that trick in school, I'd have never been in the top bunk. I know now that whoever abducted Abby probably did it because the bottom bunk was easier to reach. It should have been me in there. I should have been the one they took. So I kept learning magic because I always thought that if I got good enough, I could figure out the conclusion."

"The conclusion?"

"Making something disappear isn't enough. You always have to bring it back. I kept doing magic, and it taught me about human psychology and cold reading, and that obsession spread to criminals. I studied everything I could and, well..."

"That's why you're here now."

"That's why I'm here now. I haven't given up on finding my sister, and I never will."

THIRTY-TWO

MAYA HIT THE PAVEMENT OUTSIDE THE BLACK HORSE Tavern, and the night air slapped the intoxication right out of her.

God, had she said too much to Devon in there? Was her story now going to make its way around HQ and thus join the rumor mill she'd so desperately tried to avoid? *Poor Frost. Did you hear about her sister? No wonder she's so obsessed with missing persons.*

"Motel time," Devon said, "then we'll start fresh tomorrow."

"Actually, I might head back to the precinct for a minute. I've got some thoughts I need to get down, and I can't sleep anyway."

"It's one in the morning, Frost."

"Every hour might as well be rush hour when you've got insomnia. You go to the motel. I'll walk to the precinct. It's only fifteen minutes away, and I can get a lift back to the motel from one of the officers."

"If you insist."

"Are you all right to drive?"

"I've only had one."

"It was a double," Maya said.

"OK, two. I'm still within my limit. Don't stay up too late, and be careful. There's a killer roaming these streets."

Maya saluted her goodbye, then headed toward the precinct. Before she'd gone ten steps, she found herself standing in front of Teresa Morgan's hardware store. The crime scene tape formed Xs across the door and windows, like the place had been marked for demolition. The neon CLOSED sign was dark and would stay dark forever now.

She was halfway up the street when a battered old truck rumbled past her. A screech of brakes followed, and then the truck reversed back up at speed. Maya made eye contact with the driver, and she knew those eyes. He rolled the window down, turned down his music, and poked his head through.

"Maya?"

"Alfie. What are you doing here?"

"I could ask you the same thing."

She hadn't seen the guy since yesterday. Where had he been hiding? Maya wanted to ask, but she didn't want to come off as too interested. Becky had warned her against that, but then again, Becky was a perpetually single drama queen. Don't ask a vegetarian where the best steakhouse is, her dad had always said.

"I've been at the station. My sleeping pattern's been screwed up since yesterday, so the sheriff's letting me work odd hours. Where've you been?"

"The Black Horse Tavern with Devon. She insisted I drink. Do you know about the... development?"

"Yeah, the sheriff filled me in. Terrible business. Are you heading home for the night?"

"No, I was going to hit the station. The night's still young."

Alfie checked his watch. "It's one a.m. You want to grab a coffee to keep you alert?"

Maya was no expert in the art of flirting or even an amateur. She'd missed signs in the past—few as they'd been—that even a child would have picked up on, and a part of her was convinced that she was just born without that part of the brain. She couldn't have told if a guy was into her even if they had it tattooed on their foreheads.

Or maybe not. Because some unchartered, alien region of her cerebral cortex lit up when Alfie said those words, because he was asking to spend time with her outside of the office, and he was framing it as though he was helping her out.

"A coffee? Now? Aren't all the cafés shut?"

"Yeah, but my place is open all night."

"Your place? Wouldn't that be weird?"

Alfie shrugged. "Yeah, but a woman was cut in half. In this very street, actually. Compared to that, nothing is weird."

Maya found herself weighing options that shouldn't need weighing. Going to a near-stranger's apartment at one a.m. while a killer roamed free probably violated several protocols, both professional and personal. But then again, she'd already broken protocol by drinking with Devon, by sharing her deepest trauma with someone she'd known for two days.

Maybe it was the whiskey talking, but she had to admit that she kind of liked this guy. He looked at her like she was someone worth reversing a truck for at stupid o'clock in the morning. When was the last time someone had looked at her like that? When was the last time she'd even noticed? She didn't like Alfie in some grand romantic way, but in the simple way of wanting to know what his house looked like, what kind of coffee he made, what he thought about when he wasn't enhancing CCTV footage of murders.

"Do you live far?"

"Nope. Just in Whitechapel Avenue, five minutes away."

"Deal," said Maya.

"You sure?" Alfie asked. "I don't want you thinking I'm some creep, because I'm not."

"I'm sure." And oddly enough, she was.

THIRTY-THREE

Alfie's front room was nothing like what Maya expected from someone who called their office *the crypt*. It was warm and lived in, and as she scanned the walls, she found that Alfie Kustka was indeed full of surprises.

He brought her a drink and set it down on the coffee table in front of them. "I didn't know how you like it, so I just guessed."

"Initiative. I like it."

Alfie sat at the other end of the couch, but they both had their legs angled toward the middle. Close enough to touch, should the opportunity arise, but Maya put an end to that thought immediately. What kind of idiot got involved with someone who lived a thousand miles away?

You only have to get involved for one night, Becky's phantom voice said.

No. That had never been Maya's style, and she wasn't about to break the habit of a lifetime, not when she was here to do a job and nothing more.

"I heard about the murders tonight. Riggs told me about them, but he spared me the grim details."

"Probably for the best. It was an awful scene."

"Yeah. I didn't know the couple, but some of the guys at the office did."

Over in the corner, Maya caught sight of a football helmet in a shadow box. Beside it was a trophy. She gestured at it and said, "Where'd you get a football trophy from?"

"Football. Where else?"

"You played football?"

"Yeah. Surprised?"

"A little. You don't... look like a football player."

Alfie laughed. "Yup, people see the crap in my office and think I've never been outside, but you'd be surprised. I played for Florida State a long time ago. NCAA Division I. You a fan?"

Maya wasn't clued up on football in the slightest, but she respected anyone with a passion. Even if they were passionate about the most boring thing in the world, Maya was happy to let them talk about it until their throats went raw. "I don't know the first thing about football, other than it's on Monday nights, the same time as wrestling."

"Accurate enough."

"Were you any good?"

"I was pretty good, until I wasn't. Got a concussion when I was nineteen, and the doctors said if I took another hit like that I'd go senile in a few years. So I had to retire, but I always keep this on me." Alfie spread his hands knuckles-up and displayed a large gold ring with garnets forming the NCAA logo. "Got this in my sophomore year. We went to the Orange Bowl."

"Holy moly, look at the size of that thing."

"It's a beast for sure. Most guys keep their rings locked away safe, but I keep it on me, just to remind me that I got knocked down once but I got back up again."

Maya inspected it again. It must have been solid gold, with the initials and a football engraved on the face. God knew how much the thing was worth. "If you'd have asked me to list a million things you might be into, I'd never have guessed football."

"I guess people can surprise you."

She tried her coffee. It was a solid eight out of ten. "I'm sorry you had to retire. I guess pro football beats coding any day of the week."

"Yup, but I never wanted to be one of those peaked-in-high-school kind of guys, so I try not to bring it up too much. Aside from the ring, obviously. I don't want people to think I'm a one-hit wonder."

"That's one more hit than most people get. Embrace it."

"What about you? You're based in D.C.?"

"Oh yeah. Worst place on Earth. You ever been?"

"Closest I've been to Washington is Washington State." Alfie scratched his stubble. "Which I now realize is about two thousand miles away from D.C., so ignore me, ha."

"Yeah, I hear that a lot. It's amazing the amount of Americans who don't know they're two different places."

Alfie clicked his fingers. "I forgot for a second too. D.C. is FBI, CIA, White House. Washington is Space Needle, Green River, Seahawks. Got it."

Maya's body went rigid, like Alfie's comment had somehow electrocuted her. The coffee mug tilted in her hands, the liquid sloshing dangerously close to the rim, but she paid it no attention. Her entire nervous system had just been hijacked by two words that shouldn't have meant anything but somehow meant everything.

"Hold on. Say that again."

"What? The Seahawks? Great defense, terrible offense. Last season, though—"

"No, not that. The thing before that."

Alfie blinked, and she could practically see him rewinding the conversation in his head, trying to figure out what invisible tripwire he'd just stepped on. "The Green River? It's that... long river. It's not really green, though. It's just called that."

Maya placed her coffee down in a frenzy, then jumped to her feet. The adrenaline was singing now, and it was all because of Alfie and his bad geographical knowledge. "Alfie, I'm sorry, but I have to go. I just realized something. Something big."

Alfie stared at her like she was speaking in tongues, then rose off the sofa. "Sure, but... did I say something? Sorry, I didn't mean to—"

"No. It's not that. Trust me."

"Oh. Do you want a lift? It's too late to be walking."

"Yes, please. I need to get to the precinct."

"All right, let me grab my keys."

Alfie didn't know it, but he might have just helped her catch a serial killer.

Because she suddenly knew who this mysterious Fred was.

THIRTY-FOUR

"Frost, you alive?"

Maya jerked awake with a body full of aches and a head full of questions. She was in a chair in the office, and she could no longer feel her arms or legs. "Devon? Is that you?"

"Who else would it be? You look like hell, by the way."

She scrambled to something resembling decency as fragments of the previous night drifted back. The Hutchins couple sprawled in their bed. Green lipstick on dead flesh. CALL ME FRED. Billy Big Mouth and his marked cards. David Copperfield—or did she imagine that part? That seemed too weird to be true, but she ran with it anyway. Spilling her story about her sister and mom to Devon, and then—Alfie's apartment? What had happened after that?

She blinked herself back to reality, and her late-night scrawlings on the whiteboard gave her the answer.

Of course. She knew who Fred was.

"The Green River," she blurted out.

"What? Did you sleep in that chair all night?"

"Yes I did, but listen to me." Maya jumped out of her seat and ran over to the whiteboard. "You see this? This is what I was doing all last night. I figured it out. Or at least I think I did."

Devon raised an eyebrow. "Frost, that just says *Green River* and a bunch of names I don't recognize. What's Diva Escorts? Florida Angels? Babylon Girls? You didn't call a sex agency, did you?"

Now Maya remembered. "Yeah I did. I called a ton of them."

"We get ninety dollars a day for allowance, and that doesn't include gigolos. Christ, you only had one whiskey. You wouldn't last an hour at our Christmas parties."

"Devon, seriously, listen to me. I know where our killer is going to strike next."

Her partner sat in the same chair Maya had been sleeping in for God knows how long. She stole a glance at the clock—eight a.m. She'd gotten four hours sleep at most.

Devon said, "All right, I'm listening. Tell me everything."

"Our unsub linked the Gein murder to the Ramirez via the pentagram on his hand, right? And he purposely showed us that pentagram to give us a clue where to head next. But we weren't fast enough."

"Correct."

"So his second message—*Call me Fred* in green lipstick— is the clue we need to decipher for the third scene. Only there are no infamous American serial killers named Fred or Frederick or Freddy. At least on the level of Ed Gein or Richard Ramirez. There's Fred West, but he's British, and his crimes don't track with what we're dealing with."

"Correct again."

"And we also know that he's not going to straight-up give us his name—and he hasn't. Neither did another serial killer." Maya slapped the mugshot she'd printed out. "This guy. Gary Ridgway."

"The Green River Killer."

"Exactly. The most prolific serial killer in American history, at least by body count. Forty-nine confirmed kills, all of them sex workers, most of them strangled and left by the Green River in Washington State. Our unsub left us a message in green for a reason. That was the link."

Devon shifted from interested to skeptical in a heartbeat. "That's it? Because of green text? I don't want to accuse you of leaping here, Frost, but you might be leaping. Green could mean anything. Money, nature, jealousy."

"No, there's more than that. Look at this." Maya grabbed a crumpled printout from the desk and smoothed it out. The image was barely legible, but she'd transcribed everything she needed to below it. "The Green River Killer sent *one* letter to the press during his whole reign, and that reign lasted twenty years. One message to a Seattle newspaper in 1984. He never did interviews, never called in tips, never played games with the press like some killers do. Just this one rambling, paranoid letter."

"Which said what?"

Maya cleared her throat and began reading from the printout. "*What you need to know about the green river man. Don't throw away. First one broken and dislocate arm. Why? One placed in river had stone.* It goes on like this for forty points. Paranoid rambling about trucks and rings and all sorts of crap. But then, at the very end, after all this incoherent bullshit, he writes: *There was a book lift at Denny's, I got this out of it. It belongs to a cop. Call me Fred.*" Maya pointed to the line on the transcription.

Devon leaned forward, suddenly more interested, it seemed. "He signed it *Call me Fred*?"

"Those exact words. Barely anyone knows about this letter. It's obscure knowledge, and we know our unsub is a serial killer obsessive. The green text, the message. It all connects. Which means—"

"Our next victim is going to be a sex worker."

Maya went back to the board. "That's why I spent all of last night calling up every escort agency I could find in the area and warning them to keep their girls off the streets for as long as they could."

"Did any of them listen?"

"Some did, some didn't. Some had heard about Teresa's murder, so they believed me. Some just thought I was a religious nut. The problem we've got is that he could go for an independent worker, and there are *lots* of them around here, apparently."

"Then we need to get everyone in the precinct on it. We need to warn every single one of them."

"I thought that too, but there's another thing. Ridgway *killed* all of his victims on the banks of the Green River. He didn't just dump the bodies there. If our guy keeps things historically accurate, he'll do exactly the same, which means he'll have a specific killing ground. We just need eyes on every inch of that ground."

Devon bit her lip. "Which is? The Green River's about three thousand miles from here."

"Yeah, but the Liles River isn't. And guess what Ridgway's last victim was named?"

"What?"

Maya grabbed another printout. It showed the headshots of all of Ridgway's forty-nine victims. She pointed to the last one. "Tammie Liles."

Devon jumped out of her chair like she'd been shot from a catapult. "Dammit, Frost, good find! You might have just out-thought this asshole, and now we just need to nab the son of a bitch. We'll get a patrol on the river ASAP, and then we'll notify every escort worker in the damn state to be on alert. We'll tell them to let us know if they get any clients wanting to meet by the Liles River, and then we ambush him. Boom, done, back in D.C. by morning."

Maya's entire nervous system was on fire because if fortune was in her favor, she might have just outsmarted a game-playing psychopath. She kept her breathing steady because Devon was already operating at about eleven on a scale of ten, and someone needed to be the calm in the center of this particular hurricane.

"Yeah. He's already killed twice in two days, so if the pattern holds, he'll kill the next one tonight."

"He killed Teresa around six, the Hutchins around ten. So if we take the average, we've got around twelve hours, and that's not long at all."

"Then we better get started. Let's go ruin this bastard's day."

THIRTY-FIVE

Maya was thankful for the modern phenomenon of twenty-four-hour escort agencies because it meant she and Devon were able to contact the majority of them before midday. The last one on her list was Velvet Escorts, who'd put the phone down on her once already. She tried again.

"Velvet Escorts, how can I help you?" the receptionist asked.

"Hi, my name's Agent Frost with the Fernandina police. We believe one of your workers might be…"

"Everything is above board here, ma'am. Our ladies are date companions, not sex workers."

Frustration amplified her tone. "We don't care about your agency. There's someone out there intending to harm sex… date companions. I need you to listen to me."

The receptionist paused. "I'm listening."

"Thank you," Maya replied. "We have credible information that suggests a man is targeting sex workers along the Liles River. I'm urging every agency, including yours, to advise your employees to be extremely cautious, particularly with any bookings near the river."

"Near the river?" the receptionist asked. "How do you mean?"

Maya considered her verbiage, but she quickly decided that a direct approach would get better results. "Look, we know what goes on between your date companions and their clients. We're the police. Believe us, we know. If you get any requests for a girl to meet someone along the Liles River—particularly if the man requests meeting up in his vehicle—then I want you to call us immediately."

The receptionist went silent. Maya could hear her hesitation down the phone line. "And if such an incident takes place, our agency would not be in trouble?"

"None at all. Such a client would be a first-timer. He wouldn't be a regular. He'd contact you by phone, not email. He'd be reluctant to hand over any personal details, and any details he would give would be a lie. He'd hire a brunette, early to mid-twenties. That's as much information as I can give."

The receptionist mumbled something, then said, "All right, Detective. I understand the urgency. But I need you to assure me that the safety of our companions comes first, and they won't be subjected to any police interrogation if they're brought into this."

Maya replied firmly, "Their safety is our number one priority. We'll do everything we can to protect them and treat them with respect. But we need your cooperation. If this man contacts you or if you think he's already booked one of your companions, you must let us know immediately."

"I will. Thank you," the receptionist said.

"You too." Maya hung up. Twenty-four agencies informed, two that were uncontactable until the later hours. She made a note to call them as soon as the clock struck six p.m.

Devon pushed open the door with her cell pressed to her ear. She ended her call and said, "Bad news first. Forensic report from the Hutchins scene is minimal. Couple of cloth fibers, could belong to anything. No hair samples, no bloody footprints."

Maya didn't let the disappointment get to her. In a way, she was pleased that the scene matched the first one because it meant the man was consistent. Consistency was easier to predict, and with such a complete lack of a concrete M.O., a little uniformity meant that any later mistakes would stand out. She just hoped they wouldn't need to reach that point.

"Thank you," she said.

"That's not all. I've managed to secure us a patrol along the riverbank. Three cars, unmarked, plain clothes guys, with me and you in a car each too. If our agencies slip up, or if he hires an independent girl, the closest we've got to catching him is a car patrol. You'll have to do the math on that one, though."

"Math in progress," Maya said. She pulled up a map of the Liles River on her laptop. "The river snakes through the eastern edge of Fernandina Beach for about eight miles before it hits marshland and bleeds into the Amelia River. About one mile of it is undeveloped land."

"That's a lot of ground to cover."

"Yeah. Eight miles of river, five cars if me and you take one each. But we can't see a mile and a half of riverbank each in the dark. We're going to need to keep moving if we want to cover every inch of the riverbank."

"We better hope our unsub isn't a car guy, because if he notices the same makes and models rotating past, he's going to clock us."

Maya took a deep breath. It was a big risk, but she wasn't about to lose hope easily. "Yeah, and by the looks of it, there's some real woodland along here. Dense areas. That was the kind of places that the Green River Killer hit, so we should prioritize those."

"Five cars it is," Devon said. "We should head out about what, six p.m.?"

"Yeah. I imagine we'll be sitting around a while, but we want to be there before him. Get some guys patrolling there right now, too. I doubt he'll strike in the daylight, but we need to be sure. Should we use a helicopter?"

"No. Too flashy. It'll spook him. I'm gonna go liaise with Riggs." Devon spun, then turned back at the door. "By the way, Frost?"

"Yeah?"

"You're good at this. Keep it up."

Four words. They probably took Devon half a second to say them, and she probably didn't even think about the effect they'd have.

Two days ago, Devon had called her the rookie, tested her, dismissed her resume, and made her prove she belonged on this case. And now Devon was letting her run point on the strategy, trusting her analysis, and treating her like an actual equal instead of a data analyst cosplaying as a field agent.

Maya wanted to do this right. She wanted to make the

calls that mattered and be standing there when they cuffed this bastard. She wanted Devon to look at her the way Vernon had looked at her in the Cuckoo Oak and think, *Yeah, I made the right choice.*

It was the same feeling she used to get as a kid, practicing card tricks in the bathroom mirror for hours until her fingers cramped. Her mother would be in the living room, half-drunk, and Maya would burst in with a new trick, desperate to make her smile and pull off a miracle so her mother would forget about Abigail, just for a second, and remember she still had another daughter.

It never worked.

And so Maya had stopped performing for her after a while.

But here she was again, trying to impress someone who probably didn't need impressing. Someone who'd already forgotten she'd said anything at all.

Keep it up, Devon had said.

And this time, she intended to.

THIRTY-SIX

HE'D SEEN HER.

Frost.

She'd come out of the old couple's house, gotten in the car, and driven back to the police station. He'd followed her, and then he'd waited outside the police station like some coward on the verge of handing himself in. It was funny, he thought. He'd been fifty feet away from a building that, if he'd have entered, he'd never have left. He could have gone in, asked to use the bathroom, and they probably would have let him. Then he'd have walked back out, invisible as ever.

Nobody ever looked at him twice. The master had taught him to embrace that. Dress like every other nobody in North Florida—work boots, Carhartt jacket, trucker cap with some bass fishing logo, and you were wallpaper just like everybody else. His mother had told him he had a forgettable face, and she'd meant it as an insult, the same way she'd meant everything. But it turned out to be the greatest gift she'd ever given him.

Because Frost had seen him too when she'd came out of the house. Almost certainly. Maybe she didn't register the particulars of his appearance, but her eyeballs had met his, and they'd shared a moment that came with two people being in the same place at the same time. He'd stayed outside the police station for hours, and then he'd seen Frost come out again. She'd traveled west toward the water, and he'd followed her to Black Horse Tavern, right opposite the old woman's store. He'd watched them go inside and waited again.

His mother's voice: *What are you doing, boy? You're gonna get caught sitting here like some idiot.*

His father's voice: *Should've drowned you when you were born. Knew you were wrong soon as I saw you.*

They were in there for over an hour. When Frost came out, she was with her partner. Walked like she'd had a couple beers but wasn't drunk. He heard them talk, heard their voices. They split up, and then Frost made it about half a block before someone picked her up.

Just like that.

The fact that Frost reminded him of a streetwalker wasn't lost on him, especially with what he had planned this evening. But that was for later. Now was for reflection.

The spare room in the farmhouse had never been meant for this, but then again, nothing about his life had gone according to plan. It used to be where his mother kept her sewing machine and boxes of fabric that she'd never touch.

Now it was his trophy room.

The denim jacket hanging on a makeshift mannequin had belonged to Richard Ramirez. Not during the killings, because such an item would have been impossible to obtain, but from his time in San Quentin. A guard had smuggled it out after Ramirez died, then sold it to a collector, who'd eventually sold it to him. When he wore it, he could feel the Night Stalker's rage seeping through the fabric into his skin.

Next to it, in a small glass case he'd bought from a hobby shop, were three bent nails. The seller claimed they came from Ed Gein's farmhouse demolition in 1958. Four inches long, rusted to hell, probably held up some innocuous piece of siding. But maybe, in a perfect world, they'd been part of the workshop where Gein had done his real work.

The Gary Ridgway piece had been the hardest to find. It was a Kenworth truck key, supposedly from the vehicle Ridgway had driven during his killing years. The metal was worn smooth where a thumb would rest. How many times had Ridgway turned that key after leaving a body by the river? How many times had he driven home to his wife and kid to play the part of the suburban dad?

There were other items too, but from more obscure names. Artwork by Jeremy Jones, letters from Arthur Shawcross. He even had some earwax that Herbert Mullin had kindly mailed to him, unsolicited. As disgusting as such an act was, that was the moment that he knew these items were coming to him of their own free will. He was no longer seeking them out. They were seeking *him* out, and ever since then, he knew that the past two days had been inevitable.

As he stared at the Green River Killer's personal relic, he mentally went through tonight's plan, if it could be termed that. Because the thing about Ridgway that nobody understood, that all the documentaries got wrong, was that he wasn't smart. Not book smart, anyway. The man could barely write his own name without moving his lips. But he knew how the world worked, despite just being an average nobody. He knew that the world chewed up certain kinds of women and didn't even bother to spit out the bones. Ridgway had an appetite, and that was what he was going to channel tonight.

Not intelligence or planning or luck. Just appetite.

He realized he was sweating, so he thought back to the master. The master was a stupid name, but what else could he call him? As far as he knew, he never even revealed his real name. The master had said, "You think you're becoming them, but you're not. You're becoming what they were too cowardly to be."

Maybe. Or maybe he was just another nobody in a spare room full of expensive garbage, about to do something that would finally, finally make the voices shut up for more than five minutes.

But he had to be careful because the biggest mistakes that his heroes made was that they underestimated the police. Bundy walked into the courtroom thinking he was smarter than everyone, and he ended up in the electric chair a few years later. Dahmer thought the cops were too lazy to care about dead Black kids, and Dahmer was right until he wasn't. Even Ridgway—forty-nine bodies and two decades of freedom—got caught because of a microscope and some paint chips. All that work and discipline, and it came down to something he'd tracked in on his boots.

The master had told him, "The moment you think you're winning is the moment they're putting the cuffs on. Leave them clues, but don't let them predict you. The game ends when they know what you're going to do before you do it."

So tonight couldn't be simple. It couldn't be the obvious move.

He grabbed his burner cell, found the number, and pressed *CALL*.

Three rings in, a woman answered.

"Velvet Escorts, how can I help you?"

A tremble formed in his voice, but he swallowed it. "Hello. I'm looking for a brunette, between twenty-one and twenty-five. Slender, shoulder-length hair, and I want her to drive and met me in a public area. Is that possible?"

"Yes, sir. What location exactly?"

"On the bank of the Liles River."

"Time?"

"Nine p.m."

There was typing down the line. The receptionist went so silent he was convinced she'd hung up. "Certainly. Any other criteria, sir?"

"Yes. I want a woman that offers submissive services. I want her to be OK with being tied up." He felt comical making such a request, and the lack of any retort was even more comical to him.

"Duration?"

"One hour."

"I'll see what ladies we have available. It's two hundred for one hour, and payment can be given in person to the model, but we add a ten percent fee for that. Or you can pay by card, and we'll waive the—"

"In person," he said. "I'll pay her when I meet her."

"Very well. Let me see what ladies we have available."

A wicked smile spread across his face as he listened to

the hold music. He could see it all so clearly. Every moment leading up to the final one.

But the sweetest moment would be the look on the police's faces when they realized he'd been playing them all along.

THIRTY-SEVEN

Maya Frost had never used a police radio in her life, and they were more complex than she thought. "Car seven, any updates on your end?"

Two and a half hours into their patrol, and so far it had been a washout. She'd driven up and down the entire length of the Liles River twice now and so far had seen nothing except a stray cat. She'd just passed the boat ramp, and according to the rotation schedule she'd drawn up, she'd loop back here in another twenty minutes. By then, one of the other units would have covered it. At least in theory. Her phone sat in the cup holder with its volume maxed. The clock read 20:38.

"No sighting," the other units crackled back in unison. Devon was among them, also driving solo to maximize visibility along this eight-mile stretch. Not that it had done much good so far, but the night was young, Maya told herself.

It felt surreal, being here. Being alone. Three days ago

she'd been at her desk in D.C., cross-referencing missing persons databases and eating sad desk salad out of a plastic container. Now she was driving a police cruiser through backwater Florida, hunting a serial killer who mimicked other serial killers. She pulled up for her next five-minute bout of observance on a particular stretch of river. She was nestled in the deeper recesses, the barren lands within the woods. Meanwhile, the other units were navigating the banks accessible by the main through road.

She killed the engine and rolled down the window all of the way. Let the night sounds come in.

Her mind kept circling back to the same question: *Why these three?*

Ed Gein, Richard Ramirez, and Gary Ridgway.

On the surface, they were just infamous American monsters that had achieved the rare status of serial killer. What else did they have in common? They'd all killed women, but Ramirez also killed men. Gein and Ramirez were dead; Ridgway was still alive. Gein had a victim count of two, Ramirez had thirteen, and Ridgway had forty-nine. Was this unsub gradually increasing the victim count? Possibly, but after Ridgway, he really had nowhere to go, at least among famous American killers.

And beyond that, speaking of these three killers in the same sentence made no sense. They were too different, not just in methodology but personality.

Gein had been a shut-in. A fifty-year-old virgin who'd never left his mother's orbit, even after she was dead. He'd skinned corpses because he wanted to *become* her, to crawl inside her skin and bring her back. It was necrophilia by way of taxidermy, and it was pathetic and desperate and sad.

Ramirez had been the opposite. He was a sociopathic monster who broke into houses and killed whoever he found. No pattern, no plan. He'd been a Satanist, but only in the way a thirteen-year-old spray-painting pentagrams on an overpass was a Satanist.

Gary Ridgway, on the other hand, had been normal. That was the strangest part about him. He was married with kids and had a steady job. He'd killed prostitutes for twenty years and went home every night to eat dinner with his family. He hadn't heard voices or worshipped the devil or wanted to wear anyone's face. He'd just liked choking women to death and dumping them in the river because it got him off.

Three killers. Three completely different psychopathologies.

So what the hell was this unsub trying to achieve?

Maya had spent enough time in the data to know that serial killers didn't work this way. They had a *type*. They had something that got their rocks off and kept getting them off until death or imprisonment stopped them. They didn't hop around. They didn't borrow. Copycat killers were even rarer because the psychology didn't line up. A serial killer was a narcissist. He wanted to be *the* guy. Copycats were followers. They wanted someone else's fame because they didn't have the ego or the imagination to build their own.

But this guy was doing both. He was mimicking legends, but he was also leaving clues.

That didn't track.

Unless he wasn't just trying to be them but was trying to prove he was *better* than them.

Her phone rang. The shrill ringtone made her jump hard enough that she cracked her knee on the steering column.

Unknown number.

She answered. "Agent Frost."

"Hello, Agent Frost? It's Lana from Velvet Escorts. We spoke earlier."

Maya's heart kicked into a higher gear. "What's going on?"

"We just had a call. Someone asking for a girl by the river."

There it is.

"What did he ask for?"

"Brunette, early twenties. He wants to meet in his car on the riverbank. Said the girl needs to be comfortable with restraints."

Maya reined in her racing thoughts. She kept the adrenaline at bay for now. If this was him—and if she wanted a chance at subduing him—she had to be smart.

"What did you tell him?" she asked.

"Nothing. He's still on the line."

Her brain fired in three directions at once. If she sent units now, they'd spook him. If she waited for him to book the girl and show up, he might see the patrols and bail.

The idea hit her so fast she almost said it out loud before thinking it through.

If this killer wanted to roleplay, Maya was happy to play along.

"Lana, this might sound like a strange request, but could you connect us? His line to mine?"

A pause. "You want to talk to him directly?"

"Yes. Stay on the line but stay quiet. Can you do that?"

"I... Yes, I can do that."

"Go. Quickly."

Maya heard clicking, then dead air. Her pulse was hammering. She suddenly panicked because she knew she should try and record this conversation. But how? Did she have an app? One that would work for an ongoing call? Did she have another device she could use? No. There was nothing.

Then a man's voice manifested down the line. "Hello?"

It was flat, gravelly, and nondescript. Classic American with no hint of an accent. Maya softened her voice and conjured up what few sultry tones her Massachusetts accent could muster. "Hey, angel. Heard you're looking for company tonight?"

Silence. Long enough for Maya to wonder whether he'd hung up. Then, "You sound different than I expected."

"Well, what did you expect, sugar?"

"Older, maybe."

Maya's phone screen had adjusted to the killer's line, and the number for Velvet Escorts had been replaced with *WITHHELD NUMBER*. "I'm... twenty-four. Can you handle a young woman?"

A grunt. "Yes."

God, she wanted to be sick, but she had to build rapport. The only thing between her and this man meeting in the flesh was her ability to portray a call girl. "Good. Wanna tell me what you're looking for? Something by the river, the receptionist said?"

"What's your name?" he asked.

Maya nearly fumbled. "Marissa."

"Yes, Marissa. I want to meet by the river. Can you be there in twenty minutes?"

"Sure can. I live right by it. We could meet at my place, if you wanted."

"No. It needs to be by the river."

The hair on Maya's arms prickled. This had to be him. "You're the boss. Whereabouts?"

"What do you mean?"

"It's a long river, sweetie. I need to know where to find you." Maya bit her lip and silently scolded herself. She shouldn't have said *find*. She should have said *met* or some other vague term. There was every chance this killer knew that the police were on his trail.

"I don't know."

"What about by the boat ramp? The one that leads to... you know. The boats."

"The boathouse."

"That's it."

Another moment of silence. "Are you sure you're from around here?"

Shit. He suspects something. Time to play up her ditziness. "I'm from Boston, honey, but I live here now. Obviously."

"Hmm. Obviously. Meet me on the stretch just after the boat ramp, OK? There's a dirt path that goes down toward the bank."

"Sure. Twenty minutes. Any chance you could tell me your name, or what you look like? Or what car you're driving?"

"Why?"

Maya stumbled. On the off chance her apparent client

bailed, a physical description of her killer was a good conso-
lation prize. His name was even better. "So I know who I'm
looking for, silly."

"My car is a silver sedan, tinted windows. You won't miss
it. But you have to come alone, all right? No funny business.
You got that, Marissa?"

"Of course. See you in twenty minutes. I'm just at home
getting dolled up."

"Are you sure? Because you sound like you're outside."

Maya frantically rolled up her window. He must have
heard the trees. "Just on my balcony."

"Fine. I'm in a silver sedan. Tinted windows. You can't
miss it."

"Got it."

"Good. And by the way... my name's Gary."

The phone line went dead.

Gary.

Gary Ridgway. The Green River Killer.

Maya grabbed her radio. Her hands were shaking. *Did I
just screw that up?* She'd just conversed directly with a serial
killer. The balcony excuse had been weak. The Boston thing
had come out of nowhere. Why the hell did she say Boston?
She wasn't even from there and had no Boston accent to
speak of. And she'd pushed too hard. She'd asked too many
questions and sounded too eager. She tried too hard to
extract information instead of just booking a client. They
hadn't even talked money, and while Maya was unfamiliar
with sex worker-punter relations, she assumed it was a
subject that often came up.

Goddammit. Her breath was short, and sweat had

beaded on her forehead, but if fortune was on her side, she might have just nabbed this bastard.

"Devon, come in!" she shouted into her radio. "Are you there? Devon?"

Click. "Yeah, I'm here. What's going on?"

"The boathouse. Twenty minutes. That's where he's going to be."

"What? How do you know?"

"Because I just spoke to him on the phone. I'll explain everything later. Silver sedan, tinted windows. I'll get there first; you and everyone else stay back. If you see him enter, block the exit off."

"Go. I'll tell the others. Good work, Frost."

"Thanks, and call me Marissa."

THIRTY-EIGHT

For the next ten minutes, he was Gary.

He left his real identity—as flimsy as the notion was—and parked where the dirt road met the tree line. There was a car waiting down the path, a few feet from the edge of the riverbank. Trees cast it in darkness, but he could make out a figure inside by the dashboard light.

Good. She was here.

He flashed his headlights twice.

The other car flashed back.

Down the bank, he joined the call girl under the darkness of the trees, but he maintained a distance. He parked around thirty feet from her, rolled down his window, and took in the river's scent and the humidity of the night. Now just to wait until she came to him. If history had taught him anything, it was that luring prey was easier than chasing it.

After a moment, the door of the other car opened. A silhouette appeared, black on black, the only visible detail her locks swaying just below her shoulder.

This was her. The next canvas.

He admired the finer points as she came into view. She had dark hair, a black dress, brown boots that reached mid-calf, and a chiseled profile that could surely use a few pounds. If he had to guess, she was closer to thirty. She had a handbag around one shoulder.

Even so, the most important criteria remained firm. She would have slotted perfectly into Gary Ridgway's gallery of dead girls.

She walked toward him with her hips doing most of the work. She moved like she was on a catwalk instead of a dirt road three miles from nowhere, and that confidence irritated him. This woman was a whore, so she should move like one. She should be eager to please. She should be *nervous*, aware of her place in the food chain.

At his door, she leaned down with one hand on the frame. Up close, he could see the details of her face. Tight cheekbones and lips painted a red that was so dark they looked black in the moonlight. "So you gonna make me stand out here all night?" she asked.

Gary's hand tightened around the pistol in the door pocket. Her voice had grit, and he didn't like that. "Passenger side."

She smiled and then obliged. Her silhouette cut across the front of the car, and then she was opening the door and sliding into the seat, bringing a cloud of perfume with her. In the confines of his truck, the scent was overwhelming. He didn't know women's perfumes, but he guessed it was jasmine or vanilla or something. It was too strong, and it made her too real. Teresa Morgan had smelled like WD-40. The Hutchins couple had smelled like old people. This woman smelled like she'd gotten ready for a date, and this wasn't that.

His instructions echoed: *Dehumanize. Distance.*

But she was already talking, already invading his space, and her hand landed on his thigh like she had a right to touch him. "You seem nervous. First time?"

"No."

"Sure. You got a present for me, honey?"

He reached between the seats and found the envelope. "Two-twenty. Is that right?"

She took it and thumbed through the bills without taking her other hand off his thigh. "This feels light."

The idea of giving this woman money made him sick, but he had no intention of letting her keep it. After tonight, she wouldn't be keeping anything. "Light? It's what the receptionist told me."

"That was before the restraints deal. It's an extra hundred for that."

She was making this easier than he'd expected. "It's what we agreed."

And then she laughed. "Relax, sugar, I'm just messing with you." She put the envelope on the dash. "You really are nervous, huh? What are you so scared of?"

You, he thought. *I'm scared of you.*

Not because she was dangerous. Because she wouldn't shut up. Because she kept touching him and talking and *looking* at him, and none of it was in the script. He was supposed to be in control, but this woman acted like she was the one running the show.

"The handcuffs," he said. "They're in the glove box."

"You always so direct?"

"Yes."

She chuckled and opened the glove box without taking her eyes off him. "I appreciate efficiency." She reached inside, and his hand tightened around the pistol beside him. He didn't want to shoot her. He wanted to strangle her in true Ridgway fashion, but something told him he should get this over with quickly because she seemed the type to not go down without a fight.

"Police issue," she said as she dangled the cuffs off one finger. "You a cop?"

"No. Bought them online."

"Sure you did." She was still looking in the glove box. Her hand moved. "You know, funny thing happened today."

His throat closed up. "What?"

"Got a call. Well, a bunch of calls actually. Every girl I know got them." She turned to look at him. Her other hand came out of the glove box.

Holding a pistol of her own.

Pointed at his chest.

"Heard a rumor that the Fernandina Butcher was looking for working girls," she laughed. "Word travels fast in our circles."

Gary broke into a boiling hot sweat. Who was this woman? How did she know? Had this been a setup all along? This *bitch*. She'd played him, and the mounting rage bubbling in his stomach threatened to overspill. He was furious with her for playing the hero and furious with himself for being so damn stupid. Why hadn't he just shot this whore when he had the chance?

Unless—he still had that chance.

"I'm... n-n-not—" he stuttered. "I just wanted some fun."

He just needed to lie. He just needed a moment of distraction, and then he could get out of this. It would be messy, loud, and violent. Not what he wanted, but survival trumped perfection. The pistol had been insurance, but now it was looking like the instrument of his escape.

The woman grinned. "Shush, and put these cuffs on."

He had to do it. If she clocked the pistol, she might just put a bullet in him right away. He had to do it. Don't think. Just fire. Take the risk.

And he drew.

BANG.

THIRTY-NINE

Maya was in position with a pistol clenched in her sweaty palm. She'd set everything up, made all the arrangements, and had been prepared to take him down the second he showed his face.

But here, by the boathouse, she was alone.

Just her, the river, the dirt path.

She checked the dashboard clock: 9:17 p.m. Gary was seventeen minutes late.

Every fiber of her being was wound tight. Every shadow cast by the moonlight, every rustle in the palmetto scrub made her think he was coming. She kept glancing at the rearview mirror, half-expecting to see a figure materializing from the tree line. But there was only darkness and the stretch of dirt road behind her.

Then the radio burst to life.

"Frost, any sign of him?"

"Nothing. He's nearly twenty minutes late."

She could hear Devon's frustration through the speaker.

An hour ago, Maya had this bastard on the phone, ready to reel him straight in. Now she was starting to think the shark had dodged the hook.

"He might have gotten spooked," Devon said. "Or he was bullshitting you from the start."

Maya swept the area again. Trees. Bushes. The river glinting black in the moonlight.

"Maybe," she said. But her gut said otherwise. Something was wrong.

"Frost, hold on." Devon's voice went muffled, like she was talking to someone else. Then she came back sharp. "We might have something."

Maya sat up straighter. "What is it?"

"We've still got one car patroling. He's spotted something."

"What? What can he see?"

"I don't know. He says he's three miles south. Vehicle's dark, could be abandoned. Hold on."

Static.

Then, "Frost, we've got something, and it's—"

BANG.

Suddenly, the static from the radio erupted, sizzling like boiling oil and water. Maya felt the blood drain from her face as the loud blast settled. "Devon, what the hell was that?"

Another unit came through the radio. "Shots fired. Oak coppice. I'm on it."

Maya didn't wait for the rest. She slammed the car into drive and floored it as she tore back onto the main road. Up ahead, she spotted Devon's car and another unit doing the same. The speedometer climbed—forty, fifty, sixty—on a road that should've been taken at thirty max. She didn't care.

The trees became a blur of black on black as she followed her colleagues.

Three miles south.

He'd played them. Sent her north, sent everyone north, while he worked the other side of the river.

The bridge appeared ahead, a narrow two-lane crossing lit by a single flickering streetlight. She took it too fast, felt the suspension groan as the tires hit the seam where asphalt met concrete. The river rushed below, invisible in the dark. On the other side, she could see red and blue lights strobing through the trees.

Dammit. Be discreet. He's going to see the lights and bail.

Her radio crackled. "All units, suspect vehicle spotted. Pickup truck. Black Nissan. Oh-five model. Plates not visible."

A pickup.

Not a sedan.

He'd lied about that too.

Maya swerved around a patrol car that had stopped in the road with its driver's door hanging open. Ahead, through a gap in the trees, she saw taillights. Red, bouncing, moving fast down a dirt path that split off from the main road.

She followed.

The cruiser wasn't built for off-roading, but she didn't have a choice. The dirt path was barely wide enough for one vehicle, lined on both sides by palmettos and live oaks that scraped the doors as she pushed through. The truck ahead was kicking up a rooster tail of dust and debris that made it almost impossible to see.

She dodged and weaved through whatever lay in the road—debris, terrified animals—and kept her eye on the prize. She grabbed the radio. "I've got eyes on him. Dark pickup." Was he heading northeast? Northwest? She had no idea.

"Frost, wait for backup."

"No time. He's getting away."

"Goddammit, Frost, you're going to get yourself killed."

Seconds felt like hours as the surrounding woods became a blur of motion. The red taillights of the SUV flickered in the distance, teasing her, daring her to come closer. The suspect seemed close but out of reach, and by now, he'd know that someone was trailing him. He would be on high alert—and who was the victim of his gunshot? The narrow dirt road snaked its way through another wooded patch before opening up onto a stretch of road. Maya kept her gaze fixated on the truck's rear, using it as a magnet to pull herself closer. The moonlit path was cloaked in shadow, so she couldn't anticipate the twists and turns ahead.

Suddenly, the SUV's brake lights flared brightly. Without losing a second, it swerved sharply to the left and spat debris in its wake.

And then the unmistakable sound of gunfire pierced the night, and Maya's windshield exploded into a spiderweb of cracks. A momentary blindness clouded her vision as shards of glass flew into the cabin.

Maya instinctively ducked as her heart thumped with every bump in the road. He had a gun—and she didn't. If she wanted to win this battle, the only option she had was to ram him and push him off the road.

But as the truck began speeding to the left, a second gunshot rang out so loudly it felt like it was coming from the passenger seat and demolished what remained of her windshield. Fragments of glass rained down in front of her, and while she tried to turn in the escapee's direction, her wheels skidded along the dirt. Maya's world went into a dizzying spin and she fought to maintain control of the car as it slid off the dirt road and crashed through underbrush and trees.

The vehicle rocked, and Maya felt her head slam against the side window. The world blurred as pain shot through her skull.

Gritting her teeth, Maya forced herself to stay conscious as the car finally ground to an abrupt halt. Its front end was buried in thick foliage, and her ears were ringing like a violent bout of tinnitus. For a second, Maya struggled to make sense of her surroundings.

"Frost, come in. Are you there?"

She blinked away the dizziness and shook her head. The truck had vanished.

"Frost, report your position." Devon's frantic voice came through.

"Alive," she croaked. "Suspect got away."

"Dammit. Are you OK?"

Maya touched her head, feeling a sticky wetness. "Yeah. Didn't get the license plate. I'm sorry." She pressurized the wound with her hand but didn't dare look in the mirror to see the damage.

"Get back to the coppice. Are you injured?"

"No. I'm fine."

She wasn't fine. Her head was pounding, and her ribs felt like someone had taken a bat to them. Every time she moved, shards of glass shifted in her lap. But she couldn't just sit here. Couldn't let him win.

"Can you pick me up? My car's a little... stuck."

"Yeah. Ping me your location on your cell."

"All right, give me a second. Has our guy left anything behind?"

"Yeah he has. And it's not good."

Maya didn't have to enquire any further. She already knew what was waiting for her.

Victim number three.

FORTY

An officer had picked up Maya and dropped her at the crime scene, despite his insistence that she should get to a hospital. She'd refused, and now she stood on the riverbank with a corpse at her feet.

The nameless victim lay face-up on the moist grass. Her brown locks were swept across her upper half, and her handbag was wrapped around her shoulder. The fabric of her dress clung to her hips, accentuated by the moisture that had accumulated on her torso.

But it was the puncture of a bullet wound, visible even under the midnight sky, that told the most damning part of this woman's tale.

Devon looked Maya over like she'd just crawled out of a sewer. "Frost, you shouldn't be here. Get to the hospital."

"I'm fine."

"You've got glass in your hair and blood on your forehead. That's not fine."

"It's just a cut." Maya touched her forehead. The

bleeding had mostly stopped, but her fingers came away sticky. "I need to be here."

"You need a doctor."

"I need to figure out what happened."

"No. You just crashed a car going sixty miles an hour through the woods. Once the adrenaline wears off, you're going to feel every broken rib, and if you've got internal bleeding, you'll be dead by next week. You want that?"

"Devon, leave it," she snapped. "This woman is dead because of me."

"She's dead because that's what he planned to do."

"No. He outsmarted us. He pushed us in one direction while he struck in another. He misdirected us. I should know all about that, but he beat us. He booked two different escorts."

Devon sighed, then bent down to inspect the victim. "He shot her. Gary Ridgway didn't shoot any of his victims."

Maya joined her partner in scrutinizing the victim's death state. All she could see was a single bullet hole through the ribcage. "One penetration point, to her ribs, of all places, which meant death wasn't guaranteed. Ridgway used knives, garrotes, and his bare hands."

Devon stood back up and peered off in the distance. Around fifty feet away was a white Honda Civic, presumably the victim's. If nothing else, they could determine the victim's identity through her registration.

"He shot her because it was convenient," Devon said.

"Come on, Devon. He strung a woman up from the rafters and cut her in half with a saw. He doesn't do convenient."

"So he panicked. Something happened that didn't go to

plan, so he panicked and shot her to get it over with. Then when he saw the lights, he pushed her out of his car and sped off."

"Do you think?"

"Yeah. You ever got down to business with a handbag around your shoulder?"

"You're asking the wrong woman. Could I borrow some gloves?"

Devon handed her a pair from her pocket. Maya put them on, then gently rolled the woman's handbag over. She unhooked the latch and held it open with two fingers. "Car keys, cell phone..."

"What's that? Business cards?"

Maya pulled out a stack of glossy white cards. Written in elegant black letters was: *Krystal Larkin, Premier Companion.* Below was a phone number and email address. "That explains how he got a hold of her. She was an independent girl."

"Yup. They were less likely to know about the killer targeting sex workers."

Maya's brain worked furiously as she pieced together the disparate elements. "He wouldn't have left all of this behind, either. He couldn't do much about her car, but chances are our guy contacted her by phone. He took Teresa Morgan's phone as a countermeasure. He would have done the same here."

Devon said, "We need to devour everything on that phone. Get it to the Tech team ASAP. Then we get any surveillance from the area and check the cameras for hits on Krystal's license plate."

Maya placed the handbag's contents back from whence

they came, returning the scene to its original state for the forensics team. *Krystal Larkin*, she thought. Perhaps a stage name, perhaps not. All she knew was that this innocent woman had paid the price for Maya's error. This killer had been a step ahead every time, so it was the logical conclusion that he'd be ahead of them here, too. Why had she been so blind to the obvious?

"Devon, you see something?"

"I see blood on your head. You might have a concussion, so if you don't want dementia by age forty, get to the hospital."

"No, I mean, I will, but look. We've made a mistake."

"You're not kidding. A serial killer slipped through our fingertips."

"Devon, we interrupted him mid-M.O., which means he didn't have time to pull off his signature. At every scene he's left us a clue to the next one. But this one..."

"Was aborted. So we don't know where he's going to strike next."

Maya looked at Krystal's body. At the bullet wound that should've been something else. Something worse, probably, but something that would've told them where to look next.

By trying to save her, they'd made their job harder and perhaps sealed the death warrant of the next person without a single shred of hope to save them.

Devon was quiet for a moment. Then she said, "Would you rather we'd waited? Let him finish whatever he was doing so we could get a nice clean clue?"

"No. Of course not."

"Then stop second-guessing. We did the right thing. We

went in when we had the chance. It's not our fault he adapted faster than we did."

Maya wanted to believe that, but standing here on the riverbank, she couldn't shake off the feeling that they'd just made everything worse. She suddenly thought of those nights at the women's shelter, helping women map out escape routes, packing go-bags in secret and celebrating small victories when one of them finally broke free—it had all been to prevent moments like this. A woman, alone and vulnerable, paying the price for a man's rage.

"I'll go back to the precinct and apologize to Riggs for wrecking one of his cars. Then I'll get Alfie to check out this cell."

"Good. I'll stay here and direct forensics, and I'll ping Vernon to fast-track clearance to search the phone. Call me if you get anything."

FORTY-ONE

"My sleeping pattern is screwed up," Alfie complained as he plugged Krystal's phone into his computer. "I've gone full night shift."

It was two a.m., and Maya was sitting beside Alfie in his crypt-office. Their knees were an inch from touching, but Maya didn't seem to mind. She felt like she knew him well enough that it wasn't an issue.

"Never go full night shift."

"Definitely not. Do you have clearance to search this phone?"

"Not yet. Devon is fast-tracking the clearance."

Alfie checked his watch that Maya thought was too big for his wrist. "It's two in the morning."

"So?"

"There isn't a judge in America that's awake right now."

Maya wasn't about to let anyone throw a wrench in the works now, even an admittedly handsome man like Alfie whatever-his-name-was. "Don't worry, this is Bureau juris-diction. You're just following orders."

"Just following orders? You know who else used that excuse?"

"What is it with men and the war? You'd think you were in it."

"It's all we've got. I'm just saying—searching a cell phone without permission is asking for trouble. Believe me, I've been there."

"We have permission. Or at least, we will. Just... please? I need to look at this phone tonight, and I need your help to do it."

Alfie was quiet for a moment. Then he pulled the phone closer and started typing. "For the record, this is a terrible idea."

"Noted."

"And you owe me."

"I know."

He loaded up a software program called *VESPA*, clicked through some data that Maya could barely read, and then came to a collection of folders. "OK, so this is the contents of the victim's phone. From here we can see everything. Media, text messages, saved passwords, login timestamps, search history—everything. Where should I start?"

Maya reminded herself that delving into someone's private life was an invasion, even if that person was no longer alive. Everything here was a glimpse into Krystal's world, so Maya assured herself that she'd forget everything that wasn't meant for her eyes.

"Media. See if she somehow got a picture of her killer."

Alfie navigated to the pictures folder. The most recent

pictures were of Krystal on her bed, sans makeup. The time-stamp said they were taken yesterday. The most recent video file was of a man in a wheelchair doing flips on a skate ramp, which had been sent to her two days ago. "Wow, that's cool," Alfie said.

Maya nudged him. "Forget that. So there are no media files from today?"

"No."

"Then try her messaging apps. Our unsub must have communicated with her somehow."

"On it."

Alfie scoured through folders with unpronounceable names to what Maya assumed was her chat history. Names popped up that Maya could discern among the technical jargon: Mom, Dad, Nicky BFF, David Yoga. Alfie dug into her most recent chats one by one.

"Krystal was... Let me see... Meeting her parents on Friday, talking about gin with Nicky, and doing yoga with David Yoga this weekend. Huh, funny. He does yoga and his surname's Yoga. How about that?"

Maya ignored the attempt at humor. Nausea pricked her stomach, because if her killer had called her and withheld his number, this whole effort was a waste of time. "Try her other apps."

"I am. She only uses WhatsApp, by the looks of it. There's a chat in Signal that's three months old and one in Telegram that's even older. Her basic text messages are just full of spam, and the only male name in all of this is her yoga friend."

"Dammit." Maya's patience was already wearing thin, because what kind of escort didn't arrange her meetings through online messaging? She was no expert, but she assumed it was a given. If not for the business cards, Maya would never have guessed that Krystal was a sex worker at all.

Then it hit her. The business cards. They had an email address.

"Alfie, try her email client."

"One sec."

More folders came and went, some bringing forth unreadable data files. Into a folder entitled *PivotDataAccess,* Maya spotted the subfolder *MailFriend.* Alfie clicked inside, and up popped up the unmistakable sight of an inbox with rows of email threads filling the page.

Maya clenched her fist in premature triumph as she scanned through subject lines that left little to the imagination. *Rendezvous Tonight, Our Secret Meeting, Ready For Round Two.* When Alfie dug into each title, Maya could see the whole back and forth between Krystal and her eager clients.

"Jackpot."

"Don't get too excited. These are all for future bookings," Alfie said.

And then Maya saw the subject title: *Riverside Request.*

"There. That one."

"Riverside request. Interesting."

Alfie opened up the email exchange, and the first thing that appeared was the sender's initial message.

From: user146538@selfdestructmail.com

Subject: Riverside Request.

Dear Krystal, I hope this email finds you well. I've come across your services and am interested in meeting. I'm not one for the usual locations, hence my subject title. The Liles river-side offers privacy and a certain aesthetic that appeals to me. Would you be amenable to such a setting, ideally Sunday evening? Thank you – Gary.

This was him. The Liles River. Sunday night. The pieces aligned.

Hi Gary. Odd request! But yes I can accommodate. May I ask why the specific location? My fee is $200 per hour, plus a $50 deposit. Please let me know of any specific criteria you have for your session! – Krystal L.

Gary had replied within minutes.

I appreciate the tranquility, and it keeps prying eyes at bay. Is there any way I could forgo the deposit and perhaps pay a premium on the night?

Krystal's reply: *Unfortunately not. The deposit keeps away flakers. You can find me under KrystalLarkin96 on Paybox, Linewire and InstantPay.*

Maya read between the lines. The man calling himself Gary was trying to keep his digital footprint to a minimum. A temporary email address and a reluctance to wire cash, because doing so would leave a trail. "Devious son of a bitch," she said.

"You're not kidding. Look at the next reply. It took him nearly two hours to respond."

"Because he was weighing his options."

The reply said: *I've transferred the deposit through Paybox. I require one hour of your time. Nine PM on Sunday evening. Meet me along the oak coppice. I'll be in a black truck, and as for further requirements, I need you to be OK with light restraints. This email address will no longer be in use after tonight.*

End of conversation thread.

Maya re-read the last part again, then turned to Alfie. "He... transferred her money. Which means—"

"He pulled that money from a bank account."

"And that bank account will have his name and address."

Maya wanted to grab him. Wanted to throw her arms around him and squeeze until his ribs cracked. They were close. So close she could taste it.

"You better put on the coffee," Alfie said, "because we've got some backdoor action to do."

FORTY-TWO

Blood dripped from his knuckles into the sink and mixed with the water until it swirled pink down the drain. The mirror in front of him had a fracture from where he'd punched it, and his reflection stared back in pieces.

The detective—Frost—had ruined everything.

Two kills. Two perfect recreations. Teresa Morgan had been strung up like Gein's victim, and the Hutchins couple had been staged like Ramirez's work. And then the street-walker tonight, who should've been his Green River piece, should have been strangled and posed by the water.

Instead, he'd shot her in the ribs like some amateur and dumped her on the riverbank because the cops had come out of nowhere. He'd managed to fire off a shot while he distracted her, resulting in a messy, meaningless kill that the Green River Killer would have been ashamed of.

He turned off the faucet. Dried his hands. The cuts stung, but he barely felt it. He was too busy thinking about how close he'd come to getting caught. Frost had chased him through the woods. Had nearly rammed him off the road. He'd fired two shots through his back window just to get her off his ass, and even then she'd kept coming until he'd lost her in the dark.

She'd been on the other end of the phone too. He'd known it the second the receptionist had taken a touch too long. The questions she'd fired had been the questions of someone wanting to get to know *him*, not just a whore who wanted his money. Luckily, at that point he'd already booked Krystal separately and set up the misdirection.

And it had worked. Until it hadn't.

Somehow, the bitch had found him, and it was only by some miracle that he'd escaped. They were supposed to have found the body long after he'd fled the scene.

Out of the bathroom, he staggered into his study and immersed himself among his treasures. The room was lined with shelves: books on serial killers, crime scene photos he'd bought off sketchy websites, letters from inmates he'd corresponded with over the years. A glass cabinet held his collection of weapons. Knives, mostly. A few guns. A bone saw he'd paid three hundred dollars for because the seller claimed it had belonged to someone important. Probably lies, but he didn't care. It looked right.

The Ramirez jacket hung on the mannequin in the corner. The Gein nails sat in their case. The Ridgway truck key was on his desk.

Five kills. Five legends. That's what the master had told him. Start with the classics: Gein, Ramirez, Ridgway, then move into deeper cuts. Killers most people hadn't heard of. Killers the cops wouldn't see coming.

But now the sequence was broken.

Krystal's death had been sloppy. There was no ritual and no message left behind. He didn't even *want* to take credit for this one.

He sat down at his desk. Tried to think. The room that had once inspired him now suffocated him, and it was all the detective's fault. Not only had she interfered with his plans, but she had also stripped him of his sense of power and control. She had penetrated the veil of his illusions and brought the gritty reality to the surface.

The master had been clear: Once the plan was in motion, they wouldn't communicate. Five murders, then disappear. No contact. No loose ends. But the master hadn't planned for Frost's wanna-be-hero intervention.

The original plan had two more kills lined up. Victim four and victim five, both carefully selected, both tied to killers the FBI would have to dig through old case files to identify.

But Frost had changed the game.

She'd interrupted his work, made him look weak, and made him flee.

And he couldn't let that stand.

He picked up a newspaper clipping from his desk. Recent article, dated a week ago. Since yesterday, he'd researched everything he could about this Frost woman, and he'd found out some very interesting things.

The master's plan had been good.

But the master wasn't the one getting chased through the woods or shooting the police in a frenzy.

And the master wasn't here anymore.

He was.

And if Frost wanted to make this personal, he'd return

the favor. She would come to understand the depths of his obsession, and she'd regret the day she got involved with this.

The sequence was about to change. The detective and her pals would have no idea where to look, and he was going to lure her in, present her with the most horrific sight of her life, and truly break her spirit. Then, once he'd shattered her core to pieces, he'd leave her to wallow in her failure for the rest of her days.

Frost's transgressions had deviated him from his path, but she had also unwittingly handed him the element of surprise. Now he would operate under his own whims, unburdened by the constraints of a plan laid out by someone else.

The master could disapprove all he wanted. This was personal now.

And personal was so much more satisfying than following someone else's script.

FORTY-THREE

"You'll need to be patient. This isn't some simple keyword search," Alfie said. "Why don't you get some sleep and come back in the morning? I'll still be here."

"No chance. Not when I can get this guy's name tonight."

"That's if we're lucky. It's not a guarantee. I need to black hat this thing, and you look like you've been in a car crash."

"I have been in a car crash. What's black hat mean?" asked Maya. She felt the wound on her head, which had since stopped bleeding but now felt like a bruise had formed. She didn't have the time or energy to actually check herself in the mirror, and she'd managed to talk her way out of visiting the hospital.

"Black hat usually means hacking, but we use it around here if we're ever talking about backdoor routes, going rogue, that type of thing."

Maya glanced between the screens, watching the algorithms Alfie had sent in motion to work through the apparently vast amounts of data. The digital traces the killer left behind, though scarce, were the only lead she had at the moment. She felt a pang of anxiety, thinking of the possibility of it turning into yet another dead end. Maya looked on with barely any clue what Alfie was doing. "So what are we waiting for exactly?"

Alfie exhaled through his nose, then clenched his teeth. "Well, firstly, your perp was right. This email address he used to contact Krystal expired after twenty-four hours. It's untraceable. I can't even pinpoint the IP address he used to create it. I mean, there might be a way. The email server he used could have some vulnerabilities, but it could take hours, days to crack it, and even then it could be a dead end."

"So forget the email address. What about the payment? That's our smoking gun."

"Krystal did indeed receive a payment through Paybox from what I can see, but don't get ahead of yourself. There are a few ways he could get around it, and I hate to say it, but your guy seems to cover his tracks pretty well."

"How hard is it to check Paybox records? Are we legally allowed to look into them?"

"We don't need to," he said.

Maya wasn't sure she'd heard him right. "How do you mean?"

"Paybox is a huge corporation, and they'll have the details of every user on their books. But getting them will take a while. However, all we need is the email address he used to register with them. He wouldn't be able to use a disposable one for that. They would only accept reputable domain names. From there, we can get all the details we need."

Alfie had told her not to get ahead of herself, but Maya couldn't help it. She was already imagining marching this guy into the holding cells in chains. "How do you plan on getting the email? Wouldn't you need to access Paybox's private records?"

"Not when we've got a direct line. If I can access Krystal's Paybox account, I can see all of her transactions. I'm just running a script to get into them, because it's not as simple as double-clicking into a folder. Apps like this have multi-factor authentication, and that's what I need to bypass."

Alfie worked his magic while Maya stood up and began pacing the room. Three steps one way, three steps back. The office was too small for proper pacing, but remaining still felt impossible. Her ribs ached. Her head pounded. She'd definitely done some long-term damage, but she reasoned that that bell couldn't be un-rung, so no medical intervention would rectify that now.

"Maya, get over here," Alfie shouted.

She snapped back to attention and quickly crossed the room. "Got something?"

"Look." He tapped the screen. "Krystal has had seven deposits into her Paybox account the past two weeks. Which transaction am I looking for?"

"Three days ago, according to the emails."

Alfie clicked around. "Here. One deposit on Friday night. Fifty dollars. No one else deposited that day. Is this him?"

Maya leaned in and examined the screen, despite her not understanding the raw code in front of her. "It must be. Can you see anything about him? Name, email, anything?" The pain in her skull disappeared in the wake of Alfie's discovery. Suddenly, there was no stinging. Just a new sense of optimism.

Alfie leaned forward and clicked in a frenzy. All Maya could see were mountains of text in between lines of computer code. She prayed that the unsub's identity was hiding among the unreadable language.

"Boom!" Alfie said with a slam of his fist. He highlighted a section of the code and pointed. "Right here. Look."

Maya leaned closer as recognizable words emerged from the clutter of text.

There it was.

EMAIL ADDRESS: rmiller123@instamail.com.

A triumphant grin spread across her face. All the weariness that had been holding her back evaporated in an instant.

R. Miller. She had the killer's name.

She grabbed Alfie's shoulder and squeezed. "God damn, Alfie, you're an angel."

Maya was about to call Devon, but Alfie waved his hand. "Don't get ahead of yourself. We're not out of the woods yet," he said. "Could be an alias. We need to check a few other things first."

Maya shook off the exhilaration and composed herself. This unsub certainly knew how to cover his tracks, but she couldn't help but think this was an oversight on his part. He never intended for them to find Krystal's phone. Just like at Teresa's scene, he would have swiped it if he'd had time.

"Got it. What do you need to check?"

"Email addresses are easier to trace if they're active. I'll see if I can cross-reference it with any social media accounts, subscriptions, bank accounts. It'll l give us more info on him."

Maya bashed a keyboard every day of her life, but Alfie moved at a speed she could barely comprehend. Each click was almost music to her hears. She stepped back and gave him space because she hated it when people crowded around her station at HQ.

"While you're digging into that, I'll check out any R. Millers in the database. He might..."

"Wait, wait." Alfie gestured for her to come back. "I got something... odd."

Maya rushed back, her heart now battering her ribs at an unhealthy pace. "What is it?"

"No social medias, no subscriptions, no bank account. The money in his Paybox account must have been transferred from some other app."

Maya panicked. She anticipated a dead end. She gripped the table and said, "Please say there's a *but*."

"But," Alfie began, "the email *is* linked to a website. One website in particular."

"Which website?"

Alfie opened up a browser and pasted in a URL. A site loaded up, red text on a black background. At the top of a page was a grid with tiny photos of infamous faces lined up with a grayscale filter.

Then Maya saw the title.

In gothic font, it read:

DEATH COLLECTORS.

Below that:

Premier murderabilia for the serious collector.

"Holy sh..." Alfie said.

Maya felt her skin go cold. Goosebumps erupted down her arms and across the back of her neck. Her scalp prickled.

The faces of serial killers stared at her from their grid in the top banner. Bundy, Gacy, Dahmer, Ramirez, Gein, Ridgway, Brady, Rader.

This wasn't a memorial site or a true crime forum. This was a *store*.

Maya had barely caught her breath when she spotted the site's so-called *elite* item, gloriously highlighted in a golden frame on the homepage.

GLOVE OWNED BY THE FERNANDINA BUTCHER. PROOF OF AUTHENTICITY INCLUDED. $25,000 BUYOUT. RARE.

"Jesus Christ..." Maya said. "I'm going to be sick."

FORTY-FOUR

MAYA COULD HARDLY BELIEVE SOMETHING SO GRIM existed. She'd heard of crime scene relics, murder weapons, and prison art showing up in private collections and museums, but on the page in front of her, she saw a lock of Charles Manson's hair for sale. She couldn't imagine anyone wanting to own that for free, let alone for two thousand dollars.

"This is gross," Alfie said. He highlighted a word in the site's description at the top. "Murderabilia. I guess anyone can join and sell... whatever they want to."

The homepage was divided into sections, each showcasing mementos with high-resolution photographs. A sidebar on the left listed various categories: *Historical Killers, Cannibals, Satanic Killers, Mass Killers, Execution Artifacts.*

"Yeah. This is Ebay for murder fetishists."

Alfie looked away and grimaced. "I'm not sure I want to dig any deeper. I think I'm about to throw up."

"You and me both." Maya locked on the item from the

so-called Fernandina Butcher. What did this mean? That her unsub was selling his own murder attire for profit? The audacity of showcasing something so sinister for public consumption was beyond Maya's comprehension, and she'd seen a lot in Intelligence.

"Well, if you ever want a..."—Alfie scrolled down—"clown painting by John Wayne Gacy, you know where to look."

"I'd rather have a tabasco enema," Maya said. She had no time to ponder the moral and legal implications of such items. She had a killer to catch. "Open up the listing for that glove."

Alfie clicked on the item inside the golden frame: a high-definition, close-up photo of a black glove. The listing page opened up.

An exceptionally rare piece from the uncaptured Fernan-dina Butcher, the killer currently dominating headlines across the United States. This glove was left behind at Morgan's Hardware store in Fernandina Beach, Florida and was acquired by one of the responding officers on the scene. It is now part of the Death Collectors archive and is available for any hardcore murderabilia collectors. Authenticity is guaran-teed, and purchase includes photographs of the glove at the crime scene.

"Were the crime scene photos ever made public?" asked Alfie.

Maya was asking herself the same question. "Definitely not. No one other than the people on the scene know that the killer was wearing a glove in the CCTV footage."

"And the footage couldn't have been leaked?"

"No. We'd know if it was. *You'd* be the first to know, wouldn't you?"

"Yeah." Alfie scratched his stubble. "I don't monitor the press, but someone would have told me and asked me to take it down."

"So it has to be legit. I'm sure this industry is full of fakes and scammers, but only a certain few people know the killer was wearing gloves at the Morgan scene—and the killer is one of them."

"And it matches?" Alfie asked.

"Can't be sure. Can you pull up a still of the CCTV footage from Morgan's Hardware?"

Alfie did just that. He found a grainy still image, zoomed in on the killer's gloved hand, then switched back to his browser. "What do you think?"

There was no question about it. The glove on the killer's hand and the one on the Death Collectors site were a perfect match.

And equally important was the fact that the killer had never left any glove behind at the crime scene.

Therefore, this seller had to be him.

Maya leaned in and clocked his username. *ObsidianCollector.* "Can you dig into this seller's account? Find out some more about him?"

"Leave it with me," Alfie said. He pasted the URL into his software, bringing up more lines of text and raw code. Maya left the crypt, grabbed her laptop, and returned to Alfie's office. She loaded up the police database and searched for every R. Miller within twenty miles. She felt herself reaching the finishing line, enclosing the walls around this unsub. She had a name; now all she needed was a location. If

Alfie could pinpoint his rough address, she could have this man in handcuffs before dawn.

Her search results pinged back.

No one named R. Miller within twenty miles.

Maya scrunched up her brow. She expanded the parameters to fifty miles.

Zero results.

The unsub's behavioral profile dictated that he knew this area like the back of his hand. Therefore, he had to live here, or at the very least have lived here at some point in his life. It was impossible to be so intimately familiar with Fernandina Beach without a deep connection to it.

"Dammit," Alfie interrupted. "This site is held together by duct tape. It's as amateur as it gets."

"Can't breach it?"

The frustration dripped off of him. "The site's design is clunky and outdated, which should make it easier to get in, but it's like trying to pick a lock with gum on the key. It's got some decent protection too. Not impossible to break but time-consuming. All I can find right now is the owner's name."

"Which is?"

"Mathias Harder. Site was registered in Kingsland."

"Georgia?"

"Yeah. It's about thirty miles away."

Maya pondered that. It couldn't be a coincidence that it was so close. "Does our friend ObsidianCollector have any details in their profile or anything?"

"Nope. Can't even see past transactions, purchase history. This is very much a one-and-done kind of site. Ebay it ain't."

Maya went back to the database, back to her R. Miller problem. As she traced the keyboard, the name Mathias Harder traveled from her memory bank to her fingertips. She searched his name in the police database and expanded the parameters to cover Kingsland, Georgia.

Three names within a hundred miles.

"This ObsidianCollector guy," Alfie continued, "he seems to sell the majority of the items on this site."

Maya was checking each name one by one. The first was a twenty-two-year-old in Callahan. Too far away. Too young. This killer had delusions that had festered with age.

She looked over at Alfie, and a sudden string of realization threaded together. "Could ObsidianCollector be the site owner? It said in his glove listing that it was *part of the Death Collectors archive.*"

"That's what I'm thinking too. Eighty percent of the items on here are sold by him."

Maya ruminated on the idea. A trader of macabre artifacts. Someone who bought and sold murder relics for a living but perhaps had taken the next step in the process and begun manufacturing trophies of his own. She went back to her list. The second Mathias Harder in the database was a seventy-eight-year-old living in a nursing home in Jacksonville. Judging by the CCTV footage she had, their killer was between thirty and forty. This wasn't him either.

"Any more items from the Butcher on the site?" Maya asked.

"No. That's the only one. But the same seller has listings for a bunch of other items."

"Anything from Ed Gein, Richard Ramirez, or Gary Ridgway?"

More taps on the keyboard. "Ramirez and Ridgway, yes. Prison letters. Nothing from Ed Gein, though."

Maya got to the final Mathias Harder on the list. Thirty-five years old, based in Harrietts Bluff, wherever that was. She did a quick online search and found it was only a few miles outside of Kingsland. The mugshot attached to the record was a pale-skinned man with dark hair, shaven close to the skull. Maya regarded his small, pinprick eyes and considered that she might be staring at the face of the Fernandina Butcher.

"He's definitely in Kingsland?" Maya double-checked.

"The site was registered there, and I doubt this guy has a business address. Chances are he registered it at this personal address."

Maya scrolled down to Mathias Harder's profile. Employment history was alarmingly bare, and he'd been arrested three years ago for trespassing on crime scenes.

She breathed deeply. The past few hours felt like a fever dream. Maya was sleep-deprived, hurt, and potentially concussed, but this lead was too important to ignore.

Owner of a muderabilia website. A charge for invading crime scenes. The pieces fit.

But it wasn't enough to make an official arrest.

Maya needed to see the Butcher's glove in the flesh, to prove it was real, to solidly link this man to the death of Teresa Morgan.

"Alfie, you might have just found a serial killer," Maya said as she grabbed her jacket and keys. With any luck, she wouldn't crash the next car.

The tech analyst looked up over his glasses. "You're leaving?"

Maya noted down the suspect's address. "We took the risk, now it's time to get the reward."

"Maya, you can't be serious. You might be concussed. You've already wrecked one car tonight, apparently, and I'm not sure if you noticed, but Georgia isn't in Florida. We don't have jurisdiction there."

"No such thing as state lines in the FBI. Keep searching, night worker, and give me a call if you find anything."

Alfie rubbed his temples, then crossed his arms. "Oh, and it's three in the morning."

"Perfect. It means Mathias Harder will be home."

She was out the door. The net around the Fernandina Butcher was tightening, and Maya was determined to be the one to close it.

FORTY-FIVE

A STREETLAMP THREW WEAK LIGHT THROUGH THE morning fog. The house in front of Maya was six figures in seven-figure territory. The walls were yellowed with age. A sagging roof threatened implosion. A rusty gate was fixed ajar with its hinges all but eroded. If this house was a reflection of its owner, Mathias Harder was as disturbed as Maya suspected.

Seven a.m. The magic hour for arrests, according to every veteran cop Maya had ever met. She hadn't messaged Devon to tell her where she was because she wanted to see the look on her partner's face when she brought this killer into the precinct—solo. The only assistance Maya had called upon was that of caffeine, which had gotten her through the wee hours. She might have caught an hour of sleep while she'd been waiting in the car in this street, but she couldn't be sure. The world was a blur, and she'd somehow gotten jet lag without stepping foot on a jet.

Based on Mathias Harder's criminal record, his psychological profile matched her unsub. He was a white male, criminal past, and clearly had an unhealthy obsession with serial killers. The only anomaly was that he'd never lived in Fernandina Beach, but if the man possessed an item that only the killer could have, then she was happy to admit she'd made an error in the profile. And if he was the same man she'd chased last night, it was only an hour's journey between Fernandina Beach and Harrietts Bluff. He could easily have made the trip.

Time to head in. She still didn't have a gun, and Mathias Harder almost certainly did. It was foolish, but she prayed that even this maniac wasn't crazy enough to shoot at an FBI agent.

Maya made her way across the overgrown lawn toward the front door, then stepped back to assess the exit points. The wrap-around garden meant that if the suspect fled, he could potentially escape out of the back. The windows, still concealed with drapes, seemed to be rusted beyond the point of opening. No concern there.

She knocked.

A minute passed with no answer. Maya hammered the door again, harder this time.

With an ear to the door, she listened for signs of life.

For a moment, all she could hear was birds chirping in the nearby trees, but then there was a faint creaking sound from within. Footsteps echoed in the stillness of the room behind the door. She could hear someone beyond move closer to where she stood, then abruptly stop. The sound of rustling fabric took its place.

Suddenly, from the corner of her eye, she caught a movement in one of the windows. A quick, fleeting shadow. It seemed to hesitate, then a pair of eyes locked on to hers through the gap in the curtain. Before Maya could react, the figure retreated, replaced by dirty brown drapes.

Adrenaline surged through her system, and that feeling had become a close friend in the past three days. Her mouth went dry, and she felt a cold bead of sweat roll down the back of her neck.

Time to act.

"Mathias Harder, FBI," she shouted. "Open up."

No response, but Maya could sense him on the other side of the door, lingering like a ghost.

"Mr. Harder, we need to talk. Don't make this difficult."

Then another sound. Footsteps, but quicker now. The floorboards in what Maya assumed was his hallway creaked as the weight shifted toward the back of the house.

Which left only one conclusion: Mathias Harder was trying to flee.

She sprinted around the side of the house, leaped over a fallen tree branch, and skidded slightly on the damp grass. The side was equally as irreparable as the front, and then she emerged in a back yard flanked by a very low fence.

And there, she caught a glimpse of a man hesitantly stepping over the threshold of his back door. He was a mess of tousled hair and red eyes, and a look of sheer panic registered on his face. For a moment, their gazes locked, and Maya saw not a killer but a terrified man, cornered and unsure of his next move. The hair was longer and the skin more haggard, but it was the same man from the mugshot.

But the moment of vulnerability was shattered as Mathias spun around and made a dash back into the house, slamming the door behind him.

"Damn it!" Maya cursed under her breath. She was close, and she knew it. She leaped over the fence, sprinted to the entrance, put her weight into her right leg, and booted the old wooden door down at the first try. She burst inside, and the stench of mold assaulted her nostrils. The back hallway seemed narrower than the front, and it was lined with Victorian-style wallpaper that was on the verge of peeling.

Without hesitation, Maya moved through the house. "FBI, come out!" she shouted. An entrance led directly to a derelict living room. A two-seater sofa, scratched table, discolored carpet. No family photos, no signs of a life well-lived. Perhaps the homestead of a frantic serial killer fed by delusions of grandeur.

To the left, a staircase rose to the second floor, and she could hear muffled footsteps from above. Maya bound up them, and at the top, a narrow corridor extended with doors on either side. "Mathias, come out," Maya demanded. "We need to talk to you."

One door to her left was slightly ajar. Cautiously, Maya approached it and pushed it open with her foot. The room was barely lit by the morning light, and inside was a dusty cube of boxes, piles of newspapers, and old electronics. No place in here to hide, she thought, so she edged out and tried the next one in line.

This time, the door panels looked old and rotting, but the handle was unusually clean. Maya burst inside and rotated between the two blind corners in a second. The room's contents made themselves known, and a wave of nausea rose up in her stomach.

The items she'd seen on the screen a few hours ago had manifested into reality.

Framed newspaper clippings, glossy crime scene photographs, bizarre artifacts in glass boxes, locks of hair, amateur artwork, what looked like human fingernails in plastic bags, handcuffs, kitchen knives, handwritten letters, dental molds, even an orange prison jumpsuit draped over a faceless mannequin.

The place was a shrine to murderers. Unlike every other room in this house, this place was preserved and presented like the exhibits of a museum.

But no sign of the glove.

Behind her, she heard the softest shuffle. She spun on her heel, but it was too late. Mathias sprang from a closet with an iron bar clenched in his palm. He swung, but Maya's instincts kicked in. Adrenaline took over. She ducked below his attack, but the edge of the bar caught her on the temple and sent a searing wave of pain through her skull. The world seemed to blur and spin in a whirlpool of colors and shapes, but Maya had no time for pain. She was sharing airspace with a serial killer, and the only thing between him and a life sentence was her ability to stay alert.

Mathias swung again, but Maya dodged to one side, grabbing him by his attacking wrist to seize his grip. Maya tried to disarm him, but Mathias landed a kick to her stomach and sent her sprawling back into the jumpsuited mannequin, knocking it to the dusty floor. Maya staggered and chided herself for coming in here unarmed. The man who might have been the Fernandina Butcher continued his assault, charging at Maya shoulder-first. Her will to survive took center stage, and in an explosion of muscle memory, Maya sidestepped, pivoted, and channeled all of her remaining strength into a judo throw. Mathias's feet left the ground for a split second before Maya hurled him into one of his glass cabinets, summoning a blanket of glass shards from the heavens. The impact knocked Maya dizzy, but she climbed back to her feet, reached out, and grabbed a butcher's knife, which now lay among the fallen artifacts.

Mathias wheezed as he maneuvered to a sitting position. Blood oozed from his hands and forearms. The wildness in his expression had disappeared, and he now reminded Maya of the tweakers who lived in the tunnels around D.C. He glanced around, taking in the destroyed remnants of his shrine, and then his contemplation settled on the fallen mannequin beside him.

Maya's heart threatened to burst from her chest. She had him. The Fernandina Butcher. He was at her mercy.

But mercy wasn't what she was feeling. What she felt was rage that began in her gut and spread through her veins like poison. Rage at this pathetic man and his pathetic shrine. Rage at herself for coming here alone. Rage at every unsolved case and every missing person and every body that turned up in a ditch somewhere with no one to speak for them except people like her.

She brandished her weapon and said, "The glove. Where is it?"

He let out a pained whimper. His fingers trembled as he plucked a shard of glass from his forearm.

"Keep your hands where I can see 'em. The glove. I won't ask again."

Maya could see his pupils dilating and contracting rapidly, his body trying to process shock and pain and the sudden collapse of whatever fantasy world he'd been living in. Panic, pain, and fear all played on his face like emotions on a slot machine, all spinning and spinning and never quite landing on anything coherent.

"I'm not telling you anything," Mathias spat.

What leverage did she have? She couldn't threaten him with a bullet. Could she threaten to stab him to death?

No. Mathias would know she could never do that.

So she played the game.

With him cornered, she pulled out her cell and dialed 911. "This is Agent Frost with the Fernandina PD. Need police and medical assistance at 213 Comberford Road." She waited a second and then said, "Suspect is badly injured. Lacerations to the spine."

Mathias crawled backward. Maya stepped forward, cutting him off.

Finally, she told the person down the line, "You're asking if he's alive? Uh, that depends how fast you get here."

Maya hung up.

The implication was enough. Mathias wasn't dying, but he might be if he didn't give up the goods.

"One more time." Maya bent down and pressed the tip of the knife to his thigh. "The glove. Where is it?"

Mathias gasped, "The safe. It's in the safe. I promise."

"Good. Move and I gut you, got it?"

Mathias nodded frantically, and Maya breathed properly for the first time in days.

Now she just had to wait for backup to get here, and then she'd march the Fernandina Butcher into the holding cells herself.

The game was over—and she'd won.

FORTY-SIX

Maya's moment of triumph had been cut short just after she'd given Riggs and Devon the short version of the story. She'd told them about the cell phone, the exchange between Krystal and the killer, and the Death Collector website. And just after she'd passed them the glove from Mathias Harder's safe, Devon had flushed red and pulled Maya into an empty side room.

"Devon, I—"

"Shut up, Frost. Do you realize what you just did?"

"Yes."

"You know how stupid that was?"

Maya opened her mouth to defend her actions, then thought better of it. Yes, it was definitely stupid. "I'm sorry, but I caught—"

"I don't care if you caught Jack the fucking Ripper. You went into a suspect's house. Alone. Without backup. Without a weapon. Without telling anyone where you were going. I only found out from tech boy this morning where you'd gone, and I was about to come and find you, but then you show up here with some cops from Georgia and a guy in chains. If you'd have been killed, I wouldn't have even known where to look for your body. You realize you might have just fucked this whole initiative, right?"

"What do you mean?"

"Because this isn't some hippy free-for-all. I have to log everything we do, so how am I supposed to tell Vernon that you just disappeared into some murderer's house without any insurance in place?"

Maya was suddenly eight years old again, while her mother berated her for calling the police tip line—again—because she'd seen a van parked on their street for too long and the operator had recognized her voice and told her mother that this was the seventh time this month. "I'm sorry. I just got swept up."

"You're three days into this assignment. Three days. And you pulled a stunt that would get a veteran agent suspended. I was supposed to be mentoring you, making sure you didn't get yourself killed, and you decided to go Lone Ranger on a serial killer in another state. Vernon's going to shaft me in the ass over this."

Devon had every right to scold her. Now that the adrenaline was wearing off, Maya was starting to see what a stupid move it had been. The whole drive back from Harriets Bluff, sitting in silence while the trooper drove and Mathias stared out the window with his dead fish eyes, Maya had known she'd screwed up. But hearing Devon say it out loud made it real. "I thought I could handle it. I just wanted to... prove I could do it."

"Prove it to who? Me? Yourself?" Devon shook her head.

"This isn't about proving anything. You're lucky this guy didn't shoot you the second you stepped into his house. You got lucky. That's it."

"It won't happen again," Maya said quietly.

"You're damn right it won't because it's not just yourself you're screwing when you do things like that. It's me too. It's the whole damn Bureau. Imagine the public reaction if one of our rookie agents died in their first week. *The FBI can't even keep themselves safe, let alone everyone in America.* We already have enough problems without new agents going rogue, understand?"

"I understand. I'm sorry."

Devon turned toward the door and yanked it open. Then she turned back and said, "Oh, and this guy *better* be our killer, otherwise it's going to get worse for you."

The door slammed.

Maya's body temperature had risen to infernal levels, and so she pressed her hands to the wall to try and cool herself. The humiliation crawled under skin, but here in the sterile light of the precinct, she knew that she deserved it. In a way, Devon had gone easy on her because her partner had every right to kick her off the team.

Maya straightened up and processed the disciplinary. She'd made a mistake in how she'd done this, but the result was still good. Mathias Harder was in custody. The glove was in evidence. All she had to do now was make him talk.

A CROWD HAD GATHERED around the one-way glass outside the interrogation room because it seemed that everyone wanted to lay eyes on the man who might just be the Fernandina Butcher. Devon was among them, and she wore the expression of someone who'd just drunk concentrated lemon juice. Sheriff Riggs was there too with a cell phone stuck to his ear.

Inside the interrogation room sat a shackled Mathias Harder. Maya regarded him, and almost everything about him matched the profile of the unsub. He was the right age, had the right build, lived close enough to the crime scenes to have scoped them out before hitting them, had a serial killer obsession, and had the same build as the figure from the Morgan's Hardware CCTV footage.

However, there was only one thing that didn't add up.

"The tattoo," Devon said so loudly that all of the cops stopped and stared. "He doesn't have a pentagram tattoo on his hand, Frost."

"I know. I'm hoping it was a temporary tattoo or he drew it on with a marker."

"Yeah. I don't like how you got him, but he fits the profile."

Riggs ended his call and joined the party. He said, "Agents, I've got some guys at Harder's place. They're working with the Kingsland PD. With any luck, they'll find something that connects him to at least one of the vics."

"What about the glove?" Maya asked.

"It's with the lab, and they've found multiple sources of DNA on it. If it matches Teresa Morgan, we can charge this son of a bitch today. There's just something that's bothering me. I'm not big on profiling like you ladies, but human nature is human nature."

Maya's eyes didn't stray from Mathias. Their killer was as brazen as any psychopath in history, but he drew a line between theatrics and stupidity. He was a risk taker, but he'd covered his tracks at every turn. "I know what you're getting at, Sheriff. He went above and beyond to conceal himself, so why would he advertise his own clothing on a public website? The trail was difficult to follow, but he must have known we'd find it."

"Unless he trusted the sickos on that website not to snitch," Devon said.

"It's bold but not impossible," Riggs said. "How long are we able to hold him?"

Devon said, "He's in possession of a murderer's glove, Sheriff. We can hold him until the heat death of the universe. We don't even need solid evidence because the circumstantial evidence is enough to charge him. If he doesn't have an alibi for the past three nights, then we could get him in front of a judge before Christmas."

"Let's hope so. You guys going to do the official interview?"

Devon side-eyed Maya, then gestured for her to head inside. "Go on, Frost."

Maya's breath hitched. "What? Me?"

"You want to be the hero of the day? Get in there and get a confession, and if you do that, then *maybe* Vernon won't rip you a new asshole when you get to HQ."

Maya stared at the door. Then at Devon. Then back at the door. Her mouth had gone dry again, that same desert-throat feeling she'd had outside Harder's house, except this time she couldn't blame it on adrenaline.

"You're not coming in?"

"This is your collar, Frost. You found the website. You tracked down Harder. You kicked in his door and threw him through a cabinet. So finish what you started."

FORTY-SEVEN

"My name's Agent Frost with the FBI. You're Mathias Harder, correct?" Maya said as she pushed *PLAY* on the tape recorder. This was it. Her hands were shaking, so she balled them into fists to stop the tremor. Three days ago, she'd been sitting at her desk in Intelligence, dreaming about moments like this. Now the moment was here, and all she wanted was to run.

But running wasn't an option. This was her chance to either prove she belonged here or confirm every doubt Devon had about bringing a rookie analyst into the field.

And get justice for three people who couldn't get justice for themselves anymore.

"That's me," Mathias said.

The temperature in here was freezing because Devon had insisted that killers talked more when they were cold. There was something to be said for it because discomfort meant irritation, and irritation meant they would lash out. Amidst that rage often came nuggets of truth. "Let's talk about where you were the last three nights. And I want the truth. Because right now, everything is pointing at you, and if you can't give me something solid, this is going to go down a very unpleasant road for you."

Mathias' bushy hair dropped down in front of the black slits that passed for eyes. He pressed his wrists together and sat back in his chair. "I was at home," he said.

Maya processed his tone, trying to match it to the voice on the other end of the phone line last night. Both were nondescript, too ordinary to make any solid conclusions. "Can anyone confirm that?"

"No." He smirked.

Maya couldn't help herself. "This funny to you? Do you like being a suspect in a murder case?"

The man in front of her shrugged. "It's exciting, but it's ridiculous that you think I'm the Butcher. I don't even live around here."

"It's a one-hour drive. Not exactly a million miles away."

"Detective... Frost, is it?" Mathias asked. "Everyone knows serial killers operate in geographical comfort zones. I've never even been to this area. Why would I commit murders here?"

Maya clasped her hands together, a little offended that this kid was trying to school her on her subject of expertise.

"Don't believe everything you see on CSI," she said. "Killers regularly travel far and wide to commit murder. And just because you've never lived here doesn't mean you don't know this area."

Mathias jingled the chains around his wrists. "Babydoll, I'm Georgia through and through. Why would I leave the best state in the world for this shithole?"

Maya saw a crack. Time to get her claws in and rip it open. "Georgia through and through? Funny, you don't sound like you're from Georgia. I'm hearing mid-Atlantic, a little New Orleans."

Mathias' response was hard to read. He had an unsettling stillness about him, a sense of calm that could either be the product of innocence or a practiced façade by someone who had anticipated he'd be in an interrogation room one day. "Yes, Detective Frost, my accent might be a bit mixed. Parents moved around a lot. But what's that got to do with anything?"

"People's pasts are interesting, wouldn't you say? They shape who we become, and they often leave a trail. A trail that, given enough time, someone can follow."

"What trail? I've lived a very ordinary life, Detective. You're reaching, looking for something that isn't there."

"But there's always something there," Maya said. "You don't end up in an interrogation room, chained to a table, because you lived an ordinary life. You say you have no connection to this area, yet you're sitting here with a murderer's glove that matches CCTV footage. So either you're the unluckiest man in Georgia, or you're involved."

Now his smirk had fully disappeared. He was clearly re-evaluating, perhaps realizing that his performance wasn't as convincing as he had hoped. "Well, we'll see about that when my lawyer arrives."

My lawyer, she thought. "You don't have a lawyer. By the looks of you, I don't think your wallet would stretch far enough for that."

"Don't talk to me about money. You don't know anything about me or my resources."

"Resources? You sell murder relics to freaks. And by the looks of your site, you don't sell a whole lot of them. Maybe that's why you've engineered a little situation for you to maximize sales. Kill a few people, get noticed, sell the goods."

Mathias reddened. His jaw tensed. "That's *not* what happened. I'm *not* the Butcher."

Maya let the moment linger. She didn't like it when people spoke in absolutes because absolutes suggested innocence. Guilty parties favored a simple *yes* or *no*, but people with clear consciences addressed the accusations. *I did not kill that woman.*

"I think desperation leads people to do desperate things, and the fact that you're sitting here with no alibi, a matching glove, and now a temper doesn't look good for you."

"I didn't kill *anyone.*"

Maya regarded his body language. She could see the words tugging at his lips, fighting a war between speaking and staying quiet. She helped him along. "But...?"

"But nothing."

"Are you sure?"

Mathias wrinkled his nose. "Pretty sure."

"But not completely sure."

He looked up at the ceiling. Maya was sure she could see some shards of glass still stuck in his neck.

"Look, Mathias, we're seconds away from charging you with triple homicide, so if you don't want to end up with the lethal injection, I suggest you—"

"I talked to him, all right? I was in contact with him. Your killer. Just once."

A rod went down Maya's spine. "Excuse me?"

"He reached out to me, OK? I swear to God. He wanted to sell his glove. Sent me a picture of him wearing it at the crime scene and everything. I couldn't pass up an opportunity like that."

Maya pressed her fingers to her eyes and held back a surge of emotions. She could feel the frustration bubbling up like a volcano ready to erupt. "You're telling me a serial murderer contacted you... and you didn't tell the police?"

"I... thought it was a hoax. These guys, they get their kicks pretending to be all sorts of sick things online. But then he sent the picture, and it looked real. It looked like it could be the real deal."

"Right. And then what? You thought it was your lucky day?"

"It's not like that. I deal in memorabilia, not... not the real thing. But this could have been a big score for me, you know? The ultimate murderabilia item. I just froze, OK?"

"You froze," Maya repeated. "You're sitting on evidence that could lead to the arrest of a murderer, and you froze?"

Mathias was trembling now, and Maya didn't like it. The comments sounded like a lie, but his body language suggested they weren't. "I know how it sounds. I messed up. But I didn't kill anyone, Detective. I swear to you, I'm not the Butcher. I just... needed the money."

Mathias' admission had cracked the door open, and she could see the shadows lurking behind it. Maya had to proceed carefully, for the truth was close. She waited a moment, letting Mathias stew on his admission of wrongdoing. "Let's say I believe you. I need that picture, and I need to know how he contacted you. Email? Phone? Did you meet him in person?"

"Dark web," Mathias said with haste. "Untraceable. Where I do most of my business. I never met him. I just left a grand in my trash. The next day it's gone, and there's a glove in its place."

"Risky move," Maya said with suspicion.

"I know. But me and the Butcher, we developed a... rapport."

Maya was barely able to comprehend what she was hearing, and she couldn't be sure where the truth ended and the lie began—or whether this was all just excuses and Mathias Harder was trying to talk himself out of a death sentence.

"We're going to need access to your computer, your accounts, everything. If you're telling the truth, it's in your best interest to help us catch this man. Understand?"

Mathias nodded uncontrollably. Gone was the cockiness, and a man aware of the gravity of his predicament was left behind.

"I need to talk to my colleagues," Maya said. "We'll be seizing your equipment. We'll reconvene in thirty minutes, and I want you to tell me *everything* from start to finish, OK?"

Maya stood up, not even giving Mathias a chance to respond. She headed toward the door, where no doubt Devon was waiting on the other side, ready to give her another verbal punch to the face. Vernon was going to reprimand her, and she might have just screwed up her entire career.

Because she didn't know exactly what was going on, but she was certain that Mathias Harder wasn't the Fernandina Butcher.

FORTY-EIGHT

"WELL?" DEVON ASKED. SHE AND SHERIFF RIGGS WERE leaning against the wall.

Maya looked at Mathias Harder through the glass, then back at her partner. Her mouth went dry as bone. "He's not the killer."

"I know."

"He said he brought the glove from the real killer on the dark web."

"I heard."

Three days, Maya thought. She'd lasted three days in the field before imploding spectacularly. "What do you think?"

"I think we're getting ahead of ourselves because while you were in there, the lab confirmed that Teresa Morgan's DNA *is* on that glove."

Two conflicting emotions fought for dominance, but Maya couldn't put a name to either one. "So the glove is real, and Mathias might be the unsub after all."

"I'm going to say what I always say, Frost, and that's follow the evidence, and what does the evidence say?"

"It says that Mathias Harder killed Teresa Morgan."

Devon laughed. "No it doesn't. It says the opposite. Imagine you're a serial murderer—are you really going to keep an item you wore while committing murder in a safe in your house? If the police raided your house, that's the first thing they'd check. And advertising your *own* murder clothing online? That's... stupid."

"But it could be an elaborate insurance plan. A double bluff. Like he set all of this up just in case the police suspected him."

"Why bother? If he *hadn't* advertised that stupid glove, then nobody would have considered him in the first place. Harder is just a scumbag, and if this was the 1920s, he'd be one of those barkers trying to lure you into his freak show. He's not a killer."

Riggs showed his palms. He'd been silent until now. "Whoa, hold up a second. You two think that this creep is *innocent?*"

"He's guilty of a lot of things, Sheriff, but murder isn't one of them."

He waved off the comment and took two steps back. "I must be getting too old for this because in my day, when you found a victim's DNA on someone's glove, they probably killed them."

"He's a collector, Sheriff. Nothing more. Our killer knows this area like the back of his hand, probably lived here his entire life. Mathias hasn't. And our killer isn't motivated by financial gain; otherwise he would have robbed his victims too. He likes the attention, but he's not dumb enough to sell his own murder clothing on a public website."

Maya's analytical mind began to weigh the probabilities. It was plausible that the Butcher, proud of his work, would reach out to someone who could appreciate the art of his kills. It fit a certain profile, the type that needed to flaunt and have his ego stroked by the notoriety of his crimes. Mathias, with his murderabilia collection, made the perfect audience.

But then why Mathias' hesitation to share this with the authorities? The fear of being implicated or the thrill of being part of something so vile?

"I'm not buying it," Riggs said. "I'll get you his computer and cell phone by all means, but if they come up dry, then I'm taking this guy to the cleaners."

"You don't have to buy it, Sheriff. But we have to be thorough. If we put the wrong man behind bars, the real Butcher keeps slaughtering. Is that a risk you're willing to take?"

"And if you're wrong? If our perp is sitting right there in front of us? Imagine how ridiculous we'll look if we had a guy with hard evidence in our laps and still didn't charge him."

They both went silent, so Maya filled the gap. "If you anticipate the human mind, it leaves nothing to chance."

"Well, start anticipating because I wouldn't wanna be in your shoes if you overlook this guy because of some psychology stuff. I'll get his devices to Alfie and tell him to go for broke."

Riggs made a swift exit with his phone to his ear. Maya turned her focus back to Mathias, who now appeared small and inconsequential behind the glass. She couldn't shake the feeling that he was just a cog in the machine of this investigation, not the mastermind behind it all. She was well aware of the dangers of tunnel vision, and she couldn't afford to get this wrong. Mathias was the key that could unlock her final door, so she needed to explore this so-called *rapport* Mathias had developed with the real killer.

But first she needed to find out what secrets Mathias' computer held.

FORTY-NINE

Two hours later, Maya was back with Alfie in his crypt. His night shift was coming to an end—as he'd been quick to point out to her—but Maya had begged him to stay a little longer. Now he had Mathias Harder's desktop computer hooked up to his own.

"Anything?" Maya asked.

Alfie rubbed his eyes wearily, as if to emphasize his exhaustion to his apparent captor. "Hard drive is clean as a whistle. This guy knows how to cover his tracks. All I've got is this." Alfie opened up a JPG file and maximized it to full screen.

The image on the screen made Maya's blood run cold. It was a photograph of a gloved hand—the very same glove Mathias Harder had in his possession. But this image was different because it had been photographed at the Morgan's Hardware crime scene. Maya recognized the familiar hardwood floor and bottles of motor oil in the background. The glove was still wrapped around a gaunt hand.

More proof that the glove was the genuine article.

"Where'd this picture come from?" she asked. "Can you find the source? If it came directly from a camera roll, then Mathias could be guiltier than I thought."

Alfie scratched the back of his neck. "That's the problem. The meta data from the image says it came from an online link. Usually, I could find the source through that, but your guy is a dark web deviant."

"Mathias mentioned the dark web when I spoke to him," Maya said.

"Yeah. Mathias has the Tor browser installed on here, so he's definitely using the dark web. But it's not like regular browsers. There's no history. No saved logins. No search function. No caches. It's all encrypted, anonymously routed, the works."

Maya processed the information, feeling like this could be the end of the line for Mathias. By trying to cover his tracks, he'd incriminated himself. If she couldn't prove Mathias had been in contact with the real killer, the higher-ups in the Bureau would want to secure a charge before the weekend.

"So there's no trace of his conversations on there?"

"No. It's impossible. Anonymity is the dark web's top priority. All trails are erased as soon as they've been followed."

"Can we tell anything from his Tor usage patterns? Times he accessed, frequency, anything like that?"

"No. According to his logs, his Tor sessions last hours at a time. Impossible to narrow anything down through here. I'll keep digging, but don't hold your breath."

As Alfie worked, Maya couldn't shake a nagging thought.

The Butcher had been meticulous, always staying one step ahead. Why reach out to Mathias, of all people? Was it simply a matter of finding a willing buyer for his morbid trophy, or was there more to their connection? A measly thousand dollars was small compensation for what he offered —barely enough to survive a week these days—so perhaps there was something else at play.

If the Fernandina Butcher was as smart as Maya thought, then he might have considered the one component of his journey that other serial killers never did.

Serial murder was an endless voyage that only death or imprisonment could bring to an end. Killers were too consumed by their delusions or missions or sexual gratification to ever consider that one day they would need to hang up their weapons for good if they wanted to live a life outside of a prison cell.

But an elite select few did.

Serial offenders who were capable, aware, and not bound by impulses understood that investigators would never stop chasing them. High-profile cases were forever on the police's radar, which meant there was only one way for the killer to ensure that he could stop looking over his shoulder at every turn.

If someone else took the blame.

Maya shivered as the thought crystallized. The Fernandina Butcher, cunning and meticulous as he was, might have orchestrated a frame job. Mathias Harder, an easy target with his dark web dealings and obsession with murderabilia, could be the perfect scapegoat. With his murky online activities and lack of proof that he'd been in contact with the real perpetrator, Mathias was an ideal candidate to shoulder the blame. The Butcher could plant the glove, send the photo, and escape with his freedom while Mathias took the fall.

Thinking about it, the Butcher had pulled a similar move with Luke Kavanagh, the young hunter.

Alfie jumped in. "I've found some chat program he might have used on the dark web, but no chat history."

"Nothing at all?"

"Nope. Maya, based on this, Mathias hasn't been in contact with anyone. Are you sure your guy isn't just trying to worm his way out of this?"

The profile of the Fernandina Butcher was etched deeply in her mind, yet Mathias' actions carved out an anomaly she couldn't ignore. Mathias was a collector of the macabre but not a creator of it. His fascination with the grotesque was evident, but did it extend to the orchestration of the crimes themselves? His lack of a pentagram tattoo, the absence of any real connection to the city, and most damningly of all, the fact that he *had* this glove. No serial killer she knew had purposely kept their murder clothing and *advertised* it to the world.

Maya needed a new plan, so she put her own methodical brain to work.

To catch a predator, she might need to think like one.

If Mathias was indeed just a middleman, then he might be the bait she needed to draw the real killer out of hiding.

A plan began to take shape.

She'd already tried to set up a date with the killer and failed.

But as Becky always told her, you usually didn't get lucky until the second date.

"You found his chat program, right?"

"Yup."

"Then let's outsmart this son of a bitch. Stay here, I'll be back in five minutes," Maya said as she exited the office.

She had a new fire, new determination. She had the next move planned out before she reached the interrogation room.

And Mathias Harder, unwittingly or not, was going to help her do it.

FIFTY

Nightfall was coming, and he had work to do.

Tools first. He made sure he had everything he needed and then loaded them into what his peers might call a murder kit. The detective had left him no choice. She'd forced his hand, and now he had to commit the ultimate act of bloodshed.

Out of his study, he went back to the broken mirror and pored over his reflection. Pale skin and translucent flesh, dark circles under his eyes, and the look of a man who'd fully embraced the madness within. Any traces of Gein and Ramirez and Ridgway had all disappeared, and now he'd assumed the role of a lesser-known monster. Someone who was yet to reach the same heights as the greats but was no less barbaric.

He stood motionless for a moment, considering what came next. Unlike the others, which he'd been rehearsing in his head for years, this was all brand new, and the freshness excited him. The best monsters could adapt to the changing world, and that's what he'd do tonight.

As he mentally rehearsed each step of the night ahead, the distinctive ping of a message from his computer drew his attention. It was a notification from the depths of the dark web. His computer screen flared to life, and he saw that the tab with his Tor browser was flashing orange. He opened it up.

One new message.

He paused, collected himself, and let the unexpected rush subside. He wasn't the most tech savvy guy in the world, but even he knew that surprises from the dark web could be dangerous. His careful planning for tonight did not include interruptions, especially not at such a critical moment.

But there, he saw a familiar name.

ObsidianCollector.

Next to that: *1 new message.*

The murderabilia seller—the man who was going to solve all of his financial woes once these games were over—was back.

He eyed the new message with caution because he hadn't expected such hasty communication since their trade. The last time they'd interacted, he'd told Obsidian that he'd be in touch whenever a new item became available.

The message read: *Need more. Last item sold within 1 hour!*

He sat down in his worn leather chair, regarding the screen as though it held the secrets of life and death. After a moment of thought, he checked the collector's website and indeed found no sign of the glove for sale.

The prospect of someone owning his murder glove gave him a thrill akin to his first kill, the kill that psychology textbooks said he'd be chasing for the rest of his life. He leaned forward and began typing a reply, although he understood that he needed to balance his need for caution with the lure of profit and infamy.

Who bought it? he typed.

The reply came back in a few seconds. *A collector in Canada. Someone I trust. Had a LOT of my regular customers asking about it. Think we can sell tons more without listing on website.*

He shot back to his keyboard, preparing a reply, but then retreated. Obsidian hadn't been this eager last time. In fact, he'd been very reserved about taking in a piece of evidence relating to an active case.

Perhaps Obsidian was more money-hungry than he'd anticipated.

Or there was something else going on.

He etched out his response, choosing his words carefully. *I don't have anything to sell you.*

A minute passed. Two minutes. He could feel the presence on the other side of the screen, ruminating, equally selective about their response.

Something wasn't right. The churn in his gut. The sweat leaking from his forehead. His subconscious was speaking to him the same way it had at the riverside scene, right before he'd miraculously escaped with his life and freedom.

Finally, ObsidianCollector replied.

Anything. Clothing, jewelry, trinkets, stuff from your victims. Paying big money.

"Jewelry and trinkets?" he said aloud. He hadn't taken

any such things from the victims, and last time he'd spoken to Obsidian, he'd said that demand was low for items belonging to victims. Collectors wanted tangible connections to the predators, not the prey.

Now he was convinced.

The person on the other side of the screen wasn't ObsidianCollector.

The shift in tone, the eagerness, was out of character for the usually cautious and discerning buyer. This was someone else, someone trying to lure him into a trap.

And he had an idea who.

The same bitch who'd interrupted his third kill and nearly driven him into a ditch.

If she wanted to play a game, he'd ensure they were going to play on his terms. The best serial killers shifted plans when opportunity arose, and here an opportunity had fallen into his lap. It was nothing short of a gift from the murder gods.

I do have one thing, he typed and clicked send.

The swift reply came back. *Whatever it is, five grand, my place. Same dead drop. Midnight.*

Amusement overwrote the paranoia for a moment. He wasn't going back to Georgia anytime soon. The long drive had been risky enough with all the cameras around.

No. You'll have to come to my address in Fernandina, he wrote back.

Fine. I can do that. Tonight?

A grin spread across his face. He readied another message, but Obsidian beat him to it.

What's your address?

Oh, he'd give the detective the address. It was time to

show her a glimpse behind the mask, a fragment of truth that she certainly wouldn't be prepared for.

He typed his reply.

10pm tonight. Be online. I'll give you my address then.

He turned off his screen, stood up, and collected his things. Gloves, tools, a newfound sense of willpower. He glanced around his lair and ruminated how it was here that he had plotted his rise to infamy, and now it would serve as the starting point for his most audacious act yet. Every detail mattered tonight. There was no room for error.

Though a copycat he might be, soon the Fernandina Butcher would be categorized alongside Gein, Ramirez, and Ridgway for the rest of time.

Then he would sell his goods, make his fortune, and disappear into the night, never to be seen again.

The countdown to freedom was on.

Time to finish what he'd started.

FIFTY-ONE

MAYA READ THE MESSAGE, THE TIMESTAMP, AND THEN willed the *offline* status to switch back to *online*.

It didn't happen.

10pm tonight. Be online. I'll give you my address then.

With Mathias' help, she'd contacted the Fernandina Butcher through his dark web messaging program. She'd pretended to be ObsidianCollector and engaged in a risky dance with the real killer—for the second time. She was walking on ice because if the killer got a hint that it wasn't Mathias on the other side of the screen, he'd immediately cease contact and leave her at another dead end.

But he'd promised her an address at ten p.m. tonight.

Maya glanced at the wall clock in her office: 9:56 p.m.

"Come on, you bastard," she breathed. Her eyes flickered to her computer screen every few seconds, awaiting the next piece of the puzzle. The seconds felt like hours, tormenting her, morphing her office into a prison cell.

Her conversation with the Butcher had confirmed two

things. First, Mathias Harder wasn't her killer because he'd been locked back in the interrogation room once he'd provided access to his dark web program. Second, the killer was a Fernandina local.

Back to the clock: 9:57 p.m. She paced the room and watched the evening shift prepare their leave and the night shift arrive. Alfie had gone home this afternoon at Maya's request because she'd already kept him five hours past his shift. Devon was outside on the phone to Vernon, and Maya was glad she couldn't hear what they were talking about. Her name had definitely come up a few times, and Vernon was probably already preparing his disciplinary measures. Devon said she'd be available if need be, and if the killer kept up his pattern of killing every evening, Maya would be needing Devon pretty soon.

Unless this so-called address he was going to give her turned out to be genuine.

At 9:58 p.m., Maya went over to her whiteboard pinned with crime scene photos. So far, there'd been only been one piece of DNA evidence scraped from any of them, and that was from the killer's own glove. Some uniforms were checking CCTV cameras around Liles River to see if they could capture the truck's license plate from last night, but no hits so far. Maya wasn't holding her breath because if this killer was smart enough to misdirect the entire police department, he was smart enough to avoid cameras, even in a high speed chase.

The clock ticked over to 9:59. If this mysterious chatter stayed true to his word and gave up his address, then she'd summon the cavalry and infiltrate before the night was out. She'd played a similar game already but failed to fool him, so she could only hope that he hadn't seen through her plans this time. And the more time that went on, the more chance the killer had of overthinking. If he suffered a bout of panic or paranoia—not uncommon in serial killers during this stage of their reigns—then she could kiss goodbye to her lead and say hello to another dead end.

Ten p.m. arrived. Maya hovered over the screen again, putting faith in the killer's punctuality. She waited twenty seconds, thirty seconds. His status still read *offline* next to a red circle.

Come on, come on.

When had she last slept? Sometime this morning, in her car outside Mathias Harder's house. She'd gone past the needing-sleep stage now and was convinced she could go another twenty-four hours before unconsciousness dragged her down. Her brain then gave up the useless fact that the longest someone had ever gone without sleep was eleven days.

Another minute went by—10:01 p.m.

Had the Butcher sensed the trap? Or was he toying with her, prolonging the agony of the wait?

10:02.

10:03.

Maya breathed a deep sigh, balled her hand into a fist, and drove it into the desk. She resigned herself to the probability that her killer had vanished, perhaps in a bout of paranoia, and now she was going to stare at a red circle all night. How foolish she'd been to think that a front-page serial killer would give up his address to anyone. An address was as good as an identity, and the Fernandina Butcher wasn't going to breach his veil of anonymity to anyone, even someone he apparently trusted.

10:06 p.m. arrived. Maya moved back to her whiteboard and scoured the pictures, seeking anything she might have missed at first glance. She wrapped a hand around her temples to thwart an oncoming headache, although it achieved very little. The diminishing glimmer of hope amplified the pain that was coursing through her body, because without hope there could be no true despair.

Beyond the window, a starless night set in. Maya thought of the victims: Teresa Morgan, Elaine and Cecil Hutchins, Krystal Larkin. These four people who deserved better than what Maya had provided them. In time, she'd be the one to give their extended families the details of their respective deaths, and she'd have to look at them and tell them that she'd failed to find the person responsible. She suddenly remembered the day that the police had told her family that Abigail was officially a missing person.

As Maya dwelled on the past—something she tried not to do—something pulled her back into the present.

A sound.

A ping.

She spun around.

The red circle had turned green, and now her anonymous chatter's status was *online*.

He was back.

One new message.

Maya grabbed the mouse and clicked.

This was it. The moment she'd get a serial killer's address. She suddenly had visions of the killer toying with her, laughing at her, declaring his superiority that he'd seen through her ruse. Surely there was no way this wanted criminal would give up his own location.

But Maya was wrong.

Because his message said exactly that.

114 Whitechapel Avenue.

It felt like nails had penetrated her feet because Maya couldn't move. A sudden onslaught of electricity jolted every nerve ending in her body.

"114 Whitechapel Avenue," she repeated.

The address swirled around her mind, bringing forth a recent memory. Maya's breath hitched in her throat as she stared at the screen.

She recognized this address.

Understanding arrived in a rush. The pattern had been there the entire time, hidden in plain sight, waiting for her to step back far enough to recognize what she was looking at. Three days of data points suddenly formed a line, and that line led straight to an address she knew by heart.

She'd been at this address two nights ago.

Call me Fred.

It was Alfie's home.

FIFTY-TWO

Maya sped through the streets toward Alfie's house with Devon in the passenger seat. The pieces of the puzzle that had eluded her for so long now seemed glaringly obvious. How had she missed them? Each piece of evidence, the killer's taunts—both had been leading her to this point, yet she'd been too engrossed in the details to see the bigger picture. She didn't want to believe it, but at this point, she had no choice.

She'd sat with Alfie in his so-called crypt, inches away from him, all while he'd pretended to be the innocent tech guy just trying to help with the investigation. But really, he'd been hiding a secret.

"Frost, talk me through this, because I'm not sure what's going on."

"Alfie. He was the one who planted the idea about the Green River Killer in my head in the first place. After we went to the bar the other night, Alfie picked me up in his truck."

"He picked you up?"

Maya took a corner way too sharply. She'd already wrecked one car since coming to Florida, and at this rate, she was heading for a sequel. "Yeah. He drove past, spotted me, then invited me back to his place."

"You said truck?"

"Yes. Black."

"Like the one we saw at the river?"

"Yes. I mean, I can't be sure, but similar. And the timings match up too. All of the kills have taken place while Alfie was out of the office, and then there's the obvious. What message did the killer leave at the Hutchins scene?"

"Call me Fred," said Devon.

"It wasn't just a reference to the Green River Killer. It was his real name. Alfie. Alfred."

Maya thought back to her apartment in D.C., which now felt a million miles away. What had Becky said? *Don't trust anyone named Kyle. Or Alfie, or any guy who has an X in their name.* Maya had brushed it off as Becky's sweeping generalizations of modern men, but Maya guessed she owed her an apology. She owed a lot of people apologies, she thought, because if this killer had been right in front of her from the beginning, she could have kept three innocents alive if she hadn't been so God damn blind.

"Why would he give up his own address?" asked Devon. "This is super risky, even for our guy."

"Something tells me Alfie's project is coming to an end, and this is his end game."

The GPS said they were 0.2 miles from their destination, and Devon said, "Ditch it here. We don't want him to see us coming."

Maya planted the wheels on the curb and slammed on the brakes. She could see Alfie's house at the end of the street, and there was light in the front window and Alfie's truck in the driveway. "This might be a trap. We need to be careful."

"Yes we do."

"What's the approach? Knock? Ambush?"

Devon cocked her firearm. "The only thing I'm knocking is this guy's teeth out. We go in all guns blazing. Got it?"

"Got it."

"I'm going in first." Devon jumped out of the car and made her way up the street with Maya behind. They passed houses, parked cars, streetlamps—and then Alfie's house came into view. Maya's brain wouldn't shut up. It kept replaying every interaction with Alfie. The shy smile when she'd first met him in the kitchen. The way he'd flirted in that never-flirted-before kind of way. The enthusiasm in his voice when he'd shown her the enhanced CCTV footage. Had any of it been real?

She felt worse than stupid. Someone who'd been played so thoroughly she hadn't even noticed the strings. Alfie had fed her hints and led her by the nose through this entire investigation, and she'd eaten it up because she'd wanted so badly to prove she belonged in the field, to show Devon and Vernon and everyone else that she was more than just an analyst.

How had she not connected it sooner?

Because you didn't want to, whispered a voice in her head. *Because he was nice to you, and you wanted to believe he could look at you and not see something to manipulate.*

Maya shoved the thought down as they reached the

property line. Devon moved up the driveway in a crouch and used the truck for cover. Maya followed close by. Then they came to the front door – the same front door Alfie had opened and ushered her through like a gentleman just nights ago.

But as the thoughts collected, Maya spotted a beam of light between the door and the frame.

It was ajar.

Devon caught it too. She turned and regarded her partner. Maya didn't know.

Was this an invitation? Her anonymous chatter hadn't given her any instructions regarding the dead drop item, simply an address. Perhaps he expected his collector friend to simply walk inside?

No, Maya told herself. Alfie—or the Fernandina Butcher—wouldn't be so careless. Was it an oversight? Or another part of his game?

Devon mouthed, *We're going in.*

This was it. Time to see Alfie for who he really was.

Devon pushed the door open with her boot. It swung inward without a sound.

"FBI," she called down the hallway. "Alfred Kustka, we need to speak with you."

Nothing came back.

Inside, lavender invaded her senses. She'd smelled it the other night and welcomed it, but now it made her feel sick. She and Devon edged through the carpeted hallway, and Maya attuned her senses to that of the silent house. Was Alfie expecting his collector friend to walk inside, right into his front room?

Up ahead, the door to the living room sat ajar too. Maya

nudged her partner toward it because it was the only room in this house she was familiar with. Devon nodded and took the lead.

Maya needed answers. She needed finality.

Devon nudged the living room door with her foot. Light engulfed the hallway, and Maya found herself staring at the same trappings she'd seen two nights ago. Brown leather sofa, mahogany coffee table, football memorabilia, the smallest TV she'd ever seen.

But it was the new centerpiece that drew Maya's attention.

The lavender mixed with the coppery tang of mass blood loss, and her heart instantly turned to stone. The image before her was a picture of madness, dragged straight from her nightmares into reality.

No. Alfie was not the Fernandina Butcher.

Because his corpse took pole position on the living room floor. Bloodied, battered. He lay face-down with his arms outspread, and his left hand had been purposely positioned for Maya's eyes.

Devon edged closer, leaned down, and glared at Alfie's hand.

"Frost. Look."

She didn't need to. A wave of nausea hit her, and she stumbled backward against the wall. Alfie surely hadn't been part of the killer's plan. He'd been killed because of her.

And the killer had removed his index finger.

Just like the Bangor Ripper had done to his victims.

HE DROVE NORTH, windows down, cool night air rushing through the cab. His hands gripped the steering wheel loose and easy. Blood was still caked under his fingernails, but he'd deal with that later.

What a rush.

This kill had been different from the others. He didn't even know the guy's name or how much of a fight he'd put up, and the silly bastard had opened his door like he'd been expecting a pizza delivery. Trusting to the end. Stupid to the end.

With his knife brandished, he'd walked right in with the guy as his hostage. Same house he'd watched Frost enter two nights ago when he'd been tailing her. The fight had been brief because the guy might have been tall, but size didn't matter when metal was on your side. Three quick stabs to the chest. One across the throat.

Then the real work began.

The finger had been tricky. He'd brought pruning shears from his shed, the kind used for thick branches. They'd done the job cleanly enough. One quick squeeze, and the bone separated. The victim had been dead by that point, which was a shame, he reasoned. The Bangor Ripper had always taken his trophies while the victims were still breathing. But timing was everything, and he couldn't risk the victim making noise.

He glanced at the passenger seat. Two items sat there.

The finger was in one bag with a very nice gold ring still attached. A gift for later. He'd mail it north, send it to the person who'd inspired this whole beautiful project. He could sell it to aid his financial woes, but he'd learned his lesson in that regard. He'd need to find a more trusted buyer than

Obsidian, because by the sounds of it, Frost had Obsidian in custody. That would come later.

And next to the severed finger was something even more valuable.

Usually, such an object would be useless to him.

But with the finger, it opened up a world of possibilities.

And after he'd done that, he'd disappear into the night and become mythical, just like his heroes.

He'd won.

FIFTY-THREE

Maya felt the world spinning. The lines between hunter and hunted blurred in her mind. She'd come here to confront a monster only to find that she'd been fooled again. Her breathing was shallow, and she couldn't tear her eyes off the dead body in front of her.

Alfie Kustka.

"Frost, he's taken Alfie's finger. Like the Bangor Ripper did."

"I know."

"That's... your case."

"My case? I never worked it."

"But you solved it, and I think..."—Devon glanced back at her—"that he did this for you."

It all paralyzed her in place. The multiple failures, the fear of being outmaneuvered, of signing Alfie's death warrant just by getting close to him. But how did the Butcher know about Alfie? How did he know where he lived?

"How could the killer know that? Only a few people in the FBI know that."

"Not true. We have newsletters that go out to governments around the country. Sometimes it's posted online, and our guy knows his way around computers."

"It's my fault. I got Alfie killed."

"You didn't get anyone killed. I'll search this place to make sure no one's hiding in here. You go outside and call it in. Medics, Riggs, everyone."

"I'm sorry," she managed to say, but it was a pathetic display of remorse. No words could undo the horrors in front of her. Every decision she had made, every step she had taken in this investigation seemed to mock her now. Whoever the Fernandina Butcher was, he could somehow predict her every move, as though he had a lens that could peer into the future. Guilt wrapped her brain in a vise, squeezing the life out of her, telling her to get out of this before she subjected any more innocent people to the grave. This was her fault, and that was something she'd have to live with for the rest of her days.

"Frost, go. Hurry up."

Maya summoned movement into her limbs and rushed outside. Tears blurred her vision as she struggled to maintain her composure, but she needed to be strong and keep focus. She feverishly searched her pockets for her cell phone, then realized she'd left it in the car. She ran to it, pulled open the door, and found it in the holder. She scrolled, found Riggs' name, and went to tap.

But suddenly, the screen began to flash.

Maya gulped down saliva, feeling like she'd just inhaled a pile of rocks.

Someone was calling her.

And not Riggs or HQ.

INCOMING CALL: ALFIE KUSTKA.

FIFTY-FOUR

"Hello, Miss Frost."

The voice was distorted, unrecognizable.

Maya's throat knotted up, and words failed her. This wasn't a random taunt. The killer knew her, knew her name, and was now reaching out to her through Alfie's phone.

"Why Alfie?" she breathed.

"Necessity. I cut off his finger for you, and then I realized I could use it to unlock his phone. Funny how fate works. I've even got a nice ring for my efforts."

"This isn't a game, you piece of shit."

"You thought you could outsmart me. Your little trick at the riverbank. Posing as the collector. I saw through it all. You're not so smart."

"Intelligence is cheap," Maya said. "Hard work is the difference."

"This was just supposed to be a little fun, Detective. A roleplay session. But you had to get involved, you had to make it personal. Now look what you've done."

"What do you want from me? Why have you done this?"

"That's for you to figure out," the voice laughed. "Now I'm just calling to give you the bad news."

Hearing this voice, altered as it was, reminded Maya that the Fernandina Butcher was nothing more than a human being. He shit, sweated, and made mistakes like everyone else on Earth. He wasn't a figure of terror; he was a deluded maniac.

"Bad news," Maya repeated. Not a question.

"This is the last time we're going to do this. I just wanted to say goodbye."

Maya wasn't sure she'd heard him right. She'd profiled that once this man's mission was complete, he'd vanish into the ether and never kill again. But she hadn't expected it so soon.

"This is far from goodbye," she said.

"You don't understand, Miss Frost. This is my game, and I'm done playing. My quest is over, and I wanted to thank you for the time we've spent together. However, I can't do this forever."

"You can run all you want, but I'll always be on your trail, you understand? Ridgway thought he'd escaped too, then twenty years later..."

The Butcher hissed with venom. "Ridgway was a fool. I'm smarter than he ever was. I covered my tracks."

Maya had to keep him talking. The more someone talked, the more they revealed. You couldn't learn anything by talking, but you could learn a hell of a lot from listening. "The Bangor Ripper thought so too, and I figured him out."

"We learn. We adapt, and there'll be more of your children dead tomorrow."

"Bullshit," Maya spat. "All you've done is copy other killers. You're desperate for an identity because you don't have one of your own. You just want attention, and this is the only way you can get it. Mom didn't give you enough attention when you were a kid?"

"You've got a lot to learn," the caller said. "I haven't copied anyone. I've taken inspiration. There's a difference. But my work here is done. I've torn out your heart, and now it's time for me to say farewell."

Maya felt the Butcher slipping away. She needed to keep him hanging on, distort his sense of superiority.

"Then I guess this is goodbye," Maya said.

A moment of silence. Maya could sense she'd knocked him off balance. "That's it?" he asked. "Not going to make an idle threat? Not going to try and keep me on the line to trace my location?"

"No. You're not the first serial killer to play games with me, and you won't be the last. Stop thinking you're anything special."

He cackled down the line. "Please. I've beaten the police, carved out my legacy. There's nothing left for me here."

"Beaten the police? We've been on your ass every step of the way. Correct me if I'm wrong, but didn't you run away from me like a coward last night? Couldn't fight like a man, could you?"

Maya heard him sniffing, processing her comment. She felt her words take hold, rile something up in him. "There was only one of me and about five of you. That's not a fair fight, is it?"

Maya felt a crack in his armor, one she could dig her claws in and open up.

"Then fight me, one on one."

"Ha. Nice try, Detective. I know you and your cronies would just ambush me. I'm not an idiot."

"Who said anything about a physical fight? Try me once more. One of your little games. I've figured out every clue you've left behind so far, haven't I? Ed Gein, Richard Ramirez, Gary Ridgway, Bangor Ripper. Who's next?"

The Butcher went silent again. Maya checked her screen to ensure he hadn't hung up. Ninety seconds on the call.

"I'm sorry. I've already won. I don't have to do this. I did have a different finale planned, but I had to pivot when you nearly killed me in our car chase."

"You haven't won shit. You want to prove you're better than Gein and Ramirez and Ridgway and the Ripper? Give me a fair game. You and me, one on one. The other killers got caught. You could be the one who opposed the police and got away with it. A Jack the Ripper, a Zodiac, a Mad Butcher."

It was a risky move, goading a serial killer into a final game, but Maya knew it was her only chance. She could feel his ego swelling through the phone.

"You really want to do this, Detective? Your friend's blood is already on your hands."

Maya's heart pounded. This was it, her last shot.

"Yes," she said.

"All right, Detective Frost, you want one last game? You'll get it. What's a few less people on the face of the Earth, anyway?" the Butcher finally said. "But this will be on my terms. You'll get one clue, one chance to catch me. If you fail, I disappear forever. And trust me, you won't find me unless I want you to."

"Fine," Maya said. "Sudden death."

"Indeed. But I'll warn you, this is going to be explosive. I guess I'll get my original finale after all. I'm going to finish what I started. You've got three hours."

"Bring it on. What's my clue?"

The Butcher paused, as if savoring the moment. "I've already told you," he said.

And the line went dead.

FIFTY-FIVE

When Maya got back to Alfie's doorstep, Devon was standing there. "House is empty. Did you call in reinforcements?"

"Yes. And someone else called me too."

Devon gritted her teeth. "Who? Don't say...?"

Maya nodded. "He called me from Alfie's phone."

"And? Did you trace the call? Anything?"

"No. I don't have tracking software. But he... said some things."

"Such as?"

"That tonight was his last kill, and he was going to disappear and never be heard from again."

Devon threw her head back and sighed. "Please say there's a *but*."

"I convinced him to play one more game. With me. And he agreed. He said he'd target one more person, and I had three hours to figure out who it was."

"Three hours? What was the clue?"

Maya replayed the conversation in her head, but she couldn't latch on to anything resembling a clue. "I don't know. He said he'd already given it to me during our conversation, but..."

"Then we've got three hours to figure this out, or tomorrow we're gonna have a lot to answer for."

"No, *I'm* gonna have a lot to answer for. You weren't involved with this. This is all on me."

Devon shot a hand out onto Maya's shoulder. "We're in this together, Frost. If this guy threatens you, he threatens me too."

Maya shuffled out of Devon's touch, not in the right mindset for gestures of comfort. "Come on, Devon. You don't have to answer for my dumb decisions. I shouldn't have toyed with him like that, but I figured... it was our last chance."

"Yes I do have to answer for your dumb decisions, because it was me who chose you."

Maya wasn't sure she'd heard Devon right. "You... what?"

"It was me, not Vernon. I heard what you did with the Ripper, and I asked to be partnered with you, all right?"

The concrete under her feet seemed to tremble. Devon, who'd treated her like dead weight on the plane. Devon, who'd called her "rookie" and made her prove every single observation. Devon, who'd watched Maya crash and burn for three days straight.

"You?"

"Yes. Vernon had a list of candidates, and I chose you without hesitation."

"But... why?"

"Because I know passion when I see it. I wanted to harness it, and I have."

Guilt reared its head. Devon had believed in her. Had staked her own credibility on Maya's potential. Had vouched for her to Vernon and the entire Behavioral Unit. And Maya had thanked her by storming Harder's house, nearly dying in a collector's shrine, letting the real killer stay ahead of them and kill someone on the police force, and baiting him into committing one more murder.

She'd failed Devon. Worse, she'd proven right everyone who said that desk jockeys didn't belong in the field.

"Devon, I—"

"Shut the hell up because we don't have time for this. We have three hours to figure this out, and we're not wasting sixty seconds on guilt, capiche? None of this is your fault. You didn't slice a woman in half, you didn't slaughter an old couple, shoot a sex worker, and you certainly didn't kill your friend. You're not responsible for the actions of a lunatic. You already know this, so why do you find it so hard to tell yourself?"

"Because if I hadn't come back here with Alfie, the killer might not have known where he lived."

"And if my aunt had balls she'd be my uncle." Devon gently slapped Maya's cheek, not hard but enough to shake her out of her mental paralysis. "Look, Riggs and co. are here. So we're going to leave them to sweep the scene while we put an end to this tonight, and I don't want to spend the rest of the night with a moping little bitch. I want the brain that caught the Bangor Ripper working with me, not the one worrying about what-ifs. Got it?"

Maya took a breath. Then another. The fog in her head

started to clear. Devon was right. She'd screwed up. Badly. Multiple times. But there were still three hours left on the clock, and the game wasn't over until the final whistle.

She'd spent her whole life trying to fix the past. Trying to bring Abigail back, undo her mother's suicide. Trying to rewrite history through sheer obsession.

But she couldn't change what had already happened. Not to Abigail. Not to Teresa or the Hutchins couple or Krystal or Alfie. All she could do was stop it from happening again.

And she still had time.

"You're right. Let's find this bastard."

Devon grinned. "That's my girl. You're driving."

FIFTY-SIX

MAYA ASSAULTED THE WHITEBOARD WITH HER MARKER pen, occasionally glancing over at the crime scene photos and autopsy reports to jog her memory. She unleashed her subconscious, spilling everything out like a broken dam. So far, she'd failed at every opportunity, but now she was determined to dissect the Butcher's psychopathology and see the world through his eyes.

"All right," Devon said. She was perched on the desk behind her. "We need to figure out where he's going to strike next, right?"

"Right, but first let's cover everything, just in case we've overlooked anything."

Maya went through all of the details, piece by piece. "First victim was Teresa Morgan, killed in her own hardware store. Severed in two, hung from the ceiling like a deer. Our unsub was mimicking the crimes of Ed Gein."

"Then he showed himself on CCTV with a pentagram

tattoo on his hand. That led us to Elaine and Cecil Hutchins."

"The Hutchinses. Older couple, stabbed in their own homes, a copycat of a Richard Ramirez murder. He then left us a message in lipstick that referenced the Green River Killer."

Devon nodded. "Then he killed Krystal Larkin in his own car. We interrupted him mid-kill on the riverbank, but he fled. Because we broke his pattern, we didn't know where he was going to strike next."

Maya considered the pattern. At this point, their unsub might have pivoted from his intended sequence because of the interruption. As she scrawled the word *pivot,* she recalled her conversation with the killer on the phone.

"Devon, when I talked to the unsub earlier, he said that he had a different finale planned, but he had to pivot when I nearly killed him in our car chase."

Her partner necked her coffee then said, "So the victim after Krystal was supposed to be someone else, but he changed his mind, probably because you enraged him."

"Exactly. Then he killed Alfie." His name brought the wave of despair back. Maya benched it, silently promising to grieve him properly once she'd brought his killer to justice. Alfie deserved more than a passing mourning.

"Right, so there's one thing we can glean from all this. You said he doesn't have a strict victimology, but our guy obviously prefers women. They're easier for him to control. He killed one man, but he ambushed him while he was asleep. Our guy isn't confident in his physical ability."

"Two men. Will we get an autopsy report for Alfie before the night is out?"

"No. But our perp was mimicking the Bangor Ripper, and the Ripper blitz-attacked, so it stands to reason the Butcher did the same here. I didn't see Alfie's torso, but there was a gash across his neck. The unsub slit his throat."

"Same way the Ripper killed."

"Yup. Our guy isn't comfortable being around people. He doesn't spend much time with them at all."

"He subdues them at the first opportunity."

"Yes, and for his finale, he'd want to be in full control. That means his next victim will probably be a woman, and he'll attack them in a private space that doesn't belong to him. Our guy has never lured anyone back to his place. He probably doesn't have the social skills to do it."

Maya nodded and scrawled it all down on the whiteboard. "He knows me. He has a vendetta against me for some reason. He must have seen me at one of the scenes. If he tailed me to Alfie's place, he must have seen me outside the Hutchins house, followed us to the bar, and then seen me go to Alfie's."

"Do you remember seeing anyone? I don't."

"No."

"So our killer has it in for you. Could he target anyone close to you? Me? Riggs?"

"Possibly, but that's a major risk. We said he'd go low risk for his finale."

"You're right," said Devon. "Now you're going to have to use that memory of yours. That conversation you had with the perp tonight? You need to recall everything he said to you. Every word. Talk me through it."

Maya leaned against the whiteboard and closed her eyes to concentrate. She replayed the phone conversation with the Butcher in her mind and tried to capture every nuance and inflection in his distorted voice.

"He started with a greeting, knew my name, used Alfie's phone. He said Alfie was a necessary piece in a much larger game. He boasted about cutting off Alfie's finger to unlock his phone."

"Are there any other historical killers that cut fingers off?"

Maya rummaged through her mental database and came up with one name. "Only the Bangor Ripper in the US. One in Australia, one in the UK. Definitely none on the level of Gein or Ramirez or Ridgway."

"That's another thing," Devon said. "Our guy copies infamous killers, not obscure criminals. The Jack the Rippers and Zodiacs."

Maya shook her head, etching her new thoughts on the board. "It wouldn't be either of those. He only mimics captured American serial killers."

"Right. What else did he say?"

"He taunted me about the riverbank incident. Claimed I thought I could outsmart him, that he saw through my disguise as the collector."

"That's ego," Devon said. "He's proud of seeing through your plan. Then what?"

Maya wracked her brain, struggling to recall the exact flow of the conversation. "Then I challenged him. I told him to face me one on one. A fair fight. He resisted at first but then he gave in."

Devon leaned closer. "OK, and this is point where he'd be most manipulative. Once you set the challenge, he'd go into gamemaster mode. What did he say?"

Maya's eyes lit up as the pieces began to fall into place in her mind. "He said something weird, something that struck me as odd, but in the moment, I looked past it."

"Which was?"

"He said, *'What's a few less people on the face of the Earth, anyway?'* Then he said he was going to go out explosively."

"Explosively? You don't think he means... a literal explosion?"

Maya went to note it down but stepped back, speed-reading her notes so far. "No. He wouldn't. That's not his style at all. Serial killers and bombers are two completely disparate profiles, polar opposites. How is he going to have time to put a bomb together?"

Devon sat back on the desk. "You're right. That doesn't fit. There's no sexual component to bombing, and our guy doesn't like to admit it, but there's an element of sexual gratification here. He gets off on pretending to be famous murderers. He needs to see their bodies, be present at the moment of terror. Bombing wouldn't give him that satisfaction."

"Agreed."

"But wait," Devon interrupted. "He said, *'What's a few less people on this Earth?'*"

"Yeah. Why?"

"*People?* Not *person?*"

Maya scratched her scalp. Understanding swamped her like a rogue wave. "Shit, you think he's going to kill more than one person?"

"He's done it before, and it would be an explosive way to go out."

"Maximum impact," Maya agreed. "To show that he's better than me. He'll want to go out on a high."

Devon jumped to her feet and slammed her palm against the whiteboard. "Come on, Frost, you might not realize it, but you *know* this guy. You can close your eyes and walk in his shoes. Where's he going next? What could he possibly do that connects... all this?"

Images spun on a mental carousel. She saw the scenes, the victims, the CCTV footage, the victim's blurry profile through the back windshield of his truck. The gears began to spin rapidly, and she condensed her focus as she dove deep into the labyrinth of the Butcher's psyche.

"He's obsessed with notoriety, with outdoing those before him. He wants to be remembered."

"Frost, think about the killers he's emulated. What's their common thread?"

Maya's vision began to darken as her subconscious mind took over. In her head, she was the Fernandina Butcher, seeing the world through his eyes.

"They all sought attention, but each in a unique way." Her eyes darted across the room and connected invisible dots. "Gein, Ramirez, the Green River Killer... they all had a signature."

"And the Butcher?"

"He... takes their signatures and amplifies them."

"So if he's escalating, what's his ultimate move?"

"A famous murder," Maya spat, and she was convinced her hand moved unconsciously. "One that involves multiple victims but resonates with me personally."

Devon grabbed her by the shoulders. "You got this, Frost. Keep digging. Explosive, less *people*. What do you see?"

Maya stared at the whiteboard. She cycled through possibilities but discarded them as fast as they appeared. The killer wanted to target her. Make it personal. But she didn't live here. Didn't have family in Fernandina Beach. Didn't have friends or ex-boyfriends or childhood homes. She'd been in Florida for four days. How could he make it personal when she had no history here?

Unless he knew her history from somewhere else.

She had to think like him. Be him. Walk in his shoes the way she'd done with the Bangor Ripper.

He'd studied her. That much was obvious. He knew about the Ripper case because he'd mimicked it with Alfie. Cut off the index finger as a message specifically for her. A way to say *I know you. I know what made you famous.*

So what else did he know?

Maya's breath came faster. She felt herself slipping into that dark mental space where the world narrowed to pure analysis, where emotion shut off and only logic remained.

He'd been watching her. Following her. He'd seen her go to Alfie's house. Seen her at the bar with Devon. Maybe he'd been at the crime scenes, blending in with the crowds, the uniforms, the forensic techs. Serial killers did that. Returned to watch the investigation. Fed off the chaos they'd created.

But watching her at crime scenes wouldn't tell him enough. Wouldn't give him the intimate details he needed to make this truly personal.

Think. Think.

He'd said she'd already been given the clue during their conversation. Which meant something he'd said contained the answer. But what? She replayed it again. *What's a few less people on the face of the Earth, anyway?*

Multiple victims. Public impact. Something that would devastate her specifically.

"Wait," Maya said.

"What?"

"The killer had said something else. Something just as weird."

"Which was?"

Maya found that fragment of verbiage, one she'd forgotten about until now. "He said, '*We learn. We adapt, and there'll be more of your children dead tomorrow.*'"

"Frost, Ted Bundy said that, right before he went to the electric chair."

A tidal wave hit her, a revelation more powerful than any drug. The spark ignited a fuse, exploding, lighting up the hazy image in her mind into a clear, visible picture.

Explosive.

Persons.

Finale.

"That's it," Maya shouted. "Ted Bundy. He's going to mimic Ted Bundy—and I know exactly how."

FIFTY-SEVEN

"Ted Bundy," Maya repeated in a frenzy. It all fit, every little detail. She scrubbed out one half of the whiteboard and began loading it up with fresh information.

Devon took a step back. "Explain," she said.

Maya went back to the start, playing out recent events like a movie reel in her head. She dissected the whole thing step by step.

"Alfie's finger," Maya said. "Our killer severed it, right?"

"But you said no serial killers cut fingers off. That includes Bundy, surely?"

"Bundy didn't cut off anyone's finger, but he did take something from his victims." Maya scrawled the word RING on the board.

"Ring?"

"Our perp took Alfie's finger to unlock his phone, but he also said that he'd *gotten a nice ring for his efforts*. Alfie had a ring on his index finger. An NCAA ring. His prized possession. Bundy took jewelry from some of his victims."

Devon waved her hands in a gesture to slow down. "But wait, our killer had to cut Alfie's finger off *before* you challenged him."

"Because while I hate to admit it, this guy knows me inside out. He anticipated my move. He never intended to disappear after killing Alfie. Bundy has always been part of his sequence, and why not? The most notorious serial killer in history. It fits his pattern perfectly."

Devon aggressively rubbed her face, then cracked her neck. "What else? You're not just basing this on a ring?"

"No. Then there's his little message. *What's a few less people on this Earth?* In his prison interviews, Bundy said, *'What's one less person on the face of the Earth, anyway?'*"

"So our killer just got the quote wrong?"

"I don't think so. It was another clue, that he was going to target multiple people instead of a single person."

Devon looked over Maya's haphazard scrawling. "All right, Frost, you might be on to something here. But what Bundy murder are we talking about? He killed thirty women, so that means any young woman could be a target."

But Maya wasn't done. There was one more piece that assembled the jigsaw. "On the phone, our killer mentioned his *finale*. Bundy had a finale too. One final blow-out just before he got caught. The one where he completely lost control. The explosive finish."

"The sorority house murders. I remember. Several victims in one night."

Maya rushed to her laptop and pulled up the details to refresh her memory. "The Chi Omega sorority house murders. Bundy invaded the house, attacked four women, and killed two of them. We know our guy wants to one-up every killer he emulates, so he's going to try and take at least two lives. Maybe more, to finish what Bundy couldn't. It fits his pattern of escalation, his desire for notoriety. He wants to make a final statement, and he's picked Bundy's most infamous crime to do it."

The more Maya talked, the more she was convinced. This had to be it. The picture was too clear to be wrong.

"Omega," Devon said. "You know what omega means?"

"It's a Greek letter."

"The last Greek letter. It means *finale*."

Maya snapped her fingers. "Crap, I didn't even know. It has to be, right? This has to be his big finish." She quickly scanned Bundy's most famous crime on her laptop and consumed all of the available details. Now she just had to transpose this crime to a potential location in Fernandina Beach.

"But where might he strike? Are sorority houses even a thing anymore?"

"Not around here." Maya searched for sorority houses in the area and came up with a massive zero. Nothing even close. The nearest one was a hundred miles away in Jacksonville. She glanced at the clock: 11:30 p.m. She had ninety minutes left.

"There must have been some back in the day. I know this isn't a university town, but come on. Try historical records. Property records. These buildings don't just disappear."

Maya put her fingers to work. She pulled up the county assessor's database and started filtering. Greek life organizations. Residential properties. Anything tied to university housing or sorority affiliations.

Nothing in Fernandina Beach itself. Nothing in the surrounding neighborhoods.

"Shit." Maya wiped sweat from her forehead. The precinct felt like a furnace. Or maybe that was just her body temperature spiking as the minutes ticked away.

Maya navigated to the Nassau County Historical Society website. The page loaded slowly. She drummed her fingers on the desk while Devon paced behind her. The site had a section on historical buildings. Landmarks. Properties of note. Maya scrolled through pages of old churches and plantation houses and Victorian homes. Nothing that fit. She scrolled through, page after page, and it wasn't until page seven of the archives that something caught her eye.

Former Greek Life Housing in Nassau County.

Maya clicked.

The page loaded. A list of addresses appeared, most of them in Fernandina Beach and the surrounding area. Fraternity houses from the 1950s. Sorority houses from the 1960s and '70s. Most had been demolished or converted into apartments.

But one entry stood out.

Chi Omega Chapter House, 412 Magnolia Street, Fernandina Beach. Established 1972. Closed 1998. Current use: Haven House Women's Shelter.

A shelter. The kind of place that housed vulnerable women. Women fleeing violence. Women with nowhere else to go. Women who trusted that the walls around them would keep them safe.

"Devon, look at this."

Her partner moved in. "Chi Omega. Same name as Bundy's target."

"But look. It's a women's shelter now. A battered women's shelter."

"Didn't you say you used to work at one years ago?"

"I... volunteered at one in my twenties. Do you think...?"

"Yes I do think!" Devon said. "We need to get there right now. Check it out. How many women live there?"

Maya searched Haven House Women's Shelter online. The website popped up. "Twenty women. God, there could be kids there too."

"Then that's we're going. I'm calling backup, SWAT, everyone. We need to lock that place down."

It all fit. If the Butcher had searched Maya online, articles about her volunteering at women's shelters would have popped up. The local news in Townsend had covered it extensively, and her name popped up regularly.

But an old adage about being fooled twice came to mind. The Butcher had misdirected her at the riverside scene, and he'd summoned her to Alfie's house to witness the horror in all its glory. Twice she'd tried to best him, and twice she'd failed.

It wasn't going to happen again.

There was something else. Something she was missing. A piece of the puzzle that the killer purposely left out, just like he'd done the past two times.

"Devon, go to the woman's shelter. Evacuate everyone in there. Be as discreet as possible."

"On it. You're coming, right?"

Maya turned back to her whiteboard, looked over her notes, and took in the crime scene photos one last time. This was her last shot at catching this killer, so she had to make sure she was right. And if she was truly seeing the world through his eyes, then there was another element to this whole thing that she needed to figure out. What was known in the magic world as *kicker*. She couldn't afford another misstep. This was a game of chess, and she had to think several moves ahead.

"No," Maya said. "Secure the shelter. That's the priority for now."

Devon reached the door, then looked at her partner in confusion. "If you're not coming with me, where are you going? Don't you want to catch this son of a bitch with your own hands?"

Maya turned her attention back to the whiteboard. She scanned each detail one more time, trying to find the missing piece. Her intuition told her there was still more to this.

A serial killer role player, harnessing the essence of what made these historical killers so terrifying. Putting aside the brutality and theatrics, every crime scene was a challenge to his pursuers. It was the subtle touches he incorporated that told his true story.

I'm going to finish what I started, he'd said.

"I do want to catch him with my own hands," Maya said. "So?"

"Just go. You don't need me."

Devon was over the threshold. "I'll call you as soon as we've got something. Oh, and here you go, in case you do anything stupid again." Devon placed her Glock 17 down on the table.

"For me?"

"For you. I'll grab another one from the locker. Remember, only point your gun at something if you intend to kill it."

And her partner was gone. Maya needed to cover all

bases, but she was sure of one thing—the Butcher's mind games hadn't ended just yet.

Yes, she wanted to catch this killer with her own hands.

And that's why she wasn't going.

She had somewhere else to be.

FIFTY-EIGHT

DEVON LYNCH HAMMERED ON THE FRONT DOOR TO THE Haven House Women's Shelter, fully aware that her intrusion would not be well-received at such an hour. She glanced at her watch. One hour before time was up.

No response from anyone inside. Devon hammered again, this time with an impact one level below smashing the door off its hinges.

"FBI, open up," Devon yelled. She peered up and down the deserted street for any signs of onlookers, curious bystanders, potential murderers. Nothing but darkness in every direction.

The old door to the women's shelter began to move. It slowly creaked open to reveal a cautious face peeking out. Devon met the eyes of what she assumed was the shelter's night guard, a forty-something man, buzzed hair, weathered skin from too much nicotine.

"Special Agent Lynch," Devon said with her badge held out. "FBI."

The man peered back into the building for a moment, then asked, "Police? What are you doing here?" There was caution in his voice, the tone of someone who'd learned to distrust law enforcement.

"We believe someone has made a threat against the lives of the residents in this building. Do you work here?"

The man gently opened the door and stepped outside, as though moving out of earshot of someone else. "I'm the center manager," he said. "Todd Williams. I have a room here. I stay overnight whenever I can."

"You're in charge?" Devon asked.

"Yes. I've run this place for years."

Devon quickly assessed Todd Williams, taking in his cautious demeanor and the protective stance he held at the doorway. Time was ticking, and every second counted.

"Todd, we have credible information that a dangerous individual may target this building tonight. For the safety of everyone inside, we need to evacuate the shelter immediately. This isn't a drill."

"A threat? To this shelter? What do you mean?"

"No time to explain. How many residents are here tonight?"

Todd peered back inside again. "Just one, but I'm not allowed to leave any residents alone. We only have five girls living here, and they don't always spend the night. Why?"

Devon remembered Maya's comment from half an hour ago. *We know our guy wants to one-up every killer he emulates, so he's going to try and take at least two lives. Maybe more, to finish what Bundy couldn't.*

Devon didn't have time to dwell on it. Her priority was

to secure this place, regardless of what the behavioral profile said.

"Listen, Todd, we need to get her to safety right now. This is a matter of life and death. We'll provide protection and ensure everyone's safety, but we need to act now."

Todd hesitated for a moment, then wrapped his arms around himself to shield from the cold. "With all due respect, Agent, I can't send one of my girls to a police station or a safehouse for God knows how long. The women here have been through a lot."

Devon fought back her impatience. "Protocol says any evacuated parties need to check in to a police-designated establishment. I'm sorry, but we have to..."

"Please," Todd said, reaching out to grab Devon's wrist but clearly thinking better of it. "The girl inside, Michelle, she's had it tough. She's a new arrival, too. The last thing I want to do is scare the life out of her."

Understanding Todd's concern, Devon paused for a moment to consider her options. The safety of the shelter residents was paramount, but so was catching the unsub. And sometimes, a little human touch went a long way.

"Is there anywhere you can take her?" Devon asked. "Just for tonight?"

Todd clenched his teeth, then glanced off into the distance. "Yeah. We have a sister shelter over in Yulee. We could go there."

"All right," Devon said. "Do that, and I'll need you to tell every resident not to come here until police have cleared it, all right? I'll need the keys to this place, alarm codes, every-thing. How many entry points does this place have?"

Todd opened the door behind him, stepped inside, and

gestured for Devon to join him. He pointed to a table. "Keys are here. I'll note the alarm code for you. There are two entry points, but the back door is bolted shut. All windows are barred for security too. It's only the front door that people can enter through."

"Got it. Please get Michelle out of here."

Todd nodded and disappeared up a nearby staircase. Devon circled the downstairs area and took it all in. She became a little concerned about the lack of breachable entry points because if the killer couldn't find a convenient way inside, he might abandon ship and choose a more accessible victim. Devon planned to stake this place out until someone arrived, so she'd need to maintain an eagle eye on every corner. She familiarized herself with the layout and checked the back door to ensure it was indeed bolted as Todd had mentioned. Then she scoped out the best vantage point to watch for oncoming intruders.

Two pairs of footsteps descended the staircase, and Todd returned alongside a thin, frail woman. A brunette, barely in her twenties. She was wearing a nightgown and had a cheap coat draped over her shoulders.

"Alarm code is written down for you," Todd said as he placed a note on the table. "I'll inform everyone to keep away. Should I call you when I get to the other shelter?"

"Yes. Call the Fernandina precinct and ask for Agent Frost."

"Agent Frost," Todd repeated.

"Is anyone else scheduled to arrive tonight?"

"No," Todd said as he ushered the young girl out the door. "Just the two of them."

Devon's gaze shot to him. She wasn't sure she'd heard

him right. "Two? I thought you said there was only one girl here?"

The door was ajar, and Todd was halfway out. "I meant us two. Me and Michelle. I'll be in touch," he said as he left, gently closing the door behind him.

Devon spied Todd through a locked window, watching him escort the young girl to a vehicle and load her in the front seat. A second later, the vehicle flew off at a speed that, if Devon wasn't preoccupied, she would pull the man over for.

Todd's last comment lingered in the air. The slight shift in story, the sudden correction, the urgency to flee despite putting up resistance at first.

Just the two of them tonight.

When it came to law enforcement and whiskey, Devon always trusted her gut, and that subtle comment had given her cause for concern.

She quickly scoured the downstairs area again, ensuring that everything seemed in its place. Then she rushed to the upstairs area to double-check every room, every window, every door. Twenty years of profiling experience had honed her ability to notice even the smallest details, and Todd's inconsistency had set off internal alarm bells.

She found a small hallway, narrow and dusty, with rows of doors on either side. She charged into the first room and found two beds, two tables, one dresser.

Empty. No personal items, no sign of recent occupation.

She tried the next door in line. Another unoccupied space. Two beds neatly made, empty closets. It was as if the shelter was waiting for a crisis that had never come.

Another room, this time a musty bathroom. Yellowed

walls, shower clogged with hair. For what was supposed to be a sanctuary, Devon couldn't help but conclude that this place was in dire need of TLC.

Devon switched the light on and was immediately met with a scene that put her on high alert. The mirror above the sink was shattered, jagged shards of glass still in the basin. Among the broken pieces, she spotted smears of blood.

A portrait of rage. Knuckles against the mirror.

Vandalism? Accident? Self-harm? The product of a breakdown by a resident in the throes of distress?

Devon's heart pumped in her chest, not sure exactly what was going on but certain that something here was amiss.

She rushed back out into the corridor, trying the next door in line.

But this one was locked.

Could be a staff area, a maintenance closet, anything.

But Devon's gut told her she needed to inspect the contents. She reached into her pocket and pulled out the keys that Todd had passed her, trying each one in the lock with no success. She discarded them, stepped back, and prepared for the oncoming impact.

Channeling years of tactical entries, Devon stepped forward and drove her boot into the door just beside the lock. It shook, trembled, but didn't give way. She repositioned herself, took a moment to focus her energy, and then hit the door again with all the force she could muster.

This time, the door frame splintered, and the door swung open with a loud crack.

Devon stormed inside the pitch black chamber,

searching for a light switch. She found it, turned it on, and illuminated the vast room.

Not a maintenance closet.

Not a staff area.

Devon never found herself short of words, but the room before her rendered her mute. Adrenaline coursed through her veins, and she found herself questioning everything that she and Maya had profiled about this offender.

Because her focus was on the room's centerpiece.

A young woman lay on the floor, tape around her mouth, blood erupting from a gash in her stomach.

Devon sprang into action. She dropped down to her knees beside the girl, still rolling, still breathing. She tore off her jacket and covered the wound, then rushed to peel the tape off her mouth as gently as possible. She threw it aside as the woman coughed up a fountain of blood. Devon put her arm below her head, propping her upright.

"Stay with me," she shouted as she fumbled for her cell phone. She hammered the number in. "Urgent medical assistance needed at Haven House Women's Shelter. Stabbed victim, alive but barely. Come quickly."

The woman rolled around in Devon's arms, eyes closing then darting back open.

"You're gonna be fine, girl," she said. "Look at me. Keep breathing. Help is on the way, all right?"

Devon's training had prepared her for moments like this, but the reality of the situation was always more intense than any simulation. As she desperately tried to keep the nameless woman alive, Devon came to a simple conclusion.

Todd Williams was not just the center manager.

He was the Fernandina Butcher.

And he might have outsmarted them again.

FIFTY-NINE

IT HAD BEEN ALMOST TOO EASY.

Todd Williams turned to Michelle in the passenger seat and put one hand on her thigh. The young girl barely gave a response. By now, the drugs would have kicked in and the woman would be unconscious before they'd even gotten to their destination.

He gazed out of the window as he followed the familiar route, almost wishing that the detective had put up a little more of a fight. All he'd had to do was plant the Ted Bundy seed in her mind and she'd latch on to it, unable to see beyond the surface, just like she'd done every other time.

Still twenty minutes on his timer, but he'd already won the battle. The girl back at the shelter would be dead by now, and since she had no way of screaming, Frost's partner would never find her. She'd spend her evening at the shelter, constantly looking over her shoulder for intruders, blissfully unaware that she was sharing airspace with a dead body.

The chessmaster had struck again. He'd won the game

before it had even started. Gein, Ramirez, Ridgway, the Bangor Ripper—not even Bundy could make such a claim. His mission had been a masterclass in the art of serial murder, misdirecting police, taking lives through disparate modus operandis and racking up a body count rarely seen in the modern age. Before the night was out, he'd have seven victims to his name, cementing a legacy alongside the historical greats. By the time the devil called his number, there'd be a throne in hell with his name on it.

Michelle, sitting passively beside him, was oblivious to the dark thoughts swirling in Todd's mind. The drugs had rendered her a mere pawn in his elaborate scheme, her humanity stripped away in his eyes, reduced to a tool for his machinations. She would help him finish the story, and then he could disappear into the night, into the new life that the master had arranged for him.

Todd Williams' descent into darkness had not been an abrupt plunge but a gradual slide. He was not the center manager of the Haven House Women's Shelter, merely a lowly member of staff entrusted with the night shift. He never cared for the people he helped, simply the money. Night after night, he was subjected to the harrowing but mundane stories these women wove, each one as predictable as the last. Drugs, homelessness, endless cycles of bad decision-making that forced other people to care for them.

The once heart-wrenching tales of abuse and fear became mundane to him, and all Todd could offer was cynicism. He started to view some of the women not as victims in need of help but as burdens, unworthy of the support and care the shelter offered.

No longer content with being a passive observer in the

lives of the shelter's residents, Todd sought a more active, malevolent role. Combined with his obsession into the realm of infamous murderers, Todd started to derive a perverse sense of power and control from the idea of deciding their fates and thus playing God in a game of life and death.

But his descent into the life and crimes of historical killers had taught him a lot, including how to stay under the radar. Operate in a familiar geographical hunting zone. Frame multiple suspects for the murders along the way. And most importantly—leave the personal kills until the very end. Theories suggested that many uncaptured serial killers disappeared once they murdered the one person they'd been after all along, and that all other victims were simply decoys.

He turned to Michelle beside him, the woman who'd tried to ruin his life, the woman who'd reported him when he'd tried to make his move on her. Since then, Todd had reconciled with her, but it was all simply manipulation until he could finally have some private time with the young woman.

And what would happen after tonight? Would the police conclude that Todd Williams was indeed the Fernandina Butcher?

It wouldn't matter. Once Michelle was suitably placed, he would feign a car crash, plant the seed that both he *and* Michelle had been a target of the Butcher. Besides, Todd had no plans to stick around in Florida. Bigger things awaited him elsewhere. A new name, a new life, a new identity. The Fernandina Butcher would simply disappear, establishing his monicker alongside infamous phantoms like Jack the Ripper and the Zodiac Killer.

For him, that was achievement enough.

He glanced back at Michelle, whose head was now lolling against the window. She was the perfect picture of vulnerability. The idea of killing her back at the shelter had occurred to him, but he had to prove to Detective Frost that he could outwit her. The finale had to be grand, his own *omega*. Simply killing two sleeping women wouldn't be enough. The culmination of a serial killer's reign was perhaps the most important part, the component the world would remember.

As he drove, his mind replayed the events of the evening. The satisfaction of outsmarting the police, of playing them like pawns in his grand design, was exhilarating. He relished the thought of the headlines that would soon sweep the nation, the fear and confusion that would grip the city. He had become the author of a nightmare, and the world was his audience.

Up ahead, his destination came into view. A place he'd hunted only last night. The fools had interrupted his pattern, and he wasn't going to let that slide. That little component of his crimes felt like a loss, so he had to right that wrong. In doing so, he could realign his pattern *and* invoke the spirit of Ted Bundy in the same breath.

"Where are we?" Michelle slurred as she drifted in and out of consciousness.

He caressed her thigh again. "Just going for a drive. By the river."

"Huh?" she mumbled. "The river?"

"Yes. Don't worry. Everything's OK."

Todd's car slowed as it approached the riverbank. The secluded spot was perfect for his final act, away from prying eyes and the buzz of the city. He parked the car.

Looking at Michelle's limp form, he felt a surge of power, the same surge Bundy must have felt. This was the moment he had meticulously planned for. He got out of the car and walked around to the passenger side and opened the door. The cool night air brushed against his skin, carrying the faint murmur of the river.

Carefully, he escorted Michelle from the car. The poor woman was barely able to stand of her own accord now.

"Come down here," he said. "I've got something to show you."

As he carried her toward the riverbank, his thoughts drifted to the legacy he was about to leave behind. The Fernandina Butcher. A phantom that would haunt the annals of criminal history.

He looked down at Michelle's face, so serene in her drugged slumber. In his mind, she was no longer a person but a symbol of his ultimate triumph over the police and over the banality of his former life. Once she was dead, he would head home and began the act of purification. He would slaughter his animals, burn his farmhouse, and take his collection to another state. There, he'd sell everything he had, including the old farmland, and begin his new life.

They got to the river's edge. Michelle stumbled, but Todd kept her steady. He paused, savoring the moment. He was about to create a scene that would baffle and terrify—a mystery that would remain unsolved for eternity.

"Michelle," Todd said as he tightened his grip on her arm. "Remember when you tried to ruin me?"

The woman swayed again, teetering on the edge of the river. She grabbed hold of Todd. "Huh? No... I don't know what you mean."

"Of course," he said. Todd glanced at the tranquil water. The ripples on the surface would soon be disturbed. They had to be, in order to witness the end of Michelle's story and the birth of a legend. The waters would wash away any forensic evidence and leave behind a clean crime scene.

The Fernandina Butcher was about to make his final cut.

"Almost too easy," he said as he drew his gun.

But that was when the riverside came alive.

A piercing sound cut through the silence of the night.

"Don't move," a voice said.

In that moment, Todd Williams felt his legacy crumbling. His aspirations of infamy dissolved into the cold night air as he turned around to see Detective Frost pointing a gun at his chest.

The chessmaster had been outmaneuvered.

SIXTY

MAYA AIMED FOR HIS HEART, SUMMONING EVERY OUNCE of willpower not to pull the trigger and let justice ring with a bullet.

She had him.

There was no denying it.

The man in front of her was the Fernandina Butcher.

"Let her go," Maya yelled, "and put your hands where I can see them."

With his trimmed hair, shabby clothing, and pinprick eyes, the Butcher was nothing like Maya expected. Yet by the same token, he was exactly as she imagined: a nondescript nobody, a heap of flesh and bones. She had no time to assess his physical profile, nor did she care to. Her only goal was to incapacitate the monster before her, be it through death or chains.

The Butcher grinned, but Maya saw through it. The man in front of her was panicking, furious that she'd seen through his plan. He held on tightly to the woman beside him, a woman who looked moments away from collapsing.

"I won't ask you again," Maya shouted.

"You won't shoot," the Butcher said. "You need me alive, Detective. To answer for... for all of it."

Maya's finger hovered over the trigger. This man had taken five lives, one of whom had been a person she thought she shared something with. Not firing every round into his heart took a level of self-control she didn't know she had. "I don't need anything from you."

The Butcher pulled Michelle closer and jammed his pistol into her temple. Maya stepped to the side to adjust her aim, but the Butcher circled with her. She had no clean shot, and the chances of the insentient woman making a break for it seemed slim. By the way she was swaying in and out of consciousness, Maya guessed the Butcher had drugged her.

"How'd you do it?" the Butcher spat. The grin disappeared, replaced by tense lips and two rows of grounded teeth. "How'd you figure it out?"

Maya gauged him, looking for a square inch of flesh that she could zone in on.

Nothing.

The hostage blocked everything.

Maya steeled herself, silently promising herself that the Butcher wouldn't be leaving this riverside of his own accord.

"You told me," Maya said.

"Enthrall me. What did I tell you?"

"You said I wasn't as smart as I thought. Guess you got it wrong."

She sensed her words getting under his skin. The more she antagonized him, the more chance he had of firing at her.

At that moment, she'd strike first. She just needed to engineer a distraction.

"You cheated," he yelled. "You must have."

Maya adjusted her grip on her gun. "I should have known days ago," she said. "But it wasn't until you mentioned your finale, your little quote about less people on Earth. And you took my friend's jewelry. You were planning this finale all along, weren't you?"

"Maybe," he said. "Well done."

"You wanted me to think you were going to replicate Bundy's Chi Omega murders, but like the last two times, you had a twist. You wanted me to go to that woman's shelter while you struck elsewhere. Unlike you, I learn from my mistakes."

He tightened his grip on the woman. "You think you've figured it all out, don't you? You think you're the hero of this story?"

"Oh, we're far from done. I don't know much about you, but I know that Ted Bundy is your idol, isn't he? It was right there from the start. We traced one of your electronic payments. R. Miller? Bundy used the alias Rolf Miller during a very select period of his reign."

The Butcher's composure dropped, and his face bent into a look of disbelief. His shoulders slumped, his mouth dropping open an inch. His disguise of control was crumbling.

"So what? You think that makes you clever? Tracing a payment?"

She wasn't done dissecting this man, presenting him with the facts he thought he was smart enough to hide. "And you don't just emulate these killers; you get to their very essence. You roleplayed as Gein for weeks, tattooed your hand like Ramirez, told escort agencies your name was Gary. You wanted to *be* them, to live a day in their shoes. Bundy would be no different. You wouldn't just mimic one of his crimes; you'd channel the crux of what made him who he was—and what did Bundy like doing more than anything?"

Maya had him at her mercy. She could feel his spirit waning. Any moment now, the man would snap.

"What?" the Butcher hissed.

"Revisiting his old crime scenes. You couldn't visit any of the others because none of them are accessible now. But out here? No one can stop you coming out here. And this is the place where we interrupted your pattern, and someone as obsessive as you wasn't going to let that slide, right?"

"Am I supposed to be impressed?"

Maya maintained her steely gaze because any lapse in concentration could be fatal. "I don't care what you are, but there are a few nuggets of irony here, aren't there? Something only the most hardened serial killer researchers would be aware of."

"Oh? Do tell me."

"Ted Bundy helped police profile the Green River Killer, and now look where we are. You're here, beside a river, trying to recapture your Green River kill, and it was your attempt to channel Bundy that brought us here."

The Butcher screamed, "I'm smarter than *both* of them. You think you've outsmarted me? The night isn't over."

Maya had one final line, and then she had to make a move before the woman in the Butcher's arms collapsed. For all she knew, she could have been given a fatal dose. "That's not all, buddy. There's one more thing. Something I think a serial killer fanatic like you is really going to get a kick out of."

The Butcher's eyes narrowed. "You see, Ted Bundy was caught because he got careless, overconfident. He thought he was smarter than everyone else, untouchable. And his ego handed him a death sentence."

"And?" the Butcher asked.

Maya could see the moment of decision in his eyes, the internal struggle. It was now or never.

She had no clean shot, so the only solution was to get up close and personal.

"And you've done the same," Maya said. Without hesitation, without concern for her own life, she pushed her weight down into her ankles and charged.

She hurtled across the muddy ground, supercharged with frustration, fury, and despair. She was a human bullet, speeding through the night with ruin in sight, an unstoppable force willing to obliterate her target. Maya's heart thumped loud enough to hear. There was no room for doubt, no space for fear.

For a moment, the world became a blur, and the seconds between outset and impact were erased from time. She saw the Butcher fling his hostage to one side, and in the next moment, Maya's shoulder connected with his stomach, sending them both spinning to the ground, rolling across the wet earth in a knot that Maya's fists would untangle. Her pistol flew out of her hands upon impact, and suddenly she was on top of her suspect. She gripped his wrist, trying to prize the weapon from his hands, but the Butcher pulled the trigger, firing one gunblast after another into the night.

Maya counted. Three, four, five. She fought for the gun

again, but the recoil of the sixth blast disoriented her for a moment. The world went silent as her eardrums dealt with the shockwaves, and she suddenly felt a stinging sensation in her thigh. Warm liquid ran down to her knee, and as she quickly glanced over, she saw a rip in her jeans, blood spurting from within.

In his other hand, the Butcher had pulled a knife.

Yet Maya felt no pain. She cursed herself for not anticipating a second weapon, but there was no time for hindsight. Her determination turned into a primal instinct for survival. Ignoring the searing pain in her thigh, she focused her energy on disarming the Butcher. Her hands, slick with mud and blood, struggled for control of the knife. As she pinned his wrist to the ground, she saw the pentagram tattoo on his hand sparkling in the moonlight.

But the split-second distraction became her undoing, because the Butcher contorted his wrist and caught Maya's forearm with the tip of the blade. It dug in deep, and this time she couldn't ignore the pain. It sucked all of the energy out of her, and for a moment, she was at the Butcher's mercy. He rose to his knees, thrust them into Maya's abdomen, and sent her sprawling onto her back.

Maya lay there, disoriented, her vision blurred by the impact. A burning sensation spread rapidly from each wound, numbing her nerves and removing some of the feeling in her fingertips. Her strength ebbed away, and her body struggled to compensate for the unexpected rush.

But Maya's spirit was unbroken. She pushed herself to a sitting position, trying to determine her best move. The Butcher was tall, wiry, and seemed to possess decent strength. Even without a pistol, he could surely do some damage. As she rapidly composed herself, she saw that he was already on his feet. The knife in his hand glinted in the silver moonglow.

Maya's training kicked in. She scanned the area quickly, looking for her pistol, but it was nowhere in sight. She realized she would have to rely on her physical skills alone.

With an inhuman grunt, her attacker descended on her with his blade pointed in her direction. He mounted her, pinning her down with his knees, but Maya knew this position well. Her instincts flared, and she thrust her knees into the Butcher's spine, then used the momentum to roll forward. Her attacker rolled off, scrambling across the ground out of her range. Maya had space, so she quickly checked on the state of the hostage.

The mystery woman was crawling along the ground, out of harm's way. Barely alive but alive nonetheless. For the time being, that would have to be enough. Maya regained her footing and regarded the Butcher ten feet ahead of her. Her body ached, but her determination did not wane. The adrenaline coursing through her veins numbed the pain, and that enabled her to focus solely on the task at hand: subduing this monster.

The Butcher rose to his feet. His mask had melted away, and now she saw the true face beneath. In bouts of combat, people always revealed who they really were. Through those narrow eyes and tight cheekbones, Maya saw the face of a desperate killer, a lost soul looking for a place in a world he deemed himself too good for. She envisioned him at every crime scene, shooting, mutilating, eviscerating, slitting Alfie's throat and clipping off his finger. The thought tore her to shreds, but it brought a surge of willpower that enlivened her nerves.

She moved with precision, circling the Butcher, waiting for an opening. Her mind flashed back to her training, the countless hours of physical combat, the strategies drilled into her. She knew that one wrong move could be fatal.

"Is that all you got, Detective?"

"You really think you're going to get out of here?"

"I was planning seven victims. Looks like it's gonna be eight before the night is out."

Maya didn't have time to do the math, and there was a chance he was still trying to get into her head, even in the throes of battle.

"You didn't tell anyone you were coming here, did you?" the Butcher continued. "All alone. No one to find your body once I've finished with it."

Maya breathed heavily as she processed the comment. He was right. She'd come here on a solo mission, determined to take this man down with her own two hands. Anything else would be unsatisfactory. It was an itch she needed to scratch or it would haunt her for the rest of her days.

"No I didn't. It's just me and you," Maya said. His taunts were meant to distract, to unnerve, but Maya was beyond the reach of his words now. She knew this was a battle not just for her life but for justice, for all the lives the Butcher had brutally snuffed out.

"You make it too easy," the Butcher said, lunging forward, resuming his relentless assault. His blade sliced the air wildly and erratically, the actions of a man with no formal training. Maya dodged, evaded, spun out of harm's way, and circled him again. She needed a moment that couldn't be interrupted by steel.

"No one will remember you," she shouted.

"Too late for that."

"I've done it before, and I'll do it again. You'll be six feet underground, and someone will say your name for the last time."

The Butcher exhaled through his nose. He sprang forward again, swinging the tip of his blade inches from her flesh. Then, at the moment his final swing hit its plateau, Maya stepped forward and closed the gap.

Now was the time.

She struck him with a knee in his mid-section, gripped his wrist, and maneuvered around to his back. Maya dug her claws into his palm—a dirty tactic, but rules were out the window. The Butcher's grip released, and his knife fell from his hands, lodging itself in the muddy ground.

"You want to play dirty, you little bitch?" Maya yelled in his ear. She quickly bound his arms in a nelson hold, interlacing her fingers, locking the Butcher in place. He struggled beneath her, but her hold was ironclad. He kicked his legs back, trying to take her down by the ankles, but the night was her arena, and the riverbank was her cage. Maya locked a leg around him from the front, pushed forward, and sent him down to the ground face-first. She planted him in the dirt, smashing his nose and creating a pool of blood beneath the point of impact. Maya released her grip and rolled him onto his front, then took pole position on top of him.

Then she felt it—the compulsion to unleash justice in its most painful form. Fury itched at her knuckles, and so Maya began a relentless unquenchable assault that she knew could leave the Butcher comatose or worse. Her fist met his cheek, and teeth were dislodged. Then a second blow to his nose, followed by a third below his eye. Maya thought of Teresa, Elaine, Cecil, Krystal, and Alfie, dispensing a series of blows for each victim, for those souls that were no longer here. For those prematurely sent to the afterlife, she was their messenger, bringing disfigurement and ruin with every blow.

The Butcher's resistance waned under the onslaught. His attempts to shield himself were futile against Maya's fury. "Stop!" he spat, saliva collecting around his mouth. "Or....you'll .... never know."

Maya's arms grew heavy. She stopped, panting heavily, looking down at the man who was now barely conscious. "I don't give a shit," she said.

"All this," the Butcher gasped. "It wasn't... my idea."

Maya's body ached, and so she ceased her attack. The adrenaline began to fade, replaced by a deep, hollow feeling. She had stopped the Butcher, but the cost was written in bruises and blood, in the heaviness of her heart.

"What?" she asked.

"There's someone else." The Butcher grinned through a mask of blood. "And I know who he is."

"Shut up. It's over."

"It was him who... inspired me."

"What? Who?"

"You think you've won... but this... this is just the beginning."

Maya's knuckles were broken and bloody, but like her dad always said, you always had one more strike left in you. "What do you mean?"

"I'm not... telling."

And she delivered it with the fury of a woman scorned. The impact sent shockwaves up her arm, and satisfaction and regret came in equal measures.

The Butcher faded beneath her.

He went limp. His eyes closed in a parody of death.

Out cold.

She looked down at the man who had caused so much pain and destruction, now reduced to a defeated heap beneath her.

Maya checked the hostage. Still moving, still rolling, still alive.

She reached for her cell and dialed for reinforcement.

Game over.

SIXTY-ONE

Maya sat by the riverbank and admired the waters that were now illuminated by red and blue lights. Rivers had always reminded her of her mom's death, but tonight it didn't, and perhaps that demon had somehow been banished for good. The brain worked in odd ways, and she figured that humans would never truly understand it no matter how much they tried.

Her thigh throbbed where the bullet had grazed her. Her forearm burned where the knife had caught her. Her knuckles were split open and already swelling. Someone had wrapped gauze around the worst of it, but she'd refused the ambulance. No ambulance could bring Alfie and the others back to life, and for that she felt like she needed to sacrifice some of her own well-being.

Up ahead, Sheriff Riggs was directing the scene. There were five cruisers, one ambulance, and one forensics van. The Butcher—whose real name was still a mystery to Maya—was being held face down on the ground by three officers. Devon broke free from a group of uniforms, ambled over to Maya's spot, and took a seat, shoulder to shoulder.

"Paramedics want to check you out," Devon finally said.

"Do they?"

"You need stitches. A tetanus shot. Antibiotics."

"I bet," said Maya. "Have you talked to him?"

"Who, the paramedic?"

"No, not the paramedic."

"Oh, you mean the serial murderer in chains over there?"

"Yeah. Him."

Devon said, "We haven't exchanged numbers, if that's what you mean, but yes, I've talked to him. And yes, he fooled me back at the shelter too."

Maya asked, "What do you think?"

"I think... well, let me put it this way. Have you ever been to Paris?"

"Paris? No."

"Well, they have this thing called the Eiffel Tower. You might have heard of it."

"Of course I know what the Eiffel Tower is," Maya said.

"Ah. When I was a little girl, I was obsessed with the Eiffel Tower. I thought seeing it would change my life. I finally got to see it when I was about twelve, and guess what? I got there, and it was just... a big tower. It didn't change anything."

"So a disappointment."

"A disappointment indeed, and it's the same for our guy over there. We romanticize people like him, give them spooky names like the Ripper and Butcher and Night Stalker, and that convinces us that they're special. But look at him. He looks like ten pounds of shit in a five-pound bag, and he smells like it as well."

"Yeah, I caught that too."

"Like I said the other day, they're man children, and murder is nothing more than a temper tantrum. Don't think of him as special because he's nothing more than your garden-variety pervert. Oh, and you beat him."

"*We* beat him," Maya said. "Sorry for heading off without telling you. I didn't want to call you while you were staking out the shelter."

"In this case, I think the results speak for themselves, so don't sweat it. By the way, I called you non-stop after I met that guy at the shelter. Now I know why you didn't pick up."

"Do we know what his name is?"

Devon said, "He told me at the shelter it was Todd Williams, but he might have been lying."

It all felt a little surreal to Maya. Like she was watching all of this happen to someone else. The forensics team was already setting up markers along the muddy bank where the fight had taken place, and the woman Maya had saved was being loaded into the ambulance. Groggy but still alive.

And then two deputies hauled Todd Williams—or whatever his real name was—to his feet. Blood streamed from his broken nose. One eye was already swollen shut. He stumbled when they tried to make him walk, and they had to half-carry, half-drag him toward the nearest cruiser.

"Shit, Frost, you did a real number on him," Devon said.

Maya showed her partner her knuckles. "Pretty sure I broke something."

"You broke something all right. His face."

The unsub looked small and pathetic now. Nothing like

the monster who'd killed five people and made headlines across the country. He was just a man who'd made poor decisions and would spend the rest of his life in a prison cell at the very least.

Their battle now felt like a blur, but there was something prickling at Maya's subconscious. The Butcher had said something she hadn't expected, and it plagued her since the moment they left his mouth.

"Devon, the killer said something weird. He said there was someone else."

"Someone else? Another victim?"

"No. He said someone else inspired him to do this, and that this was *just the beginning*."

"Come on, Frost. A deluded psychopath in the throes of death is going to say some strange things. He was just trying to distract you. Nothing more."

"You think?"

"Yeah. I've had perps throw all sorts of random crap at me while I've been on top of them. They'll say anything in that moment, so don't worry about it."

Maya cast the thought aside and focused on the scene. She was more than ready to get home and hopefully sleep for about a week. "You think Vernon's going to kill me?" she asked.

"Yup." Devon used Maya's shoulder to leverage herself to a standing position, then she offered a hand to her partner. Maya took it, and Devon pulled her up. "But you're an analyst thrust into a homicide case. I'd be more concerned if you *didn't* screw up a little."

Maya laughed it off. Her first real laugh in four days. "I'll take it on the chin, as they say."

"I wouldn't worry about it. You ready to get out of here? We can be in D.C. by morning."

She took one last look at the scene. The killer was in the back of a cruiser, guarded by three officers. Crime scene markers mapped out their fight along the river. God knew how much blood and other bodily fluids they'd find there, but they had all the time in the world to process it because there'd no more victims of the Fernandina Butcher.

"I'm ready."

"Good. Precinct first to grab our things, then we'll head home. You want to go talk to him?"

"To who?"

"Our new friend. The Butcher. Todd Williams."

Maya stared at the silhouette in the back of the police cruiser. His head was lolling against the window, and all this time, he hadn't glanced over at Maya once. For a man hell bent on infamy, he should have basked in the moment, but instead he'd retreated into himself. Maya guessed that you didn't know what you truly wanted until it was right in front of you, and for years she'd have given anything for some one on one time with a psychopathic serial killer.

Now that she had it, she realized it wasn't all it was cracked up to be.

"No. Let's go home."

Devon just laughed and said, "Welcome to the club."

SIXTY-TWO

FOUR DAYS. THAT'S ALL IT HAD BEEN. IT FELT LIKE FOUR years, and Maya had begun to feel a kinship with this temporary office. But now it was time to clear it all out and quite literally wipe the board clean. Time to return borrowed space to its original state and go home.

She'd packed everything up, shredded the printouts she didn't need, put them in the recycling, and even wiped down the desk. She grabbed her jacket just as Devon appeared in the doorway.

"Christ, Frost, you cleaned this place up good."

"Everyone has a talent. Where've you been?"

"Saying goodbye to the sheriff. He's got the low-down on the unsub, if you want to know. Even searched his place from top to bottom."

Maya didn't want to humanize him any more than she already had, but part of the profiler's job was to acknowledge that serial killers had boring, human lives just like anyone else. "What did he find out?"

"So the killer's real name is Arthur Hayes. He lied about his name to me at the shelter. Forty-two years old, owns a farm about five miles away from here, although *owns* is generous because the place is apparently on its ass. He inherited it as a kid, and Riggs even remembered the whole ordeal. Hayes' mom got drunk one night, fell in the pig pen, and, well..."

Maya imagined the scene, and the first thing that hit her was how improbable that was. "Sounds like a load of crap."

"Funny you should say that, because crap was the only thing that remained of Hayes' mom. Her teeth came out the other end. If you ask me, that's where it started."

"Yeah. If she was abusive, then the killer probably pushed her in, but there's probably no way to ever clarify that. But you said he was working at the women's shelter?"

"Worked there to make ends meet because the farm was so dead. The woman he stabbed there is still alive and stable, and the woman he took hostage is fine too. She was drugged but not attacked. You got there in time."

Relief washed through Maya. Not everyone had died. Not everyone. "They find anything at his place?"

"Everything. Found his murderabilia collection in his so-called study, and the thing was massive. Letters from serial killers, artwork, relics, even had a truck key belonging to the real Green River Killer. The FBI vault is going to get a lot bigger thanks to him. What's the saying about clouds and silver linings?"

"Any links to the victims?"

"Just one, but a major one. Teresa Morgan's skinned face was hanging on a mannequin. That alone is going to get him a life sentence. Possibly a death sentence. This is Florida, after all."

Maya let go of a breath. She was worried there'd be no tangible link between the Butcher and his victims, which could have delayed prosecution by years. Thankfully, there was, as grim as such evidence was. "Thank God."

"And he's confessed to the whole thing too."

"Naturally. Someone as obsessed with notoriety as him would want to make sure the police got all of the details right. Of course he's trying to control the narrative."

"So we have him dead to rights, and that's the best we can ask for."

Maya should have felt triumphant. They had caught him. Stopped him before he could complete his twisted homage to Ted Bundy. Case closed, killer in custody, community beginning to heal. This was what success looked like.

So why didn't it feel like it?

"His farm," Maya heard herself say. "What did he grow?"

Devon raised an eyebrow. "Does it matter?"

"Maybe."

"He reared animals and grew corn, but like I said, it's been dead for years. The house is in terrible shape too. Officers said it looked like he lived in squalor."

Maya pictured it: Arthur Hayes in his rotting farmhouse, surrounded by the corpse of his family's legacy, spending free time in a shrine to serial killers, planning murders that would make him worthy of joining their ranks. A man so desperate for meaning, for recognition, for significance that he turned to the most extreme form of attention-seeking imaginable.

Pathetic. Devon had been right. He wasn't special. He wasn't brilliant. Just another damaged person who chose to inflict his damage outward rather than seek help.

But he had still killed five people and created grief that would echo for decades. The banality of his evil didn't lessen it.

"Frost, you did good here. You know that?"

"Thank you. So did you."

"It was a team effort," said Devon. "You ready to go? Plane leaves in two hours."

It *was* a team effort, but one member of the team—the most important member, in Maya's opinion—wasn't here anymore.

"Yeah, could I just... take a moment? I just need to do something. Visit someone."

"Sure. I'll finish up here."

Maya left the office and walked down the corridor she had come to know over four days. The precinct had quieted since the arrest. Officers at desks. Phones ringing. Someone laughing at a joke she couldn't hear.

She found the crypt at the end of the hall. The door stood open. Inside, the room was just as the cryptmaster had left it. Three monitors, the hard drive still running, a giant fan in the corner, a shelf of action figures, an empty goldfish bowl, and a poster for the movie *Blade Runner*.

"I'm sorry," she said.

It felt like an inadequate apology. Childish, even. But she spoke the words anyway because they were true and because Alfie deserved to hear them even if he couldn't.

Her eyes burned. She blinked hard and refused to let the tears fall. Not here or now. She had cried briefly at the river, and that was all she'd allow herself until she was home, alone.

"Alfie was a good man."

Maya turned around to see Sheriff Riggs manifest in the doorway. Hands in his pockets, he looked twenty pounds lighter than he had yesterday.

"Yes he was."

"Best tech guy I ever worked with, and I worked with a lot of 'em."

"If not for Alfie, we wouldn't have caught the killer. Alfie was the guy who traced him online. And I'm sorry to you too. It was my fault."

"Alfie died because a lunatic murdered him. That's it. That's the only reason."

"I should have... if I'd just..."

"Less of that. You think I don't know how it feels? You think in twenty-five years I haven't lost people? This is the game in the police world. You know, I've got two daughters about your age, and I tell them all the time: Never get into the cop game because sometimes we come to work and we don't go home. That's just how it is."

Maya's throat constricted. She couldn't speak.

The tears came then. Maya couldn't stop them. They spilled down her cheeks, and she hated herself for it, hated the weakness, hated that she was crying in front of Sheriff Riggs about a man she had known for less than a week.

Riggs didn't look away or tell her to stop. He just stood there patiently until she wiped her face with her sleeve.

"Sorry," she said.

"Don't be. First thing we do when we pop out of the womb—we cry. It lets the world know you're alive."

"Four days. I only knew him four days."

"Four days is more than enough. He talked to me about you. He asked if he could prioritize this case so he could work with you. Didn't know that, did you?"

Maya couldn't help but laugh. She barely knew the guy, really, but it sounded like something he'd do. "Well, now I feel even worse."

"The community around here are going to hold a vigil next week for all of the victims. All Saints Church on Cleveland Street. You should come. Closure, or whatever passes for it."

"I'll be there," Maya said and meant it.

"Good. Alfie would have liked that. Now get out of here because your work here is done."

Maya turned to leave, but something stopped her. A question that had been nagging at her since the river. "Sheriff, Devon said you scoured through Arthur Hayes' possessions. Is that right?"

"My guys did just that. They found some freaky stuff, all right."

"Did they happen to find... Alfie's ring?"

Riggs frowned. "His NCAA ring? God, he loved that thing, but no, it wasn't on the inventory. Why?"

"I was wondering... if I could have it? After it goes through evidence processing, I mean. If that's possible."

Understanding crossed Riggs's face. "You want something to remember him by."

"Yeah. I guess I do."

"Well, feel free to take one of his action figures, but we were going to ship all of his belongings to his parents."

"No, it's fine. I understand."

"But listen, I'll keep an eye out for the ring. We've still got some parts of the house to inspect, so if it shows up, I'll make sure it gets to you, all right?"

"Thank you. I really appreciate it."

Riggs stuck his hand out. "It was an honor working with you, Agent Frost, and I hope to see you again next week."

Maya shook his hand. His grip was warm and steady, the handshake of someone who had seen too much but kept going anyway. "The honor was mine, Sheriff."

She headed back to the office to help Devon finish packing. Two hours until their flight. Two hours until they left this place behind and returned to D.C., to normalcy, to whatever came next.

Welcome to the club, Devon had said.

Maya thought about that. About what it meant to be in the club, to be a real agent, to carry the burden of experiences like this one for the rest of her life.

It was terrible, and the benefits were awful.

But it was hers now. And she wouldn't trade it for anything.

SIXTY-THREE

Maya returned from the bathroom to find Devon on the phone as she stared out the window at darkness and a blinking wing light. Florida altitude had played havoc with Maya's bladder for four days straight, and apparently the return journey was no exception.

She slid back into her seat opposite Devon, catching the tail end of a sentence. "Yes sir, understood, speak soon" before Devon abruptly ended the call.

Then Maya's own cell buzzed. She found a text from Director Vernon.

Exceptional work, Miss Frost. Welcome to the BAU.

She read it twice. Three times. The words refused to feel real.

"You've got a sour face, Frost. Is there pornography on that screen of yours?"

"Far from it." Maya showed her partner the text. "Vernon doesn't sound like he wants to kill me, thank God.

I've been panicking that he was going to summon the firing squad."

"Ha. I told you. Don't worry about it."

Something seemed amiss. Two days ago, Devon had ripped Maya's head off for breaking protocol and basically assured her that Vernon was going to murder her once she got home. Now that didn't seem to be the case at all.

What had changed? Because they'd caught the killer?

Then Maya saw the wry smile on Devon's lips.

"You covered for me."

"That obvious, huh?"

"Why? I screwed up."

"Name someone who hasn't."

"David Copperfield?"

"Oh, he's screwed up plenty. Just trust me on this. If Vernon asks if I approved every move you made, just say yes. He doesn't need to know, and he doesn't even care how we do it, just that we do it and nobody from legal hassles him. All he needs to know is that we caught a serial killer in four days. End of story."

Maya tried to get her thanks out, but she couldn't quite articulate the gratitude. "That's... I owe you one."

"No, I owe you one, because let's be honest, I was kind of a bitch to you the first couple of days." Devon appeared uncomfortable, as though apologies didn't come naturally. Once again, Maya was a little stuck for words, so she decided to go for the honest approach.

"Yeah, you were."

"Ha. Well, there's a reason for that. My last partner, Agent Sam Hawkins, died on the job. He went rogue on a terrorist job we were working in Ohio. Found himself in an old building in the middle of nowhere, and boom. Gone. Explosives took him out. For that, I never forgave myself, so I don't want the same to happen to you."

The plane hit a pocket of turbulence. They both swayed slightly and said nothing until it passed.

"Jesus, that's awful," Maya said. "And for what it's worth, I get it. You were making sure I didn't get myself killed."

"Did I succeed?"

Maya touched her bandaged forearm, her swollen knuckles, felt the throb in her thigh. "Jury's still out."

That earned another laugh. Devon shook her head and looked back out the window. "Heard you're heading back to Florida next week. Riggs told me."

"Yeah. I think I owe it to the victims. And Alfie."

"You liked that guy."

Maya laughed, and now it was time to admit it. "Yeah, I did. You were right."

"I usually am. Stay at home until then. Heal your wounds. I'll make sure Vernon is happy, and if you ever want to do this again..."

Devon left the question there. The plane hummed though darkness, and below them, invisible in the night, America slept. Arthur Hayes sat in a cell, probably awake, probably replaying his crimes in his head, probably still convinced he was special. Somewhere the families of his victims tried to sleep and failed. Somewhere Sheriff Riggs sat in his kitchen, thinking about Alfie Kustka and all the other good people he had lost.

And somewhere in D.C., Raymond Vernon prepared to

integrate Maya Frost into the Behavioral Unit permanently, at least according to his vague text.

Should she?

She didn't even have to ask. She had the answer four days ago.

"Yeah, I do want to do this again."

EPILOGUE

MAYA SAT IN THE BACK ROW OF THE CHURCH AND fought to keep her composure. Grief had taken up residence on every pew. Families and friends of the victims filled every available space. Their faces looked carved from stone. Sorrow and loss and, in some cases, a quiet rage with nowhere to go.

Speakers had come and gone. Family members shared memories. They spoke of lives that had been full of promise and joy and mundane beauty before Arthur Hayes decided otherwise. Maya heard every word that echoed through the hall. She absorbed each story. But as the ceremony drew to a close, she understood that no words could do the victims justice. The Fernandina Butcher had not been mentioned once during the entire sixty minutes.

Maya would make good on her promise. Once she finished, no one would remember his name. She owed that much to everyone in this church, living and dead.

The congregation rose, and people began filing toward

the exit in orderly silence. Several hundred bodies moved as one. Maya joined the line. She scanned faces and saw pain and unanswerable questions and despair that would never heal. Some offered others unsteady attempts at comfort.

The line moved swiftly out the door, past wreaths and framed photographs and trinkets. Maya read their names in flowery script, and she knew they'd be burned into her brain for life. She had known only one of them in life. But she felt close to all of them in death.

People dispersed quietly. Some lingered to exchange condolences. Others walked away alone. The ceremony might have ended, but the journey of healing was just beginning for many, Maya thought.

She slowed down as she came to the section dedicated to one Alfred Kustka. The photographs captured contexts she had never witnessed. Alfie onstage with a guitar. Alfie in a football uniform. A yearbook photo from the mid-2000s. She remembered their brief moments together and perhaps the potential that would never be explored.

She knelt before the display, then reached into her pocket and withdrew a small pendant shaped like a football. *Florida State* was engraved on the back. She placed it carefully among the other items, and then took a moment to admire the photos. His athletic prowess frozen in time and his younger self full of dreams. These were facets of his life she had never known, and yet now they felt intimate, connected to her in ways she couldn't explain.

She rose, then looked at his smiling face one more time. She remembered his laughter and his kindness. The brief spark of something more that had passed between them.

She turned and collided with someone.

"Excuse me," she said. "I'm sorry."

"It's quite all right," a man replied. He was older with a square face, trimmed gray beard, and a full head of hair despite his age. "Emotions are high." He smiled.

"Indeed," Maya said, still regaining her composure. She watched the man peer down at Alfie's memorial, then sigh. "Did you know the deceased?"

"Me? Oh no. I'm just part of the community, but something this tragic affects us all."

Maya nodded. She felt an unexpected connection with this stranger. "It's a difficult day."

"You knew them?" he asked. She tried to place his tone. He'd said he was local, but his accent said otherwise.

"Sort of." Maya didn't elaborate. Behind him, groups of people merged toward the exit. Mourning time was over.

The man extended one hand and clasped the other over Maya's still-bruised knuckles when she took it. "Well please, take of yourself. If we ever cross paths again, my name's Felix."

"You too."

Maya released his hand—and then something clinked at her feet. She panicked, fearing she'd disturbed the memorial, so she quickly adjusted herself. Something prodded at the bottom of her shoe, so she immediately bent down and plucked it out. The last thing she wanted to do was disrupt the proceedings.

Then Maya's fingers went numb.

She was suddenly transported back to Alfie's house, back to his brown leather sofa, his trophies and his too-small TV.

Here it was, right in her hands.

A gold ring.

With an NCAA engraving.

The same one stolen by the Fernandina Butcher. The one Hayes had pried from Alfie's dead fingers.

"What the hell," Maya whispered. She stared at it. Unmistakably Alfie's. The design. The weight. The NCAA engraving.

But how had it ended up here, at the memorial? She'd been told it hadn't been found with the Butcher's possessions.

Questions raced but found no answers. All she had was the ring. A tangible link to Alfie. A piece of him returned in the most impossible way.

She rose back to her feet, finding herself alone at Alfie's memorial.

And her new conversation partner, Felix, had disappeared into the crowd.

Don't miss WHEN THE WICKED PROSPER. The riveting sequel in the Maya Frost FBI Thriller series.

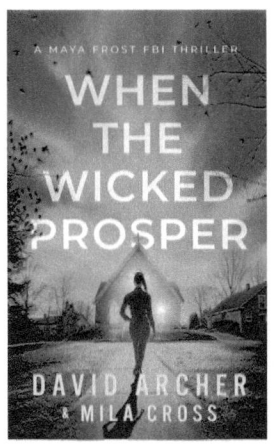

Scan the QR code below to purchase WHEN THE WICKED PROSPER.
Or go to: righthouse.com/when-the-wicked-prosper

NOTE: *flip to the very end to read an exclusive sneak peek...*

DON'T MISS ANYTHING!

If you want to stay up to date on all new releases in this series, with this author, or with any of our new deals, you can do so by joining our newsletters below.

In addition, you will immediately gain access to our entire *Right House VIP Library*, which includes many riveting Mystery and Thriller novels for your enjoyment. Including a prequel novella to this series!

righthouse.com/email

(*Easy to unsubscribe. No spam. Ever.*)

ALSO BY DAVID ARCHER

Up to date books can be found at:
www.righthouse.com/david-archer

ROGUE THRILLERS
Gates of Hell (Book 1)
Hell's Fury (Book 2)
Ice Burn (Book 3)
Judgement by Fire (Book 4)

JACOB HUNTER THRILLERS
The Kyiv File (Book 1)
The Bogota File (Book 2)
The Havana File (Book 3)
The Amsterdam File (Book 4)
The Saint Petersburg File (Book 5)

PETER BLACK THRILLERS
Burden of the Assassin (Book 1)
The Man Without A Face (Book 2)
Unpunished Deeds (Book 3)
Hunter Killer (Book 4)
Silent Shadows (Book 5)
The Last Run (Book 6)
Dark Corners (Book 7)
Ghost Operative (Book 8)
A Fire Burning (Book 9)
Dawnlight (Book 10)

Dead Ice (Book 11)
No Loose Ends (Book 12)

ALEX MASON THRILLERS
Odin (Book 1)
Ice Cold Spy (Book 2)
Mason's Law (Book 3)
Assets and Liabilities (Book 4)
Russian Roulette (Book 5)
Executive Order (Book 6)
Dead Man Talking (Book 7)
All The King's Men (Book 8)
Flashpoint (Book 9)
Brotherhood of the Goat (Book 10)
Dead Hot (Book 11)
Blood on Megiddo (Book 12)
Son of Hell (Book 13)
Merchant of Death (Book 14)
Extinction C-14 (Book 15)
A Vengeful God (Book 16)

NOAH WOLF THRILLERS
Code Name Camelot (Book 1)
Lone Wolf (Book 2)
In Sheep's Clothing (Book 3)
Hit for Hire (Book 4)
The Wolf's Bite (Book 5)
Black Sheep (Book 6)
Balance of Power (Book 7)
Time to Hunt (Book 8)
Red Square (Book 9)

Highest Order (Book 10)
Edge of Anarchy (Book 11)
Unknown Evil (Book 12)
Black Harvest (Book 13)
World Order (Book 14)
Caged Animal (Book 15)
Deep Allegiance (Book 16)
Pack Leader (Book 17)
High Treason (Book 18)
A Wolf Among Men (Book 19)
Rogue Intelligence (Book 20)
Alpha (Book 21)
Rogue Wolf (Book 22)
Shadows of Allegiance (Book 23)
In the Grip of Darkness (Book 24)
Wolves in the Dark (Book 25)
Olympus Must Fall (Book 26)
Children of the Empire (Book 27)
Wolf at the Gates (Book 28)

SAM PRICHARD MYSTERIES
The Grave Man (Book 1)
Death Sung Softly (Book 2)
Love and War (Book 3)
Framed (Book 4)
The Kill List (Book 5)
Drifter: Part One (Book 6)
Drifter: Part Two (Book 7)
Drifter: Part Three (Book 8)
The Last Song (Book 9)
Ghost (Book 10)

Hidden Agenda (Book 11)

SAM AND INDIE MYSTERIES
Aces and Eights (Book 1)
Fact or Fiction (Book 2)
Close to Home (Book 3)
Brave New World (Book 4)
Innocent Conspiracy (Book 5)
Unfinished Business (Book 6)
Live Bait (Book 7)
Alter Ego (Book 8)
More Than It Seems (Book 9)
Moving On (Book 10)
Worst Nightmare (Book 11)
Chasing Ghosts (Book 12)
Serial Superstition (Book 13)

CHANCE REDDICK THRILLERS
Innocent Injustice (Book 1)
Angel of Justice (Book 2)
High Stakes Hunting (Book 3)
Personal Asset (Book 4)

CASSIE MCGRAW MYSTERIES
What Lies Beneath (Book 1)
Can't Fight Fate (Book 2)
One Last Game (Book 3)
Never Really Gone (Book 4)

ABOUT US

Right House is an independent publisher created by authors for readers. We specialize in Action, Thriller, Mystery, and Crime novels.

If you enjoyed this novel, then there is a good chance you will like what else we have to offer! Please stay up to date by using any of the links below.

Join our mailing lists to stay up to date --> righthouse.com/email
Visit our website --> righthouse.com
Contact us --> contact@righthouse.com

facebook.com/righthousebooks
x.com/righthousebooks
instagram.com/righthousebooks

EXCLUSIVE SNEAK PEEK OF...

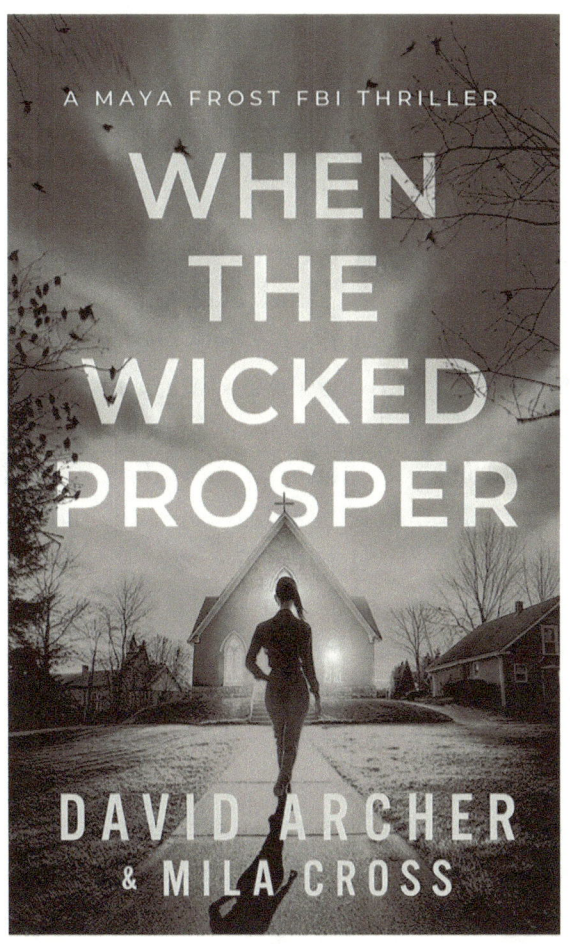

A MAYA FROST FBI THRILLER

WHEN THE WICKED PROSPER

DAVID ARCHER

& MILA CROSS

PROLOGUE

Father Downing sat on the wooden bench inside the confessional with his cassock bunched around him and a half-empty pack of Marlboros pressing against his ribs through the fabric. Giving up smoking had seemed like a good idea last month, back when he'd briefly entertained the fantasy of becoming a better man. Now three weeks into the deprivation, the dopamine hit had worn off, and it just felt like the cure was worse than the disease.

That would teach him to make rash decisions, he thought, but then again, long-term decisions hadn't paid off so well either. Twenty-five years of praising the Lord, and where had that gotten him? A one-bedroom apartment, a rusty Toyota, multiple substance abuse issues, and the lingering thought that maybe this whole Jesus thing wasn't all it was cracked up to be. Downing thought of his trip to Vegas last year, where he'd seen a magician walk on water, turn a fish into several hundred fish, and then stop and restart his pulse, essentially resurrecting himself. After that, Downing couldn't shake the thought that Jesus might have just been a trickster who was way ahead of his time.

The bench was hard beneath him. His back ached. He was fifty-three years old and felt seventy.

He needed a moment to collect himself before the next penitent arrived with their predictable sins. October was always bad for this. These were the people suddenly desperate to scrub themselves clean because they thought Jesus watched them a little closer during the run-up to Christmas.

Downing actually liked to think that Jesus did just that, but who was he kidding? If Jesus was real, he'd have dropped a lightning bolt on this church years ago. St. Andrew's was a pit, and it was time for Downing and the other priests to stop pretending otherwise. There was mold in every corner, knotweed reclaiming the exterior, and the roof would probably cave in before winter was out. Not to mention that the local faithful had reduced to single figures, which meant that the collection plate had reached an all-time low too. Back in the day, he'd steal the odd twenty from the collection plate just to keep him in liquor, but now the takings were so low that any theft would be noticeable. The diocese paid a pittance, so Downing's purse strings were tighter than ever.

A soft knock at the door.

Downing banished the intrusive thoughts and focused on the task at hand. He levered himself upright. Late-night confessional, and he still had an hour to go.

"Enter, my child," he said.

The figure, concealed by the partition between them,

slipped into the booth. Father Downing waited for the man to sit, but he remained standing. Whoever it was, he cut a sizeable silhouette.

"Bless me, Father," he said.

Downing silently willed the stranger to finish the common preface, but it didn't arrive. The times were a-changing, Downing figured. "Good evening, my son. Is it your first time here?"

"Yes. It's been a long time coming."

Downing tried to get a feel for the shapeless mass on the other side of the box. Clearly male, forties to fifties, an out-of-towner given the lack of a local drawl. Passing through town, then. Downing figured he probably wouldn't see him again after tonight.

"Well, the Lord's door is always open. He'll welcome you with open arms. Please go ahead."

The penitent cleared his throat. "Well, Father, it's a little complicated. I'm not sure where to begin."

"Why don't you start with what's weighing on you most heavily? The first step is always the hardest."

"Okay, let me think."

Downing resisted the urge to check his watch. Late-night confessionals used to be his favorite job, because when the sun went down, the good stuff came out. In his experience, nobody confessed to affairs and scandals in the cold light of day, but something about the night hours gave shame the courage to speak. Although he had to admit, even the gossip had become stale recently. It was less Jerry Springer and more Jerry from Accounting, because it was just a continuous stream of middle-aged men confessing to the fear that they'd peaked in high school. Confessions were no longer about what men *did* but what they were scared to do, and it made for long, boring discussions in which Downing was woefully uninterested.

There was still silence from the other side of the screen, long enough for Downing to wonder if the stranger had gotten cold feet. It happened sometimes. People got right up to the edge of confession and couldn't make the leap, but usually the invitation to unburden was all it took to get the confessions flowing. He prompted, "I know it's tough, but long journeys start with small steps. Is everything all right?"

"Everything's fine."

"Then take your time, my son. The Lord is patient, and so am I."

Downing shifted on the bench. The ache in his lower back intensified. He should have brought a cushion. The diocese wouldn't spring for one, nor would they spring for anything that might make his job more bearable. He'd have to pilfer one from the rectory. The urge to check his phone bubbled up, but Downing cursed himself for leaving the thing on charge in the office.

"It's just difficult to put into words," the penitent said at last. "I've actually been waiting for this for a long time."

"You've been waiting to confess for a while, is that right?"

"Yes."

Another awkward silence. In truth, Downing couldn't care less about this stranger's crisis. He could see a mile away that it was just another garden-variety white man eaten up with guilt over something that nobody else—especially not God—cared about. The thrill of spiritual voyeurism had worn off years ago, which was why Downing had to get his kicks a different way these days. "Something's been eating at you for a while. Start at the beginning."

"I did something once. Something I'm not proud of."

Downing tried not to laugh. If he had a nickel for every time he'd heard that, he'd have retired years ago. "We've all fallen short of the glory of God, but His mercy is infinite. Whatever you've done, he'll forgive you."

The irony of the statement wasn't lost on him. But what the penitent didn't know wouldn't hurt him. And Downing had long ago made peace with his own hypocrisy. It was the price of doing business in a fallen world.

"That's just it, Father. I'm not sure I want to be forgiven."

Unease skittered up Downing's spine. The petty sinners usually fell over themselves to beg for God's pardon. "I understand your hesitation. Facing our transgressions can be daunting, but God's love is greater than our sins."

"There's no one else in this church."

Downing perked up. The man's tonality suggested it wasn't a question. "No. I never said there was."

"You do these late nights alone?"

"Yes, I do."

"Why?"

"We encourage anonymity here. Hence the lack of eyes in the building."

"Does that not concern you?"

Downing's pulse picked up speed. His mouth went dry as old bones. "No it doesn't. God watches over me. Now could we talk about—"

"We're not here to talk!" the man shouted.

Downing grabbed the handle to the booth. His fingers

were trembling. Instinct propelled him to search for a weapon, despite him having never needed one in his twenty-five-year career. He frantically patted himself down and found nothing that he could defend himself with. Not even his cell phone.

He took a breath. "I understand, sir. But if you could—"

"You don't understand anything."

Beyond the partition, the man's silhouette swelled and contracted, like he was breathing heavily. Downing considered breaking out of here and grabbing one of the candle holders near the altar for self-defense. This place was full of wood and metal. Surely he could find a makeshift weapon within twenty feet?

But what if this confessant had a weapon of his own? Or a gun? Or what if trying to escape pushed him over the edge?

No. Downing had made his living talking to people at their lowest. They rarely got angry, but he'd heard a million stories like this from other priests and had just thought himself too much of a smooth talker to ever end up as that guy.

"Then what's troubling you?" Downing asked. It wasn't much of a defusion, but it was all that popped into his head. There was no Scripture now. No Father-knows-best routine.

Then suddenly, the door to the penitent's box burst open. Footsteps bounced off the floor as this anonymous confessant fled out into the church's halls. Downing strained to hear what direction he'd gone, but silence quickly descended, and he was left alone with nothing but questions and a spiked pulse rate.

Downing sat there like an idiot. What the hell was that? He tried to think rationally, but his mind couldn't catch traction. A practical joke? Some local drunk who got his kicks scaring priests?

It couldn't be. Downing knew all of the drunks in this town, and none of them sounded like that guy. And that silhouette had some mass to it, whereas the local trouble-makers were all weedy things.

He waited. Counted to thirty. Then sixty.

Nothing.

Downing's forehead began to itch. He touched it, and it came back damp.

Get out of here. The thought came from everywhere and nowhere all at once. Confessional was over for the night, and maybe forever. Someone else could do it from now on. He didn't get paid enough to deal with this.

Downing pushed the confessional door open an inch. The nave looked empty. Row after row of vacant pews. But empty didn't mean safe. He sucked in a breath. Maybe he should rush to his office and call the cops.

Don't be stupid, he told himself. He had to get out of here. Survival came first. The office was fifty feet away, but the main door was only thirty. He could be out into the parking lot and into his piece-of-shit Toyota in twenty seconds. That was the safer option. Get into space, where he could run freely if he needed to.

Downing gently opened the confessional door and crept out into the aisle. There was no sign of anyone else in here, even though he hadn't heard the main door creak open. But still, the more he looked, the more chance he had of finding someone. So, eyes locked on the prize, Downing made for the door.

He was down the aisle, past the pews. Fifteen feet. His

cigarettes knocked against his ribs with each step. His last vice. Well, not his last. Not even close. But the only one he'd tried to quit recently.

Ten feet.

The door handle gleamed in the light. Downing caught it. Escape was so close he could taste it. He could feel the evening air just beyond the threshold.

But then footsteps surged behind him. A presence at his back, cold breath on his neck. Fabric against fabric. Right behind him.

Downing didn't turn around. He turned the knob with a shaky hand. The door cracked open, and October air rushed in, sweet as wine. One more second and he'd be out, and then he'd run until he couldn't run anymore.

But then the giant hand clamped over his mouth, yanked his head back, and cold steel kissed his throat and bit deep. It severed flesh like it was nothing, and before Downing fell to the ground, he saw the ceiling, the water stains that looked remarkably like Jesus. His legs buckled, and he crumpled to the floor, twitching as his life force pumped out of him in an unstoppable torrent.

He tried to get up but couldn't. Tried to crawl, but his arms gave out. Downing's face met marble as blood filled his mouth.

Through the fog, he saw legs. Black pants. Black shoes. Then a face came into view.

No, not a face. A ski mask. Two eye holes.

And a long, dark bag snapping open in gloved hands.

A bag big enough to cram a lifetime's worth of sins into.

The last thing he thought was that he should have kept smoking. Should have enjoyed every last cigarette. Because in the end, none of it mattered anyway. Not the promises to quit. Not the prayers and certainly not the twenty-five years of lies he'd told in God's name.

The darkness rushed up to meet him, and Father Downing finally discovered what came after.

CHAPTER ONE

For the past two weeks, Maya Frost had been running.

Her route started at her apartment and ended wherever her legs gave up, which was usually somewhere near the Dairy Queen on Route 7. It was the most scenic route that Church Falls had to offer, and today she'd managed to go half a mile further than her personal best—all before nine a.m.

Not bad, Maya thought as she began the long walk home. The return journey was apparently for reflection according to other runners she'd met on her travels or to simply bask in the dopamine high, but Maya never really indulged in either. If her ankles would let her, she'd have run back home too, because even though they said women were great multi-taskers, it was hard to think about much when your legs were on fire.

Because what Maya craved at the moment was empty-headed, non-thinking bliss.

She passed the Cuckoo Oak Bar, the cops bar, the place where it had all begun seventeen days ago. Raymond Vernon —director of the FBI—had summoned her to that bar and offered her a new life. She'd accepted pathetically quickly and so was thrust head-first into a new training program that teamed newbies with veteran field agents. Maya had gone from sitting behind a desk in the Intelligence Unit to the frontlines within a matter of hours, and Maya would be lying if she said it wasn't like someone had reached into her head, pulled out her biggest fantasy, and made it real.

The reality, as fulfilling as it was, had left some scars. She'd hunted a serial killer who'd mimicked the crimes of history's most infamous murderers and taken five lives in the process. The press, in their infinite creativity, had taken to calling him the Fernandina Copycat, which Maya thought was like naming your red car Red Car.

But the lack of imagination on the media's part hadn't made a difference because Maya couldn't escape the Fernandina Copycat's name if she tried. Details of his crimes were plastered on every news site in the world, and she couldn't turn on Fox or CNN or ABC without seeing the same footage of him being marched into a detention center in Jacksonville on loop. It was the only footage of him that existed, and every network was eager to milk it.

Following the case, Maya had been awarded the mandatory ten working days leave to help her physical wounds heal, but the real wounds weren't the kind that healed in two weeks. It was the mental trauma. She'd seen a lot of despair in her time in Intelligence, but she hadn't gotten up-close with the bodies or the families who'd never see their sons or daughters or parents again until that case in Florida. She too had come close to death when she finally came face to face with the perp on that riverbank, and her brain was still playing an endless game of *what if*.

And then, of course, there was Alfie.

Alfie Kustka, a man who she'd only known for three days during her time in Florida, but three days was apparently enough to get someone killed. Alfie had been a mere tech analyst who'd operated far away from the trenches, but Maya's proximity to him had been a curse, like she was one of those Victorian-era typhoid carriers. The Copycat had found Alfie, killed him, and stolen his prized possession: an NCAA ring from his college football days.

Police had scoured the Copycat's farmhouse for that ring and hadn't found it, but last week, at a vigil for the killer's victims, that same ring had somehow dropped at Maya's feet.

How?

That was the question that had been plaguing her since the vigil, and despite her abundance of theories, none were anything close to concrete, and they ranged from the logical to the borderline paranoid. Maybe she'd knocked it off one of the memorial displays because people had left all kinds of personal stuff among the flowers and teddy bears. Football memorabilia wouldn't have been out of place. Could a friend or family member somehow have acquired it and placed it there?

Or maybe it wasn't even Alfie's ring. There were no initials engraved in it and nothing unique about it at all except the year. How many other guys had played college football and earned one of them? Thousands?

Except the police had checked with Alfie's family,

friends, anyone who might have had access to his belongings. No one mentioned having it.

Which left the theory she couldn't shake.

The stranger.

Maya had bumped into him—literally collided with him, in fact—and the ring had appeared at her feet. The stranger had taken her hand and introduced himself as Felix in an accent that didn't match his claim of being a local. He was a graying, older guy with a nimble figure and a forgettable smile, and then he'd disappeared without speaking more than a few platitudes.

She hadn't stopped thinking about that strange man because what earthly reason would he have to not just possess a dead man's ring but then drop it at Maya's feet? At that point, the Fernandina Copycat was locked up in a jail cell, so it wasn't like the killer could have put an accomplice up to the task.

But then there was the other thing.

Right as Maya was about to snap the cuffs on the killer on that riverbank, he'd mentioned that someone had *put him up to this.*

What did that mean? Maya didn't know, and that was why she needed to keep running because too much rumination on this was rewiring her brain. She was halfway home when her cell phone chirped in her pocket. Maya pulled it out and saw a number she didn't recognize flashing on the screen. She clicked ACCEPT.

"Hello?"

"Hi, is this Miss Frost? Agent Frost?" A woman's voice.

"Who's this?" Maya asked. In the law enforcement

world, you learned never to give anonymous people your name.

"My name's Jennifer Holden, and I'm a feature reporter for the Washington Post. I understand you were the person responsible for—"

"I'm sorry, I can't talk about it."

"We're only asking for a short interview, Miss Frost."

Maya sighed. This was about the tenth call she'd had in the past two weeks from reporters, and talking to the press before a perpetrator had been sentenced was a no-go in this game. Devon Lynch, the veteran agent and Maya's new partner, had warned her against it too. You stayed as anonymous as you could until the perp was dead because criminals had newspapers and Internet access in prison, and making yourself memorable to the person you'd just locked up for life was spectacularly stupid.

"We're not allowed to discuss ongoing cases. You'll have to contact the media team at the Bureau."

"I did, and they denied me."

"There's a reason for that. How did you find my name, anyway?"

"We have contacts."

"Like who? People in the FBI?"

"I'm not at liberty to say, but—"

"Then neither am I," snapped Maya and hung up. Heat prickled across her skin like a bad rash, despite it being close to freezing out here. Who did these journalists think they were? *Not at liberty* to divulge their sources but they expected her to give them the grim details of a serial killer investigation? Maya guessed that some people just couldn't comprehend that not everyone wanted to be a celebrity or cared about getting their name in the news.

Before she could pocket her cell, it rang again. Same number. Maya declined it, then she caught sight of the time on her screen. Just after nine a.m. now, and today was officially Maya's last day of leave. She was due back in the office tomorrow, and she truly had no idea what her role entailed now. Was she still in Intelligence until an active case needed her attention, or was she a full-time field agent? She figured that the director was playing this new initiative by ear, so chances were that even he didn't know.

Her cell buzzed again. Another incoming call.

She should decline again and send this persistent bitch straight to voicemail hell.

But no. She was going tell this reporter where to shove her contacts. She answered with fire already in her throat.

"I already told you, I'm not talking. If you call me again—"

"Good morning to you too, Miss Frost."

That wasn't the reporter's eager, nasal voice. It was a man's voice, and one she recognized.

"Mr. Vernon. Sir. I'm sorry," she stuttered. "I thought you were someone else."

"Clearly. Someone bothering you?"

"Yes, sir."

Vernon laughed. "Let me guess. A reporter."

"Got it in one."

"You get used to them. Well, I just wanted to ask—when are you due back in the office?"

"Tomorrow, sir."

"Is there any chance you could get to HQ today?"

Vernon asked. "Something's come up that could use your... attention."

Maya swallowed. This could only mean one thing. "Another field case?"

"I can't divulge details over the phone, but Miss Lynch is en route too. Hopefully you can read between the lines."

"Yes. I can be there. Give me one hour? I just need to head home and change."

"One hour it is. Pack your bags, and I'll see you shortly."

Vernon ended the call, but Maya continued to hold the phone to her ear. She'd barely recovered from the last case, but here she was, accepting whatever this new job was like it was a winning lottery ticket.

Pack your bags.

Yup, she was heading somewhere. Somewhere that needed her attention badly enough that Vernon was pulling her back early. Maya lowered the phone and stared at the empty trail ahead. Two weeks hadn't been enough to stop seeing Alfie's face and quiet the what-ifs.

But apparently, it was all the time she was going to get.

The smart thing would be to say she needed more time, but despite her current position, Maya Frost had never been too smart when it came to running.

CHAPTER TWO

Maya made the rookie mistake of washing her hair in the shower because it was a choice between wet hair or sweaty hair. Blow-drying it would take time she didn't have, which meant today was a ponytail kind of day.

Dressed in only a towel, Maya pulled open her closet and stared at the contents. Formal but casual. Field-appropriate. The eternal FBI wardrobe dilemma. You needed to look professional enough that local cops didn't write you off as a fed who'd never seen a real crime scene but functional enough that you could chase someone through a swamp without destroying a dry-clean-only blazer. Maya had learned that lesson the hard way in Florida, where her Ann Taylor jacket had ended up crumpled and covered in two people's blood.

Vernon had said 'pack your bags,' which meant this wasn't a meeting, so she grabbed her usual: dark jeans from Target that had enough stretch to run in but didn't look like yoga pants, multiple black tops, and enough underwear to last a week. Toothbrush. Toothpaste. Deodorant. Face wash. Moisturizer with SPF because her roommate Becky continually scolded her about sun damage, not that there was much sun in October. Hair ties. Ibuprofen. The essentials.

She grabbed her case notebook from the nightstand. Not the official one that would go into evidence but her secondary one where she wrote down the things that sounded insane. Then chargers, then she rifled through her sock drawer one more time. On the previous case, Devon Lynch had told Maya that dry socks were sometimes the difference between good days and bad days, and it had been one of those oddly-specific nuggets of wisdom that somehow stuck with you forever.

So Maya rifled through and found a few more pairs, but there, next to old underwear she should probably throw out, was a small plastic bag with a chunk of metal inside.

Alfie's NCAA ring.

She'd put it there for safe keeping, and while she'd been thinking about this damn thing for two weeks, she'd kept the actual article hidden away. Not just because it belonged to Alfie but because it reminded her that she was technically withholding evidence. Sure, there was enough evidence to put the Fernandina Copycat away for the rest of his life, but the point still held, and every day that passed made it more difficult to come clean. What would she even say now? *Hey, remember that evidence from our closed case? Funny story. It just appeared at my feet after we'd already caught the killer.*

With the bag in hand, she sat on the edge of her bed. The truth was that she knew exactly why she hadn't reported it. It would make her sound unhinged. The Copycat was in custody, and evidence falling strangely into her lap after the fact was suspicious to say the least, and part of it bordered on conspiracy theory territory. The FBI higher-ups didn't take well to conspiracy theorists because there were already enough people out there convinced the FBI was covering up everything under the sun.

Vernon had taken a chance on her, and if he caught wind of this, it could make him second-guess his decision.

Dammit, she should have just told someone about it when it happened. Devon, Vernon, even the Fernandina PD would have been fine. But now she'd committed to this secret, so now she had to either figure out the mystery or simply forget about it.

Report it now and look insane. Keep it hidden and carry the guilt. Pretend it never happened.

Those were the options, but none of them felt right.

Someone had been holding this ring before it appeared at her feet, and she needed to find out who.

Then an idea occurred to her, albeit a small, manageable idea, but it was something that might actually help her make sense of this without raising any red flags.

It was risky. Probably stupid. But it *might* just give her answers without torpedoing Vernon's and Devon's confidence in her in the process.

Then she stood up, crossed to her duffel bag, and dropped the evidence bag inside. She zipped it up, hoisted it over her shoulder and made for the door. She locked the door behind her and headed outside.

Whatever was awaiting at HQ had to be better than sitting alone with her thoughts and a dead man's ring.

Had to be.

CHAPTER THREE

As Maya ascended to the top floor of the FBI building by way of the elevator, she was reminded of that old saying: You'll care a lot less about what people think of you when you realize how seldom they do.

She'd expected a few cursory glances in the wake of her triumphant capture of the Fernandina Copycat, maybe even a few congratulatory pats on the back. The reality was that no one had even looked her way since she came through the door, which was equal parts disappointing and relieving. People were too wrapped up in their own problems to care about anyone else's. There was a Japanese word for it—the realization that everyone else was living a life as complex and vivid as your own, but Maya couldn't remember what it was. She guessed her fifteen minutes of fame had lasted fourteen minutes less than advertised, and that was fine.

The elevator dinged at the top floor, and Maya stepped out onto a marble walkway. This was executive territory, where Vernon and the other big dogs had offices larger than most people's apartments. She'd only been up here twice before, once for her initial interview and once to sign paperwork that said if she died in the field, it wasn't the Bureau's fault. Up here, she felt like an imposter, and today was no different.

"You decided to come back," a voice said.

It was the low bass tone that Maya instantly recognized as belonging to one Devon Lynch. Maya spun and found her newest friend idling, with one heel digging into the wall.

"Just call me a masochist," Maya said as she extended a hand. Devon pushed off the wall, collected her own travel bag at her feet, and returned Maya's handshake. Her red hair was tied back in a bun, and she'd opted for the black dress look, with booted heels that Maya wouldn't dare try and walk in on her bravest day.

"I'm as surprised as anyone. How are your injuries holding up?"

"Nothing a few aspirin didn't fix. What about you?"

Devon said, "All I had was a bruised knuckle, so I got off lightly. You ready to get back into this?"

"Yes. Absolutely." Maya's lips beat her brain to the punch. Maybe she should have given it some more thought, asked some more questions, like what was going to happen to her Intelligence role? Was she moving on full-time, or was she working some kind of hybrid position? Desk jockey most days, field agent when Vernon felt like rolling the dice?

While she definitely should clarify, the overwhelming urge to get back out into the field took precedence.

"Good." Devon took the lead and headed in the direction of Vernon's office. "You haven't missed much in your two weeks away."

"How do you know? Haven't you been on leave too?"

"Ha. No chance. Field reports don't write themselves, and then there's the legal reports and all the crap that comes with them. The paperwork for a case always takes ten times as long as the case itself."

"Oh. I thought you'd do it all once you came back," said Maya.

"In a perfect world, yes, but it's far from perfect, even up here on millionaire's row."

They reached the door, and Maya identified Raymond Vernon's bulk on the other side of the frosted glass. The brass plaque bearing his name had dulled to a monotone brown, and if that wasn't a fitting metaphor for Vernon's position, she didn't know what was. Devon knocked on the glass.

"Come in."

They entered, and Vernon rose from behind his desk like they'd caught him doing something he shouldn't. Maya said, "Good morning, sir."

Vernon reached over his beast of a desk and shook her hand. "Miss Frost. Good to see you again. And you too, Devon."

"At your service, Ray," Devon said. Maya wondered just how long you had to work at the Bureau to casually "Ray" the man who ran the biggest law enforcement agency in the world, but she guessed that normal rules didn't apply to Devon Lynch.

"Take a seat, both of you."

There were two leather chairs positioned in front of his desk. The agents obliged. Maya gave the room a once-over, because she hadn't had chance the previous times she was here. It was oddly sparse for an office belonging to the most powerful man in the Bureau: huge desk, commendations, American flag, a collection of leather chairs, and what looked suspiciously like a closet in the corner. Maya guessed the rumors of Vernon sleeping, washing, and dressing himself in the office might not be exaggerated after all.

"I hate to be so colloquial," Vernon continued, "but you two have done me a solid. The Fernandina case wrapped in three days gives me leverage I haven't had in years. That kind of stuff goes a long way on the Hill. The attorney general actually smiled at me last week. Do you know how often that happens?"

"Rarely, I imagine, sir," said Maya.

"Rarely is right. Congress has been breathing down my neck about our clearance rates, but this kicked them right in their teeth, especially because it was one hundred percent Bureau work. I read Devon's reports last weeks, and from what I could glean, it was behavioral profiling that led you to the perp."

Maya cast her mind back. "Behavioral with a little tech wizardry. Not just us."

"Close enough for me, and close enough that it gives my initiative program some serious steam. So the question is—" Vernon fixed Maya with a stare. "Are you ready to continue?"

Maya's brain threw up the dozen questions she'd been ruminating on. What about her Intelligence position? Was this permanent or case-by-case? What exactly were the parameters of this initiative? Any reasonable person would want clarification before diving headfirst into what she assumed was going to be a homicide investigation.

But her subconscious had already made the decision, and her lips betrayed that fact.

"Yes sir, I'm ready."

"Good," he said, "because I need you both in Bangor, Maine before this afternoon."

Devon asked, "What's in Bangor, Maine?"

"Lots of things, but most importantly this." Vernon slid two casefiles across his desk. The agents took them. Maya opened up hers and found a police report staring at back at her.

BANGOR POLICE DEPARTMENT. INITIAL INCIDENT REPORT.

Case #: 2025-10-1847.

Reporting Officer: Det. Richard Stapp.

Incident Type: Homicide.

Location of Incident: St. Andrew's Catholic Church. 147 Essex Street, Bangor, ME 04401.

Victim Name: DOWNING, Peter Joseph.

DOB: 03/14/1971.

Age: 53.

Race: White.

Sex: Male.

Occupation: Catholic Priest, St. Andrew's Parish.

Manner of Death: Homicide.

Discovery: Victim discovered by church custodian, Jeremy Marlowe, at approximately 06:45 hours upon arriving for morning duties. Victim found in nave near main entrance. Victim suffered a deep incision across throat, severing both carotid arteries, as well as multiple stab wounds to the arms, legs, and torso. Significant blood loss at scene. Church doors found unlocked. No murder weapon recovered at scene.

Victim's personal effects (wallet, keys, cellular phone) located in church office, undisturbed. No indication of robbery or sexual assault.

"We've got a dead priest," said Devon. "Isolated incident?"

"Isolated is right, but if you'll check the photographs, you'll see why this warrants our involvement."

From what Devon had told Maya, the Behavioral Analysis Unit was only summoned when one or more of three criteria was met: the crime was serial in nature, the local police had no forensic or trace evidence to go on, or the crime was so violent it suggested a psychological abnormality in the perpetrator.

Looking at the crime scene photos, Maya quickly placed this one into the third column. Peter Downing, a once-priest, had been zipped up in a body bag and left on the floor of his church.

And the body inside the bag was all but floating in a shallow puddle of blood.

"Christ in heaven, the perp really went to work on him."

Devon said, "You're not kidding. Stab wounds to every inch of his body, and judging by the blood loss, they all came in quick succession. He gift-wrapped him for us, too."

"Our unsub went into a frenzy."

Maya gave the poor gentleman in the photograph a moment of silent tribute because death was the great equalizer, and everyone deserved someone to acknowledge they'd been a person once—recognition that a life had ended violently and that it mattered, even if Maya had never met the man while he was breathing.

"Ray, any more details? How long have you had this?"

"Barely an hour. I called you two as soon as it landed on my desk, and I know you aren't officially due back until tomorrow, but I thought you might want to see the scene as it is before CSI cleans it up."

Maya subtly rolled her eyes at the wording. Vernon phrased it like he was doing them a favor. The veterans in this building always reminded her that everyone on the top floor was a politician as well as whatever other title they had.

"Fine with me," Devon said. "Frost, we can dissect this unsub on the plane. You ready?"

Maya's stomach tied itself up. It was a bizarre modus operandi to say the least, and that little fact alone was enough to confirm that this was the type of case that burrowed under your skin.

There was no question about it. She had to investigate this case.

"Ready when you are."

Maya stuffed the case file in her bag and stood up. Devon followed suit.

Vernon said, "Keep me updated from the road, and remember: Momentum is everything."

The comment caught Maya off-guard because she didn't know what he was talking about and now didn't seem like the time to inquire. So she nodded her goodbyes and followed Devon outside.

With the door shut behind them, Maya asked, "What's he mean, momentum?"

Devon checked her cell. "He means he needs the killer in chains before the week is out to prove we didn't get lucky the first time."

"Do you think we got lucky?"

"You have a favorite debut album, Frost?"

Maya blinked hard. "A what?"

"You know, a band's first album. Do you have a favorite?"

"Yeah. Guns N' Roses, *Appetite for Destruction*. Why?"

Devon said, "You have a favorite second album?"

"That's an even weirder question."

"Yeah it is. Do you have one?"

"No. I don't have a favorite second album."

"Exactly. The first one, you got nothing to lose. The second one, you got everything to prove, which is why most second albums suck. Come on, I'll drive us to the airport."

Maya vaguely understood the analogy, even if it had been delivered in that weird Devon Lynch way. It meant that the pressure was on, and there was no rookie privilege this time. She shifted her bag on her shoulder, then figured that now was her only window of opportunity to complete the task she'd dreamed up back in her apartment.

"Devon, can I meet you in the car in ten minutes? I just need to head somewhere first."

"Make it quick. The next flight to Maine is in an hour according to this stupid app the tech nerds make me use." Devon put her cell away. "Where are you going? Missing your old desk?"

Maya forced a laugh. "Something like that. I won't be long."

"Fine." Devon's tone suggested that she didn't quite buy it but wasn't going to push. "See you in the parking lot."

There was something Maya needed to do, and she had ten minutes to set it into motion or she'd spend the entire flight to Maine thinking about that ring instead of a dead priest.

CHAPTER FOUR

Most people had never seen a man juggle frozen lab mice before, but most people had never met Joe Mallory, forensic technician here at the FBI Laboratory Division. He was Maya's go-to on the rare occasions that Intelligence and Lab overlapped, and he was also, without question, the weirdest person that Maya knew.

Mallory glanced up from his workstation as Maya approached. The man was built like a linebacker who'd gotten lost on the way to the NFL, and given that beaming smile he always wore, no one would guess that he had done three tours in Iraq.

"You're either lost or you want something." Mallory grinned. He was swabbing the handle of a kitchen knife with something that looked like a Q-tip.

"Half and half," Maya said. "Or maybe I just came down to see my old friend Joe."

"Ha. I wasn't born yesterday. I was born fifty-one years ago to the day, in fact."

"No kidding? Well, happy birthday. I can't think of a better place to spend it than in... a laboratory."

The FBI's main forensics lab was in Quantico, but the D.C. headquarters and other field offices had basic forensic capabilities too. After 9/11, the Bureau had learned the hard way that chain of custody was everything, and if they lost track of evidence for even an hour, defense attorneys could use it as leverage in court. In-house forensic stations meant they didn't need to outsource testing to third parties, which meant less risk in the long run.

"Here's where I belong." Mallory turned off the lamp that had illuminated the kitchen knife. "Twelve hours on the clock, then I'll probably just stay in tonight and have French."

"French?"

"Yeah. A new French place opened up by me. It puts Chinese and Mexican food to shame. I tell you, the Europeans spare no expense when it comes to quality. I'll show you if you want."

"Vernon's shipping me off to Maine in the next hour. No idea how long I'm going to be out there, but as soon as I get back, I'll take you up on the offer."

Mallory took a seat at his computer and adjusted his glasses. "Yeah, we all heard about your Florida case. Everyone is talking about it."

"Really?"

"Yeah, but don't get a big head. Some people are just wondering not only how you became a field agent overnight, but how you got to partner with Lynch."

Maya rolled her eyes. She should have known. The politics in this place started at the top and trickled down to the bottom. "High school never ends."

"Correct. I was going to ask you about it, but I didn't want you to think I was prying."

"How do people even know about it? We've only been on one case together."

"We're the FBI. It's our job to know everything."

Maya said, "Of course. What do you want to know, anyway? It's not exactly groundbreaking stuff. Vernon thought I'd be good in the field, so he put me with the best there is. Simple as that."

Mallory rummaged through his drawers until he found a tub of something. He uncapped it and then pulled out a spoonful of powder. "That *is* groundbreaking, though. That's never happened in the history of the Bureau. And this isn't supposed to sound mean, but you've spent your whole time here behind a desk."

"So?"

"So nothing, but you can see why rumors would spread. Now stand back please, because I need to powder my knife."

Maya took a step back. "Is that what we're calling it now?"

"It's not a euphemism, I promise. Anyway, did you need something important, because this gets messy, and I could be here a while."

"I bet," Maya said. "And yes, I need your services, but I need to keep it... on the down low."

Mallory froze, then placed his spoonful of powder on the workstation. "On the down low? You remember what I just said, about everyone here knowing everything?"

"Which is why I came to you, because I know you can keep your mouth shut."

Mallory folded his arms in the universal gesture of defensiveness, and Maya didn't like that. "How down low are we talking? Is this something for one of yours and Lynch's cases?"

"Sort of."

"I don't like *sort of*. You know I'm a man of great moral fiber."

Maya unzipped her duffel and pulled out the evidence bag. The gold ring sat inside. "This."

"The hell is that? A ring?"

"Yeah. It's a ring that belonged to one of the victims on the Fernandina Beach case."

"The Fernandina Beach case? You mean that whackjob in Florida who skinned a woman's face?"

"Yes. That one."

Mallory picked up the bag and inspected the contents. "Okay, and why do I have it? Or more importantly, why do *you* have it?"

"Last week, I was at a memorial service for the victims. This fell at my feet."

"Sure it did."

"Seriously," said Maya. "I know it sounds crazy, but it did."

"Right, let's say I believe you. Why haven't you handed this over?"

This was the part where it could all go wrong. Where Mallory could decide she was crazy or reckless and march straight up to Vernon's office to report her.

"Because I think someone put it there on purpose, and I need to know who."

Mallory went quiet, which was like watching a thunderstorm pause mid-lightning strike. The man was never quiet. He talked while he worked, while he ate, probably while he slept. But now he just stood there, holding the bag up to the light like it might contain the location of Jimmy Hoffa's body. He set the bag down on the workstation but kept one finger on it, like he was worried it might try to escape.

"Someone put it there on purpose," he repeated.

"Yes."

"At a memorial service."

"Yes."

"For victims of a serial killer you just caught."

"I know how it sounds, Joe."

"I'm not sure you do because that's nuttier than my ma's fruitcake."

Something else Maya and Mallory had in common was their geographical roots. Maya had grown up forty miles north of Boston, but Mallory was pure Southie and still spoke like it. "So help me make it less nutty by figuring out where it came from."

"You want me to swab it?"

"Do whatever you have to. My prints will be on it, probably the victim's too, but see if there's a third set of prints on there. Or anything that might point to where the ring came from."

Mallory stared at her for another long moment, then opened his desk drawer and dropped the bag inside. The ring disappeared into whatever chaos lived in there, then he withdrew a piece of paper from within. He folded it in half and pressed it into Maya's hand.

"What's this?"

"A piece of paper," Mallory said.

Maya frowned. "Why are you giving me blank paper?"

"Because in about thirty seconds, you're going to walk out of here, and the security camera by the elevator is going to catch you leaving. Just like it caught you coming in. Maybe you needed a form signed. Maybe you dropped off a requisition. The point is that you came in with nothing and you're leaving with something, which means you didn't just come here to give me a dead man's ring off the record. If anyone asks, it's the ballistics report for that terrorist job in Long Island."

Maya looked down at the folded paper, then back at Mallory. "You've done this before."

"I haven't actually, and I wouldn't do it for anyone else. Don't make a habit of it, and for God's sake don't tell anyone."

They said to never trust anyone you worked with, and Maya believed that to a point. However, Joe Mallory was an exception. "I won't. Please keep it between us."

"Just call me King Tut, because I can keep things under wraps. Now get out of here."

Maya tipped her invisible hat and headed toward the exit. One job down. Now to get to Maine and inspect the body of a dead priest.

Time to record her second album and make it as good as her first.

CHAPTER FIVE

For reasons Maya had never been quite sure of, she always thought special agents flew private. But her second case in, and here she was on a commercial flight to Bangor, although they'd been treated to first class. The cabin was empty except for Maya and Devon, which was either a stroke of luck or some kind of administrative magic.

"Did you bring your cards?" Devon asked. Her partner was sitting opposite her, already two whiskeys deep, which Maya thought was headed toward excessive territory for a ninety-minute flight.

"Cards?"

"Yeah. Playing cards. For that magic stuff."

Maya rummaged through her bag. She pulled out her laptop, a pair of socks, and found a deck of playing cards hiding at the bottom. "Apparently I did."

"Do something. Blow my mind."

That was the thing about magic. It was the only hobby that you had to prove you did. Nobody asked a drummer to perform an impromptu drum session, but magicians were always put right on the spot in the moment.

"As you wish." Maya spread through the cards face-up and saw the deck was already set up for her usual opener. She flipped the deck over and spread it for Devon. "Five thousand years of magic and the pattern is still the same. Pick any card."

Devon reached in and plucked one out. "Okay."

"Good. Remember it, then pass it back." Maya cut the deck into two packets, put Devon's card on top of one, and completed the cut. Then she dribbled the cards into her left hand. "Done. Your card's somewhere in there, and now watch this."

"I'm watching."

Maya snapped her fingers, then spread through the deck slowly. "See how the backs of these cards are all red? Well, with any luck, one of them should become... blue." She came to a single blue-backed card among the reds, then made eye contact with Devon.

"Well, would you look at that," Devon said.

Then Maya did the secret move. "If you picked the only blue card in this deck, would that be a miracle?"

Devon shrugged. "As close to a miracle as can be, because I saw the back was red."

Maya flipped the card over and showed the three of spades. "That one yours?"

"Sure is. Bravo."

"But wait a minute. We're not done." Maya threw the blue card on the table, then began shuffling the deck. "Just say stop whenever you like."

Devon peered closer. "Stop."

Maya showed Devon the card she landed on. "Remember this card. Okay?"

"Okay."

She snapped her fingers again, then spread through the deck one more time. "And if fortune is in our favor, there should be one... more.... blue card." Maya reached the last card in the deck, and there was no blue card. "Umm..."

"Did you do it wrong?" asked Devon.

"Maybe, it's just that usually... ah, wait a second. I see what's happened." Maya pointed to the blue card that had been sitting on the table. "What card did you land on?"

"The Jack of Hearts."

Maya turned over the blue card sitting between them, the one that had previously been Devon's three of spades. "That's the thing about magic. It's not what you see but what you... think you see. Go on."

"Turn it over?"

"Go for it."

Devon picked up the blue card, then grinned. She threw it back on the table to reveal the Jack of Hearts. "Not bad. How'd you do that?"

Three weeks ago, in a bar in Fernandina Beach, Maya had revealed how her obsession with magic started. How her sister had disappeared twenty-five years ago, and how Maya thought that if she mastered the art of magic, she could undo the cruellest disappearing act of all. It was stupid, but kids thought stupid things, and sometimes those stupid things bled into adulthood.

"If you knew the secret, you'd be very disappointed."

"Fine. Then work your magic on this instead." Devon planted her casefile on the table. Maya scooped her cards up

and boxed them. She found her own casefile, then re-famil-
iarized herself with the details.

"Father Peter Downing, 53, white male, stabbed
multiple times, including a slit throat, and then placed in a
body bag inside the church he worked at."

"That's what it seems like to me. Where would you
start?"

Devon liked her tests, Maya had realized. She never just
seemed to provide the answer, or even a starting point.

"First, how did our unsub know Downing would be
alone in that church? I doubt he just carried a body bag
around with him until he stumbled on a victim."

"Why not?"

"Because someone walking around with a body bag
would raise suspicions, especially when news came out that
a dead body was found in a body bag. He purposely went
somewhere isolated."

"So the victim was targeted?"

"I think so," Maya said. "What do you think?"

"I think you need to keep going."

Of course. Maya wasn't getting off that easily. She looked
through the crime scene photos one more time and put
herself in this killer's head. She was in a church, alone with
the targeted victim. Why do it here? Why stab him exces-
sively? Why leave a mess and a noticeable ritual?

"You don't bring a body bag with you by accident, and
you don't stab someone to this extent by accident. Our
killer's been building this fantasy for a while, and that
fantasy is driven by rage. Excessive stab wounds suggest a
frenzy, but given that the victim is male, it's unlikely there's a
sexual component involved."

"Are you sure?"

Maya ran through her mental catalogue of historical killers, but then came to a flaw in her theory. "Okay, maybe not. Jeffery Dahmer and Colin Ireland were both men who killed other men for sexual gratification."

"But they were both gay men, so either there's no sexual component *or* our unsub is gay. Either one works in our favor."

Statistics didn't lie. The overwhelming majority of serial killers were straight men whose primary motivation was sexual gratification through violence, which meant they killed women. Male on male attacks in the serial killer realm were rare.

"Good. We can't determine whether Downing was killed where he stood because we don't have photos of the entire scene. The killer might have attacked him somewhere else in the church, put him inside the bag, and dragged him to his final position."

"The body bag," Devon said. "What do you make of it?"

Maya wracked her brain for historical precedents but came up empty. Most killers left their victims where they fell, or they transported them in tarps, blankets, car trunks, or plastic sheets. Body bags were specialized equipment.

"I can't think of any serial cases where the killer used actual body bags," Maya admitted. "Which tells us something in itself. This isn't mimicry or copycat behavior."

"So what is it?"

Maya stared at the photo of Father Downing's wrapped corpse. "It could be symbolic. A body bag is meant for the already dead. Maybe the killer saw Downing as spiritually dead before he ever touched him. Like he was just completing the process. Or it could be about transformation, like a chrysalis. The priest goes in, something else comes out."

"I hope not. There's nothing worse than a wannabe-artist."

"Or practical. The unsub might have access to body bags, which would narrow our pool significantly. Medical, funeral industry, emergency services, morgue workers." Maya tapped the photo. "I'm no expert, but I imagine these aren't cheap or easy to get. We need to first check out people who work in the death industry."

"The irony," Devon said. "What about body placement?"

Maya thought about it, and her thoughts scattered in multiple directions. "If the killer left the body there on purpose—as in, he wasn't interrupted—then it's either a message or a theatrical touch. He had the victim in a body bag, so he could have dragged him anywhere, even to his trunk and disposed of the body where no one would find it. But no, he wanted him front and center, which means he's not hiding anything. He wants credit for this."

"Which means he might escalate quickly if he doesn't get the attention he thinks he deserves." Devon closed her file and knocked back the rest of her whiskey. "When we land, we go straight to the scene. We need to see this church while it's still fresh."

"Works for me."

Suddenly D.C. seemed like a million miles away. Maya thought about the ring hidden in Joe Mallory's desk drawer, about Felix's face at the memorial, about all the questions she'd left behind. But those were problems for later. Right now, she had a dead priest in a body bag to worry about, and she wasn't quitting until she had this killer in a body bag of his own.

Scan the QR code below to purchase WHEN THE WICKED PROSPER.

Or go to: righthouse.com/when-the-wicked-prosper

www.ingramcontent.com/pod-product-compliance
Lightning Source LLC
Chambersburg PA
CBHW021122260626
47169CB00005B/1408